BEYOND THE GAP

Tor Books by Harry Turtledove

The Two Georges (by Richard Dreyfuss and Harry Turtledove)
Household Gods (by Judith Tarr and Harry Turtledove)
The First Heroes (edited by Harry Turtledove and Noreen Doyle)
Between the Rivers
Into the Darkness
Darkness Descending
Through the Darkness
Rulers of the Darkness
Jaws of Darkness
Out of the Darkness
Conan of Venarium
Gunpowder Empire
Curious Notions
In High Places
The Disunited States of America
Beyond the Gap

(Writing as H. N. Turteltaub)

Justinian
Over the Wine-Dark Sea
The Gryphon's Skull
The Sacred Land

Beyond the Gap

Harry Turtledove

TOR®

A Tom Doherty Associates Book
New York

BEYOND THE GAP

Copyright © 2007 by Harry Turtledove

This book is printed on acid-free paper.

A Tor Book
Published by Tom Doherty Associates, LLC
175 Fifth Avenue
New York, NY 10010

www.tor.com

Tor® is a registered trademark of Tom Doherty Associates, LLC.

ISBN-13: 978-0-765-31710-0
ISBN-10: 0-765-31710-9

First Edition: February 2007

Printed in the United States of America

0 9 8 7 6 5 4 3 2 1

BEYOND THE GAP

1

WHEN THE WIND blew down from the north, Nidaros felt as if the Glacier had never gone away. Two thousand years before, the spired city that ruled the Raumsdalian Empire was a mammoth-hunting camp at the southeastern corner of Hevring Lake, the great accumulation of meltwater at—or rather, just beyond—the southern edge of the Glacier.

Hevring Lake was centuries gone now. Whatever had dammed its outlet to the west finally let go, and the great basin emptied in a couple of dreadful days. The scoured badlands of the Western Marches were the scarred reminders of that flood.

The Glacier had fallen back, too. New meltwater lakes farther north marked its retreating border. These days, farmers raised oats and rye and even barley in what they called Hevring Basin. No wild mammoths had been seen anywhere near Nidaros for generations. They followed the ice north. Sometimes, though, mastodons would lumber out of the forest to raid the fields.

Back when Nidaros lived by mammoth ivory and mammoth hides and rendered mammoth fat and dried mammoth flesh, no one would have imagined forests by Hevring Lake. The Glacier was strong then, and its grip on the weather even stronger. That was tundra country in those days, frozen hard forever beneath a frosty sky. So it seemed all those years ago, anyhow.

Now, as Count Hamnet Thyssen rode up toward Nidaros, he thought about how the world changed while men weren't looking. He was a big, dark, heavyset man who rode a big, dark, heavyset horse. Over his mail he wore a jacket of dire-wolf hides, closed tight against that cold north wind.

The head from a sabertooth skin topped his helm. The beast was posed so its fangs jutted forward instead of dropping down in front of his eyes.

His thoughts were as slow and ponderous as his body. Many other men would get where they were going faster than he did, whether the journey was by land or over the stormy seas of thought. But if the way got rough, or if it petered out altogether, many other men would turn back in dismay. Count Hamnet carried on . . . and on, and on. Sooner or later, he got where he was going.

And much good it's done me, he thought sourly. His left hand, mittened in bearskin against the wind, rose to scratch at the white streak in his thick black beard. But for that streak, the beard would have hidden the great scar seaming the left side of his jaw.

He muttered under his breath. Fog puffed from his mouth and his great prow of a nose. If he'd thought faster ten years ago, he would have realized sooner that his wife was betraying him. If he'd thought faster, he might even have found a way to make her not want to betray him. And if he'd moved faster in the world, her laughing lover never would have been able to lay his face open like that.

The other man was dead.

So was his love—or so he kept telling himself, anyhow. He would have taken Gudrid back. She didn't want to come. Where she'd left him secretly before, she left him openly then. And he'd never found anyone he cared about since.

He muttered again. Gudrid and Eyvind Torfinn lived in Nidaros—one more reason Hamnet stayed in his cold stone keep out on the eastern frontier as much as he could. But when the Emperor summoned, Count Hamnet came. Sigvat II was a man for whom disobedience and rebellion meant the same thing.

As Hamnet neared Nidaros' gray stone walls, he had to rein in to let a merchant caravan come out through the South Gate. Horses and mules and two-humped hairy camels were laden with the products of the north. Some carried mammoth tusks. Others bore horns cut from the carcasses of woolly rhinos. Many in the south—and not a few in the Raumsdalian Empire— believed rhinoceros horn helped a man's virility. What people believed often turned out to be true just because they believed it. Charlatans and mages were quick to take advantage of that. Which was which . . . Hamnet Thyssen shook his head. He doubted there was any firm dividing line.

Baled hides burdened other beasts. Still others bore baskets and bundles that hid their contents. A few horses hauled carts behind them. The un-greased axles squealed. The carts bumped up and down as their wheels jounced in the ruts.

Merchants rode with the animals. Some were plump and prosperous, with karakul hats and long coats of otter or marten over tunics and baggy breeches tucked into boots of buttery-soft leather or, more often, of felt. Others were accoutered more like Hamnet Thyssen—they were men ready to fight to keep what they owned.

And the caravan had a proper fighting tail of guards, too. Inside the Em-pire, they were probably—probably—so much swank, but beyond the bor-ders bandit troops thrived. Some of the guards were Raumsdalians in chainmail like Hamnet's, armed with bows and slashing swords. Others were blond Bizogot mercenaries out of the north. The lancers looked as if they would rather be herding mammoths than riding horses. Even though they were many and he only one, they gave him hard stares as they rode past. Their cold blue eyes reminded him of the Glacier in whose shadow they dwelt.

He rode through the South Gate himself once the caravan came forth. A guard stepped out into the middle of the roadway to block his path. With upraised hand, the fellow said, "Who are you, and what is your business in the capital?" He sounded like what he was—an underofficer puffed up with his own petty authority. Most men coming into Nidaros would have had to bow and scrape before him. They might have had to grease his palm before he let them pass, too. No wonder he was puffed up, then.

The count looked down his long nose at the gate guard. "I am Hamnet Thyssen," he said quietly. "I have an appointment with his Majesty."

"Oh!" The gate guard stumbled back, all but tripping over his own feet. "P—P—Pass on, your Grace!" Petty authority punctured, he deflated like a pricked pig's bladder.

At another time—or, more likely, were he another man—that would have made Count Hamnet laugh. Here, now, he just felt sad. Without an-other word, he booted his horse forward and rode into smoky, smelly Nidaros.

He hadn't gone more than a few feet forward before a man sitting on horseback in front of a tavern rode out alongside him. "Good day, Count Hamnet," the rider said, his voice a light, musical tenor. "God grant you long years."

"I don't know you." Hamnet's eyes narrowed as he surveyed the foxy-faced newcomer. The crow's-feet at their corners deepened and darkened when he did. He shook his head. "No. Wait. Ulric Skakki, or I'm a Bizogot. Forgive me. It's been a few years." He pulled off his right mitten and held out his hand.

Ulric Skakki had an infectious grin. As he clasped hands with Count Hamnet, he said, "Don't worry about it, your Grace. I'm not offended. D'you think *I'm* a Bizogot?"

He might have been a lot of things. Though he spoke Raumsdalian perfectly, he might well not have been a native of the Empire. But a truculent mammoth-herder from the fringes of the Glacier? That, never.

Count Hamnet started forward. "Forgive me, but I have business in the city."

"I know," Ulric said. "I was waiting for you. I have the same business, you see."

"Do you?" Hamnet eyed him suspiciously. "With . . . ?" He didn't finish. His hand slipped toward the basket hilt of his sword. The basket was big enough to let him wield the blade even with a mitten. If Ulric Skakki didn't give him the right answer . . . Well, no matter what sort of trick the other man had in mind, he wouldn't profit from it.

But Ulric Skakki nodded. "Yes, with the Emperor."

Count Hamnet's hand retreated, not quite so smoothly as it had advanced. He hadn't known Sigvat had summoned anyone else. But, since he still didn't know why the Emperor had summoned him, he couldn't be surprised his Majesty had also called someone else. And Ulric was a man of parts, no doubt about it. Just what the parts added up to . . . Yes, that was a different question.

"Let's go, then," Hamnet said roughly, and rode on into Nidaros.

"Yes, let's." Ulric Skakki's voice was mild as milk, sweet as honey. He rode beside Hamnet as if he had not a care in the world. Maybe he didn't. Some men were born without a conscience, or perhaps had it sorcerously removed. Count Hamnet's still worked all too well, however much he wished it didn't.

Nidaros . . . Nidaros was worse than a maze, for a maze bespoke intelligent design. Nidaros was a jumble, surely the place where the the phrase *You can't get there from here* was born—and where it had flourished mightily ever since. Nidaros' streets and lanes and alleys twisted back on one another, worse than a mammoth's bowels in the cavern of its belly.

The imperial capital was an old town, an old, old town, which helped account for that. New cities farther south had their streets arranged in neat grids, some running northeast and southeast, others northwest and south-west. Strangers could find their way around in them with the greatest of ease. Hamnet Thyssen knew that was true; he'd done it. By the time a man learned to navigate all the quarters of Nidaros, he was commonly too old to get around with ease. You steered by smell as much as any other way. The Street of the Perfumers ran not far from the palace. The butchers' and dyers' districts gave the southern part of town, through which Hamnet and Ulric Skakki rode now, a different sort of pungency.

Because those districts were in the southern part of town, the wind from the Glacier blew their stinks away more often than not. The Glacier . . . The great shield over the north of the world . . . You couldn't see it from Nidaros any more, as you had been able to in ancient days, but its might, though somewhat lessened, still lingered. And the Glacier, and the wind from the Glacier, was the other reason Nidaros' streets behaved the way they did.

No one wanted to give the wind from the Glacier a running start. It was bad enough without one. Narrow, winding streets helped blunt its force. Nothing could stop it. Nothing could defeat it. The Bizogots, who lived and hunted out in the open far to the north of Nidaros, called it the Breath of God. Hamnet Thyssen had no love for most Bizogots, nor they for him, but he could not quarrel with them over the name.

No, you couldn't beat the wind. If you weren't a Bizogot, if you dwelt within the marches of the Raumsdalian Empire, you did what you could to blunt it. Streets twisted. Houses stood tall, and almost shoulder to shoul-der. Their steep-pitched roofs helped shed snow. Windows were small and slitlike, to hold heat in. No house, no shop, in Nidaros had a north-facing doorway. Walls unlucky enough to face north were almost always blank. Where owners could afford it, they were double, to put a dead-air space be-tween living and working quarters and the ravening wind.

Rich people on the street wore furs. The richer the man or woman, the richer—and the warmer—the fur. Poor folk made do with wool. Folk too poor to keep their capes and cloaks and greatcoats in good repair didn't last long, not in Nidaros.

"Why do you suppose the Emperor wants us?" Ulric Skakki asked after a long and not very companionable silence.

"Well, it's not for our looks," Count Hamnet answered. Ulric Skakki blinked, then laughed loud and merrily enough to make heads turn up and down the cobbled street.

Hamnet had tried to stay away from Nidaros since Gudrid started her wandering ways. He still knew how to get around the city, in a rough sort of way, but he wasn't as confident as he had been once upon a time. He found himself letting Ulric Skakki take the lead. The foxy-faced man didn't hesitate. He might be wrong, but he wasn't in doubt.

And he turned out not to be wrong, either. Hamnet Thyssen's nose told him as much even before he caught sight of the towers of the imperial palace above the rooftops. If you smelled musk and sandalwood from distant shores and rosewater in the air, you were close to the Street of Perfumers, and if you were close to the Street of Perfumers you were also close to the palace.

A deep ditch surrounded the palace's thick walls. It wasn't for storing snow, though it sometimes filled during the winter. It was, literally, the last ditch. If, God forbid, an enemy broke into Nidaros, the palace could serve as a citadel till rescuers arrived.

Or, chances are, till it falls, Count Hamnet thought morosely. Chances were that piercing the heart of the Raumsdalian Empire would kill it. Being as sensitive about omens as any less gloomy man, he held that thought to himself.

A drawbridge spanned the ditch. Guards at the outer end of the bridge lowered their spears to horizontal to bar the way. "Halt!" their sergeant called. "Who comes?"

Count Hamnet Thyssen and Ulric Skakki gave their names. "We are expected," Ulric added.

"We'll just see about that." The sentry produced a scrap of parchment and, lips moving, read through the list on it. He might have been cousin to the man Count Hamnet encountered at the South Gate—nothing was official till he said it was. In due course, he did. He nodded to his comrades, who raised their spears. "Pass on!" he said. Horses' hooves booming on the planks of the drawbridge, Hamnet and Ulric Skakki rode on.

ON THE FAR side of the bridge, unarmed attendants took charge of the newcomers' horses. Armed attendants relieved them of their weapons. Hamnet Thyssen surrendered his sword, his dagger, and a holdout knife in his right boot. Ulric Skakki wore his holdout knife in his left boot, which reminded Hamnet he was dangerous with either hand. He'd forgotten that about the other man.

After the guardsmen disarmed them, a mage came up with a knife carved of wood. He held it in his left hand and made passes with his right all the while, murmuring a spell. The language of the charm was older, far older, than Raumsdalian, itself not a young speech. The wizard used it by rote— only a vanishing handful of scholars spoke it with understanding.

Rote or not, the charm served its purpose. The wizard suddenly stopped and stiffened. He pointed to Ulric Skakki. "On his right arm!" he exclaimed.

Growling like dire wolves, the attendants seized Hamnet's companion. Sure enough, he carried a stiletto, slim but deadly, in a sheath strapped to his right forearm. "What do you have to say for yourself, wretch?" a guardsman growled, the tip of his sword at Ulric's throat.

"That among other things I am charged with ensuring that his Majesty's safety is everything it ought to be," Ulric Skakki answered. "Speak with the first minister. Use my name. If he does not confirm it, drink my blood." He sounded as calm as if haggling over buttered oatcakes.

One of the attendants hurried away. The others stayed ready to slay Ulric Skakki on the instant. Count Hamnet watched Ulric out of the corner of his eye. Even if the first minister vouched for the other man, that could mean one of two things. Maybe Ulric was telling the truth. Or maybe he and the first minister were plotting against the Emperor together.

In due course, the attendant returned. "It is as this fellow says," he said, an unhappy expression on his face. "He is one of Lord Dragnar's agents."

Hamnet wondered if he ought to speak up. Before he could, the chief guardsman said, "Oh, he is, is he? Well, let's strip him, then, and see what else he's carrying."

They didn't just peel Ulric Skakki's clothes off him. They examined him much more intimately than Hamnet Thyssen would have cared to be searched. And they found a couple of sharp-edged throwing disks that could double as armlets, as well as a long, sturdy pin—all objects that escaped the notice of the usual search spell.

By the scars that seamed Ulric Skakki's arms and legs and torso, he'd done more fighting than Count Hamnet would have guessed. By the nasty smile on his face, the guards hadn't found everything. To him, that seemed more important than standing there naked and shivering in the hallway.

That nasty smile goaded Sigvat II's attendants, as no doubt it was meant to do. At last, in a seam of Ulric Skakki's jacket, they found a nasty little saw-edged blade. "All right, now you've got all of it," Ulric Skakki said. "Can I have my clothes back? It's bloody cold."

"Get dressed," the chief guardsman said. "If it was up to me . . ." He didn't say exactly what would happen then. Whatever it was, Count Hamnet didn't think he would want it to happen to him.

Ulric Skakki dressed without another word. If he'd told the attendants and the wizard they should have done a better job of protecting the Emperor, they would have found ways to make him—and, incidentally, Count Hamnet Thyssen—sorry for it. As things were, he projected an air of silent reproach that also had to set their teeth on edge.

"Come with me," one of the attendants said when Ulric had his clothes on again.

On they went. The maze of corridors and passageways inside the palace was nearly as confusing as the maze of streets and lanes and alleys outside. Though Count Hamnet had not come here for years, he found his bump of direction still worked. "This isn't the way to the throne room," he said sharply.

"No, it's not, your Grace," the attendant agreed. "But it is the way to his Majesty's private chambers."

"Oh," Count Hamnet said, startled. In all the years he'd come to the palace, he'd been to the Emperor's private chambers only once or twice. "Can you tell me what this is about?" he asked. Whatever it was, it bore even more weight than he'd thought when the order calling him away from his castle arrived.

The attendant shook his head. "Whatever it is, his Majesty will tell you what you need to know."

Hamnet muttered as he tramped along. He had always been a man for whom the Emperor's word was the be-all and end-all in life. Now he found himself dissatisfied with having to wait for it. A slight smile pulled up the corners of Ulric Skakki's mouth, almost, it seemed, in spite of themselves. Hamnet scowled at him, thinking, *So you know that about me, do you?*

Ulric Skakki looked back blandly, the little smile still on his face, as if to say, *Well, what if I do?* Hamnet trudged ahead. He didn't like other people understanding him so well, being able to think along with him. Gudrid had taught him the hard way how dangerous that could be.

Not that he was in any great danger of falling in love with Ulric Skakki. The first thing you had to do around Ulric was keep your hands in your pockets, or else they'd get picked. And how could you love anyone you couldn't trust? Gudrid had taught him the folly of that, too. By comparison, Ulric's being of the wrong gender seemed a thing of little weight.

A palace servitor fed more charcoal into a brazier. Braziers and fireplaces scattered through the enormous building heated it . . . somewhat. Hamnet hadn't walked five paces past this brazier before a frigid breeze slithered down the back of his neck. Maybe that was just as well. In places sealed too tightly against the cold, men sometimes lay down by braziers and never got up again. Not even wizards knew why that happened, but no one doubted that it did.

"Wait here," the attendant told Hamnet Thyssen and Ulric Skakki. The man ducked through a doorway. Hamnet could hear him speaking to someone inside, but couldn't make out his words.

"Yes, yes. Send them in. I've been waiting for them, haven't I?" Count Hamnet had no trouble hearing that, nor in recognizing Sigvat II's voice. Emperors often had less cause to exercise discretion than ordinary mortals did.

Out came the attendant. He gestured to Hamnet and Ulric Skakki. They followed him into the chamber. Rather than on his throne, Sigvat II sat on an ordinary three-legged pine stool. Hamnet Thyssen, being of noble blood, dropped to one knee before his sovereign. Ulric Skakki fell to both knees—he was only a commoner.

A tall, blond Bizogot stood in the room, his back to the fireplace. His blue eyes blazed contempt; Bizogots bent the knee before God, but to no living man. This nomad from the northern steppe wore a cape made from the skin of a short-faced bear. That meant he'd killed the animal himself—Bizogot men would not use hides from beasts they had not slain. And anyone who'd killed a short-faced bear would not be likely to have much trouble with mere men.

The Emperor broke into Count Hamnet's thoughts, saying, "Rise, gentlemen." Hamnet's knee clicked as he got to his feet—one more reminder he wasn't as young as he used to be. Ulric Skakki rose as smoothly as if dipped in bear grease. Hamnet wished he hadn't had that thought; it made his eyes travel to the formidable-looking Bizogot again. The man scowled at him.

Instead of scowling back at the barbarian, Count Hamnet asked Sigvat, "How may we serve you, your Majesty?" However he and Ulric Skakki were to serve, it would involve the Bizogot in some way. The man wouldn't be here otherwise. Hamnet found the prospect less than delightful—quite a bit less, in fact—but knew he couldn't do anything about it.

"There is news from the north," the Emperor said, which was anything but a surprise. Though Hamnet Thyssen would never have said such a thing, he'd long thought Sigvat II had a gift for the obvious. Sigvat was unlikely to go down in history as one of the great Raumsdalian Emperors. No one five hundred years from now would speak of him in the same breath as Domaldi the Conqueror or Faxi Blood-Hand or even Smiling Solveig, who hadn't been much of a general—or, indeed, much of an Emperor—but who'd passed away in circumstances that proved his personal popularity.

"And what *is* the news from the north, your Majesty?" Ulric Skakki asked when the Emperor didn't go on right away.

Sigvat II looked a trifle miffed at being pushed, but he seldom looked more than a trifle miffed; he was a good-natured man. His face, round and bland, suggested as much. But Hamnet Thyssen saw something in Sigvat's eyes he'd never even imagined there before. Was it fear or awe or a bit of both? He couldn't be sure; it was too unfamiliar.

"I think," Sigvat said, "I had better let Trasamund here give it to you. He found it, and he is the man who brought it to Nidaros. Trasamund," he added, "is jarl of the Three Tusk clan of the Bizogots."

"Jarl?" Hamnet Thyssen said in surprise. "The clan chief came here himself?" He spoke to the Emperor, not to the Bizogot.

"I am the clan chief, and I came here myself," Trasamund said in excellent Raumsdalian. He looked from Count Hamnet to Ulric Skakki and back again. "Do the two of you know my clan?" He used the dual number, implying Hamnet and Ulric were a natural pair. That insulted Count Hamnet; by the pained look on Ulric Skakki's face, he liked it none too well, either.

Ulric Skakki's expression also said he knew something of the Three Tusk clan. Before he could parade his knowledge, Count Hamnet beat him to the punch. "I do," he said, stressing that *I* ever so slightly. "You dwell in the farthest north, up against the Glacier as close as any folk may go."

Trasamund grunted and nodded. Had the Raumsdalians *not* heard of the Three Tusk clan, that would have been a deadly insult—though few men this far south in the Raumsdalian Empire troubled to tell one barbarous band from another. Since Hamnet Thyssen and Ulric Skakki did know of his clan and its place in the fierce, frigid Bizogot scheme of things, the jarl accepted their knowledge as no less than his due.

"Knowing who we are and our position, then, you will know also that we travel up the Gap as far as we may," Trasamund rumbled.

"It only stands to reason," Hamnet Thyssen said, and Ulric Skakki nodded.

For long and long and long, the Glacier that capped the north of the world had been a single vast sheet. Scholars claimed it was three miles thick in spots. Count Hamnet had no idea how they knew, or how they thought

they knew, but he wasn't prepared to call them liars. He'd seen the edge of
the Glacier himself, on journeys among the Bizogots. Those shining cliffs
seemed to climb forever.

When the edge stood not far north of Nidaros, in the days before the
Raumsdalian Empire rose to greatness, the Glacier had still been a single
sheet. But, as it drew back over the centuries that followed, it drew back not
straight north, but to the northeast and the northwest. Thus what Raumsdalians called the Gap—a narrow stretch of bare ground between the two
lobes of the Glacier. The Bizogots used a word with the same literal meaning but much earthier associations.

"By God," Hamnet Thyssen said softly. "By God! Will you tell me, Jarl
Trasamund of the Three Tusk clan, *will* you tell me the Gap has cloven the
Glacier in two?"

Ulric Skakki whistled softly, a low, mournful note. Count Hamnet felt
like doing the same. There were metaphysicians, and more than a few of
them, who argued that the Gap could not possibly divide the Glacier, for the
Glacier had to go on forever. Though no metaphysician himself—far from
it—he'd always inclined toward that view himself. So did most men who'd
actually set eyes on the Glacier. It was too vast to imagine its having an end.

But Trasamund nodded. He also scowled. Plainly, he did not care to be
anticipated. Anticipated he was, though, and he would have to make the
best of it. "I will tell you this, southern man, for it is so. Do you call me a
liar?"

If Hamnet Thyssen did call him a liar, one of them would die in the next
few minutes. Hamnet was large and formidable, but Trasamund was larger
still, and stronger, and younger. All the same, Count Hamnet thought he
could take the Bizogot if he had to.

Here, though, the issue did not arise, for Hamnet shook his head. "Not
at all, your Ferocity." He invested the jarl's title with not even a grain of
irony. "No, not at all. Tell us, then—what lies beyond the Glacier?"

Hamnet leaned toward Trasamund, waiting for the answer. So did Sigvat
II. Ulric Skakki also listened intently, but seemed rather less interested.
Hamnet Thyssen wondered why. Beyond the Glacier . . . He might as well
have said, *beyond the moon*. Anything might lie there, anything at all. Some
folk said God led men into this promised land and then laid down the
Glacier to keep evildoers from following them. Some said the men here *were*
evildoers, and God had laid down the Glacier to keep them from finding the
earthly paradise that lay beyond it. Some said the men here had always been

here, and the Glacier had always been here, and nothing lay beyond it. Count Hamnet had always inclined toward that view, too, but maybe he was wrong.

"Haven't been far yet, you understand," Trasamund said. Hamnet, Ulric Skakki, and Sigvat II nodded as one man. The Bizogot went on, "What I've seen of the land beyond the Glacier looks a lot like what I'd see on this side just below it. It's tundra country, a cold steppe. The animals are strange, though. Buffalo near the size of woolly rhinos. Big wandering herds of squat, shaggy deer. Wolves bigger than coyotes, smaller than dire wolves. White bears—smaller than short-faced bears, but I think slier and sneakier, too."

"Men?" All three Raumsdalians asked the question at the same time.

"I didn't meet any. Maybe I was lucky not to," Trasamund answered. "I'd say there are some, for the animals were wary of me. They've been hunted. I have no doubt of that. But the way northwest is open. If the weather doesn't turn cold enough to make the ice sheets grow together again, it'll stay open."

"Did you see any sign—any sign at all—of the Golden Shrine?" Sigvat II asked.

Again, the Emperor and Hamnet Thyssen and Ulric Skakki leaned toward Trasamund as if a lodestone were drawing them. People who claimed this land south of the Glacier was promised to those who lived in it said the Golden Shrine was what had kept their enemies from following them all those ages ago. People who claimed this land was in the hands of evildoers or their descendants said the Golden Shrine was made to keep them in. People who claimed the Glacier went on forever mostly didn't think there was any such thing as the Golden Shrine. Count Hamnet hadn't. Now . . . How could anyone know what to believe now?

"I saw nothing of that sort myself," Trasamund answered. "But it's on account of the Golden Shrine that I came down here to Nidaros with the word. You Raumsdalians know more about old things than we do. If it's there, and if we find it . . . I wouldn't want to touch off a curse, you understand, not even knowing I was doing it. Next time I go north, I ought to have Raumsdalians along, too. Just in case, you might say."

To turn aside any curses, Hamnet wondered, *or to make sure we get our fair share of them?* Were Bizogots devious enough to think that way? Hamnet wasn't so sure about most of the barbarians. The jarl of the Three Tusk clan struck him as sly enough and then some.

"Here you have two bold men who will go anywhere a Bizogot will," the

Emperor said, nodding to Count Hamnet and Ulric Skakki in turn. "Both have traveled widely in the north of the world, and both are presently, ah, at liberty."

Hamnet Thyssen knew what that small imperial exhalation meant as far as he was concerned. It meant he would be—not happier, but less unhappy—the farther from Nidaros he went. He'd never dreamt of going beyond the Glacier, but if that didn't put enough distance between him and Gudrid, nothing could.

Odds were nothing could.

And what of Ulric Skakki? Why was he so willing to leave the Empire for parts unknown? Was he running away from someone? From something? Was he running *toward* something? In Hamnet Thyssen's experience, that was far less common, but it wasn't impossible.

Right now, Hamnet had no answers, only questions. On the journey, if they made the journey, maybe the answers would come out. Maybe they wouldn't do too much harm when they did. Hamnet could hope they wouldn't, as long as he remembered hopes were only shadows that too often vanished in the pitiless light of reality.

As he was looking at Ulric Skakki, so Trasamund the jarl was eyeing him and Ulric both. "Yes, they may do," the jarl said at last. "The name of Hamnet Thyssen is not unknown in the north, and this other fellow is a likely rogue—I have heard of him, too. But will they be enough? We Bizogots, we have likely rogues aplenty. We have warriors aplenty, too—good fighting men. I mean no disrespect to you, Count Hamnet."

Hamnet Thyssen bowed. "I take none. You do not insult me, or tell me anything I did not know, when you say I am not unique." One more thing Gudrid had taught him. If she'd found a more painful way to give him the lesson than any Bizogot jarl might, that only meant it would stick better.

As Trasamund eyed Hamnet and Ulric, so Sigvat II eyed him. "What would you, then, your Ferocity?" the Emperor asked.

"When we go through the Gap again, your Majesty, our band will have a shaman with it, the wisest Bizogot shaman I can talk into coming along," Trasamund said. "But there is wisdom, and then there is wisdom. The Empire has more of it than we do. You can afford it. You sit in towns, and what are towns but stores of *things*? Things like books, for instance. I said it before—your memories are longer than ours, firmer than ours. Give us a wizard, give us a—what word do you use?" His big head bobbed up and down as he found it. "Give us a scholar, by God!"

Now Count Hamnet studied the jarl in surprise. Not all Bizogots even realized they were barbarians by the standards of the Raumsdalian Empire. Most of the ones who did realize it answered Raumsdalian scorn with contempt of their own. To them, Raumsdalians were weak and tricky and corrupt, of use to the Bizogots not for themselves but for their *things*, the things they could make and keep and the northerners couldn't.

But Trasamund, plainly, was no ordinary mammoth-herder. He grasped something a lot of Raumsdalians couldn't—that the way writing bound knowledge across time gave the Empire a breadth and a depth of thought no Bizogot clan could even approach. Facing the unknown beyond the Glacier, Trasamund wanted people equipped to understand it—if any people were.

Sigvat II seemed taken aback. When he did not answer at once, Count Hamnet said, "Your Majesty, if a wizard and a scholar will go with us, we would do well to have them. Who knows what we may find? Who knows what we may try to understand?"

"The Golden Shrine," Ulric Skakki murmured.

Hamnet Thyssen still had no idea if there was any such thing as the Golden Shrine. An hour earlier, he would have laughed at the very idea. He wasn't laughing now. If the Gap had opened, who could say what lay beyond the Glacier? No one now—no one except Trasamund and whoever traveled with him.

And whoever lived beyond the Glacier, if anyone did. Trasamund thought so. Hamnet wouldn't have believed it, but so what? The opening of the Gap made his beliefs, and everyone else's in the Empire, irrelevant. Belief worked well enough when a man could not measure it against facts. But when he could . . . Facts crushed belief like a mammoth crushing a vole.

After a few heartbeats of thought, the Emperor nodded. "Well, your Ferocity, your Grace, let it be as you desire," Sigvat said. "We shall indeed summon a scholar and a sorcerer to accompany you. God grant they prove useful."

Trasamund and Count Hamnet both bowed. The jarl of the Three Tusk clan said, "I thank you for your kindness, your Majesty, and for your wisdom."

"It was not my wisdom—it was yours," Sigvat said. "Count Hamnet helped me see it."

"Count Hamnet has a name for good sense," the Bizogot chieftain said. "I was glad when you summoned him."

"You have heard of me, too, you said. What do *I* have a name for?" Ulric

Skakki inquired in what might have been amusement or might have been something altogether darker and more dangerous.

Trasamund took him literally, answering, "For getting in and getting out again. Where we are going, what we are doing, that may be the best name of all to have."

"Each of you will be my guest here at the palace till we find you suitable companions," Sigvat said. "I will lay on a reception and a feast in your honor tonight."

So much for wisdom. So much for good sense, Count Hamnet thought unhappily. Now he was stuck in Nidaros for God only knew how long, stuck in the same town with Gudrid and Eyvind Torfinn. He wished he could have got in and got out again. And it was his own damned fault he hadn't.

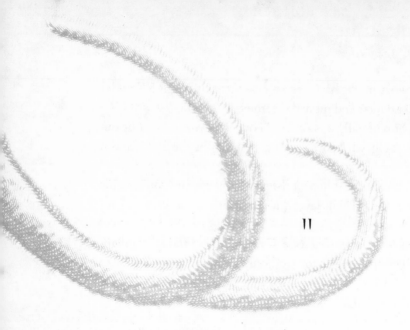

II

Torches blazed bravely. They drove night back to the corners of the dining hall, even if they did fill the room with a strong odor of hot mammoth fat. Perfumed beeswax candles spilled out more golden light and fought the tallow reek to something close to a draw.

A goblet of mead in his hand, Count Hamnet Thyssen surveyed the throng gathered at least partly in his honor. He tried to imagine some of these gilded popinjays up on the tundra, or in the endless forests to the east. That was enough to squeeze a grunt of laughter from even his somber spirit.

So far, he hadn't spotted either his former wife or her new lord and master. He snorted again, more sourly than before. He didn't think even a wild Bizogot could master Gudrid, and he didn't think many wild Bizogots would be fool enough to try.

His gaze flicked to Trasamund. Tall and fair and handsome, the jarl had already acquired a circle of female admirers. The smile on his ruddy face said he enjoyed the attention. The ruddiness on his smiling face said he'd already had as much mead—or beer, or ale, or even sweet wine from the far southwest—as was good for him. Up on the tundra, Bizogots drank fermented mammoth's milk. Count Hamnet had made its acquaintance. It was as bad as it sounded. No matter how nasty it was, the Bizogots drank heroically. *Anything worth doing is worth overdoing* summed up the nomads' view of the world.

And Bizogots wenched as heroically as they drank. That might—was all too like to—cause trouble. Hamnet drifted toward a steward. A word to the wise . . . probably wouldn't help. He held his tongue. This wasn't the first time Bizogots had been fêted in the royal palace. The steward—and the Emperor—would know what they were like.

A serving woman came by with a plate of treats—toasted deer marrow on crackers of barley and maize. Count Hamnet took one. The fatty richness of the marrow went well with his mead. Beer might have been even better, but he preferred the fermented honey.

Someone—someone with long fingernails—rumpled the hair at the nape of his neck. He whirled around. If the goblet hadn't been nearer empty than full, mead would have sloshed out of it onto the rug.

"Hello, Hamnet," Gudrid said. "I wondered if you weren't noticing me on purpose."

He knew how old she was—not far from his own just-past-forty. She didn't look it, or within ten years of it. Her hair was still black, her skin still smooth, her chin still single. Her eyes were almost the color of a lion's, a strange and penetrating light brown. They sparked now in smug amusement.

She was going to jab at him. She did whenever they met. She always wounded him, too. He did his best not to show it; that way, she missed some of the sport. So he shook his head now. "No, I really didn't see you," he said truthfully. "I'm—"

He broke off. He was damned if he'd say he was sorry. He could still feel her fingers on the skin at the back of his neck. His hand tightened on the goblet till he feared the stem would snap. Somehow, the stolen caress infuriated him worse than all her infidelities. She'd lost the right to touch him that way. No, she hadn't lost it. She'd given it up, thrown it away. She took it back for a moment only because she wanted to provoke him.

She knew how to get what she wanted. She commonly did.

Her smile said she knew she'd scored, even if she might not know just why. Her teeth were white and strong, too. That also made Hamnet want to scowl; poppy juice and henbane or not, he'd had a horrid time with a tooth-drawer the year before.

"So you're going traveling with the splendid Trasamund, are you?" she said, eyeing the tall Bizogot with admiration unfeigned and unconcealed. If she decided she wanted him, she would go after him. Yes, she knew how to get what she wanted, all right.

And what would Eyvind Torfinn think of that? Hamnet almost threw the question in her face. Then he saw she was waiting for it, looking forward to it. Whatever the answer was, it would have claws in it. He didn't feel like giving her the satisfaction. "So I am," he said stolidly, and let it go at that.

Eyvind Torfinn came up then, a winecup in his hand. He was a comfortably plump man getting close to sixty if he hadn't already got there. Maybe he wouldn't mind so much if Gudrid satisfied herself somewhere else every now and again. Hamnet drained what was left of his mead. Gudrid hadn't played him false because he failed to satisfy her. Adultery was a game to her, and she excelled at it as she did at most things.

"Thyssen," her new husband said politely.

"Torfinn," Count Hamnet returned. He had . . . not too much against the older man, who'd always seemed faintly embarrassed at acquiring his wife.

"Dear Hamnet is going exploring with the wild Bizogot." Gudrid made it sound faintly disreputable. She eyed Hamnet, ready to finish him off. "What is it you're going off to look for?" Whatever it was, by the way she asked the question it couldn't have been more important than a small coin that had fallen out of a hole in a belt pouch.

"The Golden Shrine," Hamnet answered, his voice still flat. Let her make what she wanted of that.

Her lioness eyes widened, for a heartbeat looking only human, and amazed. "But that's a fable!" she exclaimed. "Nobody really believes it's up there, or wherever it's supposed to be."

"Oh, no. That is not so. Many people do believe it." Gudrid looked amazed all over again, and even less happy than she had a moment earlier. Count Hamnet didn't contradict her; Eyvind Torfinn did. "I happen to be one of them myself," Eyvind went on. He turned to his wife's former husband. "Why would anyone think the chances of finding it now are any better than they would have been last year or a hundred years ago?"

"Because the Gap has finally melted through. Trasamund's traveled beyond the Glacier." Hamnet Thyssen usually had as little to say to Gudrid's new husband as he could. Maybe the mead was what loosened his tongue enough to make him say, "So you believe in the Golden Shrine, do you, Earl Eyvind? Why is that?"

As Gudrid had a moment earlier, he got more than he bargained for. Eyvind Torfinn didn't just believe in the Golden Shrine. He knew more in the way of lore than Hamnet thought there was to know. His talk went spinning back through the centuries, back to the days before Nidaros was even a hunting camp, back to empires far older than the Raumsdalian, back to other retreats of the Glacier—though he didn't know of any others where the Gap actually opened.

By the way Gudrid listened to him, he might have been talking about a mistress he'd kept secret from her. Maybe she thought he was, and maybe she was right; knowledge was like that for some men. Hamnet Thyssen hadn't known Eyvind was one of them. Plainly, his former wife hadn't, either. After a couple of exaggerated yawns didn't make Eyvind Torfinn dry up, she flounced off, hips working in the clinging maroon wool knit dress she wore.

Her husband never noticed. He was comparing and contrasting modern ideas about the Golden Shrine with those from bygone days. He knew more about ideas from bygone days than Hamnet Thyssen had thought any living man could. "And so you see," Eyvind Torfinn said with an enthusiast's zeal, "there is more than a little consistency about these notions through time. Not perfect consistency, mind you, but more than a little. Enough to persuade me something real lies behind all the guesswork and the legends."

What Hamnet saw was Gudrid doing everything but painting herself against Trasamund. She all but purred when the Bizogot stroked her. If her gap wouldn't open for him, Hamnet would have been very much surprised.

But that was not his worry now, for which—some of him—thanked God. He set a scarred and calloused hand on Eyvind Torfinn's shoulder. "Your Splendor," he said, "his Majesty was talking about recruiting a scholar to accompany us on the journey north. I think you are the man we need."

"I?" Eyvind Torfinn said in mild astonishment.

"Certainly. You know so much about the Golden Shrine. Wouldn't you like to put what you know to use? Wouldn't you like to see the Temple with your own eyes?" *If it's there to see,* Hamnet Thyssen added, but only to himself.

Eyvind stared at him. "I would like that very much," he said. "Whether I can make such a journey may be another question. Beyond the Glacier! I was not sure there was such a thing as beyond the Glacier. For all I knew, for all anyone knew, it went on forever."

"I had the same thought when I learned the Gap has melted through," Count Hamnet said. "But Trasamund speaks of white bears and strange buffalo and other marvels he's seen with his own eyes."

"Does he?" Eyvind Torfinn looked toward the tall Bizogot. By then Gudrid, with a sure instinct for self-preservation, no longer clung to him, even

if she did hover close by. Seeing her set her present husband down a different thought-road. He swung back toward Hamnet. "Can you stand to make
a journey with me, your Grace? I would not be grateful—I fear I would not
even be long ungrateful—if you set on me the moment we passed the Empire's borders, or perhaps even before we passed them." ·

"By God, your Splendor, by God and by my honor, I will do nothing of
the sort," Hamnet Thyssen said. "You have my oath, the strongest oath I
can give. If it is not enough to satisfy you . . . If it is not enough to satisfy
you, sir, then be damned to you. I don't know what else to say."

"If we meet danger, I am more likely to prove a liability than an asset,"
Earl Eyvind said. "I am not young. I am not strong. I am not swift or grace-
ful. I have not even practiced with a sword for many years, let alone un-
sheathed one in anger."

"You know things," Hamnet said. "You know things I did not think anyone could know. Speak to Trasamund." *Though not of your wife—she's not mine
now.* "Speak to the Emperor. Knowledge is always an asset."

"Is it?" Eyvind Torfinn raised a bushy gray eyebrow. "Are you glad knowing . . . what you know about the lady who was once your wife?"

"Am I glad? No," Count Hamnet answered steadily. "Would I rather
know the truth than live in a fool's paradise? Yes, and she played me for a
fool." *And she'll play you the same way, if she hasn't done it already, and you may
prove yourself a fool if you don't know that.*

"The Golden Shrine," Eyvind murmured. "Well, maybe, if you don't
think I would slow you up too much."

"Persuade Trasamund. I have no trouble with riding a little slower than I
might have ridden otherwise, but I'm no hot-blooded, impatient Bizogot."
*And you have put horns on me, and Trasamund—I doubt not—will put horns on you,
and if I should meet Trasamund's wife, if he has a wife . . . What a jolly gathering we
would be then.*

"Well! The Golden Shrine!" Eyvind Torfinn said, and he waddled off toward the Bizogot jarl.

SIGVAT II WAS delighted that Earl Eyvind wanted to fare north, and delighted and amazed to discover him a scholar of the Golden Shrine.
Trasamund was willing to bring him along, although amazed and less than
delighted to discover him the husband of Gudrid. Hamnet Thyssen was . . .
resigned. He would have had some strong opinions if he thought Gudrid

was coming along, but she seemed furious that Eyvind Torfinn could find the Golden Shrine more interesting, more attractive, than she.

"She will spend my money while I am gone," Eyvind said to Count Hamnet when they met two days after the reception to plan what they could. On a journey into the unknown, they couldn't plan nearly as much as Hamnet would have liked.

"No doubt you are right, your Splendor," Hamnet replied. *She will spend your reputation while you're gone, too,* he thought with mournful certainty.

"I hope I have some left by the time I get home," Eyvind Torfinn said.

"Maybe your chief of affairs should oversee your funds," Hamnet said. And who would oversee Gudrid's affairs? Hamnet Thyssen almost laughed at himself. No doubt Gudrid would take care of those on her own.

Hamnet glanced over toward Trasamund. Did the Bizogot jarl speak fluent enough Raumsdalian to make that joke, or one like it, for himself? By the smirk on his ruddy, weathered face, he did.

Earl Eyvind was either blind to what Gudrid was or resigned to it. Hamnet hadn't made up his mind which. He wouldn't have wanted to be either one, though he'd stayed blind for too long when she was his wife. Maybe he hadn't wanted to see. Considering all the strife that sprang up when he finally couldn't help it . . . He shook his head. He didn't want to consider that.

"We still need a sorcerer," Eyvind Torfinn said. He was looking ahead again to the lands beyond the ice, not to what Gudrid would do while he wasn't here to watch her. "His Majesty was wise to suggest one."

"*I* suggested one," Trasamund said in a voice like distant thunder.

"Did you indeed, your Ferocity?" For the first time, Earl Eyvind eyed the Bizogot as something more than a dangerous and dubiously tame animal. Eyvind didn't seem to have imagined a brain might lurk under that handsome, well-muscled exterior. He blinked once or twice, revising his opinion.

"I did." Trasamund proudly drew himself up straight. All Bizogots were full of ungodly gobs of pride—so it seemed to Raumsdalians, anyhow. A Bizogot jarl was apt to be proud even by the standards of his people. Having known quite a few clan chiefs among the mammoth-herders, Hamnet Thyssen had seen that for himself. And Trasamund was proud even for a Bizogot jarl.

"Well, good for you, then." Eyvind Torfinn kept his voice mild. Even if Trasamund wanted to act irascible, that mildness left him not the smallest excuse. Eyvind's gaze swung back to Count Hamnet. "And where will we come by the wizard?"

"Ulric Skakki is searching Nidaros for the best man," Hamnet answered.

"You know this Skakki, don't you?" Eyvind Torfinn said. "I confess I had not met him before. He seems . . . versatile."

"A sneak, a thief, a cutpurse, a knife in the dark, a pretty song to woo the ladies." Trasamund delivered his judgment before Hamnet Thyssen could. "A good man at your side, maybe not so good at your back." He mimed taking a knife in the kidney.

"And what do you think, your Grace?" Eyvind Torfinn asked Count Hamnet—he valued a Raumsdalian's opinion more than the jarl's.

But Hamnet said, "I think his Ferocity is a keen judge of men." He bowed to Trasamund. "I rode with Ulric Skakki once. We had some business to attend to for his Majesty—this was toward the end of the first Sigvat's days." He made a sour face. "It was one of those nasty little things you wish you didn't have to do, the kind you don't like talking about afterwards. And we took care of it, and Ulric was . . . everything you said he was, Trasamund."

"Did you let him get behind you?" the Bizogot inquired.

"No. I'd already decided that wasn't a good idea," Count Hamnet answered. "As long as I could keep an eye on him, everything was fine."

Trasamund nodded. That satisfied him. And hearing his cleverness and judgment praised pleased him no less than it would have pleased a Raumsdalian. *He likes himself pretty well,* Hamnet thought. No, Bizogots were no more immune to vanity than the folk of the Empire. Many people would have said they were less immune to it.

"How far did you travel after you passed through the Gap?" Eyvind asked him.

"I stayed beyond the Glacier for about three weeks all told," Trasamund said. "I wasn't heading out in a straight line to see how far I could go, you understand. I was wandering here and there, wandering wherever I pleased."

"Drunkard's walk," Eyvind Torfinn murmured.

"By God, I wasn't drunk!" Trasamund's cheeks flamed with anger. "I drank water all through that journey—well, almost all through it."

Eyvind held up a plump, placating hand. "No, no—I meant no offense. The drunkard's walk tries to answer the question of how far from where you start you will end up if you travel at random for such and such a time."

Trasamund's face remained thunderously suspicious. "How can anyone know that? And why would anyone care?"

"It takes a good deal of calculating," Earl Eyvind allowed. "And why? Well, people like to find out whatever they can. Haven't you seen that?"

"Didn't you come down to Nidaros, your Ferocity, because you knew Raumsdalians know more different kinds of strange things than you Bizogots do?" Hamnet Thyssen added.

Trasamund made a discontented noise down deep in his broad chest. He *had* said something like that, so he couldn't very well deny it. "I meant you people know *useful* things, though," he said. If he couldn't deny, he could deflect.

Count Hamnet looked over to Earl Eyvind. He thought the notion of a drunkard's walk sounded silly, too, so he didn't know how to defend it. "Knowledge is strange," Eyvind Torfinn said. "You never can be sure ahead of time what you may need. Someone who is going to a strange place will carry different tools on his belt. Should he not carry different tools in his head as well?"

Instead of answering him straight out, the jarl of the Three Tusk clan strode over to a sideboard and poured himself a goblet of mead. He drank it down in one heroic draught. Hamnet Thyssen suspected that was an answer of sorts.

WHEN ULRIC SKAKKI brought a wizard back to the palace, Count Hamnet's first thought was of the drunkard's walk Eyvind Torfinn had mentioned. The sorcerer's name was Audun Gilli. He didn't look or act drunk. He looked like a man drying out after a long binge instead—and not like a man happy to be drying out, either.

Count Hamnet recognized that look. He knew it better than he would have liked. He'd gone on a bender or two of his own as his troubles with Gudrid got worse. He'd been sober when he killed. That was something—not much, but something.

Of course, if he were drunk when he faced Gudrid's first lover (or the first one he caught, anyhow), the other man probably would have killed him. At the time, he would hardly have minded. Now he saw living on without her as revenge of sorts.

He also saw that Audun Gilli was in a bad way. He shouted for a palace servant. "Bring this man a mug of sassafras tea," he said, pointing to the wizard. "No, bring him about three. By the time he gets to the bottom of the last one, he may be a bit better off."

"Bring me the hair of the hound—sassafras tea be damned." Audun Gilli's voice was a sorrowful whine.

The servant looked toward Hamnet Thyssen. "Tea!" Hamnet snapped. The man bowed and hurried off. Audun Gilli's sigh said it was just one more defeat in a lifetime full of them. Count Hamnet paid no more attention to him—but then, how many people ever did? Hamnet rounded on Ulric Skakki. "By God, Ulric! Which gutter did you drag him out of, and why?"

"Why? Because he'll do what we need, that's why," Ulric Skakki answered. "More to him than meets the eye." He sounded very sure of himself. From what Hamnet remembered, Ulric always sounded sure of himself. That didn't mean he was always right, though he had trouble recognizing the difference.

"There could hardly be less to him than meets the eye," Count Hamnet said with something between a sneer and a cry of despair. "*Look* at him!"

He glared at Audun Gilli himself. The wizard flinched under that fierce stare. Audun was a small, weedy man, the sort who didn't stand out in a crowd. He had a long, weathered-looking face, a scraggly beard—brown going gray—and a nose that was his largest but not best feature. The whites of his gray-blue eyes were yellowish and tracked with red. His hands trembled.

They were a wizard's hands but for the tremor; Hamnet Thyssen could not deny that. They had narrow palms and long, delicate fingers—perfect hands for the complex passes some spells required. A wizard with the shakes, though, was like a blind archer; he was more likely to be dangerous to his friends than to his foes.

The servant came in with three steaming mugs on a tray. He'd taken Hamnet literally, then. *Good,* Hamnet thought. He thrust a mug at Audun Gilli. "Here. Drink!"

With a martyred sigh, the wizard obeyed. He did need more than one mug before Hamnet saw any improvement. He was on the third one before he seemed to see any improvement himself. "I never thought I'd be warm inside again," he murmured.

"Well, that proves he wasn't drinking mulled wine," Hamnet said to Ulric Skakki. "What *was* he drinking? Anything he could get his hands on, that's plain. And why was he drinking it by the bloody wagonload? And, since he was drinking wagonloads of anything he could get his hands on, what in God's name makes you think he's worth even a counterfeit copper as a wizard?"

"I don't do this all the time," Audun Gilli protested feebly.

"Of course you don't. If you did, you would have been dead in the gutter where Ulric Skakki tripped over you, not just lying in it." Count Hamnet rounded on Ulric. "Now answer me—or else I'll throw him out on his worthless ear and take the cost of three cups of sassafras tea out of his worthless hide."

"How can you take cost out of something worthless?" Audun asked, the first sign Hamnet Thyssen had that whatever he'd drunk hadn't curdled his wits for good.

"He's had a hard time," Ulric Skakki said. "If you'd had that hard a time, you would drink, too."

Since Hamnet *had* drunk when times got hard for him, and since Ulric Skakki probably knew as much, denying that didn't seem a good idea. Instead, Hamnet turned back to Audun Gilli. "Well?" He made that more a challenge than a question.

"My wife burned down, and my house died in the fire," the wizard said, a pretty good sign not all his wits were working the way they should have.

It was also a pretty good sign he did deserve some sympathy. "When did this happen?" Count Hamnet asked, less roughly than before.

"Three years ago," Audun Gilli answered.

Count Hamnet could feel his neck swelling. "Easy, there," Ulric Skakki said. "When he dries out, he'll be fine. He's a student of sorceries from ancient days, so he should be exactly the kind of wizard we want along if we find the Golden Shrine."

"I'll bet he's a student of ancient sorceries," Hamnet said. "He's been pickled from then till now."

"His Majesty sent me out to find a proper wizard. *Me*," Ulric Skakki replied with a touch—or more than a touch—of hauteur. "I say I've found him."

"I say you couldn't find your arse with both hands if you think so," Count Hamnet growled. They glared at each other.

Forgotten by both of them like a bone abandoned when two dogs go at each other, Audun Gilli stared at the mugs in which his sassafras tea had come. He chanted softly to himself. The language he used hadn't been spoken since long before the Raumsdalian Empire rose, but Hamnet Thyssen didn't notice that. In his quarrel with Ulric Skakki, Hamnet Thyssen didn't notice the wizard at all.

Then two of the mugs started shouting at each other in high, squeaky voices that sounded like parodies of Ulric's and Hamnet's. It wasn't ventriloquism; the mugs suddenly sported faces too much like theirs. The less than flattered models both gaped. So did the third mug, which looked like a sorrowful ceramic version of Audun Gilli.

The wizard chanted again, and the mugs . . . were only mugs again. "You see?" Ulric Skakki said triumphantly.

"I saw . . . something." However little Count Hamnet wanted to, he had to admit it.

"He's a wizard. He's a good wizard. And," Ulric went on pragmatically, "he'll be better the longer he stays sober."

"Who says he'll stay sober? We'll be drinking ale or beer or mead or fermented mammoth's milk as much as we can," Hamnet said. "Even runoff straight from the Glacier can give you a bloody flux. Have you ever been up in the Bizogot country, Ulric? Don't you know about that?"

"I've been there, all right. I know," Ulric said. Count Hamnet wasn't sure he believed him till the other man added, "We'll have to pick our way past the lands where a couple of clans range. They may remember me a little too well."

That held the ring of truth. "Why am I not surprised?" Hamnet Thyssen said. Ulric Skakki gave back a bow, as if at a compliment. Audun Gilli managed a wan smile when he saw it. Count Hamnet threw his hands in the air. When you knew you were going to lose a fight, sometimes the best thing you could do was give it up before it cost you more than you could afford to spend.

If only he'd figured that out with Gudrid. . . .

EARL EYVIND TORFINN was a friendly man. As Raumsdalian nobles were supposed to be, he was openhanded in his hospitality. He lived in a large, rambling two-story house on top of a hill in the western part of Nidaros. From windows on the upper floor, he could look out on what had been Hevring Lake when the great city was but a hunting camp.

Hamnet Thyssen knew that because Earl Eyvind insisted on inviting him to feast with the other members of the upcoming expedition. Refusing would have been churlish—Eyvind Torfinn seemed to think that his acquiring Hamnet's wife was just one of those things, certainly not important enough to get excited about. Visiting that house, though, dripped vitriol on Hamnet's soul.

Gudrid did her best to make sure that it should. She wore outfits that clung and revealed. She smiled. She sparkled. Much of that was aimed at captivating Trasamund. The Bizogot didn't prove hard to captivate. If she could wound Hamnet at the same time—well, so much the better.

He set his jaw and tried not to show he was wounded, as he would have if he'd taken an arrow in the leg. Gudrid knew better. She knew him altogether too well. When they were happy together, the way she knew him pleased him and made him proud. These days, it meant he was vulnerable.

Eyvind Torfinn seemed oblivious to the byplay. Count Hamnet wasn't sure he was, but he seemed that way. Ulric Skakki watched it with wry fascination. He didn't seem to interest Gudrid. Maybe that was because he was only a commoner, maybe because she recognized that he might be as devious and dangerous as she was herself, if less alluring. As for Audun Gilli, he took in everything with a childlike, wide-eyed fascination. But a child who drank the way he did would have been in no shape to take in anything.

Trasamund, for his part, took Gudrid's attentions as no less than his due. "That is quite a woman," he told Hamnet, plainly not knowing they'd once been man and wife. "Not as young as she used to be, maybe, but still quite a woman. Still plenty tight." The jarl leered and rocked his hips forward and back, in case Hamnet could have any doubt about what he meant.

"Is she?" Count Hamnet's voice held no expression whatever. That might have been just as well. If he had let it hold expression, what would have come out? Rage? Bitterness? Jealousy? Longing? Since he revealed even less to Trasamund than he did to Gudrid, the question didn't arise. So he told himself, anyhow.

He drank Eyvind Torfinn's wine and beer. He ate horseflesh and fat-rich camel's meat, and musk ox and strong-tasting mammoth flesh brought down from the north on ice. There was ice in the north, all right, ice and to spare. He nibbled on honey cakes and frozen, sweetened milk. And his stomach gnawed at him, and he wished he were anywhere else in all the world. Sinking into soft asphalt with dire wolves and sabertooths prowling all around? Next to this lavish hospitality, that looked pretty good.

"You hate me, don't you?" Gudrid asked one evening after everyone had drunk a little too much. By the way her eyes sparkled, she wanted him to tell her yes.

"I loved you," Hamnet Thyssen said, which was not an answer—unless it was.

The gleam grew brighter. "And now?"

Count Hamnet shrugged. "We all make mistakes. Some of us make bigger mistakes than others."

"Yes, that's true," Gudrid agreed. "I never should have wed you in the first place."

"You didn't think so then," Hamnet said, and let it go at that. If he told her she'd loved him, she would have laughed in his face. He thought she had. He was convinced she had, in fact. But he was just as convinced that Sigvat II's torturers couldn't tear the confession out of her now.

"We all make mistakes. You said it; I didn't." Gudrid was like a cat, playing and swiping and tormenting before the kill.

"And what mistake did you make with Eyvind Torfinn?" Hamnet inquired.

She breathed sweet wine fumes into his face when she laughed. "Dear Eyvind? I made no mistakes with him. He lets me do whatever I please."

"And you despise him for it," Count Hamnet said. Gudrid did not deny it; she only laughed again. Stubbornly, Hamnet went on, "Wouldn't you call wedding a man you despise a mistake?"

"Of course not. I call it an amusement." She reached out and stroked his cheek with a soft hand. "But don't worry, my sweet. If it makes you feel any better, I despise you, too."

"And Trasamund?" Hamnet asked, trying to ignore the way her touch seared his flesh.

"Ah, Trasamund." She laughed throatily and batted her eyelashes at him. "No one could despise Trasamund. He's much too . . . virile."

"He thinks you're quite something, too," Hamnet said. Gudrid laughed again, this time in complacent amusement. Hamnet added, "For someone who's not as young as she used to be." Even a man with no other tool toward revenge had time on his side.

Now her eyes stopped sparkling. They flashed instead. "You'll pay for that," she said.

Hamnet Thyssen shrugged. "I've been paying for knowing you for years. What's a little more?"

"If I tell Eyvind to stay home—"

He laughed in her face. "You hurt the Empire if that happens—not that you care, I'm sure. But it doesn't worry me at all. Your husband probably knows more about the Golden Shrine than any man alive. I know he knows more than I thought anybody could. He'd be useful to have along, yes. But he's still your husband, Gudrid. If you think I *want* his company, you'd better think twice."

She made what sounded like a lion's growl, down deep in her throat. She didn't like being thwarted, didn't like it and wouldn't put up with it. She'd taken up with Eyvind Torfinn not long after Hamnet killed her earlier lover. He judged it was at least as much to show him he couldn't get the better of her as for any attraction Earl Eyvind held.

"I suppose you know I've had your wizard as well as the Bizogot," she said. Her red-painted lip curled. "He wasn't what you'd call magical."

She told him to hurt him. She couldn't have any other reason. "You're not my worry any more," he said. It wasn't true; she would go on worrying him till his dying day. He added, "You've given us all something to talk about on the way north, anyhow."

Gudrid smiled—she liked that. "Something warm, instead of the Glacier."

Count Hamnet shook his head. "Something so cold, it makes the Glacier seem warm beside it."

Fast as a striking serpent, her hand lashed out. However fast she was, she wasn't fast enough. Count Hamnet caught her wrist before she could slap him or claw him. "Let go of me," she said in a low, furious voice.

I've been trying to, ever since I found out what you are, Hamnet thought. He opened his hand. The memory of her flesh remained printed on his palm. She didn't feel cold. Oh, no. You had to know her to understand what he meant.

Then again, he wondered if he'd ever known her at all.

"You're harder than you were," she remarked.

"If I am, whose fault is that?" he asked harshly.

"May the Bizogots eat you," Gudrid said. The mammoth-herders didn't eat men, even if a lot of Raumsdalians thought they did. A lewd question rose in Hamnet's mind. He stifled it. She went on, "May you fall off the edge of the world when you go beyond the Glacier. May one of the white bears Trasamund goes on about gnaw your bones."

His bow was stiff as a wooden puppet's. "I love you, too, my sweet," he said, and tried to match her venom so she wouldn't realize he was telling the truth—the painful and useless truth.

He must have done what he set out to do, for her laughter this time was jagged as shattered ice, sharp as sabertooth fangs. She stalked away, if stalking was the right word to use for something with so much hip action. Even without words, she reminded him what he was missing. He looked down at the rug. *As if I didn't know,* he thought, and kicked at the embroidered wool.

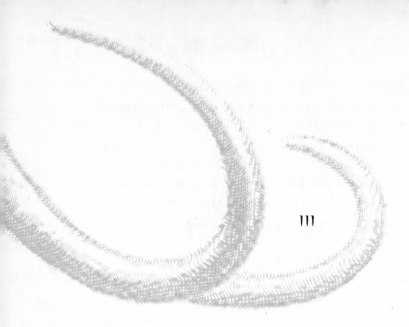

III

RIDING OUT OF Nidaros came as nothing but a relief for Hamnet Thyssen. He could deal with Ulric Skakki and Audun Gilli. He could deal with Trasamund the jarl. He could even deal with Eyvind Torfinn, though he would rather not have to. As long as he didn't have to deal with Gudrid, he felt he could do anything.

The Great North Road ran from the Raumsdalian capital toward the imperial border—and toward the Bizogot country beyond it. Armies had moved up that road more often than Hamnet could easily count, ready to repel invaders from the north. And the barbarians had spilled into the Empire more often than he could easily count, too. Its riches and the better weather it enjoyed drew them like a lodestone.

One of these days, Hamnet supposed, the Bizogots would win, and either put one of their own on the Raumsdalian throne or topple the Empire altogether. Nothing lasted forever. It seemed not even the Glacier lasted forever, although a couple of lifetimes earlier everyone would have thought the Glacier the one surely eternal thing God made.

Was God himself eternal? Hamnet Thyssen uneasily looked up into the steel-blue sky. If God himself might pass away, who rose to power after he was gone? Men intent on their affairs? Women intent on *their* affairs? (Gudrid was certainly intent on *hers*.) Or older, darker Powers God had long held in check?

What *was* the Golden Shrine, anyway?

Ulric Skakki chose that moment to remark, "A copper for your thoughts, your Grace." Hamnet was a man who made a habit of saying what was in his mind, even—perhaps especially—when no one had asked him. He told Ulric Skakki exactly what he was thinking about. The younger man blinked; whatever he was expecting, that wasn't it. He reached into his belt pouch and pulled out a copper coin. Offering it to Count Hamnet, he said, "Well, your Grace, I got my money's worth."

Hamnet solemnly stowed the coin. "We endeavor to give satisfaction. It doesn't always work, mind you, but we do endeavor." He thought of Gudrid again. But it wasn't that he hadn't satisfied her. He had, as far as he could tell. She'd wanted something else, something more, from him. Whatever it was, it seemed defined not least by his inability to give it to her.

Did her first lover, the one who laughed? Did Eyvind Torfinn? Did Trasamund? Did having them give her what she craved? *Was* having them what she craved?

If Ulric Skakki had chosen that moment to ask him for his thoughts, he would have lied without the least hesitation. He didn't mind talking about the death of the Empire, or about the death of the Glacier, or even about the death of God. The death of the one real love of his life? That was different.

Farmers weeded their young, hopeful crops of rye and oats off to either side of the road. Barley rarely succeeded north of Nidaros, even now. Wheat? Maize? Those were crops for softer, more luxurious climes. The farmers always seemed to have one eye on the north. If the Breath of God blew against them for long, their crops would wither and freeze and fail, even here. Then they would live on what they'd stored in better years, and on what they could hunt.

Or they would die. It happened, in hard years. Oh, yes—it happened.

No one hurried. Neither Trasamund nor Audun Gilli was any sort of a horseman, while Eyvind Torfinn might have been once upon a time but wasn't any more. Some of the Raumsdalians in the party might not have been anxious to leave the Empire behind—not in their hearts, anyway, no matter what their heads might tell them.

Hamnet Thyssen knew perfectly well what lay beyond the border. No-mad huts on the tundra—land crushed flat by the Glacier that had lain on it for so many centuries. Herds of half-tame musk oxen and mammoths guided—when they could be guided—by half-tame men. Meltwater lakes. Cold beyond what even Nidaros ever knew. Wind almost always from the north, almost always with frigid daggers in it. Snow and ice at any season of the year.

And then—the Glacier itself.

Yes, it was wounded. Yes, if Trasamund spoke truly, the Gap had at last pierced it to the root. Not the Glacier any more, but Glaciers, divided east and west. Count Hamnet shook his head in slow wonder at that. But still, any man who ever saw the Glacier, even diminished as it was, knew in his belly what awe meant. It went forward and back—more back than forward of late—like a live thing, but it swallowed the whole north of the world.

Well, most of the north of the world, anyhow. If the Gap ran all the way through it . . . That was why they were here.

The Golden Shrine. Hamnet glanced over at Earl Eyvind. No, he hadn't believed in the Golden Shrine. Even if he had believed in it, what difference would that have made? With the Glacier between Raumsdalia and the Golden Shrine, whether it was real might trouble scholars, but not ordinary men. Count Hamnet was not exactly an ordinary man, but he was no scholar, either, and just as glad not to be one.

Ulric Skakki puffed on a long-stemmed pipe. Tobacco came up from the warmer climes of the south. "Why do you smoke that stinking thing?" Hamnet asked. "You'll just run out of your precious weed after we've been on the road a while."

"When I run out, I'll do without," Ulric answered cheerfully. "If you don't like the smell, I'm sorry. You can ride upwind of me easily enough."

"You didn't tell me why you smoke it," Hamnet said.

"Well, maybe I didn't." Ulric Skakki smiled and shrugged. "I've got to where I like the taste, though I didn't when I started." Count Hamnet made a face. Ulric laughed. "Tell me you liked beer the first time you drank it," he said. Hamnet couldn't, and he knew it. Ulric went on, "And the smoke relaxes me, and fiddling with the pipe gives me something to do with my hands. Does that suit you?"

"Reasonable today, aren't you?" Hamnet Thyssen said with a crooked smile.

Laughing, Ulric bowed in the saddle. "I'll try not to let it happen again, your Grace." He pointed north. "Is that a serai up ahead?"

Hamnet eyed the large, low building by the side of the road. The lower half of the wall was of stone, the upper of timber. Smoke rose from three brick chimneys. "It's not likely to be anything else," Count Hamnet said.

"Well, no." Ulric Skakki's smile was so charming, it made Hamnet distrust him on sight—as if he didn't already. Smiling still, Ulric went on, "Do you think we're likely to come to another one before nightfall?"

"Mm—I daresay not," Hamnet answered. "They aren't usually set close together—if they were, they'd hurt each other's trade."

"Then shall we stop?" Ulric said.

"Why ask me?" Hamnet Thyssen returned. He knew why the others were on the expedition. Trasamund had actually gone beyond the Glacier. Eyvind Torfinn knew whatever there was to know about the Golden Shrine. If Audun Gilli could remember his own name, he was a wizard. Ulric Skakki could get his hands on anything that wasn't nailed down—and steal the nails if that looked like a good idea.

Which leaves—me, Count Hamnet thought. He could ride and he could fight and he was glad for a chance to escape the Raumsdalian Empire. All of that was well enough. But did it make him the leader? Ulric Skakki seemed to think it did. Ulric wouldn't want to lead himself—it was too much like work. But Eyvind Torfinn was a belted earl, while Trasamund was a jarl and as arrogant as anyone Hamnet had ever met. He didn't much want to lead such a motley crew.

But then Trasamund guided his horse close by Hamnet's. "Shall we stop at that serai for the night?" the Bizogot asked.

Hamnet stared. Did Trasamund think he was in charge, too? He hadn't looked for that. But he said, "Yes, I think we'd better. We won't come to another one before the sun goes down." Trasamund nodded and rode away.

Eyvind Torfinn didn't even question Hamnet's right to decide. Neither did Audun Gilli, though Count Hamnet would have been astonished if he had. *It's on my shoulders*, Hamnet thought. *And when things go wrong—and they will—the blame will land on my shoulders, too.*

DESPITE THE CHIMNEYS, the common room in the serai was smoky enough to make Hamnet Thyssen's eyes sting. Some of that smoke came from the hearthfires, some from the cookfires back in the kitchen, and some from the pipes and cigars on which more than a few of the travelers puffed.

Gnawing on a turkey leg, Trasamund said, "This is not a bad place." A tall jack of beer sitting beside his trencher of hard barley bread probably went a good way toward improving his opinion. So did the smiles he'd won from the barmaid who'd brought him the jack. He had at least some reason to hope he'd win more than smiles from her.

The food and drink suited Hamnet Thyssen well enough. The barmaid didn't interest him. He did idly wonder what Gudrid would think of

Trasamund's pursuing another woman so soon after leaving her arms. He shrugged. Chasing a barmaid wouldn't worry him unless the Bizogot got killed in a brawl over her (which seemed unlikely) or came down with an unpleasant disease because of her (the odds of which Hamnet had no way of guessing).

Eyvind Torfinn seemed content with supper, even if it was rougher than what he was used to. Audun Gilli ate more than he drank. To Count Hamnet, that made the meal a success as far as the wizard was concerned.

Hamnet shared a room with Audun. The evening was *not* a success. The sorcerer, though a small man, proved to own a large snore. Hamnet wondered if there was some sorcerous cure for that. Then he wondered if he ought to throw a boot at Audun, the way he might have at a yowling cat.

Ulric Skakki and Eyvind Torfinn had the room to one side of Hamnet's. The walls were no thicker than they had to be—Hamnet could hear the other two men talking for a long time. He wondered what they were talking about. Gudrid? As far as Hamnet Thyssen knew, she hadn't slept with Ulric. But he didn't know how far he knew.

On the other side, Trasamund had a room to himself. Except he didn't have it to himself for long. The bedframe creaked. He grunted. His companion giggled and then moaned. Hamnet found himself glad of Audun Gilli's snores. They helped drown out the amatory racket. Not long after the creaking next door reached a crescendo, it began anew. The Bizogot had stamina. By the noises his partner made, he also had technique.

How much of that technique had he had before he came south off the frozen steppe? How much had he learned inside the Empire—or, to come straight to the point, inside Gudrid? Count Hamnet ground his teeth. What *he* had right now was insomnia. He also had the firm conviction that God would have had trouble falling asleep in that room just then.

Eventually, in spite of everything, Hamnet *did* go to sleep. What that said about God's chances of doing the same . . . he was too unconscious to worry about.

A sunbeam sneaking through the slats of the shutter on the south-facing window poked him in the eye. He yawned and sat up. Audun Gilli went on snoring away. Either Eyvind Torfinn or Ulric Skakki also owned a pretty formidable snore. As for Trasamund, he really *did* have stamina. That barmaid would probably walk bowlegged for days.

Yawning again, Hamnet got out of bed. He'd slept in his clothes, as one did on the road. Instead of throwing his boots at Audun Gilli, he put them on. He did take the small pleasure of shaking the wizard awake. "You snore," he said when he saw reason in Audun's eyes.

"I do?" the wizard said around a yawn of his own. Hamnet Thyssen nodded emphatically. Audun Gilli started pulling on his own boots. "Well, your Grace, if I do, I'm not the only one here who does."

"What? Me?" Count Hamnet didn't believe it—or didn't want to believe it, anyhow. He stood on what dignity he could. "I've never once heard myself snore."

Audun Gilli started to answer that, then seemed to think better of it. He contented himself with, "Shall we get the others up?"

"Trasamund's been up most of the night," Hamnet answered, which made Audun begin and then visibly reconsider another answer. Hamnet added, "But we may as well knock. That barmaid will have to go to work soon anyhow, though I daresay Trasamund's worked her harder than the fellow who runs this serai ever did. Here's hoping she had fun."

"They don't stay till morning if they haven't." The wizard spoke more practically than Hamnet Thyssen would have expected.

Hamnet knocked on the door to the room that Eyvind Torfinn and Ulric Skakki shared. He knocked loud and long, hoping Trasamund and his lady friend would also hear. That actually worked; the barmaid scurried out of the Bizogot's chamber and down the hall toward the common room. But when Ulric opened the door, he looked more than a little put upon. "What?" he said irritably. "Is this place on fire?" Earl Eyvind appeared behind him, seeming similarly aggrieved.

"No fire—except, I hope, in the hearth," Hamnet said. "Which of you snores?"

"He does." Ulric and Eyvind both said the same thing. They pointed at each other. Eyvind Torfinn added, "As long as we're talking about snoring, was that you or Audun sawing stone last night?"

"Yes." Hamnet let him make whatever he pleased of that. "I'm going to get Trasamund moving," he went on. "Then we ought to eat and we ought to ride."

Earl Eyvind rubbed his hindquarters. Ulric Skakki sighed a martyred sigh. But neither man said no. Hamnet Thyssen knocked on Trasamund's door. "You hit ours a lot harder than that," Ulric said. *Yes, and I had my reasons, too,* Hamnet thought. Ulric went on scowling.

Trasamund was also scowling as he opened up. But when Count Hamnet said, "We should be moving," the Bizogot's glower faded. Moving was something the mammoth-herders of the north understood.

They all went off to the common room. Hamnet Thyssen was ready for oatmeal mush swimming with butter or rye crackers or barley rolls or boiled goose eggs or whatever else the seraikeeper served for breakfast.

The barmaid was already busy, hurrying from the kitchen to other travelers waiting for their food. Count Hamnet noticed her only out of the corner of his eye. He stopped in his tracks at the entrance to the common room. None of his companions tried to push past him into the big hall, either.

From her perch on a bench near a fireplace, Gudrid waved gaily to them.

SHE HADN'T COME alone. Half a dozen stalwart imperial guardsmen sat across from her and to either side. Hamnet wondered how she'd talked Sigvat II out of them. Then he decided he didn't want to know, because talking might not have had anything to do with it. A heartbeat later, he shied away from *hadn't come alone,* too.

"My sweet! What are you doing here?" Eyvind Torfinn asked—a reasonable question, and much more mildly phrased than it would have been coming from Hamnet. Still sounding reasonable, and reasonably concerned, Earl Eyvind went on, "Is anything wrong down in Nidaros?"

"No, no, no." Gudrid laughed one of her silvery laughs. And then Count Hamnet discovered that he'd thanked God too soon, for she said, "I decided I'd come along with you, that's all."

Hamnet stiffened, as if taking a sword thrust. Eyvind's jaw dropped. Even the unflappable Ulric Skakki blinked. Audun Gilli's eyes widened. And Trasamund roared laughter himself.

"That's . . . impossible," Eyvind Torfinn said. Again, Hamnet would have told Gudrid the same thing. Again, he would have used stronger language. Earl Eyvind continued, "You couldn't possibly make it to the land beyond the Glacier."

"Why not?" When Gudrid sounded innocent and sweet, you were well advised to set a hand on your belt pouch.

"Because you're a woman, that's why not," Eyvind answered.

"And so?" Gudrid said. "If I can't ride better than Audun there, I'm a musk ox. And I can shoot—*dear* Hamnet taught me how years ago. I don't pull a very heavy bow, but I hit what I aim at."

She did, too. Hamnet Thyssen knew it. Trasamund looked from him to

Gudrid and back again in surprise. No, the Bizogot jarl hadn't known of any connection between them. Hamnet hadn't thought he did.

"And besides," Gudrid went on, still sounding sweet and innocent and, if you knew her, deadly dangerous, "I'll have all you big strong masterful men to protect me, won't I? *And* these guardsmen his Majesty was kind enough to give me, too."

Some of the guardsmen looked mildly embarrassed. Others smirked. How *had* Gudrid persuaded the Emperor? And why were those men smirking?

"This is most unwise. It will not do," Eyvind Torfinn said.

"I agree. This journey will be complicated enough without, uh, complications." Ulric Skakki didn't put that well, and knew it, but also didn't leave much doubt about what he meant.

"Madness," Hamnet said.

Gudrid fluttered her fingers, literally dismissing that out of hand. "As if you'd say anything else," she murmured. Then she fluttered those slim fingers again, this time toward Trasamund. "And what does our valiant Bizogot chieftain say?"

The valiant Bizogot chieftain hadn't said much of anything. He'd listened to the backbiting with what seemed like immense enjoyment. Now he laughed once more. "Let the wench come," he said. "Why not? It will make the journey more entertaining."

"But—" Eyvind Torfinn said.

Trasamund cut him off with a slash of the hand. "I have said she will come, and she will come." He spoke with a jarl's hauteur—he didn't think Hamnet was the leader any more, then. "Raumsdalia does not have to go beyond the Glacier. Raumsdalia does not have to look for the Golden Shrine. We Bizogots can do it alone. The way north for you goes through our land."

Earl Eyvind made a horrible face, not because Trasamund was wrong but because he was right. When the Empire's needs clashed with his . . . He scowled at the Bizogot and scowled at his wife, but in the end he nodded.

Hamnet Thyssen, by contrast, started out of the common room. "Where are you going?" Eyvind Torfinn called after him. His tone suggested a drowning man watching a spar drift away.

"Home," Hamnet answered. "The Golden Shrine can rot, for all of me, and the Gap, too."

Gudrid's laugh somehow struck him as ominous. "I knew you'd get stuffy about this, Hamnet. I *knew* it. Read this." She held out a rolled parchment.

He made sure he didn't touch her when he took the parchment. She noticed him making sure, and laughed again, this time at him. He ignored her. She thought that was funny, too. The parchment was sealed in wax of imperial gold, and had stamped on it a sabertooth's head—Sigvat's seal. Hamnet Thyssen ground his teeth as he broke it.

Most of the message was in a secretary's supremely legible script.

> *To Count Hamnet Thyssen from his Imperial Majesty, Sigvat II, by God's grace Emperor of Raumsdalia. Your Grace—You are hereby requested and required to continue on your journey north to the lands beyond the Glacier and, if possible, to the Golden Shrine, notwithstanding the presence on the said journey of Gudrid, wife to Earl Eyvind Torfinn, whose intimate knowledge of conditions pertaining to the said Golden Shrine conduces to the success of the expedition of which you form a component.*

A scrawled signature, unquestionably Sigvat's, lay under the body of the letter.

"You see?" Gudrid said, languid triumph in her voice.

"I see." Hamnet folded the parchment and put it in his belt pouch—he offered no offense to the imperial letter, though his first impulse was to fling it in the fire. "And I tell you this, Gudrid: no matter what this letter says, I am not a cursed component. I am a man—my own man, by God. I'm for my own keep, too, and the journey can go hang. And so, my former dear, can you."

He trudged out of the serai and off toward the stable, not a man in a hurry but not a man about to change his mind, either. He'd almost got to the stable door when someone behind him called, "Hamnet—wait."

If that had been Gudrid, he wouldn't have waited—though he might have drawn sword on her if she tried to insist. But it wasn't. It was Ulric Skakki. "Well?" Hamnet growled. "Are you fool enough to think you can make me change my mind? If Sigvat can't do it, you aren't likely to."

"I wouldn't dream of trying, your Grace," Ulric said. Hamnet laughed harshly—he knew a lie when he heard one. Unperturbed, Ulric Skakki went on, "I just wanted to tell you one thing before you go."

"Well?" Hamnet said. "What is it? Say your say, then, and be quick about it."

"I will," Ulric said. Whom he served—beyond himself—was a mystery to Hamnet. He hadn't been in the habit of talking about himself when he and Hamnet served together a few years earlier. Evidently he still wasn't.

With a small shrug, he went on, "If you leave, if you walk away, that woman wins."

Had Ulric called Gudrid by her name, Hamnet Thyssen would have turned his back and gone into the stable, and afterwards much would have been different. As things were, he looked Ulric up and down, a glower that would have annihilated a lesser man, or a less self-assured one. Ulric Skakki withstood it with no external signs of injury.

"As if I care what that woman does," Hamnet said, and then, not at all at random, "Have you swived her, too, the way everyone else has?"

"Good God, no," Ulric Skakki answered. "No scorpion ever hatched anywhere has a sting in its tail to match hers."

That held the unmistakable ring of sincerity. But then, Ulric might well be able to sound sincere when he wasn't. It was a common gift. Even Gudrid had it. For the moment, Hamnet Thyssen chose to assume Ulric meant what he said, and growled, "Well, then, you see what my trouble is. I don't want to be within miles of that woman, let alone riding beside her. And I used to love her, which makes it worse."

"But we need you on the journey. You're the best Raumsdalian we have," Ulric Skakki said. "Eyvind Torfinn is nice enough, but he's an old foof. Audun Gilli is . . . what he is. They won't do, Thyssen."

"There's you," Count Hamnet said. "Why are you acting so modest? It doesn't seem your natural state."

"It's not," Ulric agreed. "But I'm only a commoner, and I have a strange background—to say nothing of my foreground." Was his chuckle self-conscious? Hamnet had trouble believing it. Ulric went on, "Earl Eyvind won't take me seriously. Neither will Trasamund. You've got the blood they respect."

"Gudrid might want to see it spilled. Otherwise it doesn't much impress her," Hamnet said. "And there are her bodyguards. One of them would likely serve your purpose."

Ulric Skakki shook his head. "Louts. Fools. Chowderheads. The Emperor won't send away men he can't afford to lose. He'll send the ones he doesn't care about—so that's what he's done. I know about these fellows. And I know something else."

"What?" Hamnet asked uneasily; what Ulric said made altogether too much sense.

"I know Trasamund hasn't told everything he knows about what lies beyond the Glacier."

"And how do you know that?" Hamnet inquired in sardonic tones. "I suppose you've gone beyond the Glacier yourself?"

Ulric grimaced. "Yes, as a matter of fact, I have, though it's worth my life if you say so where a Bizogot might hear. It's likely worth your life, too, so you ought to bear that in mind."

Hamnet Thyssen stared at the younger man. He did not think Ulric was lying; he wished he did. "By God, how did you manage that?" he asked.

"Carefully," Ulric Skakki answered, which had to be the understatement of the year. "Trasamund says he doesn't know if there are men on the far side of the Glacier. Either he's lying or he's not as much of a far-ranger as he'd have us believe. There are." Again, he spoke with great conviction.

"And?" Hamnet asked, as he was plainly meant to do.

"And they're dangerous. To the Bizogots, to us, maybe even to themselves. I am not making this up, Thyssen. I have seen them. We need you there."

"Then send Gudrid back to Nidaros."

Ulric Skakki shrugged sadly. "I'm sorry. I can't do that. I wish I could, but I can't."

"Mmrr." Hamnet made a noise deep down in his chest. "If you lure me on with this, Skakki, if you dangle a wiggling worm in front of me to make me swim after it, I'll kill you. Gudrid's first lover didn't believe me when I said something like that. I'd tell you to ask him if I lied, but he's too dead to give you a straight answer."

"Well, you can try," Ulric Skakki murmured. Count Hamnet sent him a sharp stare. Ulric looked back imperturbably. If Hamnet's words worried him, he showed it not at all. He didn't seem to believe Hamnet could harm him. Maybe that made him a fool. Maybe it meant he knew some things Hamnet didn't, things Hamnet might discover if he tried to make good on his threat. As if it were never made, Ulric went on, "Does that mean you're coming, then?"

The last word Hamnet Thyssen thought he would use came out of his mouth. Hating himself, hating Gudrid, and saving a little hate for Ulric Skakki, too, he said, "Yes."

WEATHER ALONG THE Great North Road seemed to get worse with each passing mile. That had to be Hamnet's imagination. Spring was advancing, the sun staying in the sky longer with each passing day. Things should have got warmer and finer, not darker and gloomier. Odds were that the cloud over the expedition was fixed above his head and no one else's.

Had he wanted other opinions, he would have asked for them. He rode apart from the other travelers, with them but not of them. Audun Gilli rode apart, too, but Audun Gilli was about as sociable as an old root. Sometimes the noble and the wizard rode side by side, but even then they were apart.

As usual, Gudrid contrived to make the world revolve around herself. The royal bodyguards, Eyvind Torfinn, and Trasamund all danced attendance on her. Ulric Skakki seemed more loosely attached to that group, but attached he was—or so it seemed to Count Hamnet's jaundiced eye, at any rate.

For most of the way north toward the frontier, things went smoothly enough. The travelers stopped at a serai each night. If they didn't have all the comforts Gudrid was used to down in Nidaros, they had most of them. Gudrid played the part of the cheerful voyager as if she'd rehearsed for years. Whatever went on in the nighttime went on without Hamnet Thyssen. He and Ulric Skakki usually shared a chamber. As far as he could tell, Ulric didn't go out of nights, so maybe the other man had given his true opinion of Gudrid.

And if he hadn't, it was his lookout.

The country got flatter and flatter as they went north, till it looked as if it were pressed. And so it was. The Glacier had crushed it till very recently. Countless shallow ponds and lakes marked the slightly—the ever slightly—lower ground. The winds mostly blew warm out of the south, but snow lingered long in the shade of the spruce and fir woods.

This far north, farmers planted their rye and oats and hoped for the best. They didn't count on them, though, not the way they did in lands longer free of the Glacier and in those that had never known its touch. They raised hogs and sheep and horses and musk oxen for meat, and they hunted. Imperial garrisons couldn't hope to live on the countryside, not in this inhospitable clime. Supplies came up by riverboat when the streams were open, and by sledge when the rivers froze.

One day, the travelers found there was no serai when they needed to stop for the evening. The one that should have been there had burned down, and nobody had got around to rebuilding it.

They'd passed a village a few miles back—a small, sullen place where a lot of the people looked to have Bizogot blood. Hamnet Thyssen didn't like the idea of turning back to the south on general principles. He especially didn't like the idea of turning around to pass the night in a miserable hole like that.

Up ahead lay . . . well, who could say what? He didn't see any village close enough to reach before the sun went down. No cloud of smoke on the horizon foretold chimneys clustered close together.

"We'll just have to spend the night in the open, under the sky," he said. "This seems about as good a place as any."

"So it does," Trasamund agreed. "Enough trees to the north for firewood, and enough to shield us if the Breath of God blows hard tonight, too. We may shiver a bit, but we won't freeze." The Bizogot jarl laughed. "Next to what we'll see farther north, we might as well still be in a serai."

Gudrid seemed excited about spending the night in a tent. She put up with chewy smoked sausage over an open fire. She drank beer without making a face, though she preferred mead and wine.

Hamnet quietly fumed. He'd hoped the first taste of rough living would send her scuttling back to the capital. That was one of the reasons he'd chosen to camp out here beside the ruins of the serai. She foiled him again.

He volunteered for the first watch. Owls hooted. Off in the distance, dire wolves howled. The wind did come from the north, from the Glacier. Ragged patches of cloud scudded across the sky, now hiding stars, now revealing them.

Someone came up behind him. He whirled. The sword that had been on his belt was suddenly in his hand. Audun Gilli froze. "You don't want to try sneaking up on me," Count Hamnet remarked. "It isn't healthy."

"So I see," the wizard said. "I am not your enemy, your Grace. I hope I am not. I do not wish to be."

"No, you are not my enemy—not unless you make yourself so," Hamnet Thyssen said. "But what are you doing here, anyway?"

"Something besides lying in a gutter clutching a jar of whatever happens to be cheap and strong," Audun answered. "Whatever happens in the north, it has to be better, wouldn't you say?"

"For you, maybe," Hamnet said. "For all of us? Who knows?"

Audun Gilli studied him for a while before saying anything. In the starlight and the dim red glow of the embers from the campfire, the wizard was only a shape in the darkness to the noble. Hamnet couldn't have been much more to Audun Gilli . . . at least, if the wizard was seeing only by the light of the world.

"You are not as hard a man as you make yourself out to be," Audun ventured at last.

"No, eh? If you'd got a little closer before I heard you, I would have cut you in half," Hamnet said. "That would have given you something to grumble about—for a little while, anyway."

"Maybe," Audun Gilli said. "But maybe not, too. I am not everything a wizard ought to be—God knows that's true, and so do I. But I am not nothing as a sorcerer, either."

Ulric Skakki had also said Audun wasn't a negligible wizard. Count Hamnet was more inclined to believe it from Ulric than from the wizard himself, whether he was negligible or not. Yes, Hamnet remembered those two chattering, bickering mugs. But that was a bagatelle. How Audun Gilli would do if—no, when—they had to rely on his magic . . . was anybody's guess.

Hamnet Thyssen didn't like going into the unknown with a wizard whose true quality was also unknown. Some sort of proper test seemed reasonable—to him, anyway. He said, "Can you divine for me why Gudrid wanted to come north? Is it just to jab spikes into my liver, or does she have some other reason, too?"

Audun didn't answer right away. When he did, he said, "Down in Nidaros, she asked me for a divination about you, your Grace."

"Did she?" Hamnet rumbled. "What did she want to know? What did you tell her?"

"I told her that, since the two of you were long separated, whatever she wanted to know was none of her business," Audun Gilli said. "As for what it was, your Grace, *you* don't need to know that. And I would not feel right about divining her reasons for you unless you think she purposes danger to the Empire."

A wizard with scruples? Hamnet Thyssen would have imagined the breed long extinct. He had a hard time imagining the breed ever existed, in fact. But here he had a specimen before his eyes.

Or did he? Was Audun Gilli a wizard with scruples or only a wizard without strength? "We'll find something else for you to do, then," Hamnet said. Audun nodded. If he'd divined what Hamnet was thinking, would he have?

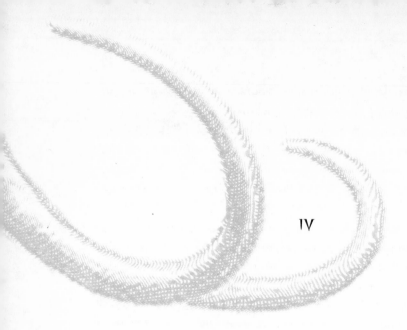

IV

D OWN IN THE distant south, where lands were rich, kingdoms and duchies and principalities marked their borders with fortresses and sometimes even walls. The northern frontier of the Raumsdalian Empire wasn't like that. There were occasional customs posts, but that was about all. The Empire didn't so much end in the north as peter out.

Past the point where even the hardiest, quickest-ripening rye and oats wouldn't let farmers put in a crop, past the broad, dark forests that lay beyond the cropland, administering the Empire grew more expensive than it was worth. There weren't enough people to build a wall in the north, and if there had been the Empire wouldn't have been able to feed the soldiers who manned it.

As for a ditch, the northern frontier lay about where the ground started staying frozen all the time. You couldn't dig a proper ditch in soil like that, no matter how much you might want to.

Every so often, then, the Bizogots broke into the Empire's northern provinces. Sometimes the Empire mustered an army farther south and drove the barbarians back up onto the frozen plains over which they usually roamed. And sometimes the invading Bizogots realized they hadn't overrun anything worth having and went back to the steppe of their own accord.

When the travelers got to, or at least near, the Raumsdalian frontier— exactly where it lay in those parts was more a matter of opinion than certain, settled knowledge—Eyvind Torfinn pointed north and east and west and said, "It's just as dreary in every direction." He wasn't wrong, and it wasn't much less dreary to the south, either.

"It won't get any prettier, either," Hamnet Thyssen said. Ulric Skakki nodded. So did a couple of the imperial guardsmen who accompanied Gudrid. They'd all been up into the Bizogot country before. None of them seemed enamored of it.

Audun Gilli looked this way and that with curiosity both avid and wary. *Probably wondering where his next snootful will come from,* Count Hamnet thought.

Before he could say anything—if he was going to—Trasamund burst into song. The Bizogot language was related to the Raumsdalian, but only distantly. To Hamnet Thyssen's ear, the tongue the mammoth-herders used was rolling and guttural and raucous. Any time a Bizogot spoke his own language, he sounded full of himself. He couldn't help it; the language itself made him sound that way.

"How much of the Bizogot tongue do you know?" Ulric Skakki asked Hamnet.

"Enough to get by," the noble answered. "They'll never think I'm a native, but one look at me and they'll know I'm not, so that doesn't matter. How about you?"

"I'm in the same sleigh," Ulric answered.

Trasamund was in full flow, going on about the Breath of God, about mammoth dung and musk-ox meat, about hunting lions in the snow, about God's curtains (which was what the Bizogots called the northern lights), about fighting enemy clans and leading away their sobbing women after a victory, and about everything else that went into a northern nomad—all in long rhymed stanzas with perfect scansion. Hamnet Thyssen didn't admire the way of life the jarl extolled, but he admired the way Trasamund extolled the life.

So, evidently, did Ulric Skakki. "How does he do that?" Ulric said. "He's no bard, but it just pours out of him."

Count Hamnet couldn't answer, because he didn't know, either. But Eyvind Torfinn said, "He has little blocks of poetry that he uses to make his big poem."

Ulric Skakki scratched his head. "Sorry, your Splendor, but I don't follow that."

"Well, listen to him when he's talking about mammoths," Eyvind said. "If he needs four syllables in front of them to pad out his line, they're always heavy-bodied mammoths. Always. That's the four-syllable epithet for mammoths. But if he only needs two syllables, then they're great-tusked mammoths. They're towering mammoths if he needs three, and black mammoths if he needs one. Those are the only epithets you'll ever hear attached to mammoths. He has others for lions and for fire and for snow and for God and for the rest of the things that go into a Bizogot's life. You see? Building blocks."

"By God," Hamnet Thyssen said. "By God!" He sketched a salute to Earl Eyvind. "I thank you, your Splendor. That's been under my nose for years, and I never saw it."

"Nor I," Ulric Skakki said.

"Wizards in the Empire will do the same thing," Audun Gilli said. "It makes spells easier to memorize."

"Do you understand the Bizogot language?" Hamnet asked.

"No, not past a few curses," Audun answered. "Maybe I will learn more." He shrugged. "Or maybe not."

Trasamund's enormous wave encompassed the whole great sweep of land ahead. "We ride!" he roared.

Ride they did. Shrubs dotted the plain. Hamnet needed a while to see that some were oaks and birches. Up here, with the cold and the wind above and the frozen ground below, they couldn't grow into proper trees. Farther north still, near the edge of the Glacier, they got no bigger than violets or daisies down in warmer climes.

A bird glided across the sky above them. *A hawk,* Hamnet Thyssen thought. But after a moment he realized he was wrong. It was an owl, a snowy owl. They often hunted by day. Everything up in the Bizogot country seemed confused.

"There are folk in the south who say seeing an owl by daylight is the worst of bad omens," Audun Gilli remarked.

"Let them come to the north country, the free country, the great country, and they will see they are mistaken," Trasamund boomed. Even speaking Raumsdalian, he sounded as if he were declaiming his song of praise.

In a low voice, Ulric Skakki said, "They might think coming to this God-frozen place was the worst of bad omens, and if they saw an owl by daylight that would only prove it."

"I shouldn't wonder," Hamnet replied, also quietly. To his way of thinking, the closer to the Glacier a stretch of land was, the madder a man had to be to want to live on it. The way the Bizogots behaved did little harm to his theory. He asked, "What's the weather like beyond the Glacier?"

Ulric made sure Trasamund wasn't paying any attention to him before he answered, "It's not much different from this, as a matter of fact."

"You surprise me," Hamnet said. "I would have expected worse."

"I expected worse myself," Ulric said. "But it seems as if the weather that blows down off the Glacier is already about as bad as it can be. Whether that amounts to a disaster or a consolation depends on your point of view, I suppose."

Hamnet Thyssen was temperamentally inclined to look on the gloomy side of things any which way. Hearing that things in these parts were as bad as they could be gave him a somber sort of satisfaction.

The snowy owl swooped. It rose again with something writhing in its claws. It wouldn't go hungry for a while—or maybe it had nestlings that would feast on the mouse or vole or rabbit it had caught. By the purposeful way it flew, Hamnet Thyssen guessed it was off to share its prey.

He glanced over at Gudrid. To his relief, she didn't notice him doing it. Her eyes were on the owl. They glowed. They sparkled. He supposed it was the pleasure of watching the kill. That was like her, sure enough. The chilly wind painted roses on her cheeks. She looked uncommonly vivacious, uncommonly beautiful. In spite of everything Hamnet knew, his manhood stirred.

Angrily, he looked away.

WHEN THE DOGS came bounding toward the travelers, Hamnet first took them for a pack of dire wolves. They were as fierce as dire wolves, baying and howling and showing their yellow fangs. They were almost as big as dire wolves; several of them looked big enough to bridle and saddle. And, by the way they loped forward, they were as hungry as their wild cousins, too.

Trasamund stood up in the stirrups and roared curses at them in his own language. Men would have cringed. The dogs took no notice. On they came.

Ulric Skakki proved himself the relentless pragmatist Count Hamnet thought him to be—he strung his bow and nocked an arrow. That seemed like such a good idea, Hamnet imitated it. He didn't think killing a couple of these brutes would scare off the rest. That could work with men, but wouldn't with beasts. But the living might feed on the dead, which would make them less enthusiastic about attacking the travelers.

Off to one side as usual, Audun Gilli muttered to himself. Hamnet Thyssen thought nothing of it; Audun spent too much time muttering to himself, maybe as consolation for drinking less. This muttering, though, proved different.

From the air in front of Trasamund came a growl that might have burst from God's throat if God happened to be a dog. Hard on the heels of the growl followed a snarl like ripping canvas, then another growl, and then some furious barks that almost deafened Hamnet and spooked his horse.

He wouldn't have made a useful archer. How was he supposed to shoot when he had all he could do to keep from getting pitched off the horse and onto his head? Next to him, Ulric Skakki also fought to stay in the saddle.

It turned out not to matter. The onrushing dogs stopped so short, they dragged their bottoms on the ground as they dug in their hind legs. They seemed to decide they had urgent business elsewhere—with their lawyer, perhaps, or at the tailor's. They ran the other way as fast as they'd charged ahead—and much less noisily.

A few more growls and woofs right behind them spurred them on their way. Audun Gilli stopped muttering. The dog the size of God fell silent, too. Hamnet Thyssen was no scholar. He left that to Eyvind Torfinn, who was welcome to it. Scholar or not, Hamnet recognized cause and effect when he saw them.

Once he persuaded his horse that the God-sized dog wouldn't devour it in the next heartbeat, he bowed in the saddle to Audun. "That was fine wizardry," he said. "You know I've had my doubts about you, but you just buried a lot of them."

"My thanks." Sweat beaded on Audun's face despite the chill. "The sounds weren't hard, though getting them loud enough took a little doing. But I think the scent worked even better."

"Good God!" Ulric Skakki said. Count Hamnet nodded—he couldn't have put it better himself. What would a dog that sounded like that smell like? Not having a dog's nose, he couldn't fully understand the answer. But he had some idea of what it must be, anyhow. A dog that sounded as if it was the size of God smelled . . . intimidating.

Trasamund pointed north. "Here come the dogs those dogs belong to. Musk Ox clan." His curled lip said what he thought of the approaching Bizogots.

The riders wore furs, as he did. But on their heads they had woolen caps in gaudy zigzag stripes. They hadn't made those themselves; the caps were products of Raumsdalian bad taste. But they'd traded for them, so they had bad taste of their own.

"Next question is, are they at war with Trasamund's clan, or does he just think they wear ugly headgear?" Ulric Skakki murmured.

"We'll find out," Hamnet Thyssen said, a sentiment that had the advantage—or, too often, the disadvantage—of being true almost all the time.

"Who are you people?" one of the oncoming Bizogots shouted. "Why are you crossing our grazing lands?" Count Hamnet hadn't heard the Bizogot language for a few years. He was glad he could still understand it.

"What did you do to our dogs?" another mammoth-herder added.

"We drove them off," Trasamund yelled back. "Better than they deserve, too. If dogs trouble us, we treat them . . . like dogs." He didn't quite tell the Musk Ox men they were dogs themselves, but he didn't miss by much, either. Bizogots lacked a lot of things Raumsdalians took for granted, but not arrogance. Never arrogance. Trasamund struck his broad chest with a big fist. "I am Trasamund son of Halkel, jarl of the Three Tusk clan. These are my friends." He threw his arms wide to include his companions from the Empire. Then he pointed straight at the man who'd challenged him. "Hinder us at your peril!"

"Subtle," Ulric Skakki murmured.

"It's how Bizogots do things," Hamnet Thyssen answered, and Ulric nodded. Hamnet went on, "In his own way, Trasamund has style." Ulric Skakki nodded again. It wasn't the sort of style Hamnet would have wanted, but that had nothing to do with anything.

The Bizogots from the Musk Ox clan reined in. It didn't look like an immediate fight—a good thing, too, because Trasamund and the Raumsdalians were likely to lose. "I am Sarus son of Leovigild," said the blond barbarian who spoke for the Musk Ox men. "I am the jarl's son." He wore a cap with rings of red and deep blue and saffron. It couldn't have got much uglier if it tried for a year. "We have no quarrel with the Three Tusk men . . . now." The concession was grudging, but it was a concession.

"We have no quarrel with the Musk Ox men . . . now." Trasamund sounded as grudging as Sarus.

"And we have no quarrel with the Empire," Sarus added after taking a look at the men—and woman—accompanying Trasamund. He didn't qualify that with a *now*. Hamnet Thyssen wasn't sure Trasamund noticed, but he did himself.

Eyvind Torfinn held the highest rank among the Raumsdalians. "Nor does the Empire quarrel with the Musk Ox clan," he said in the Bizogot tongue, speaking slowly but clearly. As well as a round man could, he bowed in the saddle.

"What did you do to the dogs?" asked the mammoth-herder who'd put the question before.

"We kept them from troubling us," Eyvind Torfinn answered.

"You have a shaman with you." By the way Sarus said it, it was not a question.

"And why should we not?" Eyvind Torfinn spoke in even terms. After Trasamund's bombast, Count Hamnet wondered if Sarus would pay any attention to him. Eyvind went on, "The world is full of spirits. The world is full of other shamans, too. Are we not allowed to ward ourselves as we would?"

Sarus mulled that. The son of the Musk Ox jarl was big and fair, like most of the Bizogots who rode with him and like Trasamund. Though he couldn't have been older than twenty-five, he had a warrior's scars and a nose that leaned to the left. "You will come to our camp," he said at last. "My father will decide."

It was not a request but a command. The only way to say no was not to speak but to fight. Sarus had more men with him than the Raumsdalians and Trasamund. Even if the northbound travelers somehow vanquished Sarus and his followers, the Musk Ox men could easily summon reinforcements. Hamnet Thyssen could not prove there were any other Raumsdalians north of the ill-defined border.

"Are we to be guests at your father's camp?" he asked before either Trasamund or Eyvind Torfinn could speak. People formally admitted to be guests had a special status among the Bizogots. They couldn't be killed for the sport of it, for instance. If any of them were female, they couldn't be thrown down on the cold ground and gang-raped for the sport of it, either.

If Sarus said no, then fighting to the death now might make a better bet than whatever the Musk Ox jarl's son had in mind. But, after no more than a heartbeat's hesitation, Sarus nodded. "Yes, you will be guests at my father's camp. You will eat of our meat and salt. You will drink of our smetyn." That was the name they gave to fermented mammoth's milk—indeed, to any fermented milk. A Raumsdalian would have spoken of bread and salt and beer or, if he was rich, of wine. But the same principle held.

"We thank you for your kindness," Hamnet Thyssen said. "We are glad to accept. Should you come to the lands we roam, we will gladly guest you there."

Sarus smiled to see a foreigner fulfill ritual so well. Trasamund bared his teeth at Count Hamnet in what looked also like a smile, but wasn't. He did not want ties of guesting to bind him to the Musk Ox clan. Want it or not, though, he was stuck with it unless he wanted to charge Sarus's clansmates singlehanded.

Maybe he wanted to. But he didn't do it.

Hamnet Thyssen chuckled, down deep in his chest. So did Ulric Skakki. Audun Gilli looked from one of them to the other. Neither offered to explain. In some clans—Hamnet didn't know if the Musk Ox was one of them—hospitality went further than meat and salt and smetyn. Some of the mammoth-herders shared their wives with guests.

And the Bizogots expected visitors to their tents to do the same if they ever appeared as guests themselves. Every so often, a Raumsdalian marriage burned like a dry, dead fir after a man who'd gone up to the frozen plains unexpectedly had to try to meet his obligations to a traveler from the north.

What would Gudrid make of such a demand? Count Hamnet suspected it would depend on what she thought of the individual Bizogot. She certainly hadn't turned her back on Trasamund—at least, not with her clothes on.

To Hamnet's relief, Sarus son of Leovigild said, "We ride, then," and wheeled his horse to the northwest, the direction from which he and his comrades had come. The Raumsdalians and Trasamund rode after him.

The dogs that had loped along with Sarus's followers clung close to their horses. They didn't trouble the travelers. Hamnet didn't hear any more barks from the outsized magical dog, but he wondered whether Audun Gilli was keeping some of the nonexistent animal's definitely existent smell in the air. No denying it—Audun was a wizard.

When the barbarians passed a herd of grazing musk oxen, most of the dogs peeled off to help tend it. The musk oxen didn't seem to need much help. Whenever men or wild beasts approached, they formed a circle with the formidably horned bulls facing out on the perimeter. Cows and calves sheltered within. The defense wasn't perfect, but what in this world was? It was usually more than good enough.

Sarus rode back to the Raumsdalians and fell in beside him. "May I ask you something?" the Bizogot said in Raumsdalian not quite as good as Trasamund's.

"You may ask. I do not promise to answer." Count Hamnet went on speaking the Bizogot tongue. He wanted the practice.

Maybe Sarus did, too, for he continued in Raumsdalian, "This woman you have with you—who is she? What is she doing here?"

Hamnet understood his curiosity. If anything, saying women from the Empire seldom came to the frozen steppe was an understatement. "Gudrid is Earl Eyvind Torfinn's wife," Hamnet answered. That was true now. What was once true didn't concern the Bizogot.

"I thought he said that, the old man. I was not sure it could be so." Sarus shrugged. "But then again, why not? Our strong old men take younger women when they can, too. So he brought her with him to keep him warm when the Breath of God blows strong, did he?"

"It is not as simple as that," Hamnet said, another good-sized understatement.

"I should say it is not!" Sarus exclaimed. "A good-looking woman who is not so old when the man who has her is . . . How much trouble has she caused you?"

"Some," Hamnet answered. "Less than she might have, I suppose. But that is not quite what I meant. Eyvind Torfinn did not bring this woman here, not the way you think. She came north because it was her will that she come north. She follows her own will, no one else's." One more understatement.

"I have heard that you imperials are soft with your women. I see it is so," Sarus said. "Beat her a few times and she will follow her husband's will, no one else's." He folded one large hand into a hard fist. "It works for us."

Hamnet had hit Gudrid when he first found out she was unfaithful to him. She tried to give him hemlock in his beer. She tried to slip a knife between his ribs while he slept. He hit her again, and told her he wouldn't do it any more if she stopped trying to do away with him. She did. Did that mean beating her worked? He didn't think so.

It didn't stop her from being unfaithful, not to him. And nothing stopped her from being unfaithful to Eyvind Torfinn, either.

What was he supposed to tell Sarus? He didn't want to admit Gudrid was once his—and his worry—so he said, "You have your ways, we have ours. Some ways work for some folk, others for others."

"It could be so," the Bizogot said politely. "But what if ways do *not* work for a folk? What then?"

"Nothing in this world is perfect," Hamnet Thyssen said, and smiled a little. Who would have dreamt that what held true for the defensive herds of musk oxen also held for women? He wondered what Gudrid would have thought of that. Not much, most likely.

"God is perfect," Sarus said. "How could God not be perfect? He would not be God."

"God is perfect," Hamnet agreed. "But is God in this world or above it?"

Sarus grunted. That was a different sort of argument. Instead of taking it up, the jarl's son said, "The Golden Shrine is perfect."

"Is it?" Hamnet said. "I have never known a man who has seen it. I have never heard a man who says he knows a man who has seen it." He had no idea what, if anything, Trasamund had told the Bizogots on his way down to Nidaros. Did they even know the Gap had melted through and Trasamund had fared beyond the Glacier? If they didn't, Hamnet was not about to tell them.

"The Golden Shrine must be perfect," Sarus said. "If God is in the world at all, he is in the world there."

"Well, maybe." Count Hamnet didn't care to quarrel. "Down in the Raumsdalian Empire, we hear all sorts of stories of lands still farther south, lands where it's like summer the whole year around, lands where there are strange animals and stranger birds. Tales about places you have not seen . . . Who knows what to believe?"

"Travelers' tales are mostly lies," Sarus said.

"Mostly, but not always," Hamnet said. "Sometimes the travelers will bring hides with them, hides of beasts that do not live in the Empire or any neighboring country. And do you know of opossums? Have they come this far north?"

"I have seen one or two." Sarus made a face. "Horrible things, like big rats with pointed faces. What about them?"

"In the olden days, when the Glacier still covered this country, they would not even come up as far as Nidaros," Hamnet Thyssen said. "As the Glacier has moved north, as the weather has grown warmer, opossums have moved north, too. The people who live south of us say the beasts once came up through their lands, and there were times when they did not know them. Opossums would have been travelers' tales in long-gone days. But now they have their own tails, and hang by them."

He hoped the pun worked in the Bizogot language. Sarus made another face, so evidently it did. "You will believe travelers' tales about these ugly animals," the Musk Ox clansman said. "But you will not believe them about the Golden Shrine or about God. What does this say of you?"

"That I believe what I see with my own eyes, what I touch with my own hands," Hamnet answered. "I already knew this about myself. Anyone else who deals with me for even a little while comes to see it is true."

Sarus thought about it for a little while. Then he nodded, as if to say he had already seen it. And then he rode away, as if to say that, having seen it, he did not find it pleasing. Hamnet Thyssen was unsurprised. He'd met that reaction before.

MORE DOGS BARKED and howled when the Raumsdalians and Trasamund rode into the Musk Ox clan's encampment. But, though the big, ferocious-looking beasts made halfhearted rushes toward the newcomers, they did no more. Count Hamnet glanced toward Audun Gilli. The wizard gave back a smile of sorts.

Maybe his magic held dogs at bay. Bizogots were another story. Men, women, and children swarmed out of their tents of musk-ox skins and mammoth hides, drawn to the strangers like iron to a lodestone. They would steal if they saw a chance. Hamnet Thyssen knew that from experience. He hoped the Bizogots wouldn't have too many chances to steal from his comrades—hoped without particularly expecting his hopes would come true.

Instead of poles, mammoth ribs and leg bones supported the Bizogots' tents. Here beyond the line where trees could grow to a useful size, wood was scarce and precious. The fires burning in braziers weren't from seasoned timber, either. They were of dried mammoth or musk-ox dung, which gave food cooked over them a certain unique piquancy.

The Bizogots claimed meat roasted over dung fires was especially smoky and juicy and flavorful. They claimed mere wood couldn't come close to matching dung in any of those ways. Travelers up from the south were dubious about their claims. Hamnet Thyssen didn't think joints cooked over dung had any marked superiority over those he was more used to. While up on the frozen plains, he generally tried not to think at all about how his meat was cooked.

Ulric Skakki had also come up here before. When he smelled the dung fires, one of his eyebrows quirked up in wry amusement. He caught Hamnet's eye and shrugged a shrug half resigned, half melodramatic. "How long will the rest of them need?" he asked, and didn't finish the question. Sooner or later, all the Raumsdalians would realize how the Bizogots had to cook.

No one needed long to realize how little the Bizogots bathed. There Hamnet Thyssen had a hard time blaming the mammoth-herders. Even in summer, warm water was a rare luxury here. In winter, water for drinking and cooking, let alone for bathing, had to be melted from snow or ice—and shedding one's clothes invited frostbite if not worse. But even if he understood why the Bizogots behaved as they did, the strong, sour reek that rose from them made his nostrils flare.

Their jarl, Sarus's father, looked like a larger, older version of the man who'd brought the Raumsdalians to the camp. Gray streaked Leovigild's greasy hair and shaggy beard. Thick, heavy gold hoops hung from his ears. A thicker golden necklace flashed against the gray and dun of his wolfskin jacket. And, when he smiled, glittering gold covered or replaced most of his front teeth. Many a Raumsdalian banker or pawnbroker would have envied his smile.

He spoke with Sarus first, to find out what arrangements his son had made with the strangers. When he knew, he turned to the Raumsdalians and Trasamund and boomed, "Welcome, my guests! Welcome! Three times welcome! Use our encampment as your own while you bide with us."

"We thank you for your kindness. We thank you for your hospitality. We thank you for your generosity," Eyvind Torfinn said politely.

"Come north and use my camp as I use yours now," Trasamund boomed back.

He and Leovigild stared at each other in what seemed part appraisal, part challenge. They had come out of the same mold, though Leovigild was out longer and had seen more hard use. "You think you're so special, traveling along by the edge of the Glacier," the Musk Ox jarl said. "All it means is, your clan couldn't get better grazing ground."

"Shows what you know, you old raven," Trasamund answered. "Every year, the Glacier falls back. All the new land that shows when it does is mine." He made a fist and thumped it against his broad chest. "Mine!" He thumped his chest again. Hamnet Thyssen had never met a subtle, re-strained Bizogot, never once.

Trasamund and Leovigild exchanged more brags and barbs. They seemed more good-natured than otherwise. Maybe that meant they both remembered the obligations guesting gave them, or maybe that they didn't dislike each other as men even if their clans did not get on well. Hamnet accepted the good humor without worrying overmuch about the wherefores behind it.

His time to worry came a little later, when Leovigild rounded on the Raumsdalians and demanded, "And you people, what are you doing north of the tree line?"

The jarl eyed him and Eyvind Torfinn in particular. He found that inter-esting. Audun Gilli was easy to ignore—the other travelers did it all the time. But Ulric Skakki was not a man who casually sank into obscurity. Neither was the leader of Gudrid's guards, a tough-looking captain named Jesper Fletti. And yet Leovigild took no notice of either Ulric or Jesper. He took no notice of Gudrid, either, but Bizogots were less likely to take women seriously (or, at least, less likely to show they took women seriously) than Raumsdalians were.

"Your Ferocity, we are explorers, come to learn what we may of your excellent country," Eyvind Torfinn said, as smoothly as he could in the Bizogots' language. "I am a scholar of days gone by. We have a wizard with us as well. . . ." He nodded to Audun Gilli, who looked surprised—even alarmed—at being singled out.

Leovigild also nodded. "Our shamans will have somewhat to say to this fellow. One or two of them speak Raumsdalian." He plainly did not expect Audun to know his language. By the look he gave the wizard, he might not have expected Audun to know anything. His attention swung back to Earl Eyvind. "What of the others, then?"

"Soldiers help guard and help hunt," Eyvind said. Leovigild accepted that with a wave. Eyvind Torfinn continued, "Count Hamnet here is an excellent man of his hands, and has traveled the cold plains before, while Ulric Skakki . . ." He ran down. How was he supposed to explain why Ulric Skakki had come north?

"I know all sorts of strange things, your Ferocity." Ulric had no trouble speaking for himself. "You never can tell when one of them will come in handy, and you never can tell which one it will be."

"Huh." Leovigild eyed him. "Strange things about slitting throats and knocking heads together and setting traps and stealing pouches, or I miss my guess." Leovigild waited. When Ulric Skakki didn't deny it, the jarl grunted. "*Thought* so." He swung back toward Earl Eyvind. "And what about the woman?"

"Gudrid is my wife, your Ferocity," Eyvind Torfinn said, a touch of sternness in his voice.

"Can't fault your taste—she looks tastable enough, in fact." Leovigild roared laughter at the look on Eyvind's face. He went on, "But what is she doing *here*?"

"I suggest you ask her yourself," Earl Eyvind replied.

"Never mind." Leovigild threw back his head and laughed again. "You just told me everything I need to know." Eyvind Torfinn looked bewildered, which only made the Bizogot laugh harder. Hamnet Thyssen had no trou-

ble following Leovigild. He meant that Eyvind couldn't tell Gudrid what to
do. The mammoth-herder wasn't wrong, either. Count Hamnet wondered
whether anyone had ever been able to tell Gudrid what to do. He doubted
it. He knew too well he hadn't.

"She is well able to take care of herself," Eyvind Torfinn said. That was
true enough; it might well have been truer than he knew.

True or not, it made Leovigild laugh even more. But then the Bizogot jarl
sobered. "Something you should know," he said, aiming a scarred forefinger at Eyvind's chest. "Something you *need* to know, by God. Need to know,
yes. The Empire is rich. The Empire has a great plenty of everything. Is it
not so?"

"Well . . ." Eyvind Torfinn hesitated. Anyone who'd lived his whole life in
the Raumsdalian Empire knew things weren't as simple as Leovigild made
them out to be. But anyone who'd spent even a little while on the frozen
plains of the north knew that, from the Bizogot point of view, the jarl was
right and more than right. The Empire *was* rich. It *did* have a great plenty of
everything.

"It is so," Leovigild said solemnly. "And because it is so, in the Empire
you can say, 'This one can take care of himself,' or even, 'This one can take
care of herself.' There is so much down in the south, one person can have
enough. It is not like that here. One person alone here is one person dead
here. Only the clans can go on. Do you understand this, Eyvind Torfinn?
Does your tastable Gudrid understand it?"

"I understand your words very well, your Ferocity," Earl Eyvind said.
Leovigild scowled and turned away. Hamnet Thyssen knew why. Eyvind
Torfinn understood what the Bizogot's words meant, yes, but they didn't
sink in for him, not at the gut level where they should have. And how much
trouble would that cause him in his travels through the north?

How much trouble would it cause Gudrid? A woman could be indepen-
dent down where trees grew and the ground wasn't frozen all the time. Up
here, where even a man was more a part of his clan than an individual? She
might find out the hard way just how different things were.

Leovigild shrugged, as if to say it wasn't his worry. "You Raumsdalians
are our guests," he said. "Even Trasamund is our guest. Eat, then, and
drink, and know that the Musk Ox clan does not stint."

When the mammoth-herders ate, they ate well. By Raumsdalian standards, they ate monumentally well. Musk-ox ribs and liver and chitterlings
and brains did not taste much different from the beef Raumsdalians ate at

home. The Bizogots made cheese from musk-ox milk. They also made butter, and ate it as a food on its own instead of spreading it on bread—they
had no bread. They used it in their lamps, too.

Mammoth had a stronger flavor than musk ox. Not all of that sprang
from the fuel over which the meat cooked; the musk ox was roasted over
burning dung, too. Count Hamnet had never quite got used to mammoth
meat, and would not have eaten it by choice. Coming up onto the frozen
plains, he had no choice. Mammoth-milk cheese also had a tang all its own.

For treats, the Bizogots ate strawberries and raspberries and blueberries
and gooseberries candied in honey. The berries that grew in this clime were
small but very sweet. Bees had to scurry like madmen in the short spring
and summer to lay in enough supplies to last through the rest of the year.
Only a little farther north, and they could not live.

Smetyn, whether made from mammoth or musk-ox milk . . . Even ale
was better, as far as Hamnet was concerned. But the sour brews warmed
him inside and told him how sleepy he was. He rolled himself in a
mammoth-hide blanket and went to bed in a tent that reeked of burning
butter.

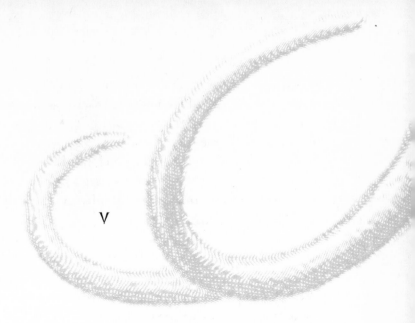

V

W HEN COUNT HAMNET woke, he needed a moment to remember
where he was. He'd been on the road for a while now, and he'd got
used to Ulric Skakki's resonant snores. He supposed Ulric was used to his,
too, for the other man didn't complain about them any more.

The lingering smell of the butter lamp told him what he needed to know.
That's right—the Bizogot encampment, he thought. In case he needed a further
reminder, the shaggy hair on the mammoth hide draped over him would
have done the job.

He yawned and stretched. A few early-morning sunbeams managed to
sneak into the tent and turn what would have been darkness into gloom.
One of those sunbeams hit Ulric Skakki in the eye. Ulric tried to twist away,
but the damage was done. His eyes opened. He sat up and looked toward
Hamnet Thyssen.

"You awake?" he asked.

"Of course not. I always talk in my sleep," Hamnet answered.

"It's too early in the morning to be funny," Ulric complained. Then he
started to scratch and started to swear. "By God, it's a Bizogot camp, all
right. Fleas, bedbugs—a copper gets you gold we're lousy, too." He
scratched some more, harder now.

Hamnet Thyssen also started scratching. All at once, he itched everywhere. "It's not a surprise," he said, trying to sound resigned instead of furious. "They don't bathe. They wander with animals all the time. There are
all these hides around, and scraps of meat . . . No wonder they've got
bugs."

"No, no wonder at all. I've been through this before. I just forgot how much I love it, that's all." By now, Ulric Skakki was probably scratching hard enough to draw blood. That wouldn't help him; it would only make him more alluring to the parasites he was trying to kill. He said, "I wonder if Audun can do anything about our little friends."

"Don't get your hopes up too high," Hamnet said. "The Bizogot shamans know something about wizardry, too, and they crawl with vermin just like the rest of the barbarians."

Ulric grunted. "Well, you know how to murder a man's hopes first thing in the morning, don't you?" He crushed something between his thumbnails. "Ha! Got one of the little bastards, anyway. . . . I just had a thought."

"Congratulations, I suppose," Hamnet Thyssen said, and then, "Oh. You expect me to ask you what it is."

"If that's not too much trouble." Ulric had no trouble being sarcastic, either.

"Not at all," Count Hamnet said politely. "So what is this thought of yours?"

"Maybe the Bizogots are so used to getting eaten alive that it's never occurred to their shamans that they don't have to. Maybe that's why they don't have any spells to hold the bugs at bay."

"Maybe," Hamnet said. "We can find out, anyhow." If he didn't sound optimistic, he wasn't.

A Bizogot dog barked at him when he came out of the tent, but not with the same ferocity the beasts had shown before. Now he'd eaten Bizogot food and slept under Bizogot blankets in a tent lit by Bizogot lamps. He was bound to start smelling like a Bizogot himself. The dog would approve of that. Hamnet didn't, but he couldn't do anything about it. And when everybody smelled the same way, nobody smelled especially bad. That was consolation, of a sort.

It was consolation for him, at least. He wondered how Gudrid would like it.

When she came out of her tent, she smelled of attar of roses. At least Hamnet Thyssen assumed the sweet fragrance came from her; it seemed unlikely to belong to Jesper Fletti or the other imperial guardsmen, and even more unlikely to belong to the Bizogot women. Some of them were pretty enough, in a fair, strong-featured way, but they cared no more for Raumsdalian notions of cleanliness than their menfolk did.

They did notice the scent that clung to Gudrid, though at first they didn't seem sure where it was coming from. "Like flowers, only more so," one of them said.

"Could we do that?" another asked. They liked the sweet smells, then, even if they didn't know much about making them.

Looking smug, Gudrid showed off the little glass bottle in which the perfume came. The Bizogot women made as much of the bottle as of the scent inside. That disconcerted Gudrid, which amused Count Hamnet. To the mammoth-hunters, glass was a trade good, rare and costly. It was one more thing they mostly did without. Life on the frozen plains was, and had to be, pared down to essentials. The Bizogots made do without pottery, too, except for what they got in trade from the south. They used baskets and hide vessels. Some of the baskets were so finely woven, they would hold water. Others, with clay smeared over them, could go into a fire without burning. That was as close as the Bizogots came to real pots.

Gudrid dabbed perfume on some of the women. Yes, the Bizogots liked it. Two or three of the big blondes tried by sleight of hand to make the bottle disappear. Gudrid didn't let that happen. She didn't mind stealing herself—anything from a new joke to a new husband—but she drew the line at others stealing from her. And she drew it successfully, and she didn't make the Bizogot women hate her when she did. In spite of himself, Hamnet Thyssen was impressed.

Leovigild was not. "More southern foolishness," he rumbled, that being the Bizogots' usual name for anything the Raumsdalians could do that they couldn't match. But his nostrils flared whenever he got a whiff of the perfume.

Trasamund also did his best not to show the perfume was anything out of the ordinary. "We've got to be moving," he said at shorter and shorter intervals. Of course, he'd gone down into the Empire. He'd met perfume before, on Gudrid and, no doubt, on others as well. He'd even learned to bathe . . . sometimes.

Leovigild and Sarus both bowed to him. "God watch over you, our guest," they said. "Stay safe, stay full, stay warm. May the Breath of God blow you here again."

"May it be so." Trasamund replied to one ritual phrase with another. "Safety and meat and warmth to you as well, and may the Breath of God bring you to my encampment, that I might guest you in answer for your kindness."

Count Hamnet would have been angry if a detachment of Raumsdalian soldiers took so long to get moving in the morning. With so many people who weren't Raumsdalian soldiers in the party, he supposed it could have been worse. He suspected days would come when it was worse, too.

The dogs chased them when they rode out of camp. Count Hamnet hadn't expected anything different. To a dog, going away meant running away, and running away meant you were prey. Audun Gilli made the Voice of Dog snarl at the Bizogot beasts. Maybe he made them smell that fearsome scent, too. They dashed back toward the mammoth-hide tents, whimpers in their throats and their tails clamped between their legs.

No sooner were they gone than they were forgotten. The plain stretched out ahead of the travelers—the plain, and then, farther north still, the Glacier.

ONE OF THE things Hamnet Thyssen forgot—one of the things any Raumsdalian forgot—was how wide, how deep, the frozen plains were. A man or woman who lived in the Empire knew variety wherever the eye fell. Here you saw forests; there, fields. Here you saw a castle; there a village; there, maybe, a town. In the east there were hills; in the west, mountains. Birds and animals accommodated themselves to the different terrain in which they dwelt. People did the same thing; a tinsmith's life in a town differed in almost every way from that of a farmer who grew grain to feed his family, while a rafter who floated great armies of logs down the Broad River toward the rich foreign cities by the Warm Sea knew yet another way to earn his bread and meat and beer.

But the frozen plains were . . . the frozen plains. Once the Musk Ox clan's encampment fell behind Count Hamnet, the wide land stretched out around him and his companions in one vast sweep, seemingly identical in every direction. When the sun shone bright, the travelers might have been insects crawling across an endless plate under an enormous dome of blue enamel.

And when the wind shifted and blew out of the north, when clouds swept down and covered the sky, Hamnet Thyssen's sense of being nothing, of going nowhere, if anything, intensified. When shadows disappeared, the very idea of direction seemed to go with them. He might have been moving in any direction at all. It didn't seem to matter.

He rode up alongside Trasamund and asked, "How do you remember you are men when you measure yourselves against . . . this?" He intended his wave to be as vast as the landscape it tried to take in. Instead, the motion only reminded him of his own puniness.

Would Trasamund understand him at all? Or did the Bizogot take his own land as much for granted as a Raumsdalian peasant took his farm? To Hamnet's relief, the jarl neither gaped nor sneered at him. "Out here in the middle of nowhere, it happens that men forget," Trasamund said.

"How do you mean?" Hamnet asked.

Trasamund said a word in his own language that Hamnet hadn't heard before. "I am not sure how to turn that into Raumsdalian," the Bizogot went on. "It means something like *to enchant yourself*. Sometimes you will find a fellow staring up at the sky, or sometimes out to where the sky and the land meet. He has forgotten everything around him. Sometimes hearing his friends will bring him back to himself. Sometimes it takes a shaman. Every once in a while"—he spread his hands—"his soul flies away for good, and who knows where it goes? This is a summer complaint, you understand."

Hamnet Thyssen nodded. "Yes, I can see how it would be." In winter up here, everything closed down. A man who spent most of his time inside one of the mammoth-hide tents with his wife and his children and his dogs and all their fleas wouldn't worry about how wide the world was. "You say it happens here," Hamnet went on. "Does it not with men of the Three Tusk clan?"

"Oh, no." Trasamund laughed at the very idea. "*Oh*, no, Raumsdalian. These folk have the plain. And so do we; I will not say otherwise. We have the plain, too, yes. But we also have the Glacier."

"Ah." If Hamnet were walking instead of riding, he would have kicked at the ground in annoyance. He didn't like seeming foolish or missing things, but he knew he had.

And then, a few hours later, the travelers were no longer alone on the plain. Jesper Fletti pointed north. "Are those . . . mammoths?" the imperial guard captain asked in an unwontedly small voice.

"Not at all," Ulric Skakki said blandly. "Those are steppe fleas. And if you're not careful, they'll step on you."

Jesper grimaced. So did Hamnet Thyssen. Audun Gilli winced. Trasamund didn't get it for a moment. He had to think in his own language, and didn't understand Raumsdalian as readily. When he did, he roared laughter. "Steppe fleas, is it? If those are fleas, then the world is their dog."

"Maybe it is," Ulric said. "Only God knows why He made it the way He did. Maybe one of these days the world will scratch, and that will be the end of the fleas—and of us, too."

"Do not tell this to a priest, unless you want to burn for blasphemy," Hamnet Thyssen said.

"Do not tell this to a shaman, either. He may decide to sacrifice you to let out the madness in your spirit," Trasamund said. He snorted. "Steppe fleas!"

There were about a dozen mammoths—a herd of females with their young. Males wandered by themselves except during the late-summer mating season, when they would use their weight and their tusks to battle one another to see which of them fathered the new generation. The rest of the year, those tusks pushed snow off the grasses the mammoths ate and broke ice atop frozen streams so they could drink.

"Do not go too close," Trasamund warned. "Otherwise we shall have to step lively to flee the steppe fleas."

He waved a challenge to Ulric Skakki. Grinning, Ulric waved back, yielding him the prize. Trasamund bowed in the saddle.

No matter how bad his puns, the jarl's advice was good. Hamnet Thyssen might have wanted a closer look at the mammoths, but he understood they didn't want a closer look at him. The travelers got near enough to let him remind himself what marvelous beasts they were.

The females stood perhaps eight feet high at the shoulder. Males were bigger—he remembered that. They looked like great shaggy boulders shambling over the plain. The females were big enough for all ordinary use. The knobs of bone they had on top of their heads gave them high foreheads and a look of greater cleverness than their cousins, the forest mastodons. As far as Hamnet knew, that look was an illusion. It was a powerful illusion, though.

Unlike mastodons, mammoths also had a hump on their backs. They sloped down from it, so that their hind legs were relatively short. They had small ears and short trunks, which made it harder for them to freeze.

And they had long, black-brown hair that often led them to be called woolly mammoths. It wasn't wool; it wasn't anything like wool. The hairs were thick and coarse—they had to be half a dozen times as thick as a man's hair. But they were long—some of them as long as a man's arm—and they grew close together. Mammoths, like musk oxen, could get through almost any weather.

One of the females lifted her trunk and blew a warning blast. It sounded something like a trumpet, something like a gargle. Another female also trumpeted. The young mammoths ran behind their mothers. They were browner than the adults.

"How do you herd them?" Audun Gilli asked Trasamund.

"Carefully," the jarl answered, laughing.

The wizard looked disappointed. "I hoped for something more than that."

Trasamund almost told him where to head in. Then the Bizogot visibly thought better of showing his annoyance. A man who offended a sorcerer could have all sorts of unpleasant things happen to him. "Well," Trasamund said, "a man on horseback is big enough even for a mammoth to notice. And a troop of men shouting and waving torches can usually get the beasts to do what they want. Usually."

"What do you do when they stampede?" Hamnet Thyssen asked.

"Try to stay out of their way, by God. Try not to get trampled and squashed," the Bizogot answered. He was joking, but then again he wasn't. After a moment, he went on, "You wave those torches around for all they're worth, too. Mammoths are like most beasts—they don't like fire."

"I have a question, too," Jesper Fletti said. He waited for Trasamund to nod his way, then asked, "How do you get the females tame enough for milking?"

"You bribe them." The Bizogot jarl spoke Raumsdalian with some relish. "There is a kind of grass that grows on some parts of the plain—*blueflower*, we call it in my language. The mammoths are wild for it. One of the things we do while we travel is pull up blueflower wherever we find it. When we set a pile of the dried grass in front of a mammoth, she will stand and eat it, and the milkers can do what they need to do. Yes, we bribe the mammoths. They might as well be people."

"Are they as clever as people say?" Audun asked.

"I don't know. How clever do people down in the Empire say they are?" Trasamund asked. "They know how to do more things than musk oxen can, I'll say that. And they remember better than musk oxen do, too."

"They have trunks," Hamnet Thyssen said. "Those are almost like hands. They let mammoths do things other animals can't."

"Yes, that's so. That makes them almost like people, too," Trasamund said. "One of these days, maybe, they'll try bribing us instead of the other way around." He chortled at his own wit. Like most Bizogots Count Hamnet had known, he wasn't shy about finding himself wonderful in all kinds of ways.

"Do any beasts besides men trouble them?" Ulric Skakki asked.

"Every once in a while, lions or a short-faced bear will take a calf that wanders too far from its mother," Trasamund replied. "Doesn't happen often, but it happens. But what really troubles them in the warmer times are bugs. In spite of all that hair, the flies and mosquitoes drive them wild."

"I've been up here. I believe that," Hamnet said. When the frozen plain thawed out in springtime—or thawed out as much as it ever did, anyhow—endless little ponds dotted the landscape. Mosquitoes laid eggs in those ponds and then rose in buzzing, biting swarms. Sometimes the clouds of them were thick enough to dim the sun. It was as if the soul of a vampire were reincarnated in a million beings instead of just one.

A baby mammoth came out from behind its mother and took a few curious steps toward the travelers. She trumpeted at it. When it didn't heed her, she walked up and thumped its side with her trunk. The blow couldn't have hurt, but it sent a message. The baby stopped.

"You see?" Trasamund said. "When the little one gets out of line, it gets whacked. So too it is among the Bizogots. We have no spoiled, whining folk among us, not like some places a man could name."

That was nonsense, as Hamnet Thyssen knew. Bizogots pulled together better than Raumsdalians. That didn't mean there were no spoiled mammoth-herders, and it didn't mean they never whined. More often than not, Hamnet would have argued the point with Trasamund. Today, he held his peace, not because he felt uncommonly generous but because Trasamund was looking right at Gudrid when he grumbled about spoiled Raumsdalians. That would have made Hamnet forgive and overlook a lot.

The expression on Gudrid's face would have made him forgive and overlook even more. Yes, Trasamund went unchallenged.

HEVRING LAKE WAS dead and gone. The scars the draining of its basin left behind would lie heavy on the land west of Nidaros for centuries to come. Farther north, new meltwater lakes formed as the Glacier retreated. Sudertorp Lake wasn't very deep, but spread across a great stretch of the frozen plain. Waterfowl by the hundreds of thousands bred at the lake's marshy edges. Foxes and dire wolves and lynxes preyed on that abundance. Even lions and short-faced bears didn't disdain geese and great white swans.

Neither did the Bizogots. The Leaping Lynx clan was camped near the eastern edge of Sudertorp Lake. At this season of the year, they won enough food with their bows and with their snares that they didn't need to wander. They had stone huts that they came back to every spring. Their clothes differed from those of the Musk Ox and Three Tusk clans. To keep themselves warm, they wore jackets stuffed with down. In really cold weather, they wore trousers stuffed with down, too, with ingenious arrangements at the knee to make walking easier and others farther up to do the same for relieving themselves.

In spring, they were glad enough to guest travelers coming up by Sudertorp Lake. They had more than they could eat themselves. So did the other clans that dwelt along the lakeshore. It made them unique among the Bizogots.

The jarl of the Leaping Lynx clan was a fat man named Riccimir. Hamnet Thyssen didn't think he'd ever seen a fat nomad before. "Eat! Eat!" Riccimir said. "You are welcome. Oh, yes—you are welcome. Your goose is cooked!"

Eyvind Torfinn, Ulric Skakki, and Count Hamnet all looked up in alarm when they heard that. "Your Ferocity?" Eyvind said.

Riccimir laughed till the tears ran down his greasy face. "Ho, ho, ho! Yes, I know what that means in Raumsdalian. A trader taught me. It is a good joke, yes?"

"As long as it *is* a joke, your Ferocity, it is a good one," Ulric Skakki said.

"It is. By God, it is. But it is the best kind of a joke—it is a true joke. We have today a great plenty of cooked goose," Riccimir said.

Hamnet Thyssen ate roasted goose till his belly groaned. Bizogots used only knives for eating tools. By the time he finished, his face was as greasy as Riccimir's. So were those of the other Raumsdalians. However much Hamnet ate, the Bizogots around him outdid him without effort. They were better at going without than civilized men, too. Moderation was not in their nature. The way they lived didn't let them be moderate.

They didn't drink to enjoy themselves, either. They drank to get drunk. Downing smetyn, that took a lot of drinking. They met the challenge with ease.

Hamnet Thyssen's head was spinning when Riccimir pointed to Gudrid and said, "I will sleep with that one tonight. I like the way she smells. Trasamund, Eyvind Torfinn, pick women for yourselves. You are the leaders. It is your right. If your friends find willing women, that is all right, too."

He spoke in the Bizogot language. "What does he say?" Gudrid asked suspiciously—that finger aimed at her and the fat jarl's leer no doubt gave her reasons for suspicion.

When Eyvind Torfinn translated for her, she let out an irate squawk. "No!" she said. "And I don't like the way *he* smells, not even a little bit."

Eyvind turned to Riccimir. "Gudrid is my wife," he said, "and trading women back and forth is not our custom."

"And so?" Riccimir said. "You are in the halls of the Bizogots now." Any other jarl would have said *the tents*. "Here you follow our customs."

"Why bed an unwilling woman?" Ulric Skakki said smoothly. "Isn't it a waste of time, with so many willing? They aren't much fun after you pin them down, either."

"Says who?" the jarl returned. "Sometimes the way they squawk and thrash fans the fire. And this one looks like fun. Pick any woman for yourself in payment, Eyvind Torfinn. We have some lively ones. You are old, but they will know how to make you think you are young."

Once that was translated, Gudrid squawked louder than ever. Count Hamnet wondered why. She spread her favors over the landscape with fine impartiality. What was one more unbathed Bizogot? She was unbathed herself, even if she did have that bottle of attar of roses.

In Raumsdalian, Jesper Fletti said, "Tell the . . . jarl we have a strong custom against forcing a woman to give herself." He probably almost said something like *Tell the barbarian*. Hamnet Thyssen found it ironically amusing that Gudrid's bodyguard was indeed guarding her body, although no doubt not in the way he'd had in mind when he set out from Nidaros.

Jesper proved wise to speak politely. Riccimir answered in fairly fluent Raumsdalian, saying, "If you talk about your customs in your land, I will listen. You have the right to do that. But you are not in your land."

"Imagine the custom of our land made you do something against your own customs," Ulric said. "Would you do it, just for the sake of fitting in?"

What kind of man was Riccimir? Ulric asked a good, sensible question. But did the Bizogot care about good, sensible questions, or did he simply want to open Gudrid's legs? If he didn't feel like listening, what could the travelers do? Not much—if it came to a fight, they were bound to lose.

The jarl scowled at Ulric Skakki. When he did, Hamnet Thyssen's hopes rose. Riccimir understood what Ulric was saying, anyway. "You are not good guests," he grumbled. "Guests should follow the ways of the hosts. Our women would not raise such a fuss over a small thing."

"A small thing?" Trasamund said. "Don't you have a big thing, Riccimir?"

"I do. By God, I do!" Riccimir answered, laughing. "We are the Leaping Lynxes, but I am a mammoth. Maybe I am too much for a woman of the south."

"Maybe you are," Ulric Skakki said, and the tension eased.

"Much help *you* were," Gudrid hissed at Hamnet Thyssen a little later.

"By God, why should I help you?" he asked in honest perplexity. "I don't want you here. I wish you'd go back to Nidaros. I don't feel anything for you any more."

He wished that were true. The hopeless mix of curdled love and fury that coursed through him whenever he thought of Gudrid chewed his stomach to sour rags and made him want either to hit something—preferably her— or stab himself. Gudrid knew it. She enjoyed it—she reveled in it. He did his best not to admit it.

Usually, his best was nowhere near good enough. Tonight, it served. "You would have let that—that savage do what he wanted to me!" Gudrid said shrilly.

"This was one of the chances you took when you left the Empire," Hamnet pointed out. "Anyone with an ounce of sense would know it. No doubt that lets you out."

She swung on him. She was very quick, but again he caught her wrist before she connected. He was much stronger than she was. It hardly ever did him any good. She said something that would have horrified a drill sergeant. It didn't faze Hamnet Thyssen.

When she tried to bite him, he shoved her away, hard. She sat down even harder, and called him a name that made the first one seem like love poetry by comparison. Again, he scarcely noticed. He rubbed his hand against his trouser leg, trying to wipe away even the memory of touching her.

"Never a dull moment, is there?" Ulric Skakki said, his voice dry.

"Why, what ever could you mean?" Hamnet Thyssen trying to sound arch and coy was as unnatural as a musk ox trying to play the trumpet. Ulric did his best not to laugh, but it was a losing battle.

Sulking, Riccimir went off with a Bizogot woman. She was younger and better built than Gudrid, and at least as pretty, even if she didn't wear perfume. The jarl stayed grumpy all the same. No doubt he would have been glad enough to lie down with her if he hadn't set eyes on Gudrid. Since he had, the woman from his own clan wasn't what he wanted any more. That made her seem like secondhand goods to him.

"Foolishness," Ulric Skakki said. "Everything that goes on between men and women is full of foolishness."

"True enough," Hamnet said. "But so what? For better or worse, we're stuck with each other." He knew too much about worse and not enough of better.

"Well, not necessarily." Ulric sent him a sly, sidelong glance. "Although I must say you're not my type." He made himself mince far better than Count Hamnet made himself sound naive.

"Those things happen down in the Empire. Not up here, not very often," Hamnet said. "When the Bizogots catch men bedding men, they make them into eunuchs and then they burn them. Not a lot of give to the mammoth-herders. Their ways are their ways. You step outside them at your peril."

"Charming people." Ulric was also a dab hand at irony.

"Aren't they?" There, at least, Hamnet Thyssen could match him.

THE LEAPING LYNX Bizogots stuffed the travelers with more roast fowl and with boiled duck and goose eggs the next morning. Riccimir seemed in a better mood than he had the night before. Maybe the buxom blonde from his own clan pleased him more than he'd thought she would. Whatever the reason, he didn't try to hinder the travelers when they mounted their horses to ride away from what was as close to a settled village as the northern no-mads came.

He couldn't resist going after the last word, though. He walked up to Gu-drid and said, "My pretty, you will remember last night forever."

"Why?" she said. "Nothing happened between us." By the look in her eye, she was glad nothing happened, too.

Riccimir ignored that look. It wasn't easy; Hamnet Thyssen envied his singlemindedness. "That is why you will remember it," he said. "You will regret that you did not come to know the mighty love of Riccimir." He struck a pose.

What Gudrid's horse did a moment later probably matched her opinion of Riccimir's mighty love. His clansmates could dry the results and use them for warmth and cooking. If she had spoken, her words probably would have given them plenty of warmth, too. As things were, her expression was eloquent enough. The jarl, convinced to the marrow that he was wonderful, never noticed.

"Are we ready?" Eyvind Torfinn said. "Perhaps we should depart, then."

"God keep you safe on your journey," Riccimir said. "May he bring you back to your homes with wealth or wisdom or whatever you seek. And may he bring you to my clan on your way south. Good will be the guesting on your return—and may the sweet one's heart be softened by then."

Count Hamnet didn't see how Eyvind Torfinn could answer that without landing in trouble with Riccimir or with Gudrid or with both of them at once. Earl Eyvind showed uncommon wisdom—he didn't try. He flicked his horse's reins and used the pressure of his knees to urge the beast forward. The rest of the Raumsdalians and Trasamund followed.

"An interesting time," Audun Gilli said, riding up alongside Hamnet and Ulric Skakki.

"That's one way to put it," Hamnet said. "Some interesting times I could live without."

"It wasn't so bad," Audun said.

"Demons take me if it wasn't!" Hamnet exclaimed.

Ulric laughed. "*He* didn't mind it, Thyssen. Didn't you see him go off with that Bizogot wench?" His hands shaped an hourglass in the air.

"No, I didn't." Hamnet couldn't remember when he'd lost track of the wizard. Audun wasn't what anyone would call memorable, so he had trouble. "When was this?"

"You were exchanging compliments with your lady love." Ulric Skakki stopped. Hamnet Thyssen had a hand on his swordhilt. He probably also had murder in his eye. He didn't mind being chaffed about many things. The list was short, yes, but Gudrid headed it. Ulric hastened to backtrack. "My apologies, your Grace. When you were quarreling with your former wife, I should have said."

"Yes. You should have." Hamnet made his hand come off the sword. He made himself look away from Ulric Skakki and toward Audun Gilli. "So. You lay down with a Bizogot woman, did you? How was it? Did you have to hold your nose?"

"I'm not so clean myself these days. After a bit, you stop noticing that." Audun grinned. It made him look surprisingly young. "As for the rest, well, the parts work the same way here as they do down in the Empire."

"There's a surprise." Ulric Skakki grinned, too.

Count Hamnet only grunted. Losing Gudrid had soured him on women. He still bedded them now and again—sometimes his body drove him to do what he wanted to despise. But he couldn't take them lightly, the way most men did.

Trasamund led them away from Sudertorp Lake. The jarl of the Three Tusk clan was not in a good humor. Since Hamnet Thyssen wasn't, either, he soon found himself riding next to Trasamund. The big blond jarl scowled at him. When he scowled back, Trasamund seemed satisfied.

After a while, Trasamund said, "That Leaping Lynx clan . . ." He didn't seem to know how to go on.

"What about them?" Hamnet asked.

"They hardly seem like Bizogots at all!" It burst from Trasamund.

They seemed very much like Bizogots to Hamnet. But he was looking at them from the outside, not from the inside the way the jarl was. Slowly, he said, "The waterfowl give them so much to eat at this season, they don't have to wander. Things are different when you can stay in one place for a long time."

"I suppose so." Trasamund went right on scowling. "It's wrong, though. It's unnatural. They . . . might as well be Raumsdalians." By the way he said it, he couldn't imagine a stronger condemnation.

"I will tell you, your Ferocity, that to a Raumsdalian they don't seem much like Raumsdalians at all," Count Hamnet said.

"They live in stone houses. They have fat people. They are like Raumsdalians." No, Trasamund had no more idea of what being a Raumsdalian meant—probably less—than Hamnet did about being a Bizogot. He also didn't know that he really didn't know what being a Raumsdalian meant.

Arguing with him would only make him angry. Hamnet Thyssen didn't try. Instead, looking out across the frozen plain, he pointed and asked, "What's that?"

All at once, Trasamund was back in his element. He forgot about the Bizogots of the Leaping Lynx clan. "That's a God-cursed dire wolf, is what that is." His voice rose to a shout. "Close up! Close up! We've got wolves! Archers, string your bows! We've got wolves!"

To Hamnet Thyssen, it was only a moving squiggle at the edge of visibility. But he wasn't at home here, any more than Trasamund knew all the ins and outs of life in Nidaros, or even in the distant keep where Hamnet would rather have spent his time. Accepting that Trasamund knew and he didn't, Hamnet braced himself for an onslaught.

He didn't have to wait long. Just as the Bizogot recognized a distant moving squiggle as danger, so the dire wolf saw distant moving squiggles as meat. It couldn't take their scent; the wind was with them. But before long, a formidable pack of dire wolves trotted purposefully toward the travelers.

Dire wolves were half again as big as their cousins that skulked through the eastern forests. Their fur was thicker, and of a paler gray so as not to stand out against the snow. Some people said timber wolves were smarter than their larger cousins. Hamnet Thyssen didn't know about that one way or the other. People also said dire wolves ate more carrion than timber wolves did. Count Hamnet thought that was true. But it didn't mean dire wolves turned up their noses at fresh meat. If Count Hamnet hadn't known that, he would have found out now.

The pack leader stood there right at the edge of bowshot, eyeing the travelers. The dire wolf grinned a doggy grin at them, long pink tongue lolling out of his mouth. Even at that distance, though, Hamnet could make out the animal's teeth, long and sharp and yellow. Dire wolves needed to be wary around men. Any animal bigger than a bedbug needed to be wary around men. But men needed to be wary around dire wolves, too.

After a moment's appraisal, the dire wolf lifted its head and let out a howl. If it were speaking a human tongue, Hamnet would have thought that howl meant, *All right. Let's try it and see what happens.*

And it seemed to mean just that. The dire wolves trotted forward again. They might have been trying to cut a weak musk ox or a baby mammoth out of the herd. Almost of their own accord, Hamnet's eyes went to Gudrid. That was a tempting thought, but he didn't suppose she would appreciate it.

"Shout at them," Trasamund called. "Sometimes you can scare them off."

Hamnet yelled at the top of his lungs. So did the rest of the travelers. Some of the dire wolves skidded to a stop. A few even went back onto their haunches. But the rest kept coming. Seeing their comrades advance, the frightened wolves got up and went on, too. It was as if they didn't want their friends to think them cowards.

In some ways, dire wolves were much too much like men.

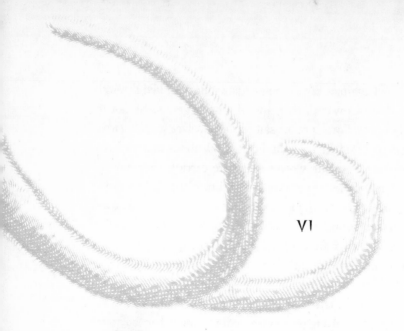

VI

TRASAMUND'S BOWSTRING TWANGED. An arrow hissed through the air. It just missed the lead dire wolf and stood thrilling in the ground. The wolf kept coming without so much as a sideways glance. Dire wolves weren't just like men. The pack leader wasted no time dwelling on what might have been. It dwelt only in the real world. Hamnet Thyssen didn't know whether to pity it or envy it.

He and Ulric Skakki let fly at the same instant, half a heartbeat behind Trasamund. Both their arrows struck the pack leader, one in the snout, the other not far from the base of the tail. "Well shot!" they cried together, at the same time as the dire wolf let out a startled yip of pain. The wolf didn't know how the men had hurt it, but it knew they had. It turned and ran from them.

The rest came on. *They* weren't hurt. And then, in short order, several of them were. Their anguished howls persuaded their fellows this was not a good place to be. When Trasamund led the horsemen forward against them, everyone still shouting, the dire wolves took it as a challenge they didn't care to meet. Unlike people, they wasted no time on useless heroics. If the travelers weren't prey, the wolves wanted nothing to do with them.

One dire wolf, struck in the eye, lay dead on the ground. "Here's meat for tonight," Trasamund boomed.

Gudrid made a revolted noise. Some of the imperial guardsmen looked a trifle green. Hamnet Thyssen had eaten dire wolf before. Nothing on the frozen plains went to waste. "It's not so bad," he said. "Just think that it's food, not where it comes from." His countrymen didn't seem convinced.

Jesper Fletti rounded on Audun Gilli. "You're supposed to be a wizard, aren't you?" the guard captain said. "Why didn't you magic away those dire wolves?"

"We were doing well enough without wizardry," Audun answered. "It takes a toll, the same as any other hard work does. If we needed it, I would have tried something. Since we didn't—well, thank God, I say."

"You're a lazy wizard, or a weak one," Jesper told him.

"No doubt," Audun Gilli said mildly. "But from now on, will you ever dare turn your back on me again? You take your chances, you know, insulting even a lazy wizard, or a weak one."

Jesper Fletti turned red. "I'm not afraid of you!"

"Then you're a fool," Hamnet Thyssen said. "And that will be enough of that."

"Who do you think you are, to tell me what I am?" Jesper demanded, glowering at Hamnet. "And who do you think you are, to tell me what to do?"

"I'm a man who recognizes fools. I'd better—I've been one often enough." Hamnet looked toward Gudrid as he answered. She deliberately looked away from him. He hadn't expected anything else. "As for telling you what to do," he went on, "well, let's see. For one thing, I outrank you. You should say, 'Who do you think you are, your Grace?' For another, I've been up here in the north before. Have you? And, for a third, I hope I know better than to get any wizard angry at me."

Jesper Fletti glowered and spluttered. Whatever he was feeling, he didn't try to put it into words. Hamnet Thyssen had landed too heavy a load of truth on him. He looked away from Hamnet, too. Gudrid did it with more panache.

"I thank you, your Grace," Audun Gilli said in a low voice.

"You're welcome. I've seen you aren't lazy or weak," Count Hamnet answered. "If he asked if you were drunk or hungover, I would have had less to say to him."

Audun's mouth tightened. "Don't you think saying something like that might make a wizard angry at you?"

"I hope not," Hamnet replied. "A man who gets angry at the truth will have a hard time in life, don't you think?"

"It could be so," Audun Gilli answered after considering the question longer and more seriously than Hamnet had looked for. "Yes, it could be so. Of course, you might say the same about a man who gets drunk whenever he finds the chance."

"Yes, you might," Hamnet agreed. "Far be it from me to deny that. But there's a simple answer, don't you think? An obvious answer, too."

"For almost every problem, there is an answer that is simple, obvious—and wrong," Audun said. Hamnet Thyssen pondered that, then inclined his head. The wizard left him with no good comeback.

Trasamund got down from his horse, tossing the reins to Ulric Skakki. He walked over to the dire wolf and butchered it. "Anyone but me want a chunk of raw liver?" he asked, holding up the dripping purplish organ. Plainly, he was ready to laugh at effete Raumsdalians when they told him no.

Gudrid gulped. When she looked away this time, she wasn't acting or posing; she was truly revolted. But Audun Gilli said, "Give me some. What better way to take in the spirit of this land?"

"I'll eat some, too," Hamnet said. "The dire wolf would have gnawed my liver. The least I can do is pay him back."

"Now that—that is spoken like a Bizogot, by God!" Trasamund said. Count Hamnet knew the jarl meant it for praise. If it felt like an insult, he could keep that to himself.

"I'll eat wolf liver. Why not? It's meat," Ulric Skakki said. He might well have eaten it before, but he didn't want Trasamund to know this wasn't his first visit to the frozen plains.

Trasamund turned to Eyvind Torfinn. "What about you, your Splendor?"

"With respect, your Ferocity, I will decline," Eyvind answered. "I have my own land, and do not wish to become mystically attuned to this one. Besides, unless starving and without choice I prefer my meat cooked."

The jarl took it in good part, saying, "Well, you know your own mind, anyway." He ate his gobbet with every sign of relish, then passed another one to Audun Gilli—the wizard was the first Raumsdalian volunteer.

Audun screwed up his face and stuffed the bloody meat into his mouth. He chewed. "Could be worse," he said once he got it down.

"At least that wasn't, 'Tastes like chicken,' " Ulric Skakki murmured.

Dire-wolf liver didn't taste like chicken. Hamnet Thyssen had no time to point that out to Ulric, for Trasamund handed him his own chunk of still-warm meat. He ate it without thinking about what he was doing, and swallowed it without too much trouble. When he saw Gudrid's mocking expression, he smiled back at her with his mouth still full. That made her turn away in a hurry.

Ulric Skakki ate his ragged slice of liver without any fuss. Jesper Fletti and the rest of Gudrid's guardsmen declined to partake. They were less smooth about it than Earl Eyvind, but Trasamund didn't harry them on account of that. He'd got three Raumsdalians to try his delicacy, which was probably three more than he expected.

Trasamund went back to his butchery. He wrapped the meat in the dire wolf's hide and tied it on a pack horse. The animal snorted and rolled its eyes at the scent of blood and the smell of dire wolf, but did not try to bolt. Trasamund left the wolf's entrails steaming on the ground.

"Let's go," he said. "Maybe the others will come back to feed on their friend."

"I think not." Ulric Skakki pointed up into the sky. "Are those just ordinary vultures, or are they teratorns?"

"Teratorns." Eyvind answered before Trasamund could. "You can tell by the pattern of white and black under the wings."

"By the size, too, when they get lower," Trasamund added. "But they won't, not while we're hanging around the offal."

Sure enough, when the travelers rode north, the three or four teratorns spiraled down out of the sky to squabble over the bounty Trasamund left behind. They were enormous birds, with a wingspan as wide as two tall men. And down in the south, Hamnet Thyssen had heard, there were bigger teratorns still, their grotesque naked heads wattled and striped in shades of blue and yellow. All vultures were ugly. Those southern teratorns seemed to take ugliness to an almost surreal level, one where even grotesqueness took on a beauty all its own.

"Do Bizogots also eat teratorn meat?" Eyvind Torfinn asked.

"If we have to. If we are starving. Otherwise . . ." Trasamund shook his head. "It is a foul bird. It eats filth and carrion. Its flesh tastes of its food, the same as any vulture's." He made a nasty face. Did that mean he was once— or more than once— hungry enough to have to eat flesh like that? Hamnet Thyssen wondered, but he didn't ask.

LIKE THE TOTEM animal for which it was named, the Vole clan was small. But the jarl of the clan, a burly fellow named Wacho, had more than his share of pride. "Oh, yes, voles are little beasts," he said. "But the frozen plain would die if not for them. Who feeds the weasels? Who feeds the foxes? Who feeds the lynxes? Who feeds the snowy owls? The vole. Give the vole its due."

Hamnet Thyssen tried to imagine someone down in Nidaros singing the praises of the house mouse. He couldn't do it. For one thing, folk in

Nidaros had plenty of other things to worry about. For another, the Bizogots were more closely attuned to nature than his own people. To Raumsdalians, house mice were nuisances, to be trapped or poisoned or hunted
with cats. To Bizogots, voles were part of the vast web of life that spread
across their land.

Who was right? Who was wrong? Hamnet shrugged. Life for the
mammoth-herders was harder than it was in the Empire. By the nature of
things, it had to be. He'd grown up in the Raumsdalian way himself, and he
preferred it. But sometimes the question was one of difference rather than
right and wrong. He thought that was so here.

As usual when a clan guested the travelers, they feasted till they neared
the bursting point. "I think the idea is to give us a layer of blubber like a
mammoth's," Ulric Skakki said, gnawing the meat from yet another musk-
ox rib.

"That's all very well," Hamnet said, "but if we don't fit into our clothes,
the blubber won't do us enough good to make up for it."

Audun Gilli started to say something. He wasn't a big man, but he had a
respectable pile of bones in front of him. Before he could speak, someone
new came into Wacho's tent—a fantastically dressed Bizogot whose jacket
and trousers were elaborately embroidered and fringed, so that he seemed
almost to be wearing a pelt. The resemblance was only strengthened by the
bear claws at his wrists and ankles, and by the bearskin mask now pushed
back from his face.

"This is Witigis," Wacho said. "He is the shaman of the Voles."

Witigis's gaze was quick and darting, more the look of a wild animal
than a man. Shamans said they had closer ties to God than Raumsdalian
priests dreamed of winning. Hamnet Thyssen wondered if Witigis was a
holy man or simply a madman. His vacant features didn't promise much in
the way of brains.

But when his gaze fell on Audun Gilli, he stiffened. So did the Raumsdalian wizard. They stared at each other. Without looking as he took it,
Witigis grabbed a rib and started chewing on the meat. Grease glistened
around his mouth. His eyes never left Audun Gilli's.

"Like calls to like," Ulric whispered.

"Maybe," Count Hamnet answered. "But if that's so, which one of them
did you just insult?" Ulric laughed, for all the world as if he were joking.

Witigis began to sing. It wasn't an ordinary song, even an ordinary Bizogot song. It had words, in the mammoth-herders' tongue, but they weren't

words that made sense, at least not to Count Hamnet. It also had hums and growls and barks and sounds that perhaps should have been words but weren't, not in any tongue Hamnet knew.

And as Witigis sang, he . . . changed. At first, Hamnet Thyssen rubbed his eyes, not sure what he was seeing. But there could be no doubt. Witigis's fringed regalia became real fur. The bear claws he wore were no longer ornaments. They grew from his fingers and toes as if they always had. After he pulled the mask down over his blue-eyed visage, his mouth opened wide to show fangs that never sprouted from any merely human jaw. Nor did his growl spring from any human throat. There he crouched on all fours—an undersized but otherwise perfect short-faced bear.

Wacho looked proud of his shaman. Trasamund nodded as if to say he had seen the like but admired the performance. The Raumsdalians all seemed a little uneasy, or more than a little.

All but Audun Gilli. He too began to sing, a calm song that might almost have been a lullaby. Count Hamnet had nearly as much trouble understanding him as he had with Witigis. Audun's words were Raumsdalian, but in a dialect so old that it came close to being another language. Hamnet needed so long to grasp one bit that several others would slip past him, uncomprehended, till he seized on another small clump of familiar sounds.

Eyvind Torfinn nodded. Whatever the wizard was singing, it was no mystery to the old earl. Hamnet Thyssen didn't suppose that should have surprised him. Any man who went searching for the secrets of the Golden Shrine would naturally come to know the old, the all but forgotten.

Audun sang on. And, little by little, the shaman lost his bearishness. His fur coat became embroidery and fringes once more. The claws he wore were only ornaments, not parts of himself. An ordinary hand—dirty, but ordinary—pushed back the bearskin mask that was only a mask. And under it lay his face. When he opened his mouth to speak, he showed a man's ordinary face.

But Hamnet Thyssen knew what he had seen. He knew it was true transformation, too, not illusion. He didn't know how he knew, but he did.

"Yes, you too have the power," Witigis told Audun.

Audun Gilli did not speak the Bizogot language. No one would ever have known it from the way he inclined his head. In Raumsdalian, he answered, "Your strength is not small." Maybe he understood with the heart if not with the head.

Witigis had given no sign of knowing Raumsdalian. "Nor is yours," he said now, in his own tongue. The two of them, the barbarian with the bear in his soul and the drunken product of a formidable civilization, bowed respectfully to each other.

"Well, well," Wacho said. "I have never seen Witigis brought out of bearness save when he himself wished it."

"How do you know he did not, your Ferocity?" Ulric Skakki asked.

The jarl sent him a sharp glance, as if to chide him for joking about a serious business. But Ulric was not joking, and Wacho saw as much. "A point, southern man," the Bizogot said. "Yes, a point. How do I know? I do not know." He glanced at Witigis. "I wonder if he knows himself."

"When I am a bear, I know little of what I do," Witigis said. "No—say not that I do not know. Say that I do not care, as a bear would not care. When I am a man again, I see what my bear-self has done. I see, and as often as not I marvel. A bear will do what a man would not. The lesson is, this does not always make the bear wrong."

"Does it always make the man wrong?" Hamnet Thyssen didn't know if Audun Gilli would have asked that question. Whether the wizard did or not, Count Hamnet wanted it answered.

Witigis blinked and looked quite humanly—though not bearishly—amazed. "Do you know, outlander, I never thought of that. I never thought about it," he said. Think about it he did, with a concentrated intensity that startled Hamnet. More than a minute went by before he continued. "No, the man is not always wrong. Sometimes a man is a fool. Sometimes a bear is a brute."

That struck Hamnet as basically honest. "I thank you," he said.

"When you change from a man to a bear, do you think God enters into you?" Eyvind Torfinn found a different kind of question to ask.

In answering, the Bizogot shaman didn't hesitate. "Not unless God comes in the shape of a bear," he answered. "When I am a bear, I am a bear not only in body but also in spirit."

"Do you still feel your human spirit when you are a bear?" Ulric Skakki inquired. "And when you are a man, do you feel a bear's spirit pawing around at the bottom of your soul?"

Witigis smiled. "You have a way with words." Ulric modestly shook his head. Again, the Bizogot thought hard before answering. "Both could be so. When I am a bear, I suppose I am a smarter bear than one who never walks on two legs. And when I am a man . . ." He shaped his hands into paws, and looked at them as if surprised the bear claws dangling from his sleeve were not part of him all the time. "When I am a man, sometimes I would rather bite and tear than talk."

Hamnet Thyssen's laugh was not particularly pleasant. "From what I have seen of men, my friend, you need not have a bear in your soul to make this so."

"If you have a bit of bear in you even when you are a man, do the women like you better for it?" Ulric Skakki grinned a sly grin.

Gudrid made a disgusted noise. Hamnet wondered why. Some of the men she was drawn to were brutes even if not shapeshifters—Trasamund sprang to mind. Did she think that was all right for her but not for someone else? Hamnet wouldn't have been surprised. Gudrid always thought rules were for other people.

As for the shaman, he grinned back. "Now and again, I have seen this to be so. Not always, but now and again. Some women like one thing, some another. You never can tell."

"No, you can't. It's almost as if they were people, isn't it?" Ulric said. Witigis scratched his head. At first, that was simple puzzlement. Then it turned businesslike. He squashed something between his thumbnails. Gudrid made another disgusted noise. Count Hamnet silently sighed. He was lousy now himself, and fleabitten, and also bitten by bedbugs. The Bizogots took all that for granted. With their attitude toward bathing, they could hardly do anything else.

"When you go from man to bear, do you leave human fleas and lice behind?" he asked Witigis. "If you stay a bear, do you get a bear's bugs?"

"You people find interesting questions, by God!" the shaman said. "I always wondered why I'm bitten less than most people. Now maybe I know."

"Maybe you do," Hamnet said.

Later, as leather drinking jacks of smetyn passed from hand to hand, he saw Witigis talking with Wacho and pointing his way. He couldn't make out what either the shaman or the jarl was saying, which annoyed him. Coming right out and asking would have been rude. Instead, he drank more than he might have otherwise.

Wacho talked with a Bizogot woman. She nodded. Then she came over and sat down beside Count Hamnet. "I'm Marcatrude," she said.

Hamnet gave his own name.

She nodded again. She couldn't have been much past twenty. She was pretty enough, and nicely shaped. If she was no cleaner than Bizogots usually were . . . Well, Hamnet Thyssen wasn't much cleaner than Bizogots usually were, either. She said, "Wacho has given me to you for the night, if you want me."

If Count Hamnet had drunk less, he might have said no. If he hadn't gone without a woman for such a long time, he might have said no, too. But he had. And, he told himself—drunkenly—refusing the jarl's kindness would be impolite.

"Where shall we go?" he asked. Bizogots worried less about privacy than Raumsdalians did. If this was going to turn into an orgy, he didn't think he could keep up his end of the bargain.

But Marcatrude didn't seem to expect it to. She set her hand on his. Even if he was drunk, he noticed she didn't have the smooth, supple skin of a pampered Raumsdalian woman—of, say, someone like Gudrid. Hamnet shook his head. He didn't want to think about Gudrid now. If he did, he might also fail to keep up his end of the bargain. If Marcatrude's palm was callused and rough from work even when she was so young, then it was, that was all. She would be soft other places, soft where it mattered.

When he got up and left the jarl's tent with her, he felt Gudrid's eyes boring into his back. Absurdly, he felt guilty, as if he were being unfaithful to her. Considering everything she'd done, that was ridiculous, which didn't make the feeling go away.

He and Marcatrude had another mammoth-hide tent to themselves. They lay down together on the cured hide of a short-faced bear. "I can blow out the lamp, if you like," Marcatrude said as he began to undress her. Drink and lust made his fingers clumsy.

"No, let it burn," he said, and then, feeling that wasn't enough, "You're so pretty, you're worth seeing."

She smiled. She had very white, very even teeth. "You say kind things," she told him. "What kind of men are outlanders?" Before long, he was naked, too. She eyed him and nodded. "You are man enough, without a doubt."

She seemed surprised when he teased her and stroked her instead of just opening her legs and taking his pleasure—surprised, but not unhappy. Far from unhappy, in fact. She purred with pleasure. That pleased Hamnet—and heated him, too.

"Oh," the Bizogot girl said softly when he went into her—a sound he thought was likely the same in any language.

He brought her to the peak an instant before he spent himself. He stroked her cheek and told her how wonderful she was. The afterglow didn't last long—it never did. What had been delight quickly turned to disgust. It wasn't that Marcatrude had a strong smell or that her hair was greasy and matted. Hamnet Thyssen took no long-lasting pleasure in Raumsdalian women, either. He'd scratched an itch, and now it wouldn't trouble him for a while. That was how he looked at it.

If a woman wasn't Gudrid, she wasn't worth bothering with.

And if a woman *was* Gudrid . . . she wasn't worth bothering with, either.

He wondered where that left him. *Nowhere good* was the only answer he'd ever found. While true, it didn't seem helpful.

"Would you like to go again?" Marcatrude asked.

"Thank you, dear, but no," Hamnet answered. To make her feel better, he added, "Once with you is like twice with anybody else."

"You *do* say sweet things," she told him, so at least he was a successful hypocrite. She didn't seem particularly put out with him for not rising to the occasion again. He had gray in his beard, so how surprising was it that once sufficed for him? Marcatrude asked, "Will you spend the night with me?"

Was that fondness, or did she aim to steal what she could while he slept? "I will," he said. "But in the morning, if anything of mine is missing, I will make you unhappy. I know how to do that, too. Do you believe me?"

If she were a man, he would have insulted her by being so blunt. But a man, even one who wasn't a mammoth-herder himself, could speak as he pleased to a Bizogot woman. Marcatrude's nod said the thought of thievery did cross her mind. "If I don't steal, will you give me something to remember you by?" she asked.

"Maybe I already did," he said, and she made a wry face at him. She might remember him very well indeed nine months from now. But that wasn't what she meant, and he knew it. He went on, "I will—if you don't."

"I said that," she told him, and pulled more skins over both of them, enough to keep them warm even though they were naked. Then she blew out the lamp. The darkness that had been hovering at the top of the tent and near the edges spread its wings and swooped.

He couldn't recall the last time he actually slept with a woman. Marcatrude's smooth warmth proved a bigger distraction than he expected. And in that darkness absolute, she could have been anyone, anyone at all, even . . . His arms tightened around her. She laughed, deep in her throat. Maybe she'd had that in mind, too.

After the second round, they both fell asleep almost at once. Hamnet woke up sometime in the night. Marcatrude's arm lay on his shoulder. Her legs were twined with his. She murmured when he disentangled them, but didn't really rouse. He lay awake a long time himself.

When morning came, he checked carefully, but found himself unplundered. He gave her a silverpiece with Sigvat II's beaky profile on it. Bizogots didn't mint coins, but they used the ones they got in trade from lands farther south.

"I thank you," she said. "May your travels fare well. I will remember you."

"And I you." Hamnet Thyssen told the truth, as he usually did. He joined with women seldom enough these days to make each of them stand out in his mind.

When the travelers rode north, Gudrid guided her horse next to Hamnet's. He didn't want her attentions. When he tried to steer away from her, though, she rode after him. "Well?" she said, a certain malicious relish in her voice.

"Well, what?" he asked. If she got it out of her system, maybe she would go away and leave him alone.

"How was it, touching her with one hand and holding your nose with the other?"

He looked at her. He looked through her. "Better than attar of roses," he said.

If she slapped him this time, he intended to deck her. If Jesper Fletti didn't like it, Hamnet intended to deck him, too, or do whatever else he needed to do. But Gudrid only laughed. "Who would have thought *you'd* turn into a liar?" she said, and rode off.

Count Hamnet stared after her. She wasn't altogether wrong. And yet . . . Even if he wasn't immune to her, he knew she was poisonous. And the Bizogot girl wasn't. In that sense, he'd told Gudrid nothing but the truth.

AS THEY DREW closer to the Glacier, they found they'd outrun spring. Sooner or later, the warm winds from the south would make it up to the very edge of the ice. A new meltwater lake was forming, there where the Glacier retreated. Grass and shrubs and flowers would burst forth from the ground for a few weeks. Streams would melt. Midges and mites and mosquitoes would buzz and breed with desperate urgency. And, when the season ended, the Glacier would have moved a few feet farther north than it had been the year before.

But spring wasn't here yet. By the look of the ground and the feel of the air, it wouldn't get here any time soon, either. Thick gray clouds blowing down from the north hid the sun. Snow lay on every north-facing slope, and on some ground that didn't face north. The hares that dug through the snow for dead grass from the last brief summer stayed white, though their cousins farther south were going brown. The foxes that hunted them were also white.

Wolves remained gray. The travelers saw a small pack of dire wolves trotting along in search of anything they could eat, from rabbits to musk oxen. The wolves saw them, too, or scented them, and came over for a closer look. Unlike the pack the travelers had met earlier, these wolves seemed to decide right away that they were more trouble than they were worth—or maybe these wolves weren't so hungry, and didn't need to press an attack. After shadowing the travelers for a while, the dire wolves loped off across the frozen plain.

"I am not sorry to see them go, the miserable, skulking things," Jesper Fletti said.

"Neither am I," Ulric Skakki said. "If they had lawyers instead of teeth, they'd be as bad as people."

Jesper gave him a puzzled look. "What's that supposed to mean?"

"What it says. I commonly say what I mean. Don't you?" Ulric was the picture of innocence. Jesper Fletti scratched his head but decided to let it drop.

"Do you enjoy baiting him?" Hamnet Thyssen asked.

"Some," Ulric answered. "He's not as much fun as you are, because he hasn't got the brains to shoot back."

"I'd think that would make him more fun, not less," Count Hamnet said.

"No, no, no." Ulric Skakki shook his head. "No sport to it."

"I see." Hamnet bowed in the saddle. "So glad to provide you with amusement. If you ever get bored with me, you can always pull the wings and legs off flies." He slapped at himself. "Enough of them at this season of the year. Too many, in fact."

Ulric slapped, too. "Way too bloody many, if anyone wants to know what I think. They don't just take pain, either, the way Jesper does—they give it out, too. That makes it a fair fight."

"If you want to be on the receiving end, you can always quarrel with dear Gudrid," Hamnet said.

"No, thanks," Ulric answered. "I'd be the unarmed one there." His shiver had nothing to do with the chilly weather. "Meaning no disrespect, your

Grace, but I don't know what you saw in her. Well, I know what you *saw*—she's a fine-looking woman, even now. But I don't know how you put up with her as long as you did."

"Everything was fine—everything was wonderful—till all of a sudden it wasn't." That was as much as Hamnet Thyssen had said about the downfall of his marriage since Gudrid left him. He scowled at Ulric Skakki, wondering how the other man tricked the words out of him. Ulric stared back blandly, as if to say he had nothing to do with it.

And, listening to himself, Hamnet Thyssen realized he'd been a fool to believe that then, and was a bigger fool if he still believed it now. Things couldn't have been all right between him and Gudrid, even if he failed to notice anything wrong. A happy spouse didn't start running around for no reason at all—which could only mean Gudrid hadn't been happy long before he realized she wasn't. How many lovers did she have that he never suspected?

Maybe things would have been different if she'd had a child or two in the first few years they were married. Well, things certainly would have been different if she had. Maybe they would have been better. He'd never know now.

Off in the distance, a bull mammoth wandered by itself. The bad bulls were probably the most dangerous animals on the frozen steppe. They were fierce and clever and swift and strong and very hard to kill.

Ulric Skakki kept looking from the woolly mammoth to Hamnet and back again. That almost made Hamnet laugh. He was strong and swift, and could be fierce. He dared hope he was hard to kill. Clever? Hadn't he just proved himself a fool in his own eyes? Didn't a teratorn, a bird that needed no more in the way of brains than what was required to sneak up on a corpse, have wits sharper than his? So it seemed to him, anyhow.

"May I ask you something else, your Grace?" Ulric said.

Harshly, Hamnet Thyssen nodded. "Go ahead."

"Do you know why your, ah, formerly beloved took it into her head to come up here?"

"By God, I don't," Hamnet exploded. "Because she does what she pleases when she pleases, and worries about it later if she ever worries about it at all. Any other questions?"

"Why didn't you kill her? You must have had your chances."

The answer to that seemed much too clear. "Because I'm a fool."

"SOON, NOW," TRASAMUND said. "Soon we enter the grazing grounds of the Three Tusk Bizogots, the grandest land God ever made." He sat up straight on his horse and puffed out his chest. He felt grand himself, and he wanted the world to know he felt grand.

Hamnet Thyssen, on the other hand, had to work to hold his face straight. He didn't know exactly where the grandest land God ever made lay, but he thought it had to be somewhere south of the Raumsdalian Empire. The Empire was far enough south for farming to be possible through most of it, though its northern reaches lay beyond the limits of agriculture. Its strength lay less in its soil than in its people. They were tested by adversity—and by raids from the Bizogots, from farther north still.

Were the rest of the Raumsdalians here thinking the same thing? Count Hamnet didn't see how they could think anything else. Yet not a one of them, not even Jesper Fletti, not even Gudrid, said a word. For one thing, whether this was God's country or not, it wasn't theirs. They needed help from the Bizogots if they were to keep on pushing north, up through the Gap. For another . . .

For another, whether this was God's country or not, spring did eventually reach it. Warm—well, warmer—breezes blew up from the south, driving back the clouds and mist and spatters of snow and sleet that had dogged the travelers for so long. The sun shone from a blue sky. If the blue was watery, if the sun didn't climb as high above the southern horizon as it did even down in Nidaros, those were details. When the clouds receded, when the mist retreated, when the sun shone, the travelers got their first clear look at something they never would have seen if they stayed down in the Empire.

The Glacier.

That wall of ice to the north might have been a mountain range. It stood as tall as many mountains. Did it reach a mile up into the sky? Two miles? Three? Hamnet Thyssen couldn't say. Here and there, storms blew dust and dirt over it, so that from a distance it looked as if it might be made of rock and soil.

But then the sun glanced off a bare patch, and that coruscating flash proved the Glacier could only be . . . the Glacier. A chill and awful majesty clung to it. "What must it be like," Ulric Skakki murmured, "to always look over your shoulder and see—that? How do you get used to it? Don't you think it's going to fall on you?"

"I would." Count Hamnet's shiver had nothing to do with the weather, which was, well, better than it had been. One enormous difference between the Glacier and ordinary mountains was that the latter ascended gradually through uplands and foothills to the peaks at the heart of the range. The Glacier, by contrast, rose sheer, which made those frozen cliffs seem even taller than they were.

A herd of woolly mammoths, no doubt belonging to the Three Tusk clan, ambled along over the snowy ground in the middle distance. By any ordinary standard, mammoths were enormous, gigantic, titanic—mammoth. Against the Glacier, ordinary standards failed. Against the Glacier, those mammoths seemed like nothing more than what Ulric Skakki had called them farther south—fleas on the hide of a white-coated world.

Hamnet Thyssen eyed Trasamund with sudden new respect. The Bizogot jarl hadn't said the land over which his clan wandered was the best or the most fertile God ever made. He said it was the grandest. Looking north from the abruptly dwarfed mammoths to the Glacier, Hamnet Thyssen decided he might be right after all.

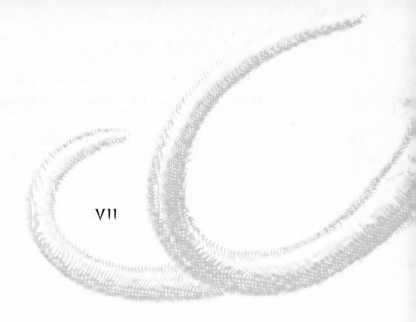

VII

TRASAMUND DID NOT know where in the large territory they roamed the rest of the Three Tusk clan would be. "It depends on the beasts," he said. "It depends on the hunting. It depends on the weather. Later in the year, they may go some way up the Gap—but not, I think, so soon."

Hamnet Thyssen looked ahead, toward the Glacier. He imagined it not just in front of him, but to either side. The thought was not comfortable— was anything but comfortable, in fact. Wouldn't he feel like a bug between two hands waiting for them to slap shut and smash it between them? The rational part of his mind insisted that couldn't happen. In spite of the rational part, he sent apprehensive glances northward.

Then he had a new thought. What would it be like with the Glacier not just to either side of him but *behind* him? Trasamund had seen that. So had Ulric Skakki. The mere idea made Hamnet dizzy. Wouldn't he think the whole world had turned upside down?

While he was looking at the Glacier, Eyvind Torfinn was peering east. Eyvind pointed. "Isn't that a horseman?" he asked.

Everyone's head swung that way. Count Hamnet was angry at himself for letting the scholar spot something before he did himself. Earl Eyvind would be worth his weight in gold when and if they found the Golden Shrine. Till then, the learned noble was so much excess baggage. So Hamnet had thought, anyway.

By the chagrin on Trasamund's face, he was having similar thoughts. Or would they be so similar? Hamnet hadn't slept with Gudrid since she married Eyvind Torfinn. Trasamund had, and hardly bothered hiding it. If

Eyvind noticed, he didn't let on. But maybe it was more a case of not letting on than of not noticing. If it was, did he contemplate vengeance on Trasamund?

What kind of vengeance could an overeducated Raumsdalian earl take against a Bizogot jarl here on the frozen plain? Hamnet Thyssen couldn't think of any. That didn't have to mean Eyvind Torfinn couldn't, though. Whatever Earl Eyvind might be, he was no fool.

Before the rider—for a rider he certainly was—came much closer, Trasamund said, "I know him. That's Gelimer. He is of my clan."

"How can you tell?" Audun Gilli asked. "By some sorcery?"

"No, no. By his size. By the way he sits his horse," Trasamund answered, shaking his head. "Do you not know your brother at some distance? Gelimer is my brother. Every man of the Three Tusk clan is my brother."

Did that make every woman in the clan his sister? Hamnet shook his head. Not in that sense—Bizogots could marry within their own clan, even if they often didn't. And, as he'd seen, they weren't shy about sporting with women from their own clan, either.

"Who comes to the land of the Three Tusk clan?" Gelimer shouted when he came within hailing distance. He was alone, and facing many strangers, but seemed fearless. After a moment, Count Hamnet shook his head. Gelimer wasn't so much fearless as righteous; he seemed certain he had every moral right to demand answers from anyone he found on the land his clan roamed.

"Hail, Gelimer. Your jarl has returned from the lands of the south," Trasamund shouted back. He urged his horse out a few paces. "Do you not know me?" *You had better know me,* his tone warned.

"By God, I do, your Ferocity," the other Bizogot warned. "These folk with you are friends and guests, then?"

"They are," Trasamund said. "They will go north into the Gap with me. They will go north beyond the Gap, beyond the Glacier, with me. They will see where God draws in his Breath to blow it out."

For a moment, Hamnet took that as no more than a figure of speech. Then he thought of the Golden Shrine, somewhere out there beyond the Glacier. If God dwelt anywhere on earth, wouldn't he dwell in or somewhere near the Golden Shrine? No, Hamnet was never a particularly pious man. But every day's travel to the north took him farther from the mundane world of the Raumsdalian Empire and deeper into the land of legend and myth. How could he afford to disbelieve, considering where he was bound?

Other thoughts ruled Gelimer's mind. Looking over the southerners, he said, "Only one woman for so many men?"

Trasamund laughed. Ulric Skakki smiled a small, tight, ironic smile. Eyvind Torfinn stiffened slightly. And Gudrid stiffened more than slightly. Seeing that, Hamnet Thyssen thoughtfully pursed his lips. He hadn't thought Gudrid understood the Bizogot language. Maybe—pretty plainly, in fact—he was wrong.

"She's not a common woman," Trasamund said. "She belongs to the old shaman here." He pointed toward Earl Eyvind. He was polite enough not to throw Gudrid's infidelities with him into Eyvind's face. His language had no real word for scholar. *Shaman* came closer than any other.

Gelimer shrugged. "Be it so, then," he said—it wasn't his worry. "But what is she doing here?"

The jarl laughed again. "What? Why, whatever she wants to, of course." He might not have known Gudrid for long, but he grasped her essence. He went on, "Where is the encampment? Is all well with the clan?"

"We are that way, about two days' ride." Gelimer pointed back over his shoulder, toward the east. "And yes, all is . . . well enough. We skirmished with the White Foxes two months past, when we found them hunting west of the third frost-heave. . . ." He told that story in some detail. Hamnet listened with half an ear. A border squabble between two bands of mammoth-herders interested him about as much as a quarrel between two coachmakers down in Nidaros would have interested Trasamund.

To the jarl, though, this was meat and drink—literally. He plied Gelimer with questions, and finally grunted in satisfaction. "You did well. You all did well," he rumbled. "The White Foxes will respect that which is right, that which is true, from here on out."

"They have a new jarl—his name is Childebert," Gelimer said. "I dare say he wanted to see what he could get away with, especially with you not here to lead our clan."

"You showed him, by God," Trasamund said. "We are Bizogots. Better, we are Bizogots of the Three Tusk clan. Do we need a jarl to tell us we let no one infringe on our rights?"

"We do not. We did not," Gelimer said. "They won't trouble us that way again any time soon."

"Which is as it should be." Trasamund sketched a salute—not really to Gelimer, Hamnet Thyssen judged, but to the Three Tusk clan as a whole.

The jarl went on, "Guide us back to the tents of the clan. We have things to do before faring north again."

"Just as you say, so shall it be," Gelimer replied.

"Of course," Trasamund said complacently. Sigvat II, Emperor of Raumsdalia, could have sounded no more certain.

THE ENCAMPMENT OF the Three Tusk clan was . . . a Bizogot encampment. Hamnet Thyssen was long familiar with them. Even if he weren't, the journey up across the frozen steppe would have taught him as much as he needed to know.

Mammoth-hide tents sprouted here and there, scattered higgledy-piggledy across the ground. Horses were tied nearby. By Raumsdalian standards, Bizogot horses were short-legged and stocky and shaggy. They needed to be, to get through the long, hard winters in these parts. Some of them would wander with the clan's musk oxen during the winter, to forage on whatever they could dig up. Others would winter in and near the tents, feeding on hay the Bizogots harvested while the weather was good, and on the frozen grasses the nomads found beneath the snow. So it went in good winters, anyway. When times were not so good, the Bizogots ate horse and rebuilt their herds as they could.

For the moment, the camp boiled with excitement. The nomads would not eat horse any time soon. They'd killed a cow mammoth not long before Trasamund and the Raumsdalians rode up, and were butchering the mountain of meat. They would roast and boil what they could, and eat it on the spot. The rest would be cut into thin strips and salted and dried in the sun and the wind.

Hamnet Thyssen eyed Ulric Skakki. "Here's to gluttony," he said. "Are you up for it?"

"I'll try my best," Ulric answered. "But any civilized man will explode if he tries to keep up with the Bizogots. They're better at stuffing themselves than we are."

"They're better at doing without than we are, too," Hamnet said. "On average, I suppose it's about the same, but they swing further in both directions than we do."

Even the arrival of their jarl, even the arrival of strangers from the south, distracted the nomads only a little. They greeted Trasamund with bloody handclasps. He took it in good part; he knew meat mattered more than he did.

Women scraped fat from the back of the mammoth hide. Some of them used iron knives that had come north in trade, others flint tools that might have been as old as time or might have been made that morning. The Bizogots never had as much iron as they wanted, and eked it out with stone tools.

Dogs danced and begged by the edge of the hide. Every so often, a woman would throw some scraps their way. The dogs yelped and snapped at the food and at one another. The women laughed at the sport.

They carefully saved the rest of the fat. Some of it would get cooked in the feast. The rest would be pounded with lean mammoth meat and berries to make cakes that would keep for a long time and would feed a traveling man.

Once the hide had not a scrap of fat or flesh clinging to it, the women rubbed it with a strong-smelling mix. Audun Gilli's nose wrinkled. "What's that stuff?" he asked.

"Piss and salt, to cure the hide," Count Hamnet answered.

"Oh." The wizard looked unhappy. "Why don't they use tanbark, the way we do?"

Both Hamnet and Ulric laughed at him. "Think about it," Ulric said.

Audun did. "Oh," he said again, this time in a small voice. Tanbark required oaks, and all the oaks grew well south of the tree line.

"What is the news?" Trasamund asked. "Who has died? Who still lives? Who is born? Who is well? Who is sick or hurt?" He had a lot of catching up to do, and was trying to do it all at once. In the Empire, that would have been impossible. The Three Tusk clan was small enough to give him a fighting chance.

"Who are these mouths up from the south?" a Bizogot asked him. That was how the Raumsdalians seemed to the locals—people who had to be fed as long as they were here. Hamnet Thyssen wondered how he liked being called a mouth. Not very well, he decided.

Trasamund named names, which would mean little to a clansman. He called most of the Raumsdalians warriors, styling Audun Gilli and Eyvind Torfinn as shamans. The Three Tusk shaman, easily identifiable by the same kind of fringed and embroidered costume as Witigis had worn, eyed them with interested speculation.

"What about the woman?" another Bizogot called. Actually, he said, *What about the gap?* That made Hamnet look north toward the gap between the two great sheets of ice that had once been one. This time, Gudrid didn't show any signs of understanding.

"Is she just yours, or can we all have her?" still another mammoth-herder asked. A woman gave him an elbow in the ribs. Was she his wife, or just jealous of competition?

"She is the old shaman's woman," Trasamund answered. Count Hamnet glanced over to see how Eyvind Torfinn liked hearing that again and again. By the fixed smile on his face, he didn't like it much. Trasamund went on, "They are all our guests. They are not to be stolen from."

"Ha!" Ulric Skakki said. Hamnet Thyssen nodded. Guest-friendship would keep the Raumsdalians' persons safe while they stayed with the Three Tusk clan. Their personal property? No. Having so little themselves, Bizogots were born thieves.

"My guests, will you feast with my folk?" Trasamund said.

"We will," answered Hamnet, Ulric, and Eyvind, the only three Raumsdalians who spoke any useful amount of the Bizogot language. "We thank you."

After the Raumsdalians dismounted, Bizogot youths led their horses off to the line where those belonging to the mammoth-herders were tied. The shaman made a beeline for Audun Gilli and spoke to him in the Bizogot tongue. His eyebrows leaped. "A woman!" he exclaimed in Raumsdalian.

"I thought you could tell the difference before they talked," Hamnet Thyssen said dryly. "She's got no beard, and that's a pretty good hint."

The shaman turned to him. "You speak your language, and you speak ours. Will you interpret for me?"

"If I can," Hamnet answered. "If you speak of secret things, I will not know your words for them, and I may not know ours, either. I am no spellcaster."

She looked at him. "You think not, do you?" While he was wondering what to make of that, she went on, "Ask his name for me, please, and tell him I am Liv."

"He is Audun Gilli," Hamnet said. He translated for the wizard.

"Tell her I am glad to meet her," Audun said. "Tell her I hope we can learn things from each other."

"I hope the same." Liv eyed Hamnet again. "And who are *you*?" He gave her his name. She shook her head with poorly hidden impatience. "I did not ask you for that. I ask who you were. It is not the same thing."

Hamnet Thyssen scratched his head. He wondered if the shaman for Trasamund's clan was slightly daft, or more than slightly. "I am a soldier, a hunter, a loyal follower of my Emperor." Did she know what an emperor was? "Think of him as a jarl ruling many clans."

"Yes, yes." Liv brushed the explanation aside. She looked at him again. She didn't just look at him—she looked *into* him, with the same disconcerting directness a Raumsdalian wizard might have shown. He tried to look away; he had the feeling she was seeing more than he wanted her to. But those cornflower-blue eyes would not release his . . . until, all at once, they did. He took a deep breath, and then another one. Facing up to her felt like running a long way with a heavy pack on his back. But all she said was, "You are not a happy man."

"No," Hamnet agreed. "I am not." She didn't need to be sorcerer or shaman to know that. Anyone who spoke with him for a little while realized as much.

He waited for her to ask him why not. But she found a different question instead, inquiring, "Why did you come to the Bizogot country?"

"You will know of the Golden Shrine." He didn't quite make it a question. He didn't quite *not* make it a question, either. Almost everyone on both sides of the border agreed that Raumsdalians and Bizogots worshiped the same God. Everyone on both sides of the border agreed they did not always worship him the same way.

But Liv nodded. "Oh, yes. What of it?"

"I came to seek it, along with your jarl."

"Oh." If he thought that would impress her, he was disappointed. Later, he found that very little impressed her, and that she admitted to even less. For now, she looked into him again. He scowled. He didn't like it, even if it was somehow not the violation it could have been. After a bit, she asked, "What do you look to find there?"

"I don't know." Hamnet Thyssen frowned. He hadn't worried about that. Finding the ages-lost Golden Shrine seemed worry enough. "Truth. Knowledge. Happiness. God."

"Yes," Audun Gilli said softly when Hamnet remembered to translate that for him.

"Maybe," Liv said. "Yes, maybe. But why do you think these things are there?"

"Where else would they be?" Hamnet burst out.

Liv didn't answer, not in words. Instead, she smiled. Hamnet Thyssen gave back a pace, and he was not a man in the habit of retreating from anything or anyone. Sober, Liv was another Bizogot—stranger than most, but apart from that nothing out of the ordinary. When she smiled . . . her whole face changed. It was as if the sun came out from behind the clouds, and hardly less dazzling. For a heartbeat, altogether in spite of himself, he fell in love.

Angrily, he turned away from her. Wizards and shamans had their tricks, yes. Try as he would, he couldn't imagine one more monstrously unfair than that.

He saw he was not the only one turning away. Audun Gilli couldn't face her, either. "She has more strength than she knows," the wizard whispered. "She has more strength than she even dreams of. What such a one would be in Raumsdalia . . ."

"What would she be but Gudrid?" Hamnet Thyssen snarled. Audun flinched as if Hamnet had hit him. Hamnet didn't care. He would rather have hit Liv. No, nothing could be crueler than reminding him of love.

LITTLE BY LITTLE, Hamnet Thyssen's temper eased. Filling his belly helped, even if he wouldn't have filled it on mammoth meat, mushrooms fried in musk-ox butter, and berries back in the Empire. Getting somewhere close to drunk helped, too, although he would have used beer or ale or mead or even wine to do the job farther south. If smetyn was what the Bizogots had, Count Hamnet would drink it.

He kept a wary eye on Liv despite his full belly and muzzy head. She didn't do anything especially noteworthy. She ate. She drank. She talked with her fellow clansmen and women, and with some of the Raumsdalians who could use her language. She left Hamnet alone. That suited him fine, or better than fine.

He wanted to ask Trasamund how long it would be before they fared north. He wanted to, yes, but the newly returned jarl was otherwise occupied. Trasamund ate enough for three hungry Raumsdalians, and drank enough for five. When he went off to the tent the Bizogots had run up for him, he went with three big blond women from the clan. Mammoth hide might be thick enough to keep out cold, but it couldn't keep in the moans and sighs that came from that tent.

"He's been away from his own people a long time," Ulric Skakki remarked.

"Well, so he has," Hamnet said. "By the sound of things, he's making some more people in there right now—or trying his hardest, anyhow."

"His hardest, indeed," Ulric murmured, and Hamnet swallowed wrong with a swig of fermented mammoth milk. Ulric had to pound him on the back to get him to stop choking.

"You're a demon, you are," Hamnet wheezed.

Ulric Skakki batted his not very long, not very alluring eyelashes. "You say the sweetest things, my dear." Count Hamnet almost—almost—sent another swallow down the wrong pipe.

Gudrid was left all alone. Worse—she was left with Eyvind Torfinn. Trasamund, at least for the time being, had forgot all about her. Now that he was back in the Three Tusk clan, he preferred his own women. That had to be a bitter pill for Gudrid to swallow. *You're not indispensable after all, my not so dear,* Hamnet thought. *Yes, the only one who cares right now is your husband. Such a comedown.* Catching his eye on her, Gudrid snapped out something he was too far away and too drunk to make out. He smiled at her, which didn't make her look any happier.

Eyvind said something to her, probably doing his best to calm her down. She snapped at him, too. He drew back, a wounded look on his usually placid features. If God had given her a sabertooth's fangs, chances were she would have bitten his head off in truth, not just as a figure of speech.

"What is the trouble?" Liv asked Eyvind. Somehow, Hamnet heard her clearly even though Gudrid's words were just noise to him. Maybe that had to do with her being a shaman. Maybe it had to do with how much he'd poured down. Drunks had selective hearing, and drunk he was.

The Raumsdalian noble only shrugged. "My wife is out of sorts," he answered. Well, so she was, but did he know why? Did he know how regularly Gudrid cuckolded him?

What would he do when he found out? Anything? That was an interesting question. Count Hamnet was glad it wasn't his worry . . . or wouldn't have been, if he didn't worry about Gudrid all the time.

"All things considered, I'd rather share a tent with you," he told Ulric Skakki when the two of them snuggled under skins for the night.

"What? Me instead of three pretty girls who aim to please? I didn't know your tastes ran in that direction, my dear." Ulric batted his eyelashes again. It made him look ridiculous, which was bound to be what he had in mind.

"No!" Count Hamnet's ears heated. His tastes didn't run in that direction, and Ulric did know it. "I was thinking of . . ." He didn't even want to say her name.

"Of Liv?" Ulric Skakki seemed bound and determined to be as difficult as he could. "I'd like her better if she bathed, but the Bizogots mostly don't. Up here, I mostly don't, either. I'd like me better if I did, too." He held his nose.

Hamnet Thyssen wouldn't have minded a bath himself, but he missed bathing less than he thought he would when he set out from Nidaros. He didn't smell any worse than the people around him, which was all that really mattered. As for Liv . . . "She's strange."

"Of course she's strange. She's a shaman, and she wouldn't be if she weren't." Ulric paused to work out whether that really said what he wanted it to. Deciding it did, he went on, "Doesn't mean she's not pretty. She has a nice smile, don't you think?"

"I didn't notice." Hamnet didn't like to lie, but telling Ulric Skakki how much he noticed Liv's smile would only leave him open for more ribbing. Instead, he said, "I wasn't really thinking of her, anyway." That was true enough.

"Who, then?" Ulric didn't need long to answer his own question. "Gu-drid? By God, you don't want to think about her, do you? I wouldn't, if I were you."

"No, I don't want to," Hamnet answered. "But what you want to do and what you end up doing aren't always the same beast."

"I always do what I want," Ulric Skakki said, which had to be a bigger lie than the one Hamnet told him. He added, "What I want to do now is go to sleep. Good night." He blew out the lamp. The smell of hot butter filled the tent. In moments, Ulric was snoring. He did what he wanted then, anyhow. Hamnet Thyssen lay awake brooding—but not very long.

PEOPLE OUTSIDE THE tent were shouting at each other. The racket pried Hamnet's eyes open. One of the people shouting was Jesper Fletti, the other Gelimer. Hamnet understood both sides of the quarrel. Yawning, he needed a moment to realize neither of them was likely to.

"Keep your hands off me, you barbarous hound!" Jesper yelled.

"What do you think you're doing, fool of an outlander?" Gelimer shouted back.

Hamnet's breath smoked when he sat up. He pulled on his boots. Not far away, Ulric was doing the same thing. Quirking up an eyebrow, Ulric said, "Maybe we ought to let them kill each other. Jesper's no great loss."

"If he hurts Gelimer, the Bizogots will want to murder all of us," Hamnet answered.

"I suppose you're right. What a pity." Ulric Skakki stood up.

So did Hamnet. The shouting outside did nothing to improve the headache he discovered on waking. "Neither one of them understands the other's language," he pointed out.

"Just as well," Ulric said. "If they knew what they were calling each other, they would have gone for their knives long since."

Count Hamnet hadn't thought of that. "We really ought to calm them down if we can," he said.

"You're no fun," Ulric told him, but they left the mammoth-hide tent together.

"What's going on here?" Hamnet said, first in Raumsdalian, then in the Bizogot tongue.

Jesper Fletti and Gelimer gave up shouting at each other. Instead, they both shouted at him. That didn't do his head any good. "This lemming-brained idiot keeps wanting to bother the jarl," Gelimer said. "Doesn't he know Trasamund's in his tent screwing like there's no tomorrow?"

At the same time, Jesper Fletti said, "This fleabitten savage won't let the lady Gudrid talk to Trasamund."

"Oh." Hamnet Thyssen's head pounded anew, for an altogether different reason.

"Oh, for God's sake," Ulric Skakki said in about the same tone of voice.

Hamnet stepped between Gelimer and Jesper. He set both hands on Jesper's shoulders. The imperial guardsman bristled at the liberty, but grudgingly allowed it from a Raumsdalian noble. "Go back to Gudrid," Hamnet said. "Tell her she can't see Trasamund now. Tell her she can't see him now even if she's seen every single inch of him before. Tell her it doesn't matter if she's a noblewoman. Tell her she's a guest among the Bizogots, and what they say goes. Tell her that if she causes any more trouble she's liable to get you killed and she's liable to get herself killed."

"Tell her that if she causes any more trouble that involves waking people up, the Bizogots may not be the ones who kill her—or you," Ulric Skakki added.

"And who *will* try to do this?" Jesper asked softly, setting a hand on the hilt of his sword. "You and who else?"

"I'm the who else," Hamnet said. Jesper Fletti looked horrified. Hamnet went on, "Tell Gudrid she can't get away with playing the spoiled brat up here. She won't hear that from me, no matter how true it is. Maybe she'll listen to you." *Or maybe she won't listen to anybody. Half the time, she doesn't.*

Jesper Fletti looked from him to Ulric to Gelimer. Abruptly, the guardsman spun on his heel and stalked away. He ducked into a tent. Count Hamnet heard his voice from inside, but couldn't make out what he said. Then Gudrid let out a screech like a lion impaled on a woolly rhino's horn.

She stormed out of the tent. She didn't stop when she saw Hamnet, but she did slow down. He looked around to make sure he still had Ulric Skakki at his back. Ulric might have borrowed some magic from Audun Gilli, for he'd just vanished. Count Hamnet sighed. Up to him, was it? Well, if it was, it was.

"Why can't I see Trasamund?" Gudrid demanded.

"Because he's still with the women from his clan," Hamnet answered. "Can't you figure that out for yourself, or are you just being difficult for the sake of being difficult?"

"Do you think I care about that?"

"Yes, I think you care about it very much. But I don't think you understand Bizogots as well as you think you do. This isn't your land. You're a guest here. Good guests have all the privileges of clan members—and more besides, because they're forgiven if they're ignorant, and clansmen and -women aren't. If they go past ignorant, though, if they get to annoying . . . God help them in that case, because no one else will."

He wished Ulric Skakki hadn't ducked out on him. If Ulric intoned something solemn like, *He's right,* it might help make Gudrid believe him. Or maybe nothing would do that. "Trasamund will listen to me," Gudrid said with her usual assurance.

"Why? Because you're special? Do you think you're any more special than any of the women he's with now?" Hamnet asked. Before Gudrid could answer or even nod, he went on, "Do you think he thinks you're more special than any of them? If you do, you're fooling yourself even worse than usual."

"By God, you are a hateful man!" Gudrid said.

"Anyone who tells you anything you don't want to hear is a hateful man," Hamnet answered. "And anybody who tells you anything true you don't want to hear is even more hateful. So I suppose I qualify, yes." He bowed.

Gudrid snarled something foul. He bowed again, as if at a compliment. Gudrid whirled and stormed off. Count Hamnet had no idea if he'd convinced her. If he hadn't, he wouldn't be sorry. She would.

But she didn't bother Trasamund. For that her former husband was duly grateful, because, whether Gudrid did or not, he knew he hadn't been joking or even exaggerating the danger. Sometimes you measured progress not by what people did but by what they didn't do. As far as Hamnet Thyssen was concerned, this was one of those times.

In due course, Trasamund emerged from his tent. He looked indecently pleased with himself—that struck Hamnet as the right word, sure enough. Gudrid went right on staying away from him. She probably thought she was punishing him. Hamnet was convinced he either didn't notice she was avoiding him or thought it was funny if he did. As long as neither of them actually *did* anything, though, that was all right.

Hamnet had no qualms about approaching Trasamund. "When do you plan on traveling north again, your Ferocity?" he asked.

"I've been going into gaps all night long." The jarl threw back his head and laughed. "Now you want me to worry about another one?"

After a dutiful grin, Hamnet said, "You were the one who came down to Nidaros. You will know best how important you think this journey is. The farther north we go, the shorter the time the weather will stay good—or even tolerable."

"I am not a child. You are not my mother. You do not need to tell me things a mother would tell a foolish little boy," Trasamund said. "This is my clan, and I have been away for a long time. I have a lot of things I need to set straight before we fare forth again."

"Is *that* what you were doing last night?" Count Hamnet murmured.

Trasamund laughed again. "By God, Raumsdalian, you've never seen anything straighter! And hard! It was hard as that Jesper's head." Had Gelimer already talked with him? Or had he come to his own conclusions about Jesper Fletti while traveling north with him? Hamnet wouldn't have been surprised. He thought the guards officer on the rockheaded side, too.

But no matter what Hamnet thought about Jesper, that wasn't the point. "If we know when we're leaving, we can be ready on the day," he persisted. "If we don't have a day, we'll just waste time."

Sending a sour stare his way, the jarl said, "You're as stubborn as that woman you used to sleep with, aren't you?"

"Almost," Hamnet answered. "It's one of the few things we have in common."

"Ha! That's what you think," Trasamund said.

"Oh, really?" Of itself, Hamnet Thyssen's hand slid toward his sword-hilt. If the Bizogot thought he would stand there and let himself be in-

sulted, that was the last mistake Trasamund would ever make. Hamnet had
stopped caring whether he lived or died after Gudrid left him. Honor was a
different story. He would uphold his own even knowing the Three Tusk
clansmen would slay him after he killed their jarl.

But Trasamund answered, "Yes, by God! You're both annoying, and
you're both here!"

Count Hamnet relaxed. He even smiled a crooked smile. The truth, by
the very nature of things, couldn't be an insult. He couldn't very well deny
he and Gudrid were both annoying. He couldn't deny they were both here,
either, however much he wished Gudrid weren't.

Then one corner of his mouth turned down. Did Trasamund think Gudrid was a nuisance when they were both in Nidaros? He chuckled under
his breath. What was that phrase the barristers used? An attractive nuisance, that was it. Chances were that summed up just what the Bizogot
thought of her.

"I am here, yes," Hamnet Thyssen agreed. "But I didn't come north to be
here, your Ferocity. I came north to pass through the Gap and go beyond the
Glacier. I thought you came north for the same reason."

Trasamund turned red. He took a deep breath. But before he could start
roaring at Count Hamnet, someone behind the Raumsdalian noble said,
"He is right, you know, your Ferocity."

That wasn't Ulric Skakki. Ulric was still nowhere to be seen. It was Liv,
the Three Tusk shaman. Trasamund glared at her, but he didn't roar. That
spoke volumes about how well respected she was. "This is none of your
business," the jarl growled.

"Oh, but it is." Liv shook her head. Her golden hair flipped back and
forth. So did the amber pendants that dangled from her earlobes. Hamnet
eyed those with a certain queasy fascination. Raumsdalian women wore ear-
rings that clipped to their ears. The Bizogots bored holes in their earlobes
through which to hang their ornaments. *They* are *barbarians,* he thought.

"How is it your affair? How?" Trasamund demanded. "We will go north.
When *I* decide, we will go north. And when we do, you will stay with the
clan. You will stay among the tents. Is that plain enough?"

"More than plain enough, your Ferocity." Liv was the picture of politeness. But she shook her head again all the same. Even some of the fringes
on her shoulders and above her breasts moved when she did. "It is more
than plain enough, but it is wrong."

"Whaaat?" Trasamund stretched the word out so he could pack the most possible scorn into it. "What do you mean?"

"I mean what I say, your Ferocity. I commonly do. I will not stay with the clan. I will not stay among the tents. I will go beyond the Glacier with you. By God, I will." Liv's face shone in the morning sun like a lamp, like a torch, like a bonfire. "By God I said, and by God I also meant. Do you not travel to the Golden Shrine? If I cannot learn of God there, where in all the world will I?"

"You can't do that," Trasamund said. Hamnet Thyssen had rarely seen him taken aback. He did now. The jarl looked as if someone had landed a solid punch on the point of his chin.

"I can," Liv said. "I will. I must. I hardly slept in the night, your Ferocity. I took divinations instead." Trasamund had hardly slept, either, but he wasn't taking divinations. Liv went on, "The answer was always the same. This is meant to be. God wills it."

Trasamund looked as if he wanted to say something unkind about God. Whatever he wanted to do, he didn't do it. Not even a Bizogot jarl dared blaspheme right out loud. You never could tell if God was listening, or what He would do if He was.

"Chances are you read the signs wrong," he said instead. That put the blame on Liv, not God.

She shook her head. "I did not, your Ferocity. Shall I do it over for you? Then you will see for yourself, and can have no possible doubt. Let me get the knucklebones, and I will ask the question aloud before I cast them."

"Never mind," Trasamund said quickly. For a moment, that surprised Hamnet Thyssen. But then he understood. If the jarl did see for himself, he couldn't possibly argue. And he plainly didn't believe Liv was making up what she claimed. He tried a different tack. "Having another woman along will cause nothing but trouble."

"How can I possibly cause more trouble than the woman who is already traveling with you?" Liv asked. Count Hamnet snorted. He didn't intend to; it was startled out of him. Trasamund sent him a baleful stare all the same. Liv eyed the jarl. "Well?"

"You are being impossible," Trasamund grumbled.

"I am following the will of God," the shaman said. "Can you tell me the same?"

"I can tell you—" Trasamund broke off. What could he tell her? That the

land beyond the Glacier was no place for a woman? Then what of Gudrid?
Scowling, Trasamund said, "I can tell you that you don't fight fair."

"When I fight, I don't fight to be fair. I fight to win," Liv said. Trasamund
turned away. She'd won this time.

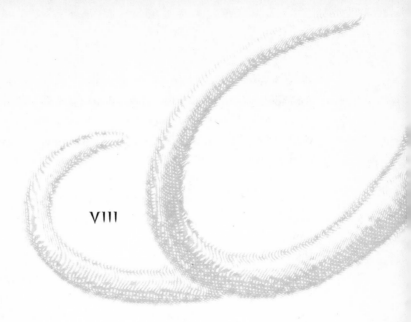

VIII

T RASAMUND WAS STILL muttering into his beard when the travelers rode north four days later. Liv, perched on a dun gelding, paid no attention to him. She rode with Audun Gilli and Hamnet Thyssen. A lot of the time, she wanted to talk shop with the Raumsdalian wizard. That left Hamnet as interpreter, and left him fuming quietly. He'd warned them he didn't know how to translate magical terms very well either way, but they both blamed him when they couldn't make themselves clear.

He tried talking with Liv about other things besides sorcery or shamanry or whatever the right name for it was. To him, the scenery was magnificent—the two great cliffs of ice, one to the northwest, the other to the northeast. Once, they'd joined together and crushed all the north under their unimaginable bulk. They were still magnificent, still awesome, still terrifying . . . to Count Hamnet.

To Liv, they were part of the landscape she'd seen every day of her life, barring fog or rain or blizzard. She took them as much for granted as anyone could. "It's only the Glacier."

"No." Hamnet Thyssen shook his head. "For me, there is no *only*."

The Bizogot woman laughed. "This is very foolish," she said. "It is always here. It will always be here. Why get excited about it?"

"If it will always be here, why is the Gap open now, when it was closed?" Whenever Hamnet said the name in the Bizogot language, he felt he was being obscene. But Liv took it in stride. Seeing as much, he went on, "Why is there a gap between the eastern Glacier and the western at all? There didn't used to be."

She frowned thoughtfully. "These are good questions. I have no answers for them. Maybe we will find the answers at the Golden Shrine."

"Maybe." Hamnet Thyssen started to ask her something else. Before he could, she asked Audun Gilli a question. Hamnet had to translate as best he could.

"Having fun?" Ulric Skakki asked him a while later.

"How did you guess?" Count Hamnet answered, so sourly that Ulric laughed. "Want to take over for me?" Hamnet asked. "You speak both languages, and you'll probably have more luck with the technical terms than I am."

"If it's all the same to you, I'd rather pass," Ulric said. It wasn't all the same to Hamnet, but he couldn't do anything about it. Ulric Skakki gave an extravagant wave of the hand. "You never get tired of this scenery, do you?"

"You do if you're a Bizogot," Hamnet answered. *It's only the Glacier,* Liv had said.

"Well, I'm bloody well not, thank God," Ulric Skakki said. "I've got plenty of things wrong with me, but that isn't one of them." Only then did he eye Liv. "She doesn't speak Raumsdalian, does she? No, of course not. You wouldn't be translating if she did."

"No, but don't forget she's a shaman," Hamnet said. "She may not need to understand what you say to understand what you mean."

"Now there's a cheery thought." Ulric glanced at Liv again. She wasn't paying any attention to him, but keeping flies off her horse with a mammoth-hair whisk. He looked relieved. In a lower voice, he said, "She wouldn't be bad if she cleaned herself up."

That was true of a lot of Bizogot women. Hamnet Thyssen shrugged. It worked out the other way around. The Bizogots never got clean. People who came among them got dirty. Then his own thoughts went in a different direction. "What's it like, passing through the Gap where it's narrowest?"

"It's like being born again," Ulric answered seriously. That startled Count Hamnet, who hadn't thought the much-traveled adventurer had room in him for figures of speech. "It really is," Ulric insisted. "You come out on the other side, and everything is different. Well, lots of things are different, anyhow. And besides, going through . . ."

"Yes, tell me about that," Hamnet said.

Ulric Skakki shook his head. "I can't. There are no words. You'll see for yourself before too long. And you won't be able to tell anybody else about it, either. It's like being in love . . . What the—?"

Hamnet Thyssen pulled savagely at his horse's reins, jerking the animal away from Ulric Skakki—and, incidentally, away from Audun Gilli and Liv. Ulric started to go after him, then saw the black scowl on his face and forbore.

"What did you say to him?" Hamnet heard Liv ask.

"Beats me." Ulric shrugged an elaborate shrug.

"Can you explain about the law of contagion in the Bizogot language?" Audun asked.

"I doubt it," Ulric said. "I can't even explain the law of contagion in Raumsdalian." He rode off, whistling. Audun muttered under his breath. Whatever he said, it didn't change Ulric Skakki into a lemming on the spot. Hamnet thought that was too bad.

He rode by himself. Ulric rode by himself. So did Trasamund. So did Eyvind Torfinn. And so did Gudrid. Audun Gilli and Liv rode together, but they couldn't talk to each other. The knot of Raumsdalian guardsmen followed Gudrid, but far enough away to keep her from screaming at them.

We're a happy bunch, Hamnet thought.

A teratorn circled high above them. With the air blowing down off the Glacier the way it did, what were the wind currents like for birds here? The huge scavenger had no trouble staying airborne, anyhow.

Audun Gilli watched the great bird soar for a while. Then he asked Liv, "Do you suppose it's an omen?"

Hamnet Thyssen had no trouble understanding him. The shaman, however, spoke no Raumsdalian. "What are you talking about?" she asked in her own tongue—which Audun couldn't follow.

The wizard threw up his hands in frustration. Then, after casting a glance of appeal that Count Hamnet stonily ignored, Audun pointed up into the sky at the teratorn. Liv pointed at it, too. They agreed on that much—and on no more. Audun tried to use gestures to explain what he meant. They didn't seem to mean anything to Liv.

To no one in particular, Ulric Skakki said, "We'd better find the Golden Shrine, and we'd better find it soon. We aren't fit to have anything to do with one another unless we find it." Unlike the wizard and the shaman, he spoke the Bizogot language and Raumsdalian, and put his plaintive comment into both languages.

"That is well said," Eyvind Torfinn said, first in one tongue and then in the other.

"Yes, true enough." Trasamund used his own language first, then unbent enough to say the same thing in Raumsdalian.

Several travelers eyed Hamnet Thyssen. He realized he was the other one who knew both the Empire's language and the Bizogots'. Liv had only the nomads' tongue. Gudrid might understand some of that, but she showed no signs of speaking it, while Audun and the guardsmen knew only Raumsdalian. Count Hamnet didn't want to say anything; he would rather have ridden along stewing in his own juices. But those stares wore him down faster than he thought they would. "Yes, yes," he said grudgingly, first in one tongue, then in the other.

"Thank you," Audun Gilli said, maybe to him, maybe to Ulric Skakki, maybe to all the men who could use both languages. The wizard added, "Will someone please translate for me?"

At almost the same time, Liv said, "Will someone please tell me what the southern wizard is trying to say about the teratorn?"

"I'll do it," Hamnet said, heaving a sigh. Ulric Skakki raised an eyebrow in surprise. Hamnet caught his eye. With malice aforethought, he went on, "Better to translate than never."

Ulric flinched. So did Audun Gilli. "What did you tell them?" Liv asked. After a moment's thought, Hamnet was able to duplicate the pun in her language. The Bizogots' tongue and Raumsdalian weren't close enough to let wordplay go back and forth between them all the time, or even very often; he felt a certain somber pride at managing here. By the look on Liv's face, she would have been just as well pleased if he hadn't. Or he thought so, anyhow, till she winked at him. That startled him into a smile of his own. "And now, about the teratorn . . ." she prompted.

"Will you tell her what I meant?" Audun Gilli asked at the same time.

"I can translate, as long as you don't both talk at once," Count Hamnet told each of them in turn. He glanced up toward the teratorn, but it had flown away.

Even so, he explained what the wizard said. Liv considered that, then replied, "If it was an omen, if it was a shadow over us, it is gone now, and we go forward without it." Hamnet Thyssen found himself nodding.

OUT ON THE frozen plain, Hamnet Thyssen had felt as if he and his companions were so many ants walking across a plate. Here between the riven halves of the Glacier, he had a different feeling, and one even less pleasant. Those great cold cliffs might have been the sides of two crates . . . and as the travelers went farther and farther north, someone—God, maybe—was pushing the crates closer and closer together. If God shoved once too often . . .

Better not to think about that.

But the thought got harder to avoid as day followed day. At its southern outlet, the Gap was more than fifty miles wide. When the travelers rode into it, they had the Glacier on the horizon to either side of them, but they could look back over their shoulders and see open land behind. And, while the Glacier serrated the horizon to east and west, there was plenty of sky above it.

With each day's travel, though—sometimes with each hour's—the Glacier grew higher and higher. Those sheer, towering cliffs ate more and more of the sky. Days were shorter than they would have been otherwise, for the sun needed extra time to climb above the Glacier to the east and sank below the Glacier to the west all too soon.

And, with each day's travel, the ground got squashier and the bugs got worse. Meltwater poured from the ice on both sides of the Glacier, more and more as days lengthened. Pools and ponds and puddles, creeks and rills and rivulets, were everywhere. Midges and flies and mosquitoes mated madly. Their offspring rose in ravenous, bloodthirsty hordes.

Gudrid veiled herself in fine, almost transparent cloth. That meant she got bitten less often than the others. It didn't mean she kept all the buzzing biters at bay.

"By God, now I know another reason why the Bizogots breed such shaggy horses," Hamnet Thyssen said, smashing a fly on the back of his hand.

"What do you mean?" Ulric Skakki asked. The bites blotching his face made him look as if he'd come down with some horrid disease.

"Well, the longer their hair, the better they do in the winters up here. That's plain," Count Hamnet said, and Ulric nodded. The nobleman went on, "But the longer their hair, the more trouble the bugs have getting at 'em, too."

"Maybe that's another reason woolly mammoths are woolly, too," Ulric said after a moment's thought. "But who bred them? They had to be here long before the Bizogots started herding them. They're still closer to wild than tamed."

"Maybe God bred them," Hamnet said.

"Maybe he did," Ulric agreed. "It would give him something to do with his time, anyway." In another tone of voice, he would have sounded blasphemous. As things were, he seemed to find the idea reasonable. When he slapped a moment later, he did sound blasphemous. And so did Hamnet Thyssen, when something that probably specialized in piercing mammoth hide bit him in the back of the neck. He didn't get the bug, which made his language fouler still.

Finding dry ground to sleep on got harder and harder. Trasamund and Liv had oiled mammoth hides to unroll beneath them as groundsheets. The Raumsdalians weren't so lucky. "If you've been this way before, you should have warned us it was a bog," Hamnet said to Ulric in a low voice.

"I couldn't—I didn't know," Ulric answered. "Everything was nice and hard then." He looked around to make sure Trasamund and Liv couldn't overhear.

"You came through here in the winter?" Hamnet Thyssen asked. "What was it like?"

"Cold," Ulric Skakki said, with feeling. "Colder than . . . Well, cold." What didn't he say? *Colder than Gudrid's heart?* Hamnet wouldn't have been surprised.

"Does the Glacier grow in the wintertime?" Hamnet asked.

Ulric nodded. "Oh, yes. *Oh,* yes. You can almost watch it happen. The way the Glacier goes forward when it's cold, you wonder how it ever goes back."

"Bad winters, it does come forward and stay there for a while. I know that," Hamnet said. "On balance, though, it's been moving back more than forward. Otherwise, the Bizogots would be herding mammoths where Nidaros stands."

"You mean they don't?" Ulric Skakki's eyebrows arched in artfully simulated surprise. "And all this time I thought . . ."

"All this time, I thought you were a chowderhead," Count Hamnet said. "And here I see I was right."

"Your servant, your Grace." Ulric bowed in the saddle. "And few clammier places have I ever been than this."

"Ow!" Hamnet Thyssen mimed squashing him like a mosquito. Ulric Skakki bowed again. Count Hamnet muttered to himself for the next quarter of an hour. In a way, that was a measure of how bad Ulric's pun was. In another way, it was a measure of how good. Hamnet forgot about the journey, even forgot about Gudrid, for a little while. He supposed that was good, too.

WHEN SOMEONE SHOOK Count Hamnet awake in the middle of the night, his first confused thought was that the northern sky had caught fire. Curtains and sheets of coruscating red and yellow and ghostly green danced there. *Oh,* he realized muzzily. *The Northern Lights.* They showed themselves only rarely down in Nidaros. He saw them more often as he traveled through the Bizogot country. Here in the Gap, he'd come a long way north indeed, and they burned more brightly than he'd ever seen them before.

All the same, he didn't think whoever was shaking him awake wanted him to enjoy their beauty. The shifting, multicolored light they shed let him see Audun Gilli crouched to one side of him and Liv to the other.

That made him reach for his sword. He didn't think they'd roused him to tell him they were running off with each other. *They'd better not be,* he thought. That would infuriate him for any number of reasons.

"What is it?" he asked, first in Raumsdalian, then in the Bizogots' language. Needing to ask twice was one more inconvenience.

"Someone," Audun Gilli whispered.

"Out there," Liv agreed, pointing north and east.

Hamnet peered in that direction. He saw nothing. "Who?" he said in a low voice. "How far away?" Again, he repeated himself so both Audun and Liv could understand.

"We don't know who," Audun answered, at the same time as Liv said, "I'm not sure how far away. But out there."

Swearing under his breath, Count Hamnet said, "Well, what *do* you know? Can you tell me if it's a Bizogot out there? Or is it a Raumsdalian?"

"We don't know." The wizard and the shaman said the same thing at the same time in two different languages. Then they did it again, adding, "Whoever it is, it's a magician."

That made Hamnet Thyssen wonder if the sword would do him any good. He held on to it. It was the only weapon he had handy, and the familiar feel of the leather-wrapped hilt in his hand was reassuring. "How do you know?" he asked.

"The touch of magic woke us." Audun and Liv said the same thing once more.

"Well, is it Bizogot magic or Raumsdalian magic?" Count Hamnet asked testily.

"I don't know," Audun Gilli said, while Liv answered, "I'm not sure." They were different there, if not very.

Then Liv said, "It might not be either one."

That made Hamnet's annoyance at being roused in the middle of the night fall away. Ulric Skakki had said he thought people dwelt beyond the

Glacier. Hamnet didn't think Ulric had told that either to Audun or to Liv. And if Trasamund believed the same thing, he was keeping quiet about it. Hamnet had trouble imagining the Bizogot jarl keeping quiet about anything for very long.

Which meant . . . Well, who could tell what it meant?

"What does she say?" Audun asked.

Muttering in annoyance at having to go back and forth, Hamnet translated.

Audun Gilli looked thoughtful. He nodded. "Why are you bothering me if this stranger is a wizard?" Hamnet asked as the new thought occurred to him. "Why didn't you deal with him yourselves?"

"We tried," Liv said in her language.

"We couldn't," Audun said in his.

So it comes down to the sword after all, Hamnet thought—sweat-stained, wear-smoothed leather against callused palm. "Well, I'll go, if you can guide me toward him," he said—the last thing he wanted was to try to stalk an unfriendly wizard by the flickering, fluttering glow of the Northern Lights.

"I'll come with you," Liv said at once.

Hamnet Thyssen wondered if he wanted a woman beside him. But if the other choice was Audun Gilli, he decided he did. This was the Bizogot shaman's country. If anyone could move through it smoothly and quietly, she could. Audun had shown himself to be a pretty fair wizard, but he couldn't move anywhere without stumbling over his own feet. And that was when he was sober. When he'd had a bit to drink, or more than a bit . . .

"You stay behind," Hamnet told him. "If you hear anything wrong or sense anything wrong, wake Ulric Skakki and Trasamund." To Hamnet's way of thinking, they were the two men likeliest to do him some good in a pinch. Audun Gilli nodded. Count Hamnet put on his boots and got to his feet. "Let's go," he said to Liv.

They hadn't gone far before she stepped in some mud and pulled her feet out with horrid squelching sounds. *So much for smoothly and quietly,* Hamnet thought. It would have been funny if it didn't endanger them both. Liv wasn't laughing. She swore as foully in the Bizogot language as Trasamund could have.

"How far away is this wizard or shaman or whatever he is?" Hamnet asked again. With no plants taller than the middle of his calf, he would have a demon of a time sneaking up on the stranger. If the fellow had a bow, he wouldn't need to be a wizard. But at that thought Count Hamnet shook his head. He wouldn't have wanted to try to gauge distances with only God's curtains to help him, and he couldn't believe any other archer would, either.

"Out beyond bowshot—that's as much as I can tell," Liv replied. "Shall I throw our shadows, to confuse him about how we're coming after him?"

"Throw our shadows? What do you mean?" Count Hamnet asked.

Instead of answering, Liv began to chant softly. Hamnet Thyssen started, for it seemed as if two manlike shapes sprang into being about fifty feet off to the left. "He will notice them. He will not notice us," Liv said. But then she added, "Unless he is a better shaman than I think he is." Count Hamnet wouldn't have minded not hearing that.

The sorcerous shadows or doubles paced along to the left of the real Raumsdalian and shaman. "Will they have any better notion of where this strange wizard is than we do?" Hamnet whispered.

Liv grinned wryly. "I wish they would."

Lightning sizzled along the ground—not a great bolt such as God might hurl down from the edge of the Glacier, but enough to fill the air with the smell of thunderstorms and enough to make the magical shadows jerk and twitch like real people caught by that brilliant lash. Hamnet Thyssen admired Liv's artistry. He blinked again and again, trying to will sight back to his dazzled eyes.

Liv pointed in the direction from which the lightning bolt had come. "There!" she said. "We will find him there! Quick!" She ran forward.

She was lightfooted, and fast as most men. Hamnet Thyssen lumbered after her, doing his best to keep up. She let out what sounded like a lynx's cry—what sounded so much like one, Hamnet wondered whether one of the beasts really spoke from her throat. He wouldn't have been surprised; Bizogot shamans and wild beasts had mystical connections he understood only dimly.

Peer as he would, Hamnet Thyssen saw no man standing or even crouching there on the frozen plain. But suddenly he heard a great thunder of wings. Some large bird—in the glow from the Northern Lights, he saw it was an owl as white as an arctic fox or hare in winter—streaked off to the north.

Liv dug in her heels and skidded to a stop. Count Hamnet charged past her, then stopped himself. The plain was empty now. He could feel it. "Our man has flown," Liv said sadly.

"Flown?" Hamnet's echo sounded foolish even in his own ears.

"Flown," the shaman repeated. "Did you not see the snowy owl just then?"

"I saw the owl," Hamnet Thyssen said. "I saw no man."

"Oh, yes, you did," Liv told him. "The owl was the man—is the man. Well, he is flown now. Wherever he lands, so long as it is far from us, he will take back his own shape. He will tell his friends, whoever they are, whatever he learned of us."

"His friends." Again, Hamnet used her words for his own. "Who are his friends? Is he another Bizogot shaman? Why would he fly north if he is?"

"He is not a Bizogot. I was not sure before. Now I am." Liv *sounded* very sure. She went on, "I do not know what he is. I do not think he comes from your folk, either—at least, his magic feels nothing like Audun Gilli's. Are there people beyond the Glacier? Maybe there are."

"Yes, maybe." Hamnet couldn't say more without telling her that Ulric Skakki had come this way before. For that matter, how could he be sure himself that Ulric was telling the truth? He couldn't, and he knew it. For him, if not for the adventurer, *maybe* was nothing but the truth.

The shaman looked north, in the direction the snowy owl had flown, toward the narrow part of the Gap, toward whatever—and whoever—lay beyond. "If there are people beyond the Glacier, they are not God's people." She sounded disappointed. "God's people wouldn't need to spy."

Count Hamnet hadn't thought of it like that. When he did, he nodded. "And if they are not God's people, if they are people like the rest of us, what does that say?"

"That they will steal whatever they can and take whatever they can," Liv replied at once. Startled, Hamnet nodded again. He wouldn't have put it that way, which didn't mean he thought the Bizogot shaman was wrong. Liv had a habit of saying exactly what was on her mind. Hamnet Thyssen tried to do that, too, which was one reason so many Raumsdalians were perfectly content to see him stay in his castle off on the edge of nowhere.

He laughed softly as he and Liv walked back to the encampment. He was much closer to the edge of nowhere here in the Gap than he could be anywhere inside the Empire. And, with the Gap melted through, he and his companions could go beyond the edge of nowhere, go into lands no one from the south could have reached for thousands of years.

The people on the other side couldn't have come down into the south for thousands of years, either. Sigvat II didn't seem worried about that. Neither did Trasamund. Hamnet Thyssen wondered why not. He knew he was.

"When the spy flew away, what did you sense?" he asked Audun Gilli when he got back.

"Is *that* what happened?" the wizard said, as if much was now explained.

"That's what happened," Hamnet said. He translated for Liv, who nodded.

"Liv made the very pretty shadow spell—I know that," Audun said. "It fooled him, too, or he wouldn't have thrown the lightning at the doubles. He would have sent it against you. But then when he realized you were still coming forward . . . Yes, it must have been a shapeshifting spell, but not one I ever met before. Nothing like any I ever met before, in fact."

"He is right," Liv said after Hamnet Thyssen translated again. "Shamans can take the seeming of a bear or a dire wolf or a lion or a musk ox or a mammoth. Sometimes it is more than a seeming—even you folk from the hot lands will know this." Count Hamnet didn't think of the Raumsdalian Empire as a hot country, but it was when measured against the Bizogot plains. Liv went on, "This magic was new to me, too. It was quicker and more complete than any I have known before. The spy did not take on the seeming of an owl. He *was* an owl."

After Hamnet turned that into Raumsdalian for Audun Gilli, he asked, "How will he stop being an owl, then?" He used both languages.

"Someone will have to make him into a man again," Liv said. "Even in owl shape, he will know enough to go back where he came from."

"What does she say?" Audun asked. When Hamnet told him, he said, "Yes, it would have to work like that. And the spy will have to hope he knows enough to go back where he came from. Otherwise, he'll catch rabbits and voles and lemmings for the rest of his days."

Now Liv had to wait for the translation. When she had it, she sketched a salute to Audun Gilli. "That can happen to Bizogot shamans, too," she said. "Some people say short-faced bears are as sly as they are because they have men's blood in them, blood from shamans who never went back to men's shape."

Count Hamnet's shiver had nothing to do with the chilly night. He tried to imagine living the rest of his life as a beast, slowly forgetting he was ever a man. Only one thought occurred to him. *How Gudrid would laugh!*

TRASAMUND GRUNTED WHEN he heard the folk from beyond the Glacier had spies on this side of the Gap. After a bit, he unbent enough to say, "If we catch them, we'll kill them." His large, hard hands opened and closed several times; he seemed to look forward to it.

"We're going up to spy on them," Ulric Skakki murmured when he and Hamnet rode a little apart from the rest of the travelers. "Why shouldn't they come down to spy on us?"

Put that way, it seemed logical enough, fair enough. But it didn't feel fair to Hamnet Thyssen. What the Empire was doing—with some help from the Bizogots—was only fitting and proper. So it looked to him, anyhow. For other folk to come down into those familiar lands, though . . . If that wasn't an invasion, what was it?

When Count Hamnet said as much, Ulric Skakki smiled one of his sardonic smiles. "Of course, we're not invading their lands when we go north of the Gap—eh, your Grace?"

"We're not invading." Hamnet waved an arm at the Bizogots and Raumsdalians riding north. "Does this look like an army to you?"

Ulric laughed. "Well, no," he said. "But does one man who turns himself into an owl look like an army to you?"

"That's different," Hamnet Thyssen insisted.

"How?" Ulric sounded genuinely curious.

Try as Hamnet would, he couldn't come up with a good answer. The only one that came to him was, *Because it's on this side of the Gap.* It was an answer plenty good enough for him. He was sure as sure could be, though, that Ulric Skakki would only laugh some more if he brought it out. And so he rode along in glum silence—and Ulric Skakki laughed at him anyway.

After a while, Ulric said, "They'll have a demon of a time trying to bring an army through here."

That touched on Count Hamnet's professional expertise. "Oh, yes," he said without a moment's hesitation. "It's not just the narrow gate they'll have to pass through. How will they keep a host of men and beasts fed?"

"Nobody can raise enough to keep a host fed till you get down into the Empire, where crops will grow," Ulric agreed. "The Bizogots would be a lot more trouble than they are if they were hosts instead of bands—and they're trouble enough as is."

"Really? I never would have noticed." Count Hamnet's voice was dry. When Ulric laughed this time, it was with him, not at him. Hamnet thought so, anyhow.

Closer and closer together came the two cliffs that marked the edges of the Glacier. Once upon a time, within the memory of chroniclers and bards though certainly not within that of living men, the Glacier had had only a southern edge. Would it really keep melting till the Gap was a broad highway—till, perhaps, there was no Glacier at all, only bare ground? Hamnet Thyssen tried to imagine that, tried and felt himself failing. Even somewhat diminished as it was, the Glacier still seemed to him a natural and all but inevitable part of the world.

As those tall cliffs of ice drew closer, they also towered higher into the sky. Count Hamnet was not a nervous man, or not a man who showed his nerves, but his voice wobbled a little when he asked Trasamund, "Are there ever avalanches up here?" He couldn't imagine how many tons of ice might come thundering down on him.

"I'm sure there are—there must be," the Bizogot jarl answered. "I've never been in one, though." He chuckled. "If I ever was, I'd be too flat to talk to you now."

"Er, yes," Hamnet said. That marched too well with what he was thinking.

And then, the next morning, he couldn't see the edges of the ice at all. He couldn't see anything. Mist shrouded the campsite. It was cold and gray and thick, thicker than he'd ever known mist to be down in the Raumsdalian Empire. The air he inhaled felt soggy. When he exhaled, he added his own fog to that which swirled around him.

"Which way is north?" he asked. His voice sounded strangely muffled.

"North?" Ulric Skakki said from not far away—but Count Hamnet couldn't see him. "In this, I have trouble being sure of up and down."

That would have been funny if it didn't hold so much truth. The air above, the air all around—the same shade of gray everywhere. It was like being in the middle of a wet sheep's wool. And when Hamnet Thyssen looked down, he could barely see his own boots.

"I ran into this myself the last time I came north," Trasamund said from somewhere in the fog. "I was stuck for two or three days, because I couldn't tell which end was up. Of course, I didn't have a shaman with me, and now we've got two."

"I know a spell for finding north," Audun Gilli said. "An iron needle floating in a cup of water will show you the way."

"What does he say?" Liv asked from farther away. Count Hamnet translated for her. When he finished, she said, "I know this spell. A Raumsdalian trader showed it to me. It may work down in your country, but not so well up here. He said it lied more and more the farther north he went."

"That's so, by God—I've seen it, too," Trasamund agreed, also in the Bizogot tongue.

Inevitably, Audun Gilli asked what they said. With a mental sigh, Hamnet translated for him, too. The wizard let out an indignant sniff. "How can a spell that works well in one place not work in another? The idea is ridiculous."

Trasamund, of course, understood Raumsdalian. "It may be ridiculous, but it's true. If you go the way you think north is, you'll smack your nose into the Glacier instead of heading on up into the Gap."

"I don't believe it," Audun said.

"Fine," Trasamund told him. "Don't believe it. Work your magic. Go the way you think is north. But watch out for your nose." He laughed. Audun Gilli sniffed more indignantly than ever. Laughing still, Trasamund went on, "Go ahead. Try your spell. We'll come along. Why not? We'll be going *somewhere,* even if it's in the wrong direction."

Hamnet Thyssen hadn't known a needle would float on water. But Audun was right—the thin one he used did. And it pointed steadily in a direction he insisted was north. Off the travelers went, moving slowly through the impenetrable fog, calling to one another again and again to keep from getting separated.

When the ground under the horses' hooves grew muckier than ever, Hamnet began to suspect Trasamund knew what he was talking about. Wetter ground meant more meltwater, and more meltwater meant they were getting closer to the Glacier. The mist did thin a little as the day wore along, and a swirl of breeze showed the great cliff of ice dead ahead and seeming unimaginably tall.

"You see?" Trasamund sounded as if he would tear Audun Gilli's head off if the wizard denied seeing.

But Audun didn't. "I see," he said sadly. He sounded chastened.

"We went more west than north, did we not?" Eyvind Torfinn said.

"Plainly." Audun Gilli sounded more chastened yet. "But we should have gone north." Was he staring at the needle as if wondering why it betrayed him? He was only a dim outline to Hamnet Thyssen, but the nobleman knew *he* would have stared at the needle that way.

Eyvind Torfinn, by contrast, sounded cheerful. "If we know the needle points somewhere close to west instead of north, then if we go in the direction the needle says is somewhere closer to east than north, we'll really be heading toward the true north after all, won't we?"

A considerable silence followed, from both Audun Gilli and Trasamund. When Audun said, "By God, your Splendor, I think we will," he seemed amazed.

Trasamund's laugh might almost have blown the fog away by itself. "By God, your Splendor, you've worked a magic to make any shaman jealous!" he boomed. "You've made a liar tell the truth in spite of himself! Well done!"

"What do they say?" Liv asked plaintively. She was the only traveler who knew no Raumsdalian. Count Hamnet translated for her. "Ah," she said when he finished. "The old man is clever."

She forgot Earl Eyvind was fluent in the Bizogot language. "I am not as old as all that, wise woman," he said in her tongue, "or at least I hope I am not."

Hamnet Thyssen couldn't see her turn red, either, but he would have bet she was blushing. "I crave your pardon," she said in a small voice.

"Come on—let's get going," Trasamund told Audun Gilli. "Your precious needle can lie as much as it pleases. You will tease the truth out of it even so."

"Maybe I will. I really think I will." Audun seemed astonished but happy. "A wizard ought to travel about with a charmed needle, and compare what it calls north to what the sky shows at a great many places. Once a chart was made, anyone would be able to use the needle anywhere and have it tell him the truth."

"That sounds like a good idea," the Bizogot jarl said. "It sounds like a good idea for somebody with all the time in the world. As much as I would like to have so much time, I don't—and neither do you."

Audun took the hint. He murmured the charm over the needle once more, perhaps to encourage it. Then he began to ride. "This way," he called. He was dimly visible through the thinning mist, but hearing him did help the others follow.

And Eyvind Torfinn's notion worked. Hamnet Thyssen saw no logical reason why it shouldn't, but plenty of things went wrong even when he saw no reason why they should.

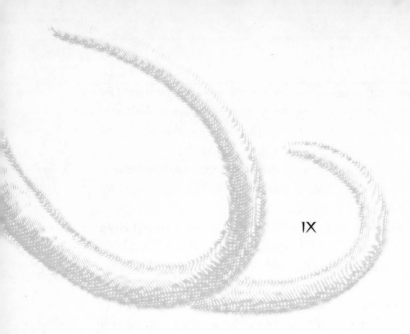

IX

O

H," LIV WHISPERED, looking first to one side, then to the other. She shook her head in awe and wonder. "Oh," she said again.

Hamnet Thyssen couldn't have put it better himself. They were passing through the narrowest part of the Gap. The ground between the two titanic ice mountains was soggy, almost saturated, with meltwater. The horses had to pick their way through the mud as carefully as they could. That meant their riders had to pay close attention to what they were doing—except they couldn't, because the spectacle to either side was too magnificent.

The Gap had melted through, yes, but not by much. The gap in the ice was only a few hundred yards wide here. It towered up and up and up to either side. How far up was it to the top of the Glacier? A mile? Two miles? Three? Hamnet didn't know. He couldn't begin to guess. A clever geometer or surveyor might have been able to figure it out, but he was neither. Far enough to be daunting—far enough and then some.

Except near noon, the shadow of one half of the Glacier or the other shrouded the Gap. The ice smoked, as ice did in warm air. But this wasn't just ice—this was the Glacier. Fingers of mist swirled and curled about the travelers, now obscuring the frozen, towering cliffs, now leaving them fully visible.

Eyvind Torfinn doffed his fur hat to Trasamund. "I thank you," Eyvind said in the Bizogot language. "By God, your Ferocity, I thank you from the bottom of my heart. I might have died without ever seeing this marvel. I've lived many years, but nothing else comes close to it."

"What does he say?" Audun Gilli asked. Ulric Skakki rode closer to him than Hamnet did, and translated Eyvind's words into Raumsdalian. The wizard nodded. "Oh, yes," he said. "I am younger than Eyvind Torfinn, but I do not expect to see anything to match this again."

"It is a wonder—no doubt of that," Ulric said. Though he'd seen it before, he had no trouble sounding impressed again. What would this passage be like in winter? One word immediately occurred to Count Hamnet. It would be *cold*. It would be narrower in the wintertime, too; as ice melted back when the sun swung north in the sky, so it grew again as days shortened. And days this far north would be short indeed come winter.

With a crack like that of a breaking branch but immensely larger, a house-sized chunk of ice broke off from the eastern Glacier and thudded to the ground. Hamnet Thyssen's horse snorted and sidestepped nervously. If he were on his feet, he thought he would have felt an earthquake. The broken piece hadn't rolled and fallen more than a bowshot's distance, either. What would have happened if it had started halfway up the Glacier? He shivered, though they weren't shrouded in mist just then. An avalanche would have happened, that was what.

Jesper Fletti's head kept whipping back and forth, back and forth, too. The guards officer didn't seemed awed by the spectacle of the Glacier to either side of him; he acted more like a trapped animal. "It's like being in a box," he said hoarsely. "In a box."

And it was, with the opening ahead so narrow. Some people didn't like being closed in. Who did, really? But it had to bother Jesper more than most people. Hamnet wondered how he liked sleeping in the tight, enfolding blackness of a mammoth-hide tent. Maybe it worried him less if he couldn't see it.

Count Hamnet might have asked another man. He might have consoled another man. He might even have consoled Jesper Fletti under different circumstances. He had nothing against Jesper as a guards officer; Sigvat II needed able men, and Jesper plainly was one. But he'd come north to protect Gudrid, and that meant Hamnet had as little to do with him as he could.

Ulric Skakki also looked to left and right. There in the narrows of the Gap, what else could a man do . . . unless he chose to look up and up and up at one half of the Glacier or the other? Hamnet Thyssen had tried that once. He didn't do it any more. It gave him the uneasy feeling he would fall *up* the Glacier. He knew he wouldn't. But what he knew and what his eyes told him were two different things, and any man had trouble disbelieving his eyes.

"I think the Gap is a little wider here than it was an hour ago," Ulric said. "Are we really past the narrowest part?"

As soon as he asked the question, the travelers all started making the same calculation. "I do believe we are," Trasamund said.

Jesper Fletti drew in a loud, deep breath, as if being past the narrows meant his chest wasn't squeezed as tightly as it had been before. He probably thought it wasn't. That was as much in his mind as Hamnet's fear of falling up the Glacier. But, in many ways, what felt real *was* real.

"By God!" Audun Gilli exclaimed. "If we keep going—when we keep going, I mean—we'll put the Glacier behind us. We'll have to look south to see it. That seems . . . unnatural."

"It may seem unnatural, but it's so—I've done it," Trasamund said. "And believe me, Raumsdalian, it's much stranger for me than it ever could be for you. I've always had the Glacier to the north of me whenever I turned my head. The Glacier was—*is*—the northern horizon for me. When I rode down to the Empire and it disappeared behind me, the sky looked wrong. The world looked wrong. Seeing it in the south—that's worse than wrong. It's . . ." He paused, groping for the word in Raumsdalian.

"Perverted?" Gudrid suggested.

The Bizogot jarl nodded. "Yes, that's what I wanted to say. I thank you. Seeing the Glacier behind me is perverted."

"Translate for me," Liv said to Hamnet Thyssen. "What do they say?" Count Hamnet did. The shaman's eyes widened. "The Glacier behind us?" she whispered. "I hadn't thought of that. It's wrong, it's impossible—and it's going to happen, isn't it?"

"If we keep going, how can it help but happen?" Hamnet replied. He found the word Gudrid had used the most fitting to describe what that would be like. He also found it much too fitting that she should have been the one to come up with that particular word.

"It seems mad," Liv said. "When you have a fever, when the world whirls round and round so you don't know what's real and what's a dream—then you might think you'd gone north of the Glacier. Otherwise?" She shook her head. "Not a chance."

"Except you're going to do it," Hamnet Thyssen said. "We're all going to do it. Maybe this is the part of the world where everything goes mad. Look at Audun Gilli's enchanted needle."

"Yes, that was strange—*is* strange," Liv agreed. "If we go far enough north of the Glacier, will the needle point south when it's trying to tell us north?"

Hamnet blinked. He hadn't thought of that. "Maybe it will," he aid. Then he turned the thought into Raumsdalian and passed it on to Audun.

It made the wizard blink, too—blink and then start to laugh. "Who knows?" he said. "What I want is the chance to find out."

LITTLE BY LITTLE, the space between the two halves of the Glacier widened, as it had narrowed before. Jesper Fletti became his old self again. "I don't feel as if everything is pressing in on me any more," he said. "I don't feel as if I have to do this"—he made pushing motions with both hands—"to hold the ice mountains apart."

"That wouldn't do you any good," Count Hamnet pointed out.

"Oh, I know, your Grace. I know it here." Jesper tapped his head. "But I don't know it here, or here." His hand went to his heart, and then to his belly.

"When will we see something different?" Gudrid said. "Everything looks the same as it did on the right side of the Glacier."

However much Hamnet wanted to quarrel with his former wife, he couldn't, not because of that. Everything on this side of the Glacier looked the same to him as it had on the other side, too.

But Trasamund shook his head. "Oh, no," he said, and then, "Oh, no," again, as if to stress how much he disagreed. "Some of the flowers and plants here—I've never seen anything like them down in the lands we know."

"Marsh plants?" Gudrid sniffed. "I don't care anything about marsh plants. I want to see something *interesting*. Where are your white bears? Where is the Golden Shrine?" She rounded on Eyvind Torfinn. "Where *is* the Golden Shrine? You're supposed to know about these things."

She talked to her husband the way she might have talked to a majordomo back in Nidaros—as someone who did know about things, yes, but who had better not presume to be her equal. And Eyvind Torfinn put up with it. Gudrid had ways of making men put up with things. Earl Eyvind coughed and said, "You must understand, my dear, this is the first time a real exploring party has come north of the Glacier—this is the first time an exploring party *could* have come north of the Glacier. We don't know just where the Golden

Shrine is. Truth to tell, we don't *know* it's here at all. We hope to find out."

That made good sense to Hamnet Thyssen. He thought it would quiet Gudrid down, but she only sniffed again. "What nonsense!" she said. "All we need to do is grab somebody up here and squeeze him. On this side of the Glacier, they'll know just where the silly old Shrine is."

Count Hamnet stared. So did Ulric Skakki. Eyvind Torfinn looked as amazed as if a teratorn were writing in the sky with characters of fire. Even Trasamund, who had his full measure of straightforward Bizogot brutality, seemed taken aback. But then he guffawed. "You've got all the answers, don't you, my sweet?"

"Well, this isn't a very hard question," Gudrid said.

Trasamund laughed some more. Earl Eyvind held his head in both hands. He'd spent most of his life looking for lore about the Golden Shrine. He knew how much he didn't know. Gudrid had no idea about any of that. Instead of untying a knot, she wanted to slash it through with a sword. Maybe that would work. On the other hand . . .

"If we grab a local and squeeze him, that won't make his clan love us," Ulric Skakki observed.

But nothing fazed Gudrid. She waved the worry aside. "Who says he has to get back to his clan? We leave him out for the dire wolves, or whatever they have here."

"I would not care to approach the Golden Shrine with blood on my hands," Eyvind Torfinn said.

"If we can't find it without doing whatever we have to do, then we'll do it, that's all." Gudrid sounded very sure of herself. She commonly did.

"Remember the owl," Audun Gilli said. "Whoever lives here has powers of his own. We are only visitors. We would do well to remember that."

She looked down her straight nose at the wizard. "Who here is the man, and who the woman?" Audun blushed like a child.

But even Jesper Fletti shook his head. "The sorcerer is right," he said. "We're a long way from the Bizogot country, even, and a demon of a lot farther from the Empire. We couldn't fight a war up here. Keeping any kind of army supplied as it goes up through the Gap . . ." He shook his head. "I wouldn't care to try it."

Gudrid only sniffed again. She didn't worry when someone disagreed with her, because she was always sure she was right. "What are we going to do?" she said. "Turn around and go home without finding the Golden Shrine? I don't think so."

Hamnet Thyssen feared they would have to do exactly that. Summer didn't last long up here. The Bizogots knew how to winter next to the Glacier, but he and his countrymen didn't. They'd never had to. Before they froze and starved, they would need to head back to a more tolerable clime.

The Golden Shrine . . . He looked around, as if expecting to spy it on the northern horizon. That made him laugh at himself. They weren't even out of the Gap yet. This ground had lain under the Glacier for years uncounted. Wherever the Golden Shrine might be, it wasn't here.

And he had no idea what it would look like if and when they did find it. It would, presumably, be white. Past that . . . Past that, who could say? He pictured it as standing all alone on something that looked like the frozen plains where the Bizogots roamed. He pictured it that way, yes, but he knew his picture might be wrong. Maybe it would be the center of a town, maybe even the center of a city like Nidaros. Then, like Jesper, he shook his head. That seemed unlikely. How would you feed a town—how would you feed anything more than a band of nomads—in country like this?

Despite all his logic, he scanned the northern horizon again. He stiffened in the saddle. His finger stabbed out. "What's that?"

"Lion," said Ulric Skakki, who rode not far away.

"I suppose so," Hamnet said. That small shape in the distance did move with a sinuous, feline grace.

"It's seen us," Trasamund said. Sure enough, the big cat trotted toward the travelers.

The closer it got, the more they stared at it. "By God," Audun Gilli said, "that's no lion!"

"It isn't," Jesper Fletti agreed. "What is it? It's no sabertooth, either—it doesn't have short hind legs the way they do."

"It is something new," Eyvind Torfinn said. "It is a creature from beyond the Glacier." Awe suffused his voice.

A creature from beyond the Glacier. That was plenty to awe Hamnet Thyssen, too. And it was a singularly deadly-looking creature. It looked more like a lion than anything else, but it was bigger than any lion Hamnet had ever seen. It was so big, it surely had to be a male, but it did not bear a mane.

Audun Gilli was right—it was no lion. Instead of a tawny coat, it had a pale golden one, broken by dark stripes that helped confuse its outline till it came quite near. When it yawned, it displayed formidable fangs, but more like a lion's than a sabertooth's.

It trotted alongside the travelers for a while, but showed no inclination to attack. In fact, it showed no inclination to come within bowshot of the horses. Hamnet Thyssen had seen similarly wary lions down in the south. "It knows men," he said. "It knows what weapons can do."

"Looks that way," Ulric Skakki said. "Well, no great surprise, not after some of the other things we've seen—and not after your magical owl."

"Not mine," Hamnet said. "Liv woke me up, so I helped chase it away."

"That'll do." Ulric pointed out toward the big striped cat. "Do you suppose they hunt in prides the way lions do?"

"I hadn't thought about that," Hamnet said. "We'll find out. Where there's one of those things, there are bound to be more."

"Well, you're right about that," Ulric Skakki said. "They might as well be tax collectors, except they don't take such big bites."

"Heh," Count Hamnet said, for all the world as if Ulric were joking.

The striped cat studied the travelers with as much curiosity as they showed it. Coming up from the other side of the Glacier, did they smell strange? Hamnet knew he smelled bad. All the travelers did, and got worse by the day. But he had no reason to believe anyone on this side of the ice was any more fragrant.

After a few minutes, the striped cat seemed to decide the humans were too alert to make good prey. It trotted purposefully off toward the northwest, leaving the horses behind. The animals seemed glad it was gone. Whatever the travelers smelled like to the cat, it smelled like danger to the horses.

"Was that a real cat?" Trasamund asked. "Or was it a man in cat shape, spying on us like the owl?"

He spoke first in his own language, then in Raumsdalian. Both Liv and Audun Gilli looked surprised. "I felt nothing out of the ordinary," the Bizogot shaman said.

Audun looked a question at Hamnet Thyssen, who translated for him. Audun nodded. "I thought it was an ordinary animal, too," he said. Hamnet translated that into the Bizogot tongue for Liv.

"I'm glad to hear it," Trasamund said, again in both languages. "And by God, I hope you're right."

THEY'D COME SO far north, full darkness never descended on the world. Not long before midnight, the sun sank below the horizon in the far northwest. Not long after midnight, it rose again in the far northeast. During its brief journey below the edge of the earth, the northern sky stayed light. Nothing deeper than twilight settled over the land, and only a few of the brightest stars came out—and then not for long.

Ulric Skakki made a joke of it, saying, "They won't be afraid to see owls by daylight here."

"No, they likely won't." Hamnet dropped his voice. "But you were up here in the wintertime before. What's it like then?"

Ulric turned and pointed almost due south. With a melodramatic shiver, he said, "The sun comes up there." Then he swung his arm from slightly east of south to slightly west. "And it goes down there. And it never gets higher in the sky than this." He held thumb and forefinger a couple of inches apart. "It's like two or three hours of late afternoon in the middle of the day. It's dark the rest of the time, dark and bloody cold. You see by the stars and the Northern Lights—when there are Northern Lights—and the moon. When the moon is full in wintertime, it does what the sun does in high summer, so it's in the sky a lot. Better than nothing, I suppose. The further from full it is, the shorter the time it stays up."

Hamnet Thyssen tried to imagine darkness spread across the landscape for almost the whole day. "You must have slept a lot," he said.

"Well, what else is there to do?" Ulric asked in reasonable tones. "You ride, and you hunt, and you roast what you kill, and you sleep. You don't even have to hunt so much in the winter, because the meat doesn't spoil. You just have to make sure the wolves and the bears and the foxes and the big striped cats don't steal it."

"That must be fun," Count Hamnet observed.

"Oh, sometimes." Ulric Skakki smiled crookedly. Then he nodded to Hamnet. "You ought to come up here in wintertime yourself, your Grace, just to see it. It might appeal—darkness suits you, eh?"

"What's that supposed to mean?" Hamnet asked. Ulric Skakki's shrug was a small masterpiece of its kind. However much Hamnet fumed, he didn't ask the other man to explain himself again. He knew too well what Ulric had to mean. Darkness crouched at the center of his soul. It had for years. He feared it always would.

He'd never been a cheery, outgoing man. He never would be; he didn't need sardonic Ulric to remind him of that. But what his former wife did to his spirit was like a wound that wouldn't heal. The spiritual pus that leaked from it infected his whole spirit.

"I know what you need," Ulric said.

Hamnet Thyssen scowled at him. "I need you to shut up and go away," he growled.

"You need to fall in love." Ulric went on as if he hadn't spoken. The adventurer's grin was bright, charming, and altogether infuriating.

"I really need you to shut up and go away." Hamnet Thyssen's laugh came harsh as a raven's croak. "You damned fool, what are the odds?" He tried to imagine himself in love again. Imagining himself wringing Ulric Skakki's neck was much easier.

Ulric laughed again, too, a light, airy sound that made Count Hamnet wonder how such different things could have the same name. "You won't do it if you don't go looking for somebody, that's for sure," he said.

"And if I do go looking for somebody, what'll she do?" Hamnet demanded. "Betray me the same way Gudrid did, that's what."

"Well, maybe you—" Ulric Skakki broke off, not from fear but from a certain self-protective caution. "You have murder in your eye, your Grace. Perhaps you should put it back in your pocket or wherever you usually keep it."

"You were going to say, 'Maybe you had it coming,' weren't you?" Hamnet said thickly. "Why shouldn't I kill you for that, you son of a whore?"

"Because it may be true even if you don't like it?" Ulric sounded as light and carefree as usual, but his hand hovered near his swordhilt.

Hamnet Thyssen's hand dropped to his. "You lie," he said. "I didn't do anything to deserve having horns put on me."

"No one ever does," Ulric Skakki said. "No one ever does, if you listen to him tell it. Or her—plenty of women sing the same sad song. 'No, I didn't do anything.' But people get horns put on them every day of the week, every week of the month, every month of the year. Meaning no offense, your Grace, but maybe doing nothing was your problem."

"What nonsense are you spewing now?" Hamnet said.

Ulric sighed. "I might have known you'd see it that way. By God, I *did* know you'd see it that way. Sometimes you have to try, whether you think it'll do any good or not." He turned away—but he kept an eye on Hamnet Thyssen even so.

"Doing nothing," Hamnet muttered in disgust. As if that meant anything! Gudrid played Eyvind Torfinn for a fool, too. Did that mean he was doing nothing, too? Count Hamnet glanced over toward Eyvind. At the moment, he was trimming his nails with a clasp knife, and making heavy going of it—the years had lengthened his sight, so he had to work at arm's length.

With what kind of man *would* Gudrid be happy? Count Hamnet couldn't imagine. By all the signs, Gudrid couldn't, either. Hamnet glared at Ulric Skakki. He thought he had all the answers, did he? Well, he wasn't half as clever as he thought he was.

Was he?

NORTH AND WEST, north and west. Hamnet Thyssen hadn't realized there was so much land beyond the Glacier. He'd thought the ground on the far side of the ice would be an afterthought, an appendage to the real world, the world he was familiar with. After all, the Raumsdalian Empire, the Bizogot steppe, and the lands to the south of those that Sigvat II ruled added up to a vast sweep of terrain. Why would anyone—or even God—need more of the world than that?

It all seemed perfectly logical. It probably was—but how much did logic have to do with truth? Not as much, plainly, as Hamnet would have wished.

"Do you have any idea where the Golden Shrine is?" he asked Eyvind Torfinn when they camped one evening, waving a hand as if to say it might be anywhere.

"I don't believe it's on the other side of the world," Earl Eyvind answered. "Past that, I'm afraid I can't begin to tell you."

"How do you know it's not on the far side of the world?" Hamnet asked.

"Because once upon a time—God only knows how long ago—we went there, and we remembered," Eyvind said. "I don't think we could have got to the Temple if it were so far away from the lands we know."

Count Hamnet grunted. "Well, I suppose that makes sense," he said, and then, surprising himself, "What does Gudrid say about the journey?"

"I think she wishes she never came." Eyvind Torfinn took the question in stride. "I told her back in Nidaros she would feel this way." He shrugged. "No one ever listens to advice, so the best advice I can give is not to give any."

"If I take it, I prove I listened," Hamnet said. "But if I advise anyone else to take it . . ."

Eyvind Torfinn looked at him, blinked, and started to laugh. He tried to stop, but seemed to have some trouble. "Oh, dear," he said, and laughed some more. "*Oh*, dear." Finally, with a fit of coughing, he made the laughter break off. "Well, well. I never expected to come up with such a neat paradox. I should be proud of myself."

Liv walked up to the two of them. "Why did the old man have a fit?" she asked Hamnet Thyssen.

That made Earl Eyvind cough some more, if not so comfortably. "I'm not as old as all that," he told the Bizogot shaman in her language.

She was somewhere in her late twenties—so Hamnet guessed, anyway. To her, Earl Eyvind probably *was* as old as all that. *To her, I'm getting on toward being an antique myself,* Hamnet thought uncomfortably, though he wasn't far past forty. The idea annoyed him more than it had any business doing. Then Liv bowed to Eyvind Torfinn. "I cry your pardon," she said. "I meant no insult, and I forgot you knew the Bizogot tongue so very well."

"You thought you could talk behind my back in front of me," the Raumsdalian noble said, an indulgent note in his voice. "Well, I forgive you—and I think I just made another paradox." The key word came out in Raumsdalian; the nomads didn't have the idea.

"Another what?" Liv asked, frowning.

"A paradox is something that says two things at the same time when they both can't be true at once," Eyvind Torfinn answered. Count Hamnet eyed him in admiration, knowing he couldn't have defined the word so well in the Bizogot tongue.

But the shaman's frown deepened. "Show me what you mean," she said.

"All right, by God, I will," Eyvind Torfinn said. "I have heard Bizogots say Raumsdalians lie all the time. You will have heard this, too, I'm sure."

"I do not believe it," Liv said politely.

"You are kind. You are gracious. But suppose it is true. Can you do that?" Eyvind waited till Liv nodded. Then he smiled. "All Raumsdalians tell lies all the time. Always. Right?" Liv nodded again. Eyvind jabbed a thumb at his own chest. "I am a Raumsdalian. I say I am a liar. But when I say I am a liar, *am I telling the truth?*"

"Yes," Liv said, and then, at once, "I mean, no." She paused a little longer. "I mean, yes." Her blue eyes started to cross. "It's maddening! It's mad!" she exclaimed. "It goes round and round, like a musk ox with the staggers. Where does it stop?"

"Good question," Hamnet said. His eyes were starting to cross, too.

"It stops wherever you want it to stop," Eyvind Torfinn said. "Or else it doesn't stop at all. That's what a paradox is."

"What do you use it for?" Liv asked.

Earl Eyvind's smile got wider. "Why, for whatever you want."

"For confusing people," Hamnet Thyssen said.

"It can do that." Liv eyed Eyvind Torfinn with more respect than she usually showed him. "You say you made up one of these horrible things?"

"Two of them, as a matter of fact," he answered, not without pride.

"You bear watching," Liv said, and walked away.

"Would you rather bear watching or watch bears?" Count Hamnet asked.

"Yes," Eyvind Torfinn said. Hamnet walked away, too.

"Deer!" Trasamund pointed west. "A herd of deer!"

Hamnet Thyssen's eyes followed that outthrust finger. The deer he knew didn't travel in herds. They were mostly solitary creatures that lived in the forests east of the Raumsdalian Empire. Every so often, they came out and fed in orchards and fields. He'd hunted them often enough to savor the taste of venison slowly simmered in ale and herbs.

These, he saw at a glance, were beasts different from the ones he'd known down in the south. *The warm south,* he thought, although he hadn't conceived of the Empire as such a warm place before his travels in the north. It was warm enough up here now, with the sun in the sky almost all day long. But what it would be like come winter . . .

Better to think about the deer. They were thicker-bodied and shorter-legged than the ones he knew, and of a pale dun color that blended in well with the ground over which they wandered. Their antlers were large and sweeping, but didn't have such sharp tines as those of the forest beasts he'd hunted. And . . . "Are they all stags?" he asked. "The deer I know, the does have no horns."

"More likely, the does here do grow antlers," Eyvind Torfinn said. Count Hamnet found himself nodding. He couldn't imagine such a large herd of male animals ambling along so peacefully.

"We'll eat well tonight, by God," Trasamund said with a nomad's practicality. Hamnet Thyssen nodded again. With so many of these strange deer going by, they would surely be able to knock over one or two.

And they did. The animals seemed untroubled, unafraid, as the men approached them. Getting into archery range was the easiest thing in the world. Jesper Fletti looked up from butchering one of the slain deer, his arms crimson to the elbows. "It's as if they never saw people before, and didn't know we were hunting them," he said.

"Either that or they're already tame, and don't worry about people because they're used to having them around," Ulric Skakki said.

"I don't think so." Naturally, the guards officer liked his own ideas better than someone else's.

Count Hamnet looked sharply at Ulric Skakki. Whether Jesper did or not, Hamnet knew Ulric had come beyond the Glacier before. "Did you meet these tame deer in the wintertime?" he asked in a low voice.

Ulric nodded. "I did. They act like musk oxen on the Bizogot plain—they scrape up the snow and eat what's underneath."

"And do people herd them, the way the Bizogots herd musk oxen and mammoths?" Hamnet asked.

"I can't prove that. I didn't see people with them," Ulric answered. "But there are people here, unless that owl you and the sorcerers flushed turned back into a white bear instead. And I don't think white bears herd deer, however much they might want to."

"No doubt you're right." Hamnet Thyssen looked around. "I don't see any signs of herders, though."

"Neither do I," Ulric said. "We must be on the edge of the country they usually wander. But that owl says we aren't the only ones who know the Glacier really has broken in two at last."

There was a disturbing thought. Hamnet looked around again. The only people he saw were the travelers with whom he'd come so far. But what did that prove?

"All we can do is go on," Hamnet said.

"No—we could go back," Ulric said. "We might be smart if we did. We've seen there's open land beyond the Glacier. What more do we need?"

"What about the Golden Shrine?" Hamnet asked.

"Well, what about it?" Ulric Skakki returned. "If you know where the bloody thing is, your Grace, lead the way."

"You know I don't," Hamnet Thyssen said irritably.

"Yes, I know that," Ulric said. "And I know I don't know where it is. Neither does Eyvind Torfinn, however much he wishes he did. Neither does Trasamund. Neither does Audun Gilli. And neither does the Bizogot shaman."

"Liv," Hamnet said.

"That's right." Ulric Skakki nodded. "And if I don't know, and if they don't know, then nobody up here from the other side of the Glacier knows—and nobody down there *on* the other side of the Glacier knows, either. And what are the odds of finding something if you don't know where in blazes to look for it? Rotten, if you ask me. So why waste time up here and maybe get caught by the weather—or by the folk who herd these deer? Better to take what we know and head back, isn't it?"

Hamnet Thyssen frowned. He might be the nominal leader of the Raumsdalians here, but he knew too well what a painful word *nominal* was. Eyvind Torfinn had a higher degree of nobility than he did, and a mulish scholarly autonomy. Audun Gilli might obey or might go off and pick wildflowers or look for something to drink. Ulric Skakki listened to himself and no one else. Jesper Fletti and his guardsmen listened to Gudrid first. As for Gudrid, if she listened to anyone under the sun—by no means obvious— she didn't heed her former husband.

Then there were the Bizogots, whom Hamnet couldn't even claim to command. No one commanded Trasamund, who was as much a sovereign as Sigvat II. Hamnet thought that if he told Liv to do something, she might . . . if she decided it was a good idea.

Wonderful. That may make one. Hamnet sighed. "Do you really suppose I could persuade the others to turn back?" he asked.

"How do you know if you don't try?" Ulric Skakki replied. Count Hamnet sighed again. That sounded sensible, reasonable. Both men knew it wasn't, which only made it more irritating.

"I'll try," Hamnet said. "That'll teach you."

THE SMELL OF roasting meat brought another striped hunting cat—or maybe the first one the travelers saw—back to investigate. They yelled and threw things at the animal and frightened it away. But it didn't go far. It skulked around out of bowshot, as if to say it claimed the scraps.

After Hamnet bit into a rib, he was willing to let the beast have them. The meat was tough and not very tasty. What flavor it had, he didn't much care for. The deer had been feeding on something that left it unappetizing. Hamnet had found the like in gamebirds, but never before in deer.

He used the poor meat to help make his point. "Now that we've found out what this country is like, shouldn't we head back to our own side of the Glacier and let the people there know?" he said, waving the rib bone for emphasis.

"Makes sense to me." Ulric Skakki did what he could to support the argument he'd proposed himself.

Everyone else metaphorically tore it limb from limb. "We have not found the Golden Shrine yet," Eyvind Torfinn declared, as if it were right around the corner—as if this vast, flat plain *had* corners.

"You have not seen a white bear yet, either," Trasamund added. "They're fine hunting, better even than the short-faced bears back on our own side of the Glacier." Considering how dangerous short-faced bears were, Hamnet Thyssen was anything but convinced that he wanted to meet anything worse. If he did, it was liable to end up hunting him, not the other way around.

No sooner had that thought crossed his mind than Gudrid said, "Besides, we haven't met the people who live beyond the Glacier."

"All the more reason to leave now, wouldn't you say?" Count Hamnet replied. Ulric Skakki nodded.

No one else could see it. Liv couldn't understand it, because the discussion was in Raumsdalian. Hamnet wondered what excuse his countrymen and Trasamund had. Were they merely foolish, or were they willfully blind? He glanced over at Gudrid. People would have asked the same thing of him when she first started being unfaithful. No doubt they had asked it—behind his back.

In those days, no one could have persuaded him she was anything but true. Here in the long-shadowed summer evening of the land beyond the Glacier, he himself could not persuade the others danger might lie ahead.

X

DEFEATED AND DEPRESSED, Hamnet Thyssen strode away from the campfire. The sun had set at last, but he was in no danger of getting lost. The northern horizon remained white and bright; the light was still good enough to read by. But he didn't feel like reading, even if he'd had a book. He wished he could keep walking, and leave behind the fools who didn't want to listen to him.

"Hamnet Thyssen!" As Liv often did, she spoke his given and family names as if they were part of the same long word. "Please wait!" she added.

After a moment, he did. She hadn't ignored him; she hadn't understood a word he was saying. Well, save for Ulric Skakki, neither had the rest, even though they and he used the same language. "Not your fault," he admitted.

"What was the argument about?" she asked, adding, "No one would slow down and translate for me. I really have to learn Raumsdalian, don't I?"

"It might help," Hamnet said. "If I can learn your language, I don't think there's any reason you can't learn mine. As for the argument, I thought we should turn around and go home while the going is good. Ulric Skakki thought I was right. Everyone else thought I had a mammoth turd where my brains ought to be."

The Bizogot shaman laughed. "You have an accent when you speak our tongue, Hamnet Thyssen, but that is something a man of my clan might say."

"What? That we should go home?" He misunderstood her on purpose.

"No, about the mammoth turd and—" Liv broke off. Her eyes flashed. "You are teasing me. Do you know what happens when you tease a shaman?"

"Nothing good, or you wouldn't want to tell me about it," Hamnet answered. "Tell me something else instead—do you think we ought to head back?"

"Probably," Liv answered. "What else can we do here, unless we happen to stumble over the Golden Shrine?"

He stared at her. He thought she was the most wonderful woman in the world. Of course he did—she agreed with him. "By God," he exclaimed, "I could kiss you!"

Liv waited. When nothing happened, she said, "Well? Go ahead."

He stared at her again, in a different way. She wasn't a bad-looking woman, not at all, but he hadn't thought she would take him literally. No—he hadn't thought she would *want* to take him literally. Since his troubles with Gudrid, he'd had trouble believing any woman would be interested in him.

Carefully, so as not to offend, he kissed her on the cheek. She raised an eyebrow. She was grimy and none too fresh, but he hardly noticed. All the travelers, himself included, were grimy and none too fresh. "Well?" he said, when she stood there looking at him with that eyebrow halfway up her forehead.

"Not very well, as a matter of fact," Liv told him. "You can do better."

You'd better do better, lurked behind the words. He managed a crooked smile of his own. "Who knows what you'd do to me if I told you no? You were just talking about how it's dangerous to anger a shaman."

In saying he didn't want to anger her, he managed to do just that. Her frown put him in mind of a building storm. "I do not force you to this, Hamnet Thyssen," she said. "If you care to, you will. If you don't . . ." She didn't go on, but he had no trouble filling in something like, *Be damned to you.*

Angry at himself and her both, he did kiss her, not much caring if he was gentle or not. "Well?" he said again, tasting a little blood in his mouth.

"That is better." Liv paused. "Different, anyway."

Count Hamnet bowed. "Thank you so much."

"My pleasure—a little of it, anyhow." The Bizogot woman could be formidably sarcastic.

The one person except Ulric who thought the same way he did—and here he was quarreling with her. How much sense did that make? Not much, and he knew it too well. He fought his temper under something close to control. "Will you tell Trasamund you think we ought to go south?" he asked.

"Is this what you ask after you kiss a woman?" Liv snapped. "Would you ask Gudrid the same question after you kiss her?"

"I would never kiss Gudrid." Hamnet's fury kindled for real. "And if, God forbid, I did, I would ask her who she'd just kissed before me and who she planned on kissing next." He spat at Liv's feet.

He thought that would infuriate her in turn. Instead, it sobered her like a bucket of cold water in the face. "Oh," she said in a small voice. "I did not mean to tease you, either. I am sorry."

"Let it go," Hamnet said roughly. "Just—let it go. But do talk to the jarl, because that really is important."

Liv bit her lip and nodded. "It shall be as you say." Then, without a backward glance, she went off toward the camp. Slowly, Hamnet Thyssen followed.

THE BEAR THE travelers saw scooping salmon from a stream was not white. It was brown. It was also the biggest bear Hamnet Thyssen had ever seen. Oh, some short-faced bears might have been as tall at the shoulder as this monster, but they were long-legged and quick. This beast was built like an ordinary woods bruin, but on an enormous scale.

It showed formidable teeth when the riders drew near. With a little coughing roar, it stood between them and the fish it had caught. "It doesn't trust us," Ulric Skakki said.

"Maybe it's met men before," Audun Gilli said.

"Maybe it just knows what we're likely to be like," Count Hamnet said.

Trasamund eyed him sourly. "And now you'll go, 'It's a great big bear! We should all turn around and run home!' "

Hamnet Thyssen looked back, his eyes as cold as the Glacier. "Demons take you, your Ferocity," he replied in a voice chillier yet.

"No one talks to me that way!" Trasamund had no more control over his temper than a six-year-old. "I'll kill the man who talks to me so."

After sliding down from his horse, Count Hamnet bowed with ironic precision. "You are welcome to try, of course. And after you have tried, the demons will take you in truth." He was not afraid of the Bizogot. Trasamund was big and strong and brave but not, from everything Hamnet had seen, particularly skillful. And even if he were . . . Hamnet Thyssen would not have been afraid, because whether he lived or died was a matter of complete indifference to him.

Trasamund also dismounted. He drew his sword, a two-handed blade

that could have severed the great bear's head from its shoulders. A blade like
that could cut a man in half—if it bit. Hamnet's own sword was smaller and
lighter, but he was much quicker with it.

Ulric Skakki rode between them. "Gentlemen, this is absurd," he said.
"You are quarreling over the shadow of an ass."

"By no means," Hamnet Thyssen said. He intended to add that he saw
the ass before him. The more furious Trasamund got, the more careless he
would act. He was proud of being a Bizogot like any other. That a Raumsdalian might goad him into foolishness because he was so typical never
once crossed his mind.

It crossed Ulric Skakki's, though. "That will be enough from you," he
snapped before Hamnet could speak. Then he rounded on Trasamund.
"And as for you, your Ferocity, you owe his Grace an apology."

"I will apologize with steel." The jarl swung his sword in a whirring,
whirling, glittering circle of death.

"You *are* a bloody fool," Ulric said.

"Shall I kill you, too?" Trasamund asked. "I do not mind. Take your place
behind that other wretch, and I will dispose of you one at a time."

"If I have to, I will," Ulric Skakki said. "Personally, I don't think you'll get
past Count Hamnet. If by some accident you should, I know you won't get
past me. Count Hamnet, I believe, fights fair. I promise you, your Ferocity, I
don't waste time on such foolishness."

"Do you *want* to die?" Trasamund sounded genuinely curious. "If you
do, I promise I can arrange it."

"Get out of the way, Ulric," Hamnet Thyssen said. "Believe me, I can
take care of myself." He had no intention of backing down—or of dying.
Surprises happened, accidents happened, but he didn't think any would
this time.

Trasamund seemed to realize for the first time that he was not only serious but murderous, that he wasn't just fighting to save his honor or to keep
from seeming a coward but because he expected to win. "You are making a
mistake, Raumsdalian," the Bizogot jarl warned.

"I don't think so," Hamnet answered. "And there's been too much talk already." He trotted toward Trasamund, ready to dodge around Ulric Skakki's
horse.

"Hold!" That cry didn't come from Ulric—it came from Liv. The shaman
pointed one forefinger at Hamnet, the other at Trasamund. They might
have been drawn bows. "You are both behaving like men who have lost their

wits. Either you are mad, or some sorcery in this country has struck you daft. Whichever it is, you shall not fight."

"No one tells me what to do. No one, by God!" Trasamund growled. He set himself to meet Hamnet Thyssen's onslaught, or perhaps to charge himself.

"I will curse the man who strikes the first blow. I will doubly curse the man who draws the first blood. And I will triply curse the man who slays." Liv sounded as determined as the jarl. Bizogots didn't commonly do things by halves.

Eyvind Torfinn was murmuring a translation for Audun Gilli. The Raumsdalian wizard said, "My curse also on anyone who fights here. We need to stick together."

"I fear no curses," Trasamund said, but the wobble in his voice belied his words.

Hamnet Thyssen really did fear no curses. He was already living under a curse, and she'd chosen to travel with him to the land beyond the Glacier. But Ulric Skakki guided his mount between Hamnet and the Bizogot again. "I think Liv is right. I think this land must be ensorceled," he said. "Otherwise his Ferocity would see he needlessly insulted a man who was only trying to do what he thought right—would see that and make amends for it."

He looked toward Trasamund. So did Hamnet Thyssen, who didn't care whether the Bizogot apologized or not. One way or another, Hamnet would go forward. All paths felt the same to him, and all had only darkness at the end.

The Bizogots had a word for that, where Raumsdalian didn't. The mammoth-herders called it *fey*. Maybe that word was in Trasamund's mind when he said, "This Hamnet dares to offer himself to my sword, to let it drink his blood. That being so, he cannot be such a spineless wretch after all. If I said something hasty, my tongue was running faster than it should have, and I am sorry for that."

"Your Grace?" Ulric said.

Part of Count Hamnet wanted to fight in spite of everything. But hearing Trasamund back down was startling, almost shocking. It shocked him enough to make him ground his sword. "That will do," he said with poor grace, and turned away.

"Good!" Eyvind Torfinn beamed. "Very good!"

Was it? Hamnet wasn't convinced. He wondered whether he'd stopped a fight with Trasamund or just put it off for another day. Trasamund muttered to himself as he slid his sword back into its sheath. Was he wondering the same thing?

THEY WENT ON, but not so far, not so fast. It was as if the quarrel about whether to go on or turn back had wounded the urge to advance without quite killing it. The plodding pace left Hamnet Thyssen less happy than either a forthright advance or a retreat would have.

"We'll never find the Golden Shrine at this rate," he said to Eyvind Torfinn.

"I don't know if it will matter whether we go fast or slow, if we go north or south or east or west," Earl Eyvind said.

"What's that supposed to mean, your Splendor?" Hamnet asked. "It sounds . . . mystical." He didn't feel like trying to penetrate another man's mysticism. To him, mysticism was even more opaque than magic, which after all had practical uses.

Eyvind Torfinn didn't help when he went on, "The Golden Shrine will be found when it is ready to be found. Till then, we can search as hard as we please, but we will pass it by. When we are ready, when it is ready, we will know, and it will be found."

"Wait," Count Hamnet said, scratching his head. "Wait. The Glacier has blocked the way north for how many thousand years?"

"I don't know. For a good many," Eyvind said calmly. "What of it?"

"Well, how could the Golden Shrine know anything about us?" Hamnet Thyssen asked. "We hardly know anything about it. Till I heard the Gap had melted through, I wasn't sure I even believed in the Golden Shrine. I'm *still* not sure I do."

"Don't worry about whether you believe in the Golden Shrine," Eyvind Torfinn said. "The Golden Shrine believes in you, which is all that really matters."

Instead of answering him, Hamnet Thyssen jerked his horse's head to one side and rode away. If Earl Eyvind wanted to talk nonsense, he was welcome to, as far as Hamnet was concerned. If he wanted anyone else to take him seriously when he did . . . that was another story altogether. Or was it?

Count Hamnet found himself looking in every direction at once. If the Golden Shrine was somehow sneaking around out there keeping an eye on him, he wanted to catch it in the act. Rationally, that made no sense at all.

He needed a little while to realize as much, but eventually he did. Yet out here beyond the Glacier, things weren't necessarily rational . . . were they?

He saw nothing that looked like the Golden Shrine—not that he knew what the Golden Shrine looked like. The country was the same as it had been since the travelers came through the Gap—a steppe for the moment green and spattered with flowers, but with all the signs of winter to come. Here and there, snow lingered on slopes that didn't see much of the sun. Here and there, frost heaves made miniature hillocks—the only real relief in the landscape.

"You call those pingoes, don't you?" Hamnet Thyssen asked Liv, pointing to one that reared a good hundred yards above the surface of the plain. A thin coating of dirt and clinging plants protected the ice core from melting in the sun.

"That is a pingo, yes," she answered. "Pingo is the name for such things in our language. That pingo is taller than most of the ones in Bizogot country."

"I wonder what makes them," Hamnet said.

"They *are*," the shaman responded. "How can they be made, except by God?"

"Sudertorp Lake is a lake because of meltwater from the Glacier," Hamnet said.

"Yes, of course." Liv nodded. "God made it so."

"Many, many years ago, Nidaros, the capital of the Empire, sat by the edge of Hevring Lake," Hamnet said. "Hevring Lake was a meltwater lake, too. Then it broke through the dam of earth and ice that held it, and it drained, and it made a great flood. You can still see the badlands it scoured out. One of these days, Sudertorp Lake will do the same thing."

"It may be so, but what of it?" the Bizogot shaman said.

Stubbornly, Hamnet Thyssen answered, "The land does what it does for reasons men can see. I can understand why Hevring Lake emptied out. I can see that Sudertorp Lake will do the same thing when the Glacier moves farther north. I don't have to talk about God to do it. So what shaped a pingo?"

Liv looked at him. "Speak to me of the Glacier without speaking of God. Speak of why it moves forward and back without speaking of God. Speak of how the Gap opened without speaking of God. Speak of the Golden Shrine without speaking of God."

Count Hamnet opened his mouth, but he did not know what to say.

"You see?" Liv told him, not in triumph, but in the manner of someone who has pointed out the obvious.

"Well, maybe I do," he admitted. "Or maybe I simply don't know enough about the Glacier to speak of it without speaking of God."

"I know what your trouble is," she said. Hamnet didn't think he had trouble, or at least not trouble along those lines. No matter what he thought, the Bizogot woman went on, "You live too far south, too far from the Glacier. You do not really feel the Breath of God in the winter, when it howls down off the ice. If you did, you would not doubt."

Bizogots always spoke of the Breath of God. Count Hamnet had gone up among the mammoth-herders in winter, but never in a clan like Trasamund's that lived hard by the Glacier. He wasn't sorry. The cold he'd known was bad enough that he didn't want to find out about worse.

It was as cold outside as it was in my heart, he thought. Could anything be colder than that? He didn't believe it. He wouldn't believe it.

But he didn't want to quarrel with Liv, either, and so he said, "Well, you may be right."

"I am." She had no doubts. She reached out and tapped his arm. "Tell me this—does your shaman, that Audun Gilli, does he think terrible thoughts about God, too? If he does, how can he make magic work?"

"I do not know what Audun Gilli thinks about God," Hamnet answered. "I never worried about it."

"You never worried about God. You never worried about what he thinks of God." Liv sounded disbelieving. "You southern folk are strange indeed."

"If you want to know someone from the south who thinks about God, talk to Eyvind Torfinn," Hamnet said.

Liv rolled her eyes, which told him she already had. "He tells me more than I want to hear," she said. "He says now one thing, now another, till I don't know whether my wits are coming or going."

"You see? We cannot make you happy," Hamnet Thyssen said.

"That is not so," Liv said. "I am happy—why shouldn't I be? But I am confused about what you think. Of the two of us, you are the unhappy one."

She wasn't wrong. Hamnet tried to avoid admitting that, saying, "What I think about God has nothing to do with whether I am happy or not."

"Did I say it did?" the Bizogot shaman returned. "All I said was that you were not happy, and I was right about that. I am sorry I was right about it. People should be happy, don't you think?"

"That depends," Count Hamnet said. "Some people have more to be happy about than others."

"Do you want to be happy?" she asked, and then, with Bizogot bluntness, "Do you think I could make you happy, at least for a while?"

He couldn't very well mistake the meaning of that. He could, and did, shake his head before he even thought about it. "Thank you, but no," he said. "Women are what made me the way I am now. I do not believe the illness is also the cure."

Liv looked at him for a moment. "I am sure you were a fool before a woman ever made one of you," she said coolly, and swung her horse away from his. Even if she'd stayed next to him, he had no idea how he would have answered her.

WHEN LIV MADE a point of avoiding him after that, it came as something of a relief. She gave him the uneasy feeling she knew things he didn't know, and not things her occult lore had taught her, either.

He wondered just how big a fool she thought he was. He didn't feel like a fool, not to himself. All he'd done was tell her the truth. If that was enough to anger her . . . then it was, that was all.

After Liv stayed away from him for a couple of days, Gudrid rode up alongside him. He tried to pretend she wasn't there. It didn't work. "It's your own fault," she said, sounding as certain as she always did.

"You don't know what you're talking about," Hamnet Thyssen answered stonily, but under the firm words lay a nasty fear that she really did.

Her rich, throaty laugh only made that fear worse. "Oh, yes, I do," she said. "I don't know what you see in that Bizogot wench, but plainly you see something. God couldn't tell you why—she smells like a goat."

"So does everybody up here—including you," Hamnet said. Just then, as if to mock him, the breeze brought him a faint whiff of attar of roses. If Gudrid smelled like a goat, she smelled like a perfumed goat.

He couldn't even make her angry. She just laughed some more. "As if you care," she said. "You chased her too hard, and you went and put her back up, and it serves you right."

Hamnet Thyssen gaped. That was so wrong, on so many different levels, that for a moment he had no idea how to respond to it. "You really have lost your mind," he said at last.

"I don't think so." Gudrid, in fact, sounded maddeningly sure. "I know you better than you know yourself."

"Oh, you do, do you?" Hamnet scowled at her. "Then why didn't you know what you'd do to me when you started playing the whore?"

Gudrid yawned. "I knew. I just didn't care."

He wanted to kill her. But if he did, she would die laughing at him, and he couldn't stand that. "You came all this way to torment me, didn't you?"

Gudrid buffed her nails against the wool of her tunic—an artful display. Everything she did seemed carefully calculated to drive him mad. "Well, I wasn't doing anything else when Eyvind decided to come," she answered.

Cursing, Hamnet Thyssen rode away from her. He really might have tried to murder her had she followed. She didn't, but her laughter pursued him.

AS THEY DID south of the Glacier, woolly mammoths roamed the plains here. The travelers gave them a wide berth. Hamnet would not have wanted to go mammoth hunting with the men and weapons they had along. If they were starving, if no other food presented itself—then, maybe. As things were, he found the great beasts better admired at a distance.

"Mammoths make me believe in God," Trasamund said one bright midnight. The Bizogot jarl was roasting a chunk of meat from one of the swarms of deer that shared the plain with the mammoths. "They truly do. How could mammoths make themselves? God had to do it."

"You could say the same thing about mosquitoes." Eyvind Torfinn punctuated the observation by slapping. "You could even say God liked mosquitoes better than mammoths, because he made so many more of them."

"No." Trasamund smiled, but he wasn't in a joking mood. "Any old demon could come up with your mosquito. A mammoth, now, a mammoth takes imagination and power. Isn't that so, Thyssen?"

Hamnet started. He sprawled by the fire for no better reason than that he didn't feel like sleeping. "I don't know what God does, or why," he answered. "If he tells me, I promise you'll be the first to hear."

Ulric Skakki thought that was funny, whether Trasamund did or not. "If God talks to anybody, he'll probably talk to you, your Grace," he said. "Me, I don't wonder so much where these mammoths came from. I wonder who herds them, and when the herders are going to show themselves."

"Haven't seen anyone yet," Trasamund said. "And the mammoths seem wild."

"How can you know that?" Eyvind Torfinn sounded curious, not doubtful. He usually sounded curious.

"One of the ways we tame them—as much as we do tame them—is to give them berries and other things they like," the jarl answered. "They're clever animals—they soon learn we have treats for them. They sometimes come up and try to get treats from us whether we have any or not."

"Back in Nidaros, my cat will do the same thing," Eyvind Torfinn said. "I don't think I would want a woolly mammoth hopping into my lap, though."

That did make Trasamund laugh, but he said, "These mammoths don't seem to think we have berries for them, so I would guess no one tames them."

Ulric Skakki made a dubious noise. Liv didn't look convinced, either; they were speaking the Bizogot language, so she had no trouble following along. Hamnet Thyssen also had his doubts.

"Could people tame mammoths some different way?" Ulric asked.

Trasamund looked down his nose at him. "People *could* do all kinds of things," the Bizogot replied. "They could waste their time with foolish questions, for instance."

"Thank you so much, your Ferocity," Ulric Skakki murmured.

"Any time." Trasamund was too blunt to recognize sarcasm, or maybe too sly to admit to recognizing it.

"We know there are people here," Liv said. "Either that or the owls in the land beyond the Glacier are sorcerers in their own right." *She* understood what sarcasm was about, even if not all Bizogots did.

Trasamund refused to let it bother him. "Maybe there are. We haven't seen any people here. That's all I can tell you."

"We have not seen the Golden Shrine, either," Eyvind Torfinn said. "Nevertheless, we are confident it's here somewhere."

"Well, people are probably here somewhere, too," Trasamund allowed with a show of generosity. "I don't think they're anywhere close by, though. You worriers are just trying to use this to get me to turn around and go back." He glowered at Hamnet Thyssen.

"Don't look at me that way," Count Hamnet said. "I didn't even take sides in this argument. You know more about mammoths than I do." *You ought to. Your hide and your skull are thick enough.*

Even though he didn't say that out loud, Trasamund sent him another suspicious stare. The Bizogot was clever enough to know when someone was thinking unkind thoughts about him. Why wasn't he clever enough to know they were thinking those thoughts because he was acting like a fool?

Instead of going back, they went on, though at the slow, halfhearted pace they'd been using for quite a while. One day seemed much like another—

broad plains ahead, behind, and to all sides. People said the sea looked that way, too. Count Hamnet couldn't speak about that; he'd never seen the sea. He did know the low, flat landscape bored him almost to the point of dozing on horseback.

One herd of deer, one herd of mammoths, one flock of ptarmigan or snow buntings came to look much like another, too. The travelers didn't see many of the great striped cats or enormous bears. He wasn't sorry about that, not even a little.

Another reason days all seemed the same was that they blended into one another so smoothly. A stretch of bright twilight for a couple of hours bracketing midnight, and then the sun came up again. You could travel whenever you pleased, rest whenever you pleased, sleep whenever you pleased.

And then, almost before Hamnet consciously realized it, real night returned to the world. The sun didn't come up quite so far in the northeast, didn't set quite so far in the northwest. It stayed below the horizon longer, and dipped farther below. Hamnet got reacquainted with stars he hadn't seen for weeks.

Birds sensed the change before he did. The sky was a murmur, sometimes a thunder, of wings. Flocks from even farther north began coming down upon and past the travelers. They knew winter was on the way, though the sun still shone brightly and days were, if anything, warmer than they had been when summer first began.

When the deer began to grow restless, even Trasamund acknowledged that the time to think things through had come. "We should turn around and head for the Gap again," he said, as if no one had ever suggested that before. "We are not going to find the Golden Shrine. Time to put away things of legend and remember the real world."

Ulric Skakki shook his head. "What a foolish idea! I think we should keep on wandering west through this godforsaken country till we come to the edge of the world and fall off it."

Trasamund glared at him. "Is that a joke? I don't hear anyone laughing."

"Then maybe it's not a joke," Ulric answered. "Maybe turning around is a good idea. Maybe it should have seemed like a good idea to you before this afternoon."

"I know when to turn back," the Bizogot jarl rumbled. "I always said I would know when to turn back."

"People say all sorts of things," Ulric Skakki observed. "Sometimes they mean them. Sometimes they don't. You never can tell ahead of time."

Glaring still, Trasamund said, "When we set out again come morning, I will ride south and east. Others may do as they please. Anyone who wants to fall off the edge of the world is welcome to, as far as I am concerned. Nobody will miss a slick-talking Raumsdalian, not one bit. Some folk are too clever for their own good."

Some folk are too stupid for their own good. But Hamnet Thyssen shook his head. Trasamund, whatever else you could say about him, was nobody's fool. *Some folk are too stubborn for their own good.* Yes, that fit the Bizogot better.

Hamnet wondered whether Trasamund would have decided to turn around sooner if he himself and Ulric and Liv hadn't kept trying to talk him into it. He wouldn't have been surprised. Trasamund was just the man to dig in his heels and try to go in the direction opposite the one other people urged on him. Count Hamnet was that kind of man himself, so he recognized the symptoms—here, perhaps, more slowly than he might have.

That night was the darkest one Hamnet remembered since passing beyond the Glacier. Maybe his own gloom painted the sky blacker than it was. Maybe the moon's being down added to the way the heavens seemed uncommonly unreachable, the stars small and dim and lost.

And maybe he was feeling something that was really in the air. Audun Gilli and Liv both woke screaming around midnight. That set Gudrid screaming, too. She only wanted to know what was going on, which seemed reasonable enough, but she made an ungodly lot of noise trying to find out.

"Too late!" Audun said.

"Much too late!" Liv agreed. They stared at each other, their eyes enormous and seeming filled with blood in the dim light the embers shed.

Hamnet Thyssen needed a moment to remember that neither of them understood the other's speech. The knowledge sent ice stabbing through him that had nothing to do with the enormous walls of ice he'd passed between.

"Do you hear them, your Ferocity?" Ulric Skakki asked.

"I'd have to be deaf not to," Trasamund answered, which was true enough. "They both had nightmares. So what?" He was not going to be impressed. No matter what happened, he wouldn't be—he was too determined.

"No, by God," Count Hamnet said. "They didn't have nightmares. They had the same nightmare. Do you think that's good news?"

"I don't think I can do much about it any which way," Trasamund said, and that was also true. He yawned—not quite theatrically, but not quite naturally, either. "About the only thing I can do that will help at all is go back to sleep, so I will . . . if the rest of you let me." He rolled himself in his blanket and turned his back on the fire—and on the rest of the travelers.

"What was it?" Hamnet Thyssen asked Liv, who lay closer to him than Audun Gilli did.

Whatever it was, it shook her enough to make her forget their quarrel. "It was . . . bad," she answered. "It was coming for us. I don't know what it would have done. I didn't want to find out. Maybe I was lucky I screamed myself awake."

"Maybe you were," Hamnet said. "If it comes on us in the waking world, can we get away so easily?"

"The waking world and the other one are less separate than you seem to think," the shaman said. "They touch, they blend, they mingle. You can't always say for sure that something is part of the one but not of the other."

Being a man who liked things neat and orderly, with each one in its proper slot, Hamnet Thyssen would like to have argued with her. Here in this land beyond the Glacier, here with the chill of winter in his heart, he found he couldn't. He couldn't sleep again, either, despite the snores rising from Trasamund.

The Bizogot jarl headed back toward the Gap faster than he'd gone before. No matter what he said there in the darkness, he worried about what Audun Gilli and Liv sensed, too.

Everything seemed normal for the next couple of days. Trasamund swore when a herd of mammoths crossed the travelers' path. A moment later, he swore again, in awe and amazement. The great beasts carried men atop them.

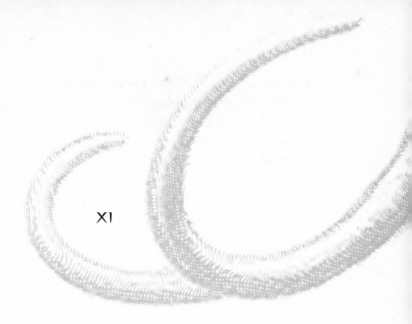

XI

WHEN TRASAMUND'S CURSES ran dry, he said, "But they can't do that." Hamnet Thyssen was inclined to agree with him. The idea of herding woolly mammoths was astonishing enough from a Raumsdalian point of view. The idea of taming them to the point where they could be ridden . . . Count Hamnet didn't know whether to be impressed or appalled. He ended up both at once, a stew of emotions that left him queasy.

Some of the mammoth-riders carried lances long enough to skewer someone in front of their enormous mounts. Count Hamnet wouldn't have wanted to try that—how much did one of those things weigh? Others had quivers on their backs. Still others seemed unarmed. After a bit, Hamnet saw that they were the men actually in charge of controlling the mammoths. They had iron-tipped bone goads with which they whacked the enormous animals to get them to do what they wanted.

What they wanted, right then, was to get a closer look at the travelers from the far side of the Glacier. The column of woolly mammoths swung into a line and bore down upon the Raumsdalians and Bizogots as smoothly as one of the Emperor's cavalry squadrons.

"Will you look at that?" Trasamund murmured. "Will you *look* at that?" He sounded as overwhelmed, and as full of yearning, as a boy on the edge of manhood staring at a beautiful woman and contemplating wonderful things he'd never imagined before. His eyes were as big and wide as the youth's might have been, too.

Hamnet Thyssen did not expect he would ever master the art of riding mammoths. He didn't feel he was suffering any great loss, either. His attention focused not on the shaggy beasts but on the men who rode them.

He did not like their looks. The closer they came, the less he liked it. They were not unhandsome—just the opposite, in a fierce half-eagle, half-lion sort of way. They had swarthy skins, big scimitar noses, proud cheekbones, and gleaming dark eyes. They wore their black beards in elaborate curled waves that rippled halfway down their chests, and their hair in neat buns at the napes of their necks.

Those gleaming eyes, though . . . Hamnet hoped his imagination was running away with him, but he did not like what he thought he saw in them. The Bizogots were hard. They had to be, living where they did, where so many things were so scarce. They mostly weren't cruel for the sake of cruelty. Hamnet Thyssen wasn't so sure about these strangers.

One of the men cupped his hands in front of his mouth and shouted something. To Hamnet's ear, it was just guttural nonsense. "I am sorry, my friends, but I don't understand you," Eyvind Torfinn answered in Raumsdalian.

"Do you speak my tongue?" Trasamund called in the Bizogot language.

More harsh-sounding gibberish came from the strangers. Eyvind and the Bizogot jarl both spread their hands to show they could make no sense of it. Ulric Skakki rode up alongside Count Hamnet and said, "I wonder if they would understand if Audun or Liv hooted like an owl."

"I wouldn't be surprised," Hamnet answered.

One of the strangers got down from his mammoth and approached the travelers from beyond the Glacier. He used the beast's long hair for handholds. The mammoth let him, which impressed Hamnet of itself. The man wasn't very tall, but he had some of the widest shoulders Hamnet had ever seen. He was built like a brick, all muscle everywhere.

He wore furs and leather, as the Bizogots did, but there the resemblance ended. The Bizogots wore clothes that fit tightly, while his jacket and trousers were loose and baggy, perhaps to let him stuff in extra padding if he wanted to. He had on enormous felt boots, into which he tucked the bottoms of his trousers. With footgear so large, his gait was more waddle than walk, but it was an impressive waddle.

He stopped about twenty feet in front of Trasamund and said something. "I don't understand you," the Bizogot jarl said.

Hamnet Thyssen didn't understand him, either, but he had a pretty good notion of what the stranger was saying. If it wasn't something like

Who are you and what the demon are you doing on my land? he would have been very surprised.

The stranger paused and scowled. He looked as if he hated everyone in the world, but especially Trasamund. He said the same thing over again, louder this time. He seemed to think everybody ought to understand his language, and ought to speak it, too.

"I still don't understand you," Trasamund told him.

This time, the noises the stranger made were different. They seemed angrier—no mean feat, when his whole vocabulary sounded angry. Either he was calling the jarl several different kinds of idiot or he was swearing at him—maybe both at once.

Audun Gilli rode forward a few paces. The stranger snarled something that sounded vile at him, too, and jumped back and drew a long, straight sword. Its highly polished edge glittered in the sunlight. He stood ready to fight and kill, ready to attack, even though Audun was surely the most inoffensive-looking of the travelers.

"No, no." Audun even sounded inoffensive, which Trasamund might not have. "You misunderstand, my friend. I come in peace." He held up his right hand, palm open—a gesture anyone on the far side of the Glacier, from the Bizogots to the folk who dwelt in the hot countries well south of the Raumsdalian Empire, would have understood.

If this stranger understood it, he didn't want to let on. He growled something that sounded unflattering. He brandished the sword again, but didn't rush the wizard. He looked even more scornful than he had when he was snarling at Trasamund. Maybe that was *because* Audun seemed so inoffensive; the Bizogot, at least, pretty plainly knew how to take care of himself.

Then Audun said, "I am a sorcerer." If Hamnet Thyssen had known he was going to do that, he would have tried to stop him—he didn't want to show these people too much (or anything at all) before he had to. He was briefly relieved to remember that the stranger seemed to know no Raumsdalian. "Maybe I can find a spell to let us understand each other," Audun went on, as if doing his best to give Count Hamnet heart failure.

Hamnet wasn't the only one who wished Audun would keep his mouth shut. "He's a trusting soul, isn't he?" Ulric Skakki whispered.

"He's a trusting fool, is what he is." Hamnet didn't bother keeping his voice down.

If Audun Gilli heard him, he paid no attention. That the mammoth-riding strangers could be dangerous didn't seem to cross the wizard's mind.

He just saw them as people with whom he couldn't speak—and maybe as a way to let him seem important to his comrades.

"I'm a sorcerer," he repeated. This time, he showed the bad-tempered barbarian—so Hamnet reckoned the man, anyhow—just what he meant. "Behold, I shall become invisible," he said, as if the stranger could understand him (and Hamnet had no sure proof the man could not).

Audun reached into his belt pouch and drew forth an opal. The stone sparkled in the sun, showing glints of red and blue and silver. The wizard began to chant. The opal seemed to draw more and more sunlight to itself as the spell went on. It sparkled brighter and brighter. Before long, it grew too dazzling for Hamnet Thyssen to look at. He had to turn away. And, since he could not look at the stone, he could not look at the man who held it, either. Audun was effectively, if not actually, invisible.

Looking away from Audun Gilli, Count Hamnet looked toward Liv. She watched the Raumsdalian wizard with avid interest. Her lips moved silently, perhaps in a charm of her own that let her go on looking at Audun and the opal after Hamnet Thyssen and the others close by had to avert their gaze.

Then Hamnet glanced in the stranger's direction. He screwed up his face and squinted at Audun—better that, he seemed to say, than to admit he was dazzled. But at last narrowed eyes availed him no more. He had to turn away.

When he did, he shouted back toward his comrades, who still sat on their mammoths. One of them stirred. They were more than a bowshot away, so Hamnet Thyssen could not tell exactly what their wizard or shaman or whatever he was did. Whatever it was, it served his purpose. The opal in Audun Gilli's hand shattered into fragments. The dazzling, coruscating light that flowed from it died.

"You see?" the stranger said in the Bizogot tongue. "You think you are so high and mighty, but in truth you are only a maggot like all your foul kind."

Audun Gilli stared at his hand, and at the tiny bits of opal still left in it. The mammoth-rider's speech meant nothing to him, because he did not speak the Bizogots' language.

But it meant something to Trasamund. "Who do you call maggot, dog?" the jarl demanded. "I asked if you knew my speech, and you would not give me a yes or a no."

"I give you nothing," the stranger said. "It is what you deserve. Soon enough, it is what the Rulers will give all who are not men."

Trasamund turned red. "You say I am no man?" he growled. The stranger nodded. "What am I, then?" Trasamund asked, his voice suggesting bloodshed would follow if he didn't like the answer.

The stranger only yawned. If he was trying to be offensive—and no doubt he was—he was succeeding. "Vermin," he said.

"Why, you flyblown son of a mammoth turd!" Trasamund shouted. He started to climb down from his horse. "By God, I'll kill you for that!"

"Wait, both of you," Eyvind Torfinn said in the Bizogot tongue. "We are newly met. We should not war. There is no quarrel between our folk."

"There is a quarrel between this wretch and me," Trasamund said.

"No, there is no quarrel," the stranger said. "The Rulers do not quarrel with lesser breeds. How could we? We do not quarrel with dogs, either. I, Parsh"—he jabbed a thumb at his own broad chest—"say this, and I speak the truth. We do not waste our time lying to lesser breeds, either."

"And I, Eyvind Torfinn, say you are provoking us on purpose."

Parsh yawned in his face. "I care nothing for what you say. Soon enough, your folk, whoever they are, will bend the knee before the Rulers. If they do not, we will destroy them as easily as Samoth there destroyed your silly wizard's stone."

"*These* are the people who hold the Golden Shrine?" Ulric Skakki whispered to Count Hamnet. Not much bothered Ulric—or if it did, he didn't let it show—but he sounded scandalized now. Hamnet wasn't surprised; the notion horrified him, too.

"Maybe they don't," he whispered back. "We don't know where the Golden Shrine is, and we don't know how much land these, uh, Rulers rule. Maybe they just talk big."

Talk big they did. "You will come to our encampment," Parsh said. "My chief will want to see what manner of lesser men you are."

"And if we don't care to come with you?" Eyvind Torfinn asked.

"However you please." Parsh shrugged broad shoulders. "But in that case, we will have to kill you here." Now he didn't sound boastful. He sounded matter-of-fact, like a man who had to talk about getting rid of mice.

Hamnet Thyssen eyed the mammoths and the men riding them. He didn't like the idea of fighting warriors aboard such immense animals. They outnumbered the travelers from the far side of the Glacier. And . . . "Audun!" Hamnet called in Raumsdalian. "How good is their sorcerer?"

"I heard you have more than one kind of animal grunts," Parsh said in the Bizogot tongue. "Well, that won't do you any good, either."

"He . . . is not weak," Audun Gilli answered reluctantly.

That would have been Hamnet's guess. But he didn't want to have to go with a guess here. He wanted to be sure. Now that he was, he said, "Let's go with them. We need to learn more about them before we decide what to do."

"When we get to wherever they camp, I will take care of this Parsh," Trasamund said—in Raumsdalian.

The man from the Rulers caught his name, even if he didn't understand the words surrounding it. His grin displayed strong white teeth. Hamnet Thyssen couldn't decide whether his canines were uncommonly sharp on their own or they'd been filed to points. Neither notion seemed attractive to contemplate.

"We will go with you to your camp," Eyvind Torfinn told Parsh.

"Oh, what an honor!" Parsh said. "The vole consents to travel with the—" The last word was one in his language. He bowed mockingly. "Thank *you*, most gracious and generous vole."

Hamnet Thyssen had disliked Parsh on first sight. The more he saw of the stranger, the more he despised him. He was sure that was exactly the impression Parsh was trying to create. Well, Parsh knew how to get what he wanted, all right.

"To travel with the what?" Earl Eyvind asked.

"With the *tiger*," Parsh repeated. "The big, striped cat. Are you too ignorant to know of tigers? By the gods, you must be fools indeed!"

"Fools for putting up with your noise," Trasamund said. He might have been less enamored of Parsh than Count Hamnet was.

"Come," the man of the Rulers said. "Come now, or be killed where you stand."

They came.

THE CAMP WAS not like anything Hamnet Thyssen expected. He'd looked for the same sort of dirt and disorder that always marked a Bizogot encampment. He didn't find them. Tents stood in neat rows. Mammoths and deer were tethered in neat lines. Some of the deer had saddles and reins. The Rulers didn't seem to ride horses. Come to think of it, Hamnet hadn't seen any horses except for the ones with his party since traveling beyond the Glacier. Parsh hadn't shown any curiosity about them, but Parsh didn't seem to show curiosity. The only thing he showed was arrogance.

That irked Count Hamnet. It infuriated Trasamund. As soon as he got down from his horse, he roared, "Parsh! Where are you, Parsh, you bastard child of a rabid fox and a palsied rabbit? Come get what you deserve!"

He didn't have long to wait. Parsh marched up to him and bowed. "Here I am, creature. How do you care to die? Name your pleasure, and I will oblige you."

"Bizogot stand-down," Trasamund said at once.

"I do not know what foolish games barbarians play," Parsh said scornfully. "Tell me what this is, so I know whether it is fitting."

"We stand here," Trasamund said. "One of us hits the other in the face. Then it's the second man's turn. Last one who can still get up and swing wins."

For the first time since Hamnet set eyes on him, Parsh actually looked pleased. "This is good sport—very good sport for a savage. How generous of you to give me the chance to amuse myself so." He shouted in his own guttural language. His countrymen sounded interested and approving, even if Hamnet couldn't understand a word they said. Parsh returned to the Bizogot tongue to ask, "How do we decide who goes first?"

"Go ahead," Trasamund said as men of the Rulers gathered to watch the stand-down. Hamnet Thyssen saw no women in the encampment. "Do your worst, hound, and then you will see what a nothing it is."

Hamnet wouldn't have said that, not against a foe as plainly powerful as Parsh. He would have tried to claim the first blow, or at least an even chance at it. Parsh actually smiled. "Your funeral," he said, and likely meant that in the most literal way.

"Talk is cheap," Trasamund said. "What do you do to back it up?"

Parsh hit him. Hamnet thought that blow might have felled a mammoth, let alone a man. Blood poured from Trasamund's nose. He swayed, but quickly straightened. "Well, when will you begin?" he asked.

"You fool! I did," Parsh said.

"Oh, that? I thought you sneezed," the Bizogot jarl said. Samoth the wizard or shaman or whatever he was turned Trasamund's words into the language of the Rulers. The strangers buzzed among themselves. They clearly weren't used to outsiders as proud as themselves. Trasamund went on, "Well, then, I'll just have to hit you back."

Parsh didn't flinch from the blow. He did stagger. He bled from the nose, too; his seemed to have changed shape. But he managed a laugh. "A mosquito bit me," he said.

"Any that did would sick you up afterwards," Trasamund jeered. Parsh hit him again. His head snapped back. He spat blood, and a tooth. "Keep at it," he told Parsh. "You may wake me yet."

He slugged the man from beyond the Glacier. Parsh lurched and blinked a couple of times. "A love pat," he said thickly, and then he too spat red.

"You dream," Trasamund said, "for I love you not."

"Then love—this." Parsh threw another right. Trasamund went to one knee. Slowly, he got to his feet. He shook his head, as if to clear it. Parsh looked quite humanly surprised—he hadn't thought the Bizogot would be able to stand up.

Trasamund shook his head. "I love it so well, I'll give you one like it." He shook his head again. "No, I'll give you one better." He smashed his fist into Parsh's face. The man from the Rulers swayed but stayed upright. Even so, the nasty light in his eyes went out. He wasn't enjoying the game any more, only hoping to get through it—as Trasamund was.

It went on for a long, painful, miserable time. Both Trasamund and Parsh went down repeatedly; each man struggled to his feet each time. Parsh kept punching with his right hand. After a while, Trasamund switched to his left.

Trasamund's traveling companions stayed quiet through the contest. The men of the Rulers cheered Parsh at first. As it became clear the victory wouldn't be easy if it came at all, they subsided into uneasy silence, too.

One of Trasamund's eyes was swollen shut. He could open the other one a little. He peered through what had to be a blurry slit at Parsh, who was in no better shape. "Here," the Bizogot mumbled through pulped and puffy lips. "This time . . ." He cocked his left fist.

Parsh watched it with fearful concentration. Maybe he saw that Trasamund was putting everything he had left into this one blow, for as the Bizogot's left fist shot forward Parsh started to duck. He wasn't quick enough, not after the punishment he'd already taken. The blow caught him square on the point of the chin. He crumpled and lay motionless.

"Aii!" Trasamund groaned. "I think I've gone and broken my other hand now."

That would have mattered had the fight gone on. But Parsh could not get up. For a moment, Hamnet Thyssen wondered if he was dead. Only the slow rise and fall of his chest said life still smoldered in him.

Trasamund turned away. "Wait!" the wizard from the Rulers—his name was Samoth—said in the Bizogot tongue.

"What for?" Trasamund could hardly stand on his own feet, let alone talk. His wits had to be scrambled. He'd taken a fearful beating. That he'd given a worse one seemed almost beside the point.

"You beat him," Samoth said. "Now kill him."

"What the demon for?" Trasamund said. "This wasn't to the death. It was last man standing. Here I am. God knows how, but here I am. He almost knocked my head off a couple of times there." Now that he'd won, he could pay tribute to a formidable foe.

But Samoth shook his head. "When we fight, we fight to the death. Anything less is a disgrace. He would have killed you. You would do him a favor by killing him. That he should lose to a lesser breed . . ." He translated his words into the gutturals his own folk used. Their fierce faces somber, the men of the Rulers nodded.

"No." Trasamund shook his head—and almost fell over on account of it. "That's his worry, not mine. I don't want his blood now. I just want to wash mine off my face and to tie up my hands. Where have you got some water, and maybe some cloth or some leather lashings?"

"I will take you," Samoth said, reluctant respect in his voice. "Come with me."

Trasamund walked with the rolling, lurching gait of a drunk. That he walked at all amazed Hamnet Thyssen. After what the Bizogot jarl had taken, his being alive amazed Count Hamnet. "Maybe I'd better go along," Ulric Skakki remarked, "just to make sure everything is on the up and up."

"Not a bad idea," Hamnet said. Silent as a snowy owl, Ulric slipped away.

Hamnet waited by Parsh, curious to see what would happen when the savage woke up and found he had lost. After a quarter of an hour, one of the Rulers poured a mammoth-hide bucket of water over Parsh's head. Parsh moaned and spluttered and jerked. His eyes came open. He looked around and realized he was lying on the ground.

Horror on his smashed face, he did his best to stand. He needed three tries before making it to his feet. Even then, he swayed like a tall tree in a storm. "Where is the Bizogot?" he asked blurrily. "Did he fall? If he didn't, I will hit him again."

No one answered when he spoke the Bizogot tongue. Increasing alarm in his voice, he asked what was probably the same question in his own language. One of his countrymen gave back a few scornful words.

Parsh shook his head. He said something else. The other man of the Rulers turned his back on him. Parsh swung toward Hamnet Thyssen. "Is it so? Can it be so?" he asked in the Bizogot language. "Did he beat me? How could he beat me?"

"He beat you," Hamnet answered. "Your chin was strong, but his was stronger."

"One of the lesser breeds cannot beat a man of the Rulers. It cannot be done," Parsh said. His own battered state was proof positive that it *could* be done, but he seemed to be talking about laws of nature, not particular cases. He shook his head, then grimaced; after the beating he'd taken, he had to wish he were dead. Hamnet Thyssen had reason to remember that thought. "It cannot be done," Parsh repeated.

"It was," Count Hamnet said.

Instead of answering, Parsh looked at his countryman, who kept on giving him his back. That seemed to make up his mind for him. "It cannot be done," he said for the third time. "I must make amends." He pulled his belt knife from its sheath and stared at the blade.

If he'd tried to go after Trasamund, Count Hamnet would have stopped him. Hamnet didn't think that would be hard; Parsh could barely walk and speak, let alone fight. But the man of the Rulers did nothing of the sort. He spat between his own feet, a gesture of vast contempt. Then he looked up into the sky—and then, before Hamnet or anyone else could stop him, he slashed the knife across his throat.

Blood spurted, scarlet in the afternoon sun. Parsh crumpled. No one could hope to stanch that wound. The man of the Rulers thrashed on the ground for a little while, then lay still in death.

Only after he died did his comrade deign to turn around and acknowledge him again. The other man of the Rulers closed the dead and staring eyes. He said something in his own language.

"I don't understand you," Hamnet Thyssen said, which was true on every level he could think of. Parsh's countryman spread his hands to show he knew nothing of the Bizogot language.

Trasamund and Samoth returned a few minutes later. Samoth eyed Parsh without surprise. "Redeemed himself, did he?" the wizard said.

"By God!" Trasamund muttered. "You are a hard-hearted folk." He looked down at his bandaged hands. "And a hardheaded folk, too."

"Do you want his weapons?" Samoth asked. "Such is the rule when one of us beats another. I do not know what the rule is when someone of a lesser breed beats a man of the Rulers. I do not think it happens enough for us to need a rule."

That was a compliment of sorts. Maybe the Bizogot jarl would have been wiser to show he saw as much. Or maybe not; the Rulers, arrogant themselves, seemed to appreciate arrogance in others—when those others could back it up. Trasamund had. "I didn't mean for him to die," he said, peering through puffed and slitted eyes at Parsh's gory corpse. "I only wanted to wipe out an insult."

"What better way to wipe it out than in blood?" Samoth returned. Trasamund shrugged. Then he grimaced. Even the little motion had to hurt.

HAD TRASAMUND NOT beaten Parsh, Hamnet Thyssen wondered if the Rulers would have fed the Bizogots and Raumsdalians. As things were, the men from beyond the Glacier treated the travelers, if not like themselves, then at least with a certain circumspection. *We may be beasts,* Count Hamnet thought, *but we've shown we're beasts with claws and fangs.*

The meat came from the deer that roamed these plains. Maybe the Rulers were fancy cooks in encampments that held women and children. Here by themselves, the warriors cooked about the same way Bizogots or Raumsdalian soldiers would have—they roasted their meat over flames. The flames came from a fire of dried dung, as they would have in the Bizogot country. Instead of holding the meat on sticks, the men used skewers made from mammoth bone. Again, the Bizogots would have done something similar, though they sometimes got wood in trade from the Empire. Hamnet Thyssen judged no trees grew anywhere close to lands the Rulers ruled.

They did have salt; perhaps the edge of a sea lay not too far off, or perhaps it came from an outcrop of rock salt. And they had spices the likes of which none of the travelers had ever tasted. The black flakes the curly-bearded men sprinkled on the meat reminded Hamnet Thyssen of chills because they bit the tongue, but their flavor was different.

Eyvind Torfinn thought so, too. "What do you call this spice?" he asked the leader of the Rulers, a hawk-faced, middle-aged man named Roypar.

Roypar scratched his cheek and then tugged at the gold hoop he wore in his left ear. None of the other men of the Rulers wore such an ornament. Was it a badge of rank? A sign of wealth? Was there a difference? Count Hamnet wasn't sure about that, even among Raumsdalians. Among the Rulers? He could only guess.

"Is name of *pepper,*" Roypar answered. He spoke only a little of the Bizogot tongue. In any case, the important word came from his own speech.

"Pepper." Earl Eyvind repeated the unfamiliar name several times. Roypar nodded. Over meat, he seemed less ferocious than his fellows had before. "Do you raise this yourself?" Eyvind inquired. "Or do you trade for it?"

"Trade," Roypar said. "Is come from far away." He pointed south and west. "Far, far away. Many days, many months."

"I see," Eyvind Torfinn said gravely. "And how far in that direction do the Rulers rule?"

"Long way. Very long way," Roypar replied. Was he clever enough to dodge Eyvind's probe or too naive to notice it was a probe at all? Hamnet Thyssen couldn't tell. That made him guess Roypar might be clever, even if he had no proof.

Eyvind went on, "And do you have it in mind to stretch your rule to the south and east now that there is a way through the Glacier?"

Now Roypar looked at him as if he were a witling. "Well, of course," said the chieftain or officer or whatever he was. "Of course. We are the Rulers. Where we can reach, we rule."

"Anyone who tries to rule the Bizogots will be sorry," Trasamund said. His voice was still a thick mumble through split and swollen lips. "Maybe you can kill us. Maybe we kill you instead." The roasted venison was tough. He chewed slowly and carefully, and on the side where he hadn't just lost a tooth.

"Maybe." That wasn't Roypar; it was Samoth the sorcerer. "You are strong. You are fierce. But your magic"—he sneered—"your magic is nothing much."

Audun Gilli had no idea what he was saying; the Raumsdalian wizard knew nothing of the Bizogot language. Liv, of course, understood Samoth well enough. She'd said next to nothing herself up till then. Now, swallowing a bite of meat, she looked across the smoky fire at Samoth and hooted three times like an owl.

He jerked as if bitten by a mosquito the size of a falcon. "So you had somewhat to do with that, did you?" he growled. His comrades who could follow the Bizogot tongue sent him curious looks. Maybe he hadn't told them he'd had to fly from the travelers' magic down in the Gap.

Liv gave him a sweet smile. "Why, yes," she said, all innocence. "We did."

Samoth muttered into his curled mat of beard. Hamnet Thyssen sent Liv a small nod. He thought she'd found a fine way to prick the Rulers' pomposity. They were so very, very sure of themselves—anything that made them doubt was bound to be on the right track.

Ulric Skakki was sitting next to Audun. When the wizard whispered to him, he provided a translation. He hadn't spoken long before Audun Gilli twitched as violently as Samoth had. "Nothing much!" Audun said in Raumsdalian. "By God, I'll—"

"You'll shut up, is what you'll bloody well do," Ulric said, much more sharply than he was in the habit of speaking. Audun blinked at him, and then did shut up, though his eyes said he didn't understand why Ulric required it of him.

Hamnet Thyssen did. Ulric Skakki's little finger understood more of intrigue than all of Audun Gilli put together. If Audun showed Samoth how good a wizard he could be, that would alert the Rulers to a problem they didn't know they had right now.

And Hamnet Thyssen also saw something he wasn't sure whether either Ulric or Audun did. If Audun tried to impress Samoth and failed again, as he'd failed with the opal . . . That would give the travelers a serious problem.

"So you aim to bring our folk under your rule, do you?" Eyvind Torfinn asked Roypar. Now the Count frowned, wondering if the other Raumsdalian noble wasn't pushing too hard.

"Is right," Roypar said complacently. The Rulers ruled other folk. To him, that was a law of nature.

Voice elaborately casual, Eyvind Torfinn went on, "Perhaps you would do well to let us return to the south, then, so the Bizogot jarls and my Emperor, apprised of your imminent arrival, can prepare for you the most appropriate and honorable reception."

Count Hamnet suddenly stopped thinking of Eyvind as an old man wise only in the things that had to do with books. He was an intriguer in his own right. Ulric Skakki's abrupt alertness argued that he was thinking the same thing. By the smug look on Roypar's face, he thought Eyvind Torfinn meant the Bizogots and the Raumsdalian Empire would get ready to surrender as soon as they found out the Rulers were on the way. Hamnet Thyssen would have been mightily surprised if that was what Earl Eyvind really had in mind.

Would Parsh have seen otherwise? He was much more fluent in the Bizogots' language, which argued that he had understood foreigners better than his superior. It didn't matter now, though, not when he was dead—he hadn't understood Trasamund, or at least the strength of Trasamund's jaws and of his fists, well enough.

Samoth stirred. The wizard said something in the language of the Rulers. *I have to learn that tongue if I can,* Hamnet Thyssen thought. Roypar snorted and shook his head. Samoth spoke again, more urgently this time. He saw that Eyvind Torfinn wasn't as submissive as he seemed.

He saw it, yes, but he couldn't make Roypar see it. The chieftain sounded angry when he answered this time. Samoth bit his lip. He muttered into his beard, then subsided—for the moment. A couple of men of the Rulers stirred and eyed Roypar in exactly the same way Hamnet Thyssen would have eyed him if he'd belonged to their folk. A leader who got a wizard angry at him was either a man of extraordinary personal qualities and confidence . . . or a blustering blowhard.

Which was Roypar? Hamnet admitted he couldn't know. Judging a man he'd just met, a man from a folk with whom he was not in the least familiar, a man who barely had a language in common with him, was a fool's game. *Well? Aren't I a fool?* Hamnet asked himself with wry amusement—the only kind he knew these days.

His gaze flickered to Gudrid. She was watching Roypar with the sort of fascination that raised Count Hamnet's hackles. He quickly looked away. His eyes went to the chieftain, too. He thought a clever man would have seen through Eyvind Torfinn's ploy, so maybe he'd been wrong before. Samoth had seen through it—and much good it did him.

"You go south, yes," Roypar said. "You go. You tell your folk, the Rulers come. You tell, bring out gold, bring out women, bring out fine mammoths, fine deer for Rulers to take."

"Deer?" Eyvind Torfinn's frown said he wasn't sure he'd understood the stranger.

"Deer." Roypar nodded. "For riding. Deer."

"Oh. Of course. Deer." Butter wouldn't have melted in Earl Eyvind's mouth. No, the Rulers knew nothing of horses. Hamnet Thyssen didn't know much of the deer they rode, either, but the animals weren't as large as horses and didn't seem as strong. On the other hand, the Rulers could do things with mammoths that even the Bizogots only dreamt of.

Strangers, Hamnet thought. It was a truth he always had to bear in mind. The Bizogots were cousins to the Raumsdalians. All the folk south of the Glacier were in effect their neighbors if not their kin. But had his folk's ancestors ever had anything to do with the forebears of the Rulers? Surely not since the Glacier last ground down out of the north.

How long ago was that? How many thousands of years had gone by since? Count Hamnet had no idea. Eyvind Torfinn might be able to make a pretty good guess. So might Audun Gilli, come to that; sorcerers needed a better notion of the distant past than most people. It was a long, long, *long* time—Hamnet was sure of that.

Roypar pointed toward the travelers' horses, which were tied alongside the riding deer the Rulers used. "Why you cut horns off your big deer?" he asked. "You no use horns to fight with?" No, he didn't understand about horses at all.

Neither did Samoth, who said, "And how did you remove the antlers so neatly? There is no trace of a scar. After we rule you, that is a trick your leeches must show us." He had as much confidence as any other man of the Rulers.

"There is no trick, I fear," Hamnet Thyssen said. "The animals are born without antlers." He didn't see how the truth could hurt here.

Samoth smiled—unpleasantly. "I might have guessed. Not likely that the lesser breeds could know anything important that we do not."

None of the travelers said anything. Even if they had, Samoth and the rest of the Rulers there wouldn't have heeded them. The Rulers knew what they knew, and didn't want to know anything else—even if it happened to be true.

Later in the evening, Hamnet Thyssen noticed Roypar trying to talk to someone who spoke even less of the Bizogots' tongue than he did. Hamnet took a couple of steps toward the chieftain, thinking to be helpful. Then he heard Gudrid's throaty chuckle, and drew back without drawing Roypar's notice or hers. He slept not a wink all night.

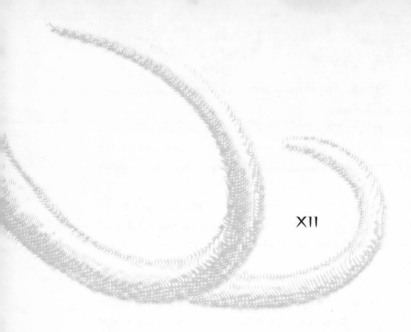

XII

WE WILL RIDE south and east," Eyvind Torfinn said, no irony audible in his voice. "We will let the other Bizogot jarls and the Raumsdalian Emperor know that the Rulers follow behind us. We will make sure our lands are ready to meet you as you deserve."

"Is good," Roypar said. "Is very good." By Samoth's expression, he didn't think it was very good, but he held his peace. Roypar led here. Anyone else challenged him at his own peril.

Parsh's body lay where it had fallen. "Will you burn him?" Hamnet Thyssen asked. "What is your custom with your dead?"

"He will lie there till the foxes and bears and tigers have feasted on him," Samoth answered. "He failed as a man—he deserves nothing better than to feed beasts. No doubt his spirit, when it is born again, will be born into the body of such a one."

"You believe in reincarnation, then?" Eyvind Torfinn asked eagerly. "Have you evidence to support your belief?"

Trasamund and Hamnet Thyssen had to drag Eyvind away from the wizard of the Rulers. If they hadn't, he would *not* have ridden south and east. He would have stayed there and plied Samoth with questions for as long as the sorcerer could stand it.

Hamnet glanced over to Roypar. The chieftain looked unmistakably pleased with himself. The Rulers thought of themselves as conquerors beyond compare. Had he lain with a woman of a lesser breed the night before? Hamnet guessed he had. Gudrid showed nothing one way or the other. She was good at making her indiscretions discreet—unless she dropped the mask and showed them off.

Hamnet looked away. She laughed softly. So she knew what he was thinking, did she? She'd always been good at that. Hamnet Thyssen turned his back, which only made her laugh again, louder this time. *Too bad*, he thought.

Roypar really did let them ride away. That surprised Count Hamnet. It seemed to surprise and dismay Samoth, who muttered into his thicket of beard. The way he muttered sparked suspicion in Hamnet even before the Rulers' encampment dropped below the horizon behind the travelers. He rode over first to Audun Gilli and then to Liv, asking each of them, "Is the wizard back there tracking us by magic? Are we taking along some little spell that lets him spy on us?" He had to repeat himself, using Raumsdalian and then the Bizogots' language. He wished the two people among the travelers who knew sorcery could understand each other. As happened too often in life, what he wished for had nothing to do with what he got.

Ulric Skakki understood him both times he asked the question. "You have a nasty, distrustful turn of mind, your Grace," Ulric said—in the Bizogot language, a choice Hamnet found interesting. "I only wish I'd thought of that myself."

"Don't worry," Hamnet said. "You would have before long."

"That kind of spell is possible, I suppose." Audun Gilli didn't seem to think Samoth had actually done such a thing.

Liv did. "Yes, of course. A sorcerous flea, you might say, coming along with us. Maybe it will bite, too, when the time is right."

"Can you find it?" Count Hamnet asked. "Can you kill it?" Again, he had to use the mammoth-herders' language and then his own.

So did Ulric Skakki when he added, "Can you find it and kill it without letting Samoth know it's gone?" Hamnet Thyssen thumped his forehead with the heel of his hand. Now he was angry that Ulric had an idea before he did.

"Who knows what all shamanry the strangers have?" Liv said. "They think it is stronger than ours. They may be right—remember how Samoth shattered Audun's opal. But we can try."

"What does she say?" Audun Gilli asked. "I heard my name in that, whatever it was." When Count Hamnet translated for him, he sniffed. "I am sure I could have stopped Samoth if I'd been looking for him to do that. Liv worries over nothing."

Now the Bizogot shaman wondered why Audun was using her name. Hamnet Thyssen turned Audun's words into her tongue. She sniffed on a note almost identical to the one the Raumsdalian sorcerer had used. "He says I worry over nothing, does he? Well, he thinks there is nothing to worry about, and that worries me."

It worried Hamnet Thyssen, too. Having the two sorcerers squabble again also worried him, the more so since they had to do their squabbling through him or through Ulric. Hoping to distract them, he said, "The flea," first in the Bizogot language, then in Raumsdalian.

"Trust a Bizogot to think of fleas," Audun said. Since he was scratching as he spoke—he didn't seem to notice he was doing it—he proved Raumsdalians weren't immune to the pests. Count Hamnet's itches already told him that.

"Never mind the snide cracks," Ulric said. "Can you find the magic?" Now he used Raumsdalian, and didn't translate for Liv. She sent Hamnet a look of appeal. He didn't translate, either. She glared at him.

"If it is here, it should be simple enough to find," Audun Gilli said.

"Please go ahead and do it, then," Hamnet Thyssen said, and then, to Liv, "I would also like you to check." By now, he was resigned to going back and forth between languages.

"I will do it if Audun fails." The Bizogot shaman glanced over at the Raumsdalian wizard. "I wish we could understand each other. It might mean much if we have to work together. Would you teach me Raumsdalian, Hamnet Thyssen?"

"If you like," Count Hamnet answered. "You will have to learn the fancy magical terms from Audun, though. I might make mistakes, and mistakes in that kind of thing can be dangerous. I am no wizard, but at least I know it."

"You're right," Liv said. "I should have started learning your language a long time ago, but you and I didn't always get on well."

"Ulric Skakki could have taught you, or Eyvind Torfinn—or Trasamund, come to that," Hamnet said.

"I think you are more patient than they are," Liv said. Hamnet doubted whether anyone in the world was more patient than Eyvind Torfinn. He didn't want to say so, not when Liv paid him such a compliment.

Audun Gilli, meanwhile, was rummaging through the pouches he wore on his belt. He muttered and mumbled as he rummaged—all in all, he might have posed for a picture of a distracted wizard. At last, though, he came up with what he needed and seemed to come back to the real world.

"Here is the dried head of a plover," he said, and held it up. Hamnet Thyssen looked away from the sunken eye sockets. Audun Gilli went on, "It has the virtue that, if used with the proper spell, it prevents deception."

"What does he say?" Liv asked. Hamnet translated for her. She nodded, though a little doubtfully. "We use a different bird for what sounds like the same charm," she said, "and a certain stone as well." She shrugged. "Well, let us see what his shamanry shows."

Audun Gilli held up the plover's head in his left hand. He made passes with his right while chanting in Raumsdalian almost too old-fashioned for Count Hamnet to understand. A moment later, Hamnet blinked. Were the bird's eyes suddenly bright and shiny and full of life? So it seemed.

And the dead, dried plover's head cried out, too—a shrill piping, such as the live bird might have used when frightened. "Well, well." Audun Gilli's voice rose in surprise. "We *do* have ourselves a flea, you might say."

"Where?" Hamnet Thyssen asked.

"That will take another charm," the wizard replied. He might have asked the plover's head a question. And it seemed to answer him, and to twist in his hand to point the way. It pointed straight toward the horse Gudrid was riding. "Well, well," Audun Gilli said again. "This could be, ah, awkward."

"Yes." Hamnet Thyssen was even less eager to break the news to his former wife than Audun seemed to be. Liv couldn't do it; she and Gudrid had no language in common. Hamnet looked at Ulric Skakki. "Would you be so kind as to . . . ?"

"I'll remember you in my nightmares," Ulric said with a grimace. But he rode over to Gudrid. She accepted his arrival as no less than her due. The way she looked at the world, everything revolved around her and paid her tribute.

Ulric spoke. Hamnet Thyssen couldn't make out exactly what he said; despite morbid curiosity, the Raumsdalian noble didn't go close enough to eavesdrop. Count Hamnet did note the exact instant when Ulric shifted from pleasantries and small talk to the reason he'd gone over to Gudrid. She stiffened in the saddle, then started to laugh. "But that's ridiculous!" she said—Hamnet had no trouble hearing her.

Shaking his head, Ulric Skakki went on talking quietly, doing his best to explain why it wasn't ridiculous. His best wasn't going to be good enough. Hamnet knew his former wife well enough to be sure of that.

And he was right. Gudrid shook her head, too. "I don't know where you get your ideas," she said, "but you can go and put them back there again, because you don't have the faintest notion what you're talking about." She made as if to ride away from Ulric Skakki.

He was not so easily detached. Unlike Gudrid, he still didn't make a lot of noise. But he did point in Eyvind Torfinn's direction. Earl Eyvind was chatting with Jesper Fletti, and not paying any particular attention to Gudrid at the moment. Hamnet Thyssen had a pretty good notion of what Ulric was saying. *Don't be difficult, or I'll tell your husband what you were doing last night.* If that wasn't it, Count Hamnet would have been astonished.

Gudrid was astonished, but not in any pleasant way. "You wouldn't dare," she said shrilly. That was the wrong answer to give Ulric Skakki. He twitched the reins and guided his horse away from hers, toward Eyvind Torfinn's. "Wait!" Gudrid screeched.

Courteously, Ulric did wait. The look Gudrid sent him was anything but courteous. Ulric was either made of stern stuff or a fine actor—maybe both—because he seemed undamaged.

"Do what you want to do," Gudrid snapped, and she might have added, *And demons take you afterwards.*

Again, Ulric affected not to notice. He bowed in the saddle and said something else too low for Hamnet to catch. Then he turned and called, "Liv, sweetheart, would you do the honors here?" He used Raumsdalian, even though Liv didn't speak it. But she had no trouble with his come-hither gesture. And Gudrid, of course, understood both the gesture and the words. She had plenty of reasons for disliking Liv, chief among them that the Bizogot shaman was the only other woman in the party. And now Liv was going to do something sorcerous around her, and she couldn't stop it? She had to hate that.

Hamnet Thyssen almost sent Ulric a formal salute. The adventurer had found a very smooth way to avenge himself.

Liv smiled at Gudrid, and kept the smile although Gudrid didn't return it. Even without a language in common, Liv was bound to know some of what Gudrid felt. What did she feel herself? Hamnet had never had the nerve to ask her.

For the moment, the Bizogot woman seemed all business. She murmured to herself and made several swift passes at Gudrid and the horse. "Ah!" she said brightly. "There it is." Hamnet and Ulric understood her. Gudrid didn't. Liv pointed at Gudrid's tunic. She gestured. "Take it off."

"What?" Gudrid didn't speak the Bizogot language, but that wasn't all that kept her from understanding. Ulric Skakki translated for her. "What?" she said again. "Take off my clothes for this chit of a girl? No!"

If you didn't take off your clothes for the Ruler, we wouldn't have this worry now, Hamnet thought. He almost said it out loud. To his surprise, he didn't. He liked Eyvind Torfinn better than he'd ever imagined he could, and didn't care to shame the older man.

Liv had no trouble figuring out what *No!* meant, even if she knew hardly any Raumsdalian. She didn't argue with Gudrid. She just dragged her off her horse. Gudrid let out a startled squawk. Both women thumped down on the dirt. Gudrid tried to fight back, but she'd never really learned how. Liv knew exactly what she was doing. Gudrid screamed and swore, which helped her not a bit. The Bizogot shaman quickly and efficiently stripped the tunic off her—and if she gave her a black eye and a split lip while she did it, wasn't she entitled to a little fun?

Gudrid was bare beneath the thick wool tunic. Hamnet Thyssen set his jaw and looked away. He knew what Gudrid's breasts were like—knew them by sight, knew them by touch, knew them by taste. He also knew he would never touch or taste them again. And he had no interest in seeing them again under such circumstances—or maybe he couldn't stand to look.

Liv seemed to care about as much for Gudrid's charms as she would have for those of a musk ox. She murmured a spell over the tunic. Suddenly, she stiffened. "Here it is!" she said. "Just a little fetish, but it will do."

"What on earth is going on?" Eyvind Torfinn said.

Ulric Skakki and Audun Gilli did the explaining. Despite his regard for Earl Eyvind, Hamnet didn't have the heart—or the stomach—for the job. He also wanted to involve himself with Gudrid as little as he could. She screeched at her husband, but warily. She didn't want him to know what she'd been doing the night before. No one else seemed eager to tell him, but that didn't mean no one would.

Eyvind Torfinn plucked at his beard. "This would have been easier if you'd given the shaman your tunic without kicking up such a fuss, my dear," he said at last.

"But she was rude! She was horrid!" Gudrid said.

Liv, meanwhile, had detached the fetish and was eyeing it with what looked like professional admiration. "An ermine's eye and a young hare's ear," she said. "The spell that animates them is not one I would use, but I am sure it will do the job. Samoth has no trouble spying on us as long as we carry this, no trouble at all. He will know just where we are."

"Are there any more charms on the tunic?" Eyvind Torfinn said in the Bizogot tongue. "If there are none, will you please give it back to my wife and let her dress?"

"Oh, very well." Liv, plainly, didn't think Gudrid deserved to wear the tunic. She all but threw it at the Raumsdalian woman. Gudrid pulled it on. The look she gave Liv would have melted lead.

"You may want to be careful," Hamnet Thyssen said in the Bizogot tongue. "You have embarrassed her. She will look for revenge."

"She is welcome to look," Liv said indifferently. "People look for all kinds of things. Whether they find them . . . That is another story."

Audun Gilli came up and examined the fetish. Slowly, he nodded. "Oh, yes. Not one I recognize in detail, but the principle is plain." He scratched his head. As often happened, what started as a thoughtful gesture turned into a hunt. After crushing something between his nails, he went on, "We should not destroy this."

"He is right," Liv said after Hamnet translated. "That Samoth would surely sense it if we did."

Audun Gilli began to whistle. The tune was strange and discordant—hardly a tune at all, Hamnet Thyssen thought till a short-eared arctic fox walked up to Audun. The wizard patted the animal as if it were a dog. It let him touch it; it even wagged its tail. Then he took a rawhide lashing and tied the fetish around the fox's neck. That done, he whistled a different tune. The fox suddenly seemed to realize where it was and the company it was keeping. With a horrified yip, it dashed away.

"Not bad," Liv said. "Not bad at all. The shaman of the Rulers will realize something is wrong when he tries to listen with the hare's ear, but that may take a while. We spoke mostly Raumsdalian here, and he does not know that tongue."

After translating again, Hamnet Thyssen said, "Their wizard does not admit to knowing our tongue, anyhow. Does Roypar speak Raumsdalian, Gudrid?"

"No," she answered automatically. Then she backtracked. "I mean, how the demon do I know whether he does or not?"

"You have a better chance of knowing than any of the rest of us," Count Hamnet said in a voice with no expression at all to it. The glare Gudrid sent him made the ones she'd given Liv seem downright loving by comparison.

Eyvind Torfinn looked as if he wanted to ask questions. If he had, Hamnet wouldn't have lied to him, though he knew the older man might not be-

lieve everything—or anything—he said. His home truths would have made
Gudrid even happier than she was already. But Earl Eyvind seemed to think
better of it. Maybe he would question Gudrid in private. Maybe, as he
looked to have done before, he would decide he didn't really want to know.
Whatever his reasons, he stayed quiet.

The travelers resumed their journey toward the Gap. Samoth could not
spy on them any more. Hamnet Thyssen hoped he couldn't, anyhow.

SUMMER UP IN the Bizogot country was a brief and fragile flower, one
that bloomed late and withered early. Even in and around Nidaros, the
Breath of God could blight crops in almost any month of the year. Knowing
all that, Hamnet was still shocked by how fast the weather turned—and
turned on the travelers—here beyond the Glacier.

Birds streaming south were the first warning. Only a few days after they
fled, the earliest snow flurries dappled the plain. The sun came out again
and melted the snow, but more fell a couple of days after that. The sun came
out once more. This time, though, the snow stuck longer. Hamnet Thyssen
could see his breath even at noon. Something in the sky had changed.
Leaden was too strong a word, but he could tell at a glance it would not be
warm again for a long time.

Trasamund took snow in stride. But even he kept looking north. "We
want to get as far as we can before the first blizzard catches us," he said.

"Blizzards!" Gudrid made it into a curse—blizzards did curse this
northern country. "Why did I ever decide to come here?"

To drive me mad, Hamnet Thyssen thought. That was not mere sarcasm;
he was all too sure he had the right of it. But she'd finally had more discom-
fort and danger than even tormenting him was worth. She should have
thought of that sooner. They were still on the far side of the Gap. She might
need to go through quite a bit more before they got back to the Bizogot
country, let alone anything resembling civilization.

The travelers had to stop to let a herd of buffalo pass in front of them. As
Trasamund had said back in Sigvat's chambers, these were bigger beasts
than the ones that roamed the prairies of the Raumsdalian Empire. They
were a lighter brown than their—cousins?—on the other side of the Glacier. And their horns, at least three times as long as those of the animals
Hamnet Thyssen knew, swept out and forward instead of curling up.

"We don't want to spook them," Ulric Skakki said. His foxy features
twisted in distaste. "That could be . . . unpleasant."

"They'd squash us flatter than a herd of mammoths could," Trasamund said. "There are a lot more of them."

Packs of wolves trotted along with the buffalo, prowling after stragglers. Again as Trasamund had said, the wolves on this side of the Glacier were smaller than dire wolves. But they seemed quicker and more agile, like woods wolves back home. Hamnet Thyssen also saw a . . . a tiger, the Rulers had called it. It might be able to pull down a buffalo all by itself. But it moved aside when the wolves came too close. It could kill several of them, without a doubt. Just as certainly, it was no match for a pack.

An hour and a half went by before the last stragglers from the buffalo herd ambled past. "Well," Eyvind Torfinn remarked, "we have all the dung we need—or we would if it were dry."

Trasamund didn't see the joke. "Plenty more that's been on the ground for a while." When it came to survival, he was altogether singleminded.

And he was right. The travelers had no trouble finding fuel for the evening's fire. As usual, they set out sentries all around. Maybe Roypar's wasn't the only band of Rulers in this part of the plain. Maybe other kinds of men lived around here, too. Strangers couldn't be sure. Better to take no chances.

One of the guardsmen who'd come north with Jesper Fletti and Gudrid shook Hamnet Thyssen awake in the middle of the night. "Sorry, your Grace," the man murmured, "but I'm glad to get some sleep myself."

"It's all right," Hamnet said around a yawn. "Well, it's not all right, but it's necessary." He yawned again, and climbed to his feet to make sure he didn't go back to sleep. He went out and took a position a bowshot away from the fire. It was cool out there, but not really cold; they seemed to be between storms.

But another one was coming. The gibbous moon wore a halo. That meant rain or snow down on the other side of the Glacier; he had no reason to think things worked differently here. And the air smelled and tasted damp. Tomorrow afternoon, maybe tomorrow night . . . That was his guess.

Off in the distance, a wolf howled, and then another and another and another, till it sounded as if a chorus of demons were howling at the haloed moon. These wolves had voices higher and shriller than those of the dire wolves he was used to, which to his ear only made them all the more unearthly. *I suppose they're wolves,* he thought uneasily. With only his ears to guide him, he couldn't prove they weren't demons. But he'd seen wolves trailing the long-horned buffalo, and he hadn't seen any demons—or he couldn't prove he had, anyhow.

The chorus of yowls and yips and howls quieted, then picked up again, even louder and wilder than before. It went on and on. Hamnet Thyssen looked back toward his comrades. How anyone could sleep through that hellish racket was beyond him, but they seemed to have no trouble.

Once he thought he heard an owl through the wolves' din. That really alarmed him, where the wolves only annoyed him. The wolves might possibly be demons, but even if they were he had no reason to think they were more interested in the travelers from the far side of the Glacier than in, say, the Rulers. A seeming owl, though, might be Samoth the wizard in owl's plumage flying out after the travelers on discovering his fetish had failed.

Hamnet Thyssen peered into the night, looking now this way, now that. Try as he would, he couldn't spot the owl, if owl it was. He muttered to himself, wondering what that meant. Was it just an owl that called once and then fell silent? Or was it Samoth mocking him, mocking all the travelers, and trying to spook him?

If it was the wizard, he was doing a good job. Hamnet chuckled mirthlessly. Even if it wasn't the wizard, he was still doing a good job.

Because Count Hamnet was searching for the owl that might or might not have been there, he didn't notice soft footsteps behind him till they drew very close. Then he whirled, hand flashing to the hilt of his sword. "Who the—?" he blurted, and then went on, "Oh, it's you." He felt foolish.

"Yes, it's me," Liv said quietly. "I'm sorry. I didn't mean to startle you."

"It's all right," Hamnet said. "You *shouldn't* have startled me. I should have heard you coming sooner." Now he was angry at himself, not at the Bizogot shaman.

"The wolves woke me." She pointed back toward the fire, which had died back to embers. "The others are snoring away. I don't know how they do it."

"I was thinking the same thing not long ago," Count Hamnet said. "Did you hear the owl, too?"

Liv nodded. "I hope it was only an owl." Hamnet almost told her that thought matched his, too, but judged her too likely to know it already. She went on, "I think it was. But even if it wasn't, we've made Samoth work harder than he expected to. Showing him we're not to be despised can't hurt."

"I hadn't looked at it that way," Hamnet said. "Of course, he'll despise us anyway. We aren't of the Rulers, so how can he help it?"

"They make much of themselves, sure enough." Liv's voice was troubled. "I hope they don't have good reason for their bragging and boasting and preening."

"From what I've seen, people who brag a lot are usually trying to convince themselves even more than other people," Hamnet said.

"Yes, that's so. It's one of the things shamans find out about people." Liv cocked her head to one side. "How did you come to see it?"

"By getting to be as old as I am and keeping my eyes open," Hamnet answered with a shrug. "I don't know what else to tell you."

"Plenty of people older than you who never notice such things," the Bizogot shaman said.

Hamnet Thyssen shrugged. "Plenty of people are fools." He laughed harshly. "I'm a fool, too, but not that particular way. You can be a fool all kinds of different ways."

"How are you a fool?" Liv's voice was serious; she really meant the question.

But Hamnet Thyssen only laughed some more, on an even more bitter note than before. "How do you think? She's asleep over there by the fire."

Liv glanced back toward the rest of the travelers. "How long since the two of you parted?"

"Sometimes it seems like a thousand years. Sometimes it seems as if it happened this afternoon," he said. "Sometimes it seems like both at once. It's worst then."

"She is . . ." Liv paused, looking for words. "If she were a Bizogot, she wouldn't last long. You Raumsdalians have more room for useless people than we do."

"Gudrid's not useless." Hamnet Thyssen's mouth twisted. "Ask Eyvind Torfinn if you think I'm wrong. Ask Trasamund. Ask Audun Gilli. Go back and ask Roypar. God! You can ask me, too." He remembered the last time he'd lain with her. He hadn't known it would be the last then. *I should have*, he thought. *She yawned when we finished, and she wasn't sleepy*. She'd slipped out of the castle the next day. He hadn't seen her since, only heard about her . . . till Sigvat II summoned him to Nidaros.

In the pale moonlight, Liv's face was unreadable. "You never found another woman after that, plainly," she said.

"I sleep with women now and again. You know I do," Hamnet said.

"That isn't what I meant," she said. "You never found one who mattered to you."

"No. I never did," Hamnet Thyssen agreed. "I can't say I've looked very hard, though. If things go wrong once, that's bad. If things go wrong more than once . . . If things go wrong more than once, why do you go on living?"

"Why do you think they would go wrong?" Liv asked.

"Why? Because they already did once. I have practice being stupid, you might say." Hamnet tried to make a sour joke of it. Even with that, he was surprised to be saying as much as he was.

"Not all women are like Gudrid," Liv said.

"No doubt you're right," he answered. "But how do I tell beforehand? I didn't think Gudrid was like Gudrid, either, you know."

"Do you think I am like her?" Liv asked quietly.

He laughed once more, this time in sheer surprise. "No," he answered. "I can think of a lot of things I might say about you, but that isn't one of them."

"Well, then," she said.

Well, then—what? But he needed only a heartbeat to realize he was being thick. He put an arm around Liv. She sighed and pressed herself against him. "Are you sure?" he asked.

"How can anyone ever be sure?" she said. "The chance seems good, though. And if you don't bet, how do you expect to win?"

Hamnet Thyssen didn't look at things that way. To him, not betting meant you couldn't lose. He hadn't even thought of winning. He still didn't, not really. He wondered how badly he would get hurt, some time later on. But later didn't seem to matter, not right this minute. He bent his head to Liv—not very far, because she was a tall woman.

Nothing either one of them did after that was surprising—only the things men and women have done as long as there have been men and women. They surprised each other a few times, because neither of them knew the other that way. Those weren't bad surprises; they were both trying to see what pleased the other.

"Easy, there," Hamnet whispered after Liv dropped to her knees. "Not too much of that, or . . ."

She paused. "I wouldn't mind."

"I would," he said, and laid her down on the clothes they'd shed. She inhaled sharply when he went into her, and wrapped her arms and legs around him. He thought he would spend himself almost at once, especially after what she'd been doing, but instead he went on and on, almost as if he were outside himself. Liv's breath came short; her back arched. He covered her mouth with his when she started to cry out—that might have brought the other travelers on the run. Her joy came, and then, a moment later, his.

She kissed him on the end of the nose. Then she said, "You're squashing me," sounding, well, squashed.

"Sorry." He took his weight on his elbows and then leaned back onto his knees. All at once, he noticed it was chilly. It must have been chilly all along, but he'd had other things on his mind. "We'd better get dressed," he said.

"Yes, I suppose so." Liv seemed sorry, which made him feel about ten feet tall. Then she remarked, "That woman was the fool," which made him wonder why he didn't float off the ground and drift away on the breeze.

He glanced back toward the fire. No one was stirring around it. Either the other travelers hadn't noticed what was going on or they were too polite to let on that they had. Which didn't matter to Hamnet Thyssen. Hardly anything mattered to him right then.

"There. You see?" Liv effortlessly picked up the conversation. "It just . . . makes things better for a while."

"For a while," Hamnet admitted.

Liv laughed. "That's all it does," she said. "I'm not trying to steal your soul or anything like that."

"No, eh?" Hamnet Thyssen wanted to laugh, too, and happily, which didn't happen every day—or every month, either. "You may have anyhow." He meant it for a joke. It didn't come out like one.

She shook her head. "That wouldn't be good. I have enough trouble taking care of myself. I don't want to take care of anyone else."

"You'd better be careful," he said.

"Why?"

"If you aren't, we'll end up getting along. Who knows how much trouble that might cause?"

"Oh." Liv smiled. She squeezed his hand. "I'll take the chance. And now I think I'd better go back by the fire, before anyone else wakes up and notices I'm gone."

"Good idea, but I think people will notice anyway before long," Hamnet said.

"Do you? Why should they?"

"Because I'm going to be wandering around with a foolish grin on my face, and I've never done that before," he answered.

"I don't care who knows," Liv said. "I wouldn't have done it if I did. Do you?"

"When Gudrid finds out, she'll try to find some way to spoil things." For a moment, Count Hamnet sounded as mournful as he usually did.

"What can she do?" Liv sniffed scornfully.

Hamnet Thyssen only shrugged. Liv sniffed again, and stood on tiptoe to kiss him, and walked back toward the fire. He didn't want to let her go, but the moon and the slow-wheeling stars said he had to stay on watch a while longer.

Before he went back, clouds rolled out of the northwest and hid the moon and stars. After that, he was on his own guessing the hour. The storm he'd seen coming in the halo around the moon was here before he'd expected it.

He went back when he thought it was midnight and cautiously shook Ulric Skakki awake. Being cautious when waking Ulric was a good idea; the adventurer had a habit of rousing in a hurry, and with a weapon in his hand—sometimes with a weapon in each hand.

Here, he just grunted and groaned and yawned, much as Hamnet Thyssen might have. "Is it that time already?" he asked around another yawn.

"Somewhere close, anyhow." Hamnet waved at the cloudy sky. "We're going to get the bad weather sooner than I thought."

"It has that look, doesn't it?" Yawning one more time, Ulric Skakki got to his feet. "Well, if it starts snowing too hard to let me see my way back here, I'll just scream my head off."

"You do that," Count Hamnet said. Ulric clapped him on the back and trudged away from the dimmed remains of the fire. They'd both been joking and not joking at the same time. Snowstorms like that weren't impossible up here, any more than they were in the Bizogot country or in the northern reaches of the Empire. Hamnet didn't think this storm would be one of those—the wind didn't have that sawtoothed edge to it—but you never could tell.

You never can tell, he told himself as he rolled himself in his mammoth-hide blanket. Of all the things he hadn't looked for, finding happiness—even if it proved only a few minutes of happiness—here beyond the Glacier stood high on the list.

Looked for or not, here it was, and he would have to figure out what to do about it. So would Gudrid, no matter what Liv thought. She hadn't left him to make him happy. She'd left for her own sake. "Well, too bad," he mumbled, and fell asleep.

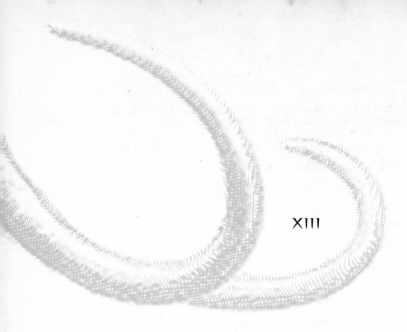

XIII

I T WAS SNOWING when he woke up the next morning. Fat white flakes
danced in the air. Nothing else in all the world moved like snow on the
breeze. If he hadn't seen too much of it, he might have marveled more. *I'm
old and jaded,* he thought. His joints creaked as he climbed to his feet and
stretched.

But he didn't feel old and jaded when he looked over toward Liv. She was
already awake, and talking to Trasamund. She broke off to nod and smile
and wave to Hamnet. He smiled back. He no doubt grinned like a fool, as
he'd thought he might. He didn't care.

When had he last made love with a woman who mattered to him as a
person, who wasn't just a willing body when his urges got too strong to ignore? The last time he made love with Gudrid—that was when. He'd had
nothing but relief since. He'd nearly—more than nearly—given up hope of
ever having anything more than relief.

Almost of themselves, his eyes went to Gudrid, who was toasting meat
over the fire. Someone must have built it up again while he slept. Gudrid
was watching him, too. Her gaze swung from him to Liv and back again.
She laughed a light, mocking laugh and held her nose for a moment.

Ever since Gudrid left him, she'd been able to make his blood boil without even trying. Every woman he'd lain down with since, he compared to
her. Every one of them he'd found wanting in some way or other. Now . . .
Now he smiled at Gudrid, too, and waved to her, and blew her a kiss. He
didn't care what she thought, and, in not caring, he felt as if a curse were
lifted from his back. He and Liv would do what they did, go where they

went—if they went anywhere—and that would be that. And if Gudrid didn't like it . . . well, so what?

Up till this moment, he'd never been able to think *so what?* about Gudrid, not since she first went to bed with another man. He shook his head—that wasn't right. Not since he found out she'd gone to bed with another man. If Liv let him finally not care about what Gudrid had done, what she was doing, which gift could be more precious?

He didn't even turn his back on his former wife. He didn't have to. All he had to do was not take her seriously. He'd needed too long—much too long—to realize that. And Gudrid must have seen the knowledge on his face. She'd always been able to read him like a codex. That, unfortunately, wouldn't go away as if it were a lifted curse.

Her eyes narrowed. So did her lips. Hamnet Thyssen sighed, and fog burst from his mouth and from his nostrils. Gudrid could put up with anything but being ignored.

Ulric Skakki came up and greeted Hamnet with a yawn. "I hope your watch was more exciting than mine," he said, and yawned again.

Well, yes, Hamnet thought, but that wasn't what he said. "You don't want a watch to be exciting," he remarked. Most of the time, that was true. But there was excitement, and then there was excitement.

"You don't want to think you'll fall asleep every bloody minute, either," Ulric said. "I hope I can doze on horseback today." Yet another yawn split his foxy face.

"Let's get going," Trasamund said. "The sooner we're back on our own side of the Glacier, the better."

"If our wizards were worth anything, they could talk with people there while we're still here," Gudrid said. "I suppose that's too much to ask, though." She sneered at Audun Gilli, and twice as hard at Liv. The Bizogot shaman couldn't understand what she said, but didn't like the way she said it. Liv glared back at her. That, of course, was just what Gudrid wanted.

"Come, my sweet—be reasonable," Eyvind Torfinn said. If that wasn't a forlorn hope, Hamnet Thyssen had never heard one. Eyvind went on, "No wizard can keep in touch with colleagues over such a distance."

"I'll bet the Rulers can do it," Gudrid said.

"If they can, they're even more dangerous than I think they are." That wasn't Eyvind Torfinn or Count Hamnet or Ulric Skakki. It wasn't Audun Gilli or Trasamund, either. It was Jesper Fletti, and the guard chief hardly ever let loose an opinion, let alone one that went against the woman he was charged to guard. The look Gudrid sent him was nearly as poisonous as the one she'd aimed at Liv.

"Jesper's right," Eyvind Torfinn said, which failed to make him the apple of his spouse's eye. "These new barbarians seem to be pretty good at war—at least, I never imagined anyone could ride a mammoth."

"Neither did I," Trasamund said. "This is something I must try when I get back to my clan grounds and finish healing. To ride a mammoth . . . That would be better than anything." Now he was the one Gudrid's gaze scorched. Since he'd ridden her, Hamnet understood why she might be miffed.

She went right on fuming as they started south and east. She hadn't managed to make the rest of the travelers resent Audun or Liv—particularly Liv, if Hamnet was any judge at all.

The snow went right on falling. Hamnet wondered if it would stop any time before spring. That wasn't his worry, though. All they had to do was get back on their own side of the Glacier ahead of the Rulers, and he thought they could. The mammoth-riders did not seem to have neared the Gap in any large numbers. Roypar and Samoth and the rest would probably have to go back to their main camp or heartland, wherever that was, and persuade their superiors that they'd found something interesting and important. That wouldn't happen in a day or a week or, chances were, a month, either. The Bizogots and the Empire would have some time to get ready.

And how will we use it? Hamnet wondered. Would the Bizogot clans join together under a jarl of all jarls? Would the Bizogots let Raumsdalian soldiers come up onto the chilly plain? Would Sigvat II see a threat from the land beyond the Glacier? Not long before, people had doubted there was any such thing as land beyond the Glacier. Hamnet Thyssen had doubted it himself. Now he had a new doubt—that the Bizogots and Raumsdalians would do anything about the Rulers till urgent danger forced them to.

When he said as much to Ulric Skakki, Ulric only shrugged. "The sun will come up tomorrow, too," he remarked.

"Curse it, I'm not joking," Count Hamnet said.

"Neither am I," Ulric replied. "No one gets excited about a danger he hasn't seen himself."

He was probably right. No, he was certainly right. Hamnet Thyssen knew human nature too well to think anything else. He wished he could have another view of things—it would have given him more hope for the Empire's safety.

A herd of deer like the ones the Rulers rode made the travelers hold up. It wasn't as large as the herd of buffalo had been not long before, but Hamnet still started fidgeting before it passed them by. Nor was he the only one. "Are the Rulers trying to slow us down?" Audun Gilli murmured.

"What does he say?" Liv asked Count Hamnet. They'd ridden close together since leaving camp. Gudrid sneered and tossed her head. Hamnet pretended to ignore her. He taught Liv bits of Raumsdalian, as she'd asked him to do. Most of the time, though, he simply enjoyed her company. He wasn't used to doing anything like that. Now he translated for her. She thought it over, then shook her head. "I don't believe it. We've already been through the reasons why the Rulers couldn't reach the Gap ahead of us, no matter how much they might want to. And this is the time of year when animals are on the move, looking for better pasture."

Now Audun asked, "What does she say?"

Again, Hamnet did the honors, adding, "I think she's probably right."

"Well, of course you do." That wasn't Audun; it was Gudrid. "But what would you think if you used your head and not your crotch?"

"You would know more about that than I do," Hamnet said.

Audun Gilli ignored the sniping. Hamnet Thyssen abstractly admired him for that; it took concentration—or possibly blindness. "Yes, I suppose she is likely to be right," the wizard said. Hamnet translated that into the Bizogot language for Liv, who smiled.

On came the deer, emerging from the snow like materializing ghosts and then vanishing into it as if expelled from the everyday world once more. They knew where they were going, whether the travelers did or not. So Hamnet thought for a little while, anyhow. But then he shook his head. It might not be true at all. Chances were that one deer at the front knew, and the others simply followed. Or maybe—and here was a frightening thought—the deer at the front had no idea where he was going, but the others followed anyhow. Were deer that much like people? Hamnet Thyssen wouldn't have been surprised.

At last, they were gone. But for their tracks and dung, but for the receding footfalls that the snow and wind soon muffled, they might not have been there at all. "Come on," Trasamund said. "Let's get moving. We'll go till it gets dark." It definitely did get dark now, even on days when skies were clear. Days shrank and nights stretched and grew. Before long, the sun would become no more than a midday intruder peeking up over the southern horizon and then disappearing again.

The travelers hadn't ridden long before Gudrid held up her hand and said, "I think we're going in the wrong direction. Shouldn't we be heading that way?" She pointed toward what Count Hamnet thought was the northeast.

"No, that's not right, I fear," Trasamund said.

"I believe the Bizogot is correct, my sweet," Eyvind Torfinn added.

Gudrid wasn't convinced—or wasn't about to let herself be convinced. She pointed again. "I'm sure the Gap lies there."

"We're going the way I think is proper, by God, and we'll keep on doing it." Now Trasamund had a harder time staying polite. That he'd bothered even once said Gudrid had a hold on his affections. *Affections—that's one word for it,* Hamnet Thyssen thought with a wry grin. The Bizogot jarl went on, "Besides, I've been here before, and nobody else has. If I don't know the way, who does?"

Ulric Skakki stirred, but didn't say anything. He did smile at Hamnet, who nodded back. *We know something you don't know,* went through Hamnet's head—one of the simple pleasures any man could enjoy.

But Gudrid wasn't mollified. Maybe she really thought they were going in the wrong direction, or maybe she just wanted to be the center of attention. "You're going to get us lost," she said shrilly. "Lost in the middle of all this—this *nothing*!" Her wave took in the whole world on this side of the Glacier.

"Really, my dear, Trasamund knows more about these things than you do," Eyvind Torfinn said in tones no doubt meant to be soothing.

"You're against me, too!" Gudrid burst into tears.

"What is her trouble? She sounds like she needs a kick in the arse," said Liv, who had a straightforward view of the world even for a Bizogot.

"She thinks we're going in the wrong direction," Hamnet Thyssen said. He didn't think that was Gudrid's only trouble, but it was the only one he felt like talking about.

Liv rolled her eyes up to the heavens. "She couldn't find her way back to the Gap by herself if someone soaked the path in mammoth fat and set fire to it. She's making noise for the sake of making noise."

Hamnet thought she was doing that, too. He shrugged. "If Eyvind Torfinn wants to calm her down, he's welcome to try." *And good luck to him, too,* he added, but only to himself.

Earl Eyvind did his well-meaning but ineffectual best. "Really, my love, I have every confidence in Trasamund's sense of direction. He is right—he

knows this terrain better than you do. And he is more familiar with traveling over roadless country in the snow."

"Oh, you're a fine one to talk about a sense of direction," Gudrid said in
a deadly voice. "You can't even find *up*." Her sneer and the way she gestured
left no one wondering what she meant—not even Liv, who spoke no
Raumsdalian.

Hamnet didn't know what he would have done after an insult like that.
Eyvind Torfinn swung his horse away from Gudrid's. "When you can be civilized, perhaps we'll talk some more," he said. "Perhaps." The repetition
told how wounded he was.

Gudrid, just then, cared for no one's wounds but her own. "I still say it's
wrong!" she cried. "We'll be lost!"

"Enough!" Trasamund thundered. "If you were my wife, it would have
been *enough* a while ago, let me tell you."

"When did you ever get enough?" Gudrid jeered. Trasamund turned the
color of hot iron. Hamnet was amazed the snowflakes striking him didn't
steam. "If your sense of direction was as bad there as it is here—"

"Why don't you go your own way, if you're so set on it?" Ulric Skakki
asked Gudrid before anything worse could happen. "The rest of us can go
with Trasamund, and we'll see who gets to the other side of the Glacier
first." He smiled as if he meant the suggestion seriously.

The look Gudrid sent him should have sunk him deep underground
even though the world up here was frozen solid not far below the surface.
Of the travelers, he was, or at least affected to be, most nearly immune to
her. "You hate me!" she shouted. "Everyone hates me!" She burst into
tears.

Eyvind forgot her gibe and did his best to soothe her. His best wasn't
nearly good enough. Hamnet smiled at Liv. She smiled back, a certain
knowing look in her eye. She might guess he was thinking she wouldn't
throw a tantrum like that. And if she did, she was right.

Audun Gilli, meanwhile, fiddled with his ensorceled needle floating in a
bowl of water. Chanting his spell and watching the way the lodestone
swung, he nodded to himself. "The magic confirms it," he said. "The Gap is
that way." He pointed the way they were riding, the way Gudrid questioned.

She rewarded him with a sneer a mustachioed stage villain in a melo-
drama would have been proud to claim for his own. "Oh, yes—a lot *you*
know about it," she said. "The last time you tried that spell, you almost ran
us straight into the Glacier, if I remember right."

"You do," Audun said steadily. "I've learned where I made my mistake. Can you say the same?"

Now she gaped at him in astonishment mixed with fury. She couldn't have thought he had enough spirit to talk back to her. Since Hamnet Thyssen hadn't thought so, either, he couldn't blame her . . . for that.

"Enough of this blather," Trasamund declared. "I am riding on toward the Gap. Anyone else is welcome to come along. Anyone who thinks I'm heading in the wrong direction is welcome to go where she pleases, as friend Ulric said." That *she* made Gudrid scowl all over again. The Bizogot jarl plainly thought no one else thought him misguided.

And he was right. Everyone rode along with him—even Gudrid, though she bit her lip in anger and humiliation. Hamnet wondered what she would do next to show how important she was—and how much trouble it would cause.

THE SNOWSTORM DIDN'T seem to want to end. Even this early in the season, it claimed the land beyond the Glacier for its own. Hamnet Thyssen didn't mind. He was used to snow himself, though neither Liv nor Trasamund would have been much impressed with his claims.

That wasn't the only reason he didn't mind so much. He was sleeping warmer of nights than he'd ever imagined he would be. There was little room for privacy in the encampments the travelers set up. Liv didn't mind; there was little room for privacy in a Bizogot camp, either.

He woke up mornings with a smile on his face. He wasn't used to that. It made muscles that hadn't been used much for a long time ache from the unaccustomed exercise.

Ulric Skakki teased him about it, saying, "What have you got that I don't?"

"A lady friend?" Count Hamnet suggested; the idea bemused him, too.

"Well, yes. I know *that*." Mock indignation filled Ulric's voice—Hamnet hoped it was mock indignation, anyhow. "But why have you got her?"

"For the beauty of my plumage and the sweetness of my song?" Hamnet suggested.

Ulric looked at him, then slowly shook his head. "You haven't just gone around the bend," he said. "You've gone right past it, you have." He steered his horse away from Hamnet as if afraid whatever the noble had was catching.

Hamnet doubted that. In his experience, happiness wasn't contagious.

He certainly hadn't caught much of it himself. Now that he had a little, he kept taking it out and picking it up and looking at it from all angles, as if it were some strange animal that lived on this side of the Glacier but not on the one with which he was more familiar.

Doing that, he discovered something he would perhaps rather not have known—the thing he was examining proved not to be quite perfect after all. It wasn't that he didn't enjoy making love with Liv. A man would have to be dead not to enjoy that. But what they did had something missing compared to what he'd done with Gudrid.

Something . . . He worked at that as a man might work at a piece of meat stuck tight between two teeth. Trying to find it almost drove him mad, as the meat would have when it didn't move. Whatever it was, it wasn't the pleasure of the act itself. Liv was at least as good a lover in those terms as Gudrid.

Something . . . Listening to Gudrid bicker with Eyvind Torfinn over roasted deer ribs one evening all at once made Hamnet stare and stare. Gudrid noticed; she usually did. "What's your problem?" she snapped. She could go from scolding her new husband to scolding the one she'd discarded without missing a beat.

"It's nothing, really. I'm sorry," Hamnet Thyssen answered, and looked away. That made Gudrid blink; he shot back more often than not. But, with a shrug that was almost a wriggle, she returned to making life difficult for Earl Eyvind. They weren't really squabbling *about* anything. They were just going back and forth, the way Gudrid did with any man with whom she was involved.

Hamnet Thyssen, meanwhile, still stared, but not at Gudrid anymore. He looked into the fire, marveling at his own blindness. *So that's it,* he thought.

When he'd made love with Gudrid, especially toward the end when the two of them were falling apart, he'd always had to win a fight before she gave in. It wasn't physical; sometimes it wasn't even verbal. But it was always there between them—the idea that he had to overcome her before she yielded herself to him. He'd got used to it, to the point where it became part of what he thought of as lovemaking.

With Liv, it wasn't there. It didn't need to be there. As far as he could tell, she really wanted him. She didn't have to be persuaded or coerced or whatever the right word was. She just . . . wanted him. And if the missing frisson of winning the fight stayed missing . . .

"Well, goodbye to it," Hamnet muttered. If that was what his trouble was, he didn't need it, not one bit.

LIKE MOUNTAIN RANGES farther south, the Glacier didn't waste much time shouldering its way up over the horizon. As soon as the snowstorm blew through and clear weather returned, there it was. The sweep to the south that marked the Gap lay almost exactly in the direction where Trasamund and Audun Gilli had said it would. Gudrid maintained a discreet silence.

A short-eared fox trotted along just out of bowshot of Hamnet Thyssen, then streaked off after a hare. Both beasts were losing their summer coats and going to winter white. Before long, only their noses and eyes would mark them against the drifted snow.

Every night seemed longer and darker than the one before. The Northern Lights began to dance, higher in the sky than Hamnet Thyssen had ever seen them. "I wonder what makes them," he murmured to Liv as they lay side by side under a mammoth skin.

"We say God warms His hands with them," Liv told him. He liked the poetry of the answer. He also liked the way Liv found to warm her hands a little later. If they were cold, they would have heated; that part of him, lately, had felt as if it were on fire. He hadn't realized a man his age could do so much. Of course, for several years he hadn't wanted to do much at all.

Birds went white for the winter, too. A snowy owl swooped down on a ptarmigan the next morning and carried it away. Count Hamnet hadn't noticed the ptarmigan, but the owl did.

Higher and higher rose the Glacier—and then it vanished as another snowstorm blew down on the travelers from behind. This one would have been a formidable blizzard in Nidaros, but the Bizogots took it in stride. That made the Raumsdalians try to do the same, lest Trasamund and Liv think them soft.

"Was it like this when you came up here before?" Hamnet asked Ulric Skakki. With the wind roaring and moaning, the only way to talk was to ride close together and bawl in each other's ears.

"No," Ulric answered. "It was worse."

"By God!" Hamnet said. "How?"

Ulric Skakki's hat came down over his forehead. A wool muffler covered his mouth and nose. Only his eyes were exposed to the weather. People said eyes by themselves didn't show much. They'd never seen his. "Believe me, your Grace, it had no trouble at all," he said. "The wind doesn't always blow toward the Glacier. Sometimes it comes down off it. Sometimes the wind blowing toward it runs smack into the wind coming down off it. If you think this is bad, imagine a tornado full of snow."

"I'd rather not," Hamnet Thyssen said. Down in the southern part of the Raumsdalian Empire, tornadoes could level a town or scatter a castle's stones across the countryside. Some of those stones had to weigh as much as a mammoth. The savage winds picked them up and flung them anyway.

No wonder weatherworkers have so much trouble, Hamnet thought. How could a mere man hope to control anything so strong?

Ulric Skakki's thoughts ran in a different direction. "When we get down to the right side of the Glacier," he said, "do you think anyone will believe us when we tell people what we've found?"

"The Bizogots will," Hamnet said. "They don't complicate things that don't need to be complicated."

"Or sometimes even things that do," Ulric said. "And the Bizogots move by clan, not as one folk. Even if they do believe, how much good will it do us? They'll spend more time quarreling among themselves than doing anything about the Rulers."

As far as Hamnet Thyssen was concerned, the Bizogots' disunity was a boon for the empire. If they ever found a jarl who could unite them all, they might prove deadly dangerous to Raumsdalia. They might also prove deadly dangerous if they decided to join the Rulers instead of fighting them.

"Will his Majesty pay attention to the word we bring?" Ulric Skakki persisted.

"He sent out this expedition. He let some of his guardsmen come along with it," Hamnet Thyssen said. And how *had* Gudrid managed that? Did she sleep with Sigvat to persuade him? Hamnet forced his mind back to the question at hand. "If the Emperor isn't convinced—"

"We're all in trouble," Ulric finished for him.

"Maybe. Maybe not, too," Hamnet said. "All we know about the Rulers is from their bragging and the little we saw."

"They don't just herd mammoths. They really tame them, the way we tame horses," Ulric said. "Samoth is a stronger wizard than Audun Gilli dreams of being."

"Well, yes." Hamnet Thyssen looked around to make sure Audun was out of earshot. "But how much does that say about the one, and how much does it say about the other?"

Ulric Skakki gave him a dirty look—and well he might have, when he'd dragged Audun Gilli from the gutter for the journey beyond the Glacier. "Audun will be fine when we really need him."

"I hope so. We all hope so," Count Hamnet said. "But the Rulers are a problem, and you're right—no one who hasn't seen them can understand how big a problem they could be."

"Well, that may take care of itself," Ulric said.

Hamnet frowned. "How do you mean?"

"By next year, chances are that everyone will have seen them, don't you think?" Ulric said. Hamnet only grunted, like a man who takes a fist in the pit of the stomach. Ulric Skakki seemed to think that a full answer. And so perhaps it was.

BEFORE LONG, HAMNET Thyssen wondered whether he and the other travelers would make it back to the Gap, let alone through the narrow opening that was the only way home. The two sides of the divided Glacier shaped a funnel with that opening as the sole outlet. All the bad weather beyond the Glacier seemed to pour into the funnel—and had no way out.

Snow piled up thick on the ground. This, sages said, was how the Glacier formed in the first place—snow that fell faster than it melted, that never melted from year to year, that hardened into the solid Glacier as the weight of more snow above it squeezed out the air. Finding or forcing a way through got harder by the day.

"Are we going to have to wait till the blizzards stop?" Hamnet asked Trasamund.

"I hope not," the Bizogot answered. Hamnet Thyssen had wanted more. Maybe his face said as much, for Trasamund went on, "This is new for me, too, you know. I'm used to weather that has more, ah, room to move around."

"Think on the bright side," Jesper Fletti said. "If we freeze to death or starve to death up here, chances are the Rulers will, too."

"Oh, joy." Hamnet Thyssen did not like Jesper, and so he took a certain sour pleasure in showing up the other man. "That isn't so, anyhow. The Rulers aren't likely to come through the Gap during winter. Chances are they'll travel when the weather is good—or as good as it gets up here."

Like the rest of the travelers, Jesper was bundled up so only his eyes and a bit of his forehead and the bridge of his nose were exposed to the air. By the way his rime-whitened eyebrows came down and pulled together at the center, Count Hamnet's dart hit home.

"One way or another, we'll manage." Trasamund didn't sound worried— but how a leader sounded and what he really thought could be two different things, as Hamnet knew full well. The Bizogot continued, "If we have to, we'll build shelters from snow blocks and wait it out. We've got plenty of deer flesh on the horses' backs."

"Have we got enough fodder to keep the beasts alive for long?" Hamnet asked, knowing the answer was no. By the way Trasamund grimaced, he knew the same thing. "Can we go forward on foot if the horses die?" Hamnet continued.

"We can, yes," Trasamund said. "It wouldn't be fast, and it would be dangerous. Hunting in thick snow's not easy, and you need to eat a lot, or the weather sucks the strength out of you like a vampire."

"You have a way with words, your Ferocity." By the way Jesper Fletti said it, that wasn't necessarily praise.

"We hope for the weather to get better, that's all." If bluff, hearty Trasamund could offer nothing more, he was worried, or worse than worried.

Hamnet Thyssen let his horse fall back alongside Ulric Skakki's. "You came back through the Gap in the wintertime," he said, making it sound almost like an accusation.

"Guilty," Ulric agreed, so he caught the tone despite the howling wind.

"How?" Hamnet asked.

"I waited for a spell of decent weather, and one came along before I got too hungry," Ulric answered. "Then I squirted through as fast as I could go. The weather on the other side was a lot milder, I will say."

"Well, I believe that." Hamnet Thyssen saw no way for the full fury of this storm to squeeze through that narrow opening. "What were things like where the two halves of the Glacier came closest together?"

Ulric considered. "Windy."

"Thank you so much. I never would have guessed." Hamnet laid on the sarcasm with a shovel. Ulric Skakki only chuckled. He probably grinned, too; the way his eyes narrowed suggested as much. But he too kept himself well covered up, so Hamnet couldn't be sure.

"You'll find out," Ulric said. "Either that or the good weather won't come soon enough—in which case, our meat will stay fresh till the animals find it next spring."

"You always did know how to cheer me up," Hamnet Thyssen said. Ulric laughed. For a moment, the wind howling down from the north let Hamnet hear his mirth. Then the frozen blast seized the laughter and flayed it on knives of ice and swept it away.

Hamnet wished he thought Ulric were joking. They could die up here. If they did, no one would know but the striped cats—the *tigers*—and the wolves and the little foxes . . . and possibly the Rulers, if they came this way when brief spring and summer set this land ablaze with flowers.

Asking a wizard to work against such weather was asking too much. Count Hamnet already understood that—understood it in his bones, which grew colder by the moment. He did wonder whether Audun Gilli or Liv could work *with* it, could craft some sort of preserving spell that would keep the travelers not quite frozen to death till the storm eased enough to let them travel some more.

Steering his horse over to Liv's was a pleasure of sorts. If he was going to die, he preferred dying in good company. When he asked her his question, she said, "It would be a charm like keeping meat fresh, wouldn't it?"

"Yes, it would," he answered, while his hope sank. He hadn't wanted to hear *would be*. That meant she had no spell ready to use. He wasn't really surprised, only disappointed. If she'd known of such a spell, chances were she already would have been poised to use it.

"Maybe it will turn out all right anyhow," Liv said.

"Maybe it . . . will." Hamnet Thyssen started to bellow his answer, as he'd been bellowing all along. Halfway through, he realized he didn't need to. The wind was dying. The snow was easing. Back in Raumsdalia, romance writers threw storms that conveniently stopped into about half their tales. People laughed at them, because most of the time storms weren't nearly so considerate.

Most of the time—but not always.

"Well, well," Eyvind Torfinn said, as he had a habit of doing. "Well, well." He said it—and Hamnet Thyssen heard him. One of the horses snorted and shook its head, sending snow flying. Count Hamnet heard that.

He looked around. He felt as dazed and drained as if he'd fought in a battle. The aftermath of a battle, though, was horror, with the cries of the wounded and the stenches of blood and ordure filling the air, with maimed and slaughtered men and beasts sprawled on the ground, with ravens and vultures and teratorns spiraling down out of the sky to glut themselves on flesh before it grew cold. The aftermath of the storm . . . was one of the most beautiful things Hamnet Thyssen had ever seen.

Everything was white.

As far as the eye could see—and it could see farther with each passing moment—everything was covered in snow. Even the travelers were mostly shrouded. Hamnet almost dreaded having the sun come out. Shining off so much whiteness, it would be bound to blind. The Bizogots sometimes wore bone goggles that let in only narrow slits of light to fight against snow-blindness. Hamnet wished for a pair of his own.

To either side, the Glacier loomed up. It was white, too, whiter than he'd ever seen it. The blizzard covered the dirt that clung to the sides of the ice, covered the plants that sometimes grew in crevices when the weather warmed. The way Hamnet's breath smoked reminded him it was anything but warm now.

Trasamund shook himself like a bear emerging from hibernation. The snow he dislodged made the comparison seem more apt. "Well, now I *know* where south is, by God," he said in a voice not far from a bear's growl. "Let's get to the Gap as soon as we can, and leave the worst of this behind us."

On they rode. Gudrid's back was uncommonly stiff. She wasn't used to getting mocked over and over again for making a mistake; that was something she was more in the habit of doing to other people. Trasamund didn't care. He'd taken what she gave him, and he gave back nothing. No, Gudrid wasn't used to that at all.

What would she do about it? What *could* she do about it? Nothing that Hamnet could think of, not now, not unless she never wanted to see Nidaros again. But if they got down into safer country . . . Hamnet wondered whether to tell Trasamund to watch his back.

In the end, he decided not to. The Bizogot jarl was a grown man, able to take care of himself. That he'd turned the tables on Gudrid proved as much. If he couldn't see that she might want revenge, he was a fool. To Count Hamnet's way of thinking, Trasamund *was* a fool, but not that kind of fool.

The sun came out and shone down brightly. Hamnet blinked and narrowed his eyes against the glare. But for the snow everywhere, the blizzard might never have happened. The air grew . . . warmer, anyhow. The travelers slogged on toward the Gap.

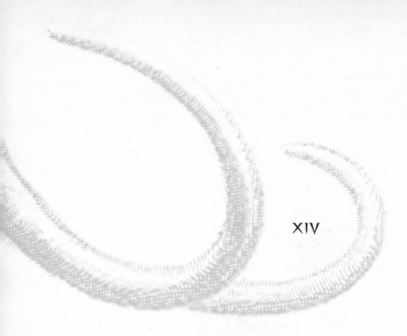

XIV

Hamnet Thyssen spread his arms wide. Liv laughed at him. "You can't span the Gap with your hands, my love," she said. "It's narrow, but not that narrow."

"I suppose not," Hamnet said. But the urge remained. With those cliffs, those mountains, of ice going up and up and up, the gap between them still seemed tiny—and, on the grand scale of things, it was. But a tiny gap was oh, so different from no gap at all. And then Hamnet stopped and gaped, really hearing in his mind everything Liv had said. "What did you call me?"

"I called you my love," she answered. "You are, aren't you?"

"By God!" The idea still startled him. But he had to nod. "I am, yes. And that would make you mine."

"Well, I should hope so." The shaman sent him a sidelong look. "Not much doubt about what we've been doing, is there?"

"Er—no," Hamnet Thyssen said, and she laughed at him. He didn't think it was so funny. He'd lavished all sorts of words of love on Gudrid.

Much good it did him.

Since his love for Gudrid foundered—no, since her love for him did, if she ever knew any—he hadn't wasted such words on any other woman. He would have sickened himself if he had. Now, with Liv, he could affirm he was her love and she his without wanting to bend down over the snow.

After the travelers got beyond the narrowest part of the Gap, after they returned to the regions Bizogots and Raumsdalians had known since time out of mind, they left the worst of the winter weather behind them, or almost behind them. It was as if they were in the front room of a house where the door wouldn't close all the way. The icy wind gusted and roared at their backs, but ahead of them the sun shone.

"Down in Nidaros, it's hardly even autumn yet," Eyvind Torfinn said wistfully.

"It will be cold enough on the plains, by God." Trasamund's breath smoked as he answered. "Cold enough, yes, but not so cold as this."

"As the Gap widens out, your Ferocity, could we perhaps steer away from the very center of it?" Eyvind asked. "That way, the worst of the blast from the north will pass alongside of us instead of blowing through us." Maybe his shiver was exaggerated for effect; on the other hand, maybe it wasn't. Hamnet Thyssen was cold, too.

But Trasamund shook his head. "By your leave, your Splendor, I'll take a cold breeze on my kidneys. I don't care for that, but I can live with it. If chunks of ice decide to come down, they'll squash me like a louse. The two halves of the Glacier are still too cursed close together—a really big avalanche'll squash us no matter where we are. Still and all, I'd sooner keep the risk as small as I can."

"Makes sense," Ulric Skakki said.

Reluctantly, Eyvind Torfinn nodded. "Yes, I suppose it does. I was hoping for the chance to be warm. Like his Ferocity, though, I should much prefer not to be flat."

Ulric looked back toward the narrowest part of the Gap. It was almost like looking back toward a dragon's mouth, except that what it belched was not fire but scudding clouds and snow. In thoughtful tones, Ulric asked, "Could a big avalanche in the right spot still block the Gap, do you think?"

"Wouldn't be surprised," Trasamund answered. "But I don't think God will give us one. God expects people to solve their own problems. He doesn't go around doing it for them."

Hamnet Thyssen found it hard to quarrel with that. But Audun Gilli inquired, "What good is such a God?"

"Well, I don't know that anyone would say he didn't make the world and all the things in it," Trasamund answered. "It'd be a little hard to get along without this old world, even if your kidneys do get cold."

"Do you suppose God made the Rulers?" Hamnet Thyssen asked, not altogether seriously but more so than he would have wanted.

"If he did, he was having a bad day," Ulric Skakki said. "If he didn't, some demon or other was having a good day. Which choice do you like better?"

"I don't like either one of them," Count Hamnet said.

Ulric Skakki chuckled. "All right, then—which choice do you like less?"

"Both," Hamnet answered, and Ulric laughed out loud.

The Gap slowly widened. Little by little, Hamnet Thyssen lost the urge to push the halves into which the Glacier had split farther apart by brute force. When he looked ahead, he saw the gap between the ice mountains stretched farther and farther apart. It still wasn't hospitable country, being flat and often marshy, but he'd known worse.

However flat and dull the countryside was, it brought a broad smile to Trasamund's face. "This is my homeland!" he boomed when the travelers camped one evening. "This is the land of my clan! We have roamed here forever!" He thumped his fist against his chest to emphasize the words.

"Forever, to him, means longer ago than his grandfather could remember," Hamnet Thyssen whispered to Ulric Skakki behind his hand.

"No doubt," Ulric whispered back. "I'm surprised he doesn't drop his trousers and dump out a pile of dung to mark his territory, the way mammoths will sometimes." They both smiled. But they were careful not to laugh. Trasamund was not a man you wanted to insult to his face unless you were ready to put your life on the line. Parsh had found that out.

Gudrid had different thoughts about dung. "I want to get back to the Empire," she said. "If you knew how sick I was of eating food cooked over turds . . ."

"It may not be pleasant, but when the other choice is not eating at all, you do what you need to do," Eyvind Torfinn said.

Had no one else added anything, it might have rested there. But Trasamund said, "Me, I like meat roasted over a dung fire better than what you get down in the south, where you cook with wood. The flavor's better."

"All what you're used to," Earl Eyvind said with a smile.

But Gudrid screwed up her face into a horrible grimace. "What you mean is, meat roasted over a dung fire tastes like dung. We've been eating dung ever since we left the Empire!"

She wasn't wrong. The same thought had crossed Hamnet Thyssen's mind once or twice. He wished she wouldn't have said it, though. Now he *really* had to think about it. By the looks that crossed some of the other Raumsdalians' faces, they felt the same way.

"What does she say?" Liv asked. Count Hamnet didn't much want to translate; that made him think about it, too. But Liv only shrugged and said, "Otherwise, we would starve—and fire is clean."

When Hamnet heard that, he nodded. "You have a good way of looking at things," he said. Fire *was* clean, even if it was fire from . . . He shook his head. He didn't want to go down that road. *Fire is clean,* he told himself, and left it there.

ULRIC SKAKKI SHOOK him awake in the middle of the night. "Sorry to do this to you, your Grace," he said, "but I need my time in the bedroll, too."

"Who says?" Hamnet demanded through a yawn. Ulric laughed. Count Hamnet yawned again. Ulric stayed there by him till he got to his feet. Who hadn't seen a man fall back to sleep instead of going out to stand sentry?

Muttering—and still yawning—Hamnet Thyssen trudged away from the embers of the fire (*the dung fire,* he thought, and wished he hadn't). Off in the distance, he could see the Glacier on either side of the Gap. It seemed almost magical under moonlight, and made him wonder if it shone from within with a glow of its own. The sensible part of him knew better, but around midnight that part wasn't at its best.

Like all the sentries, he stationed himself north of his sleeping comrades. If trouble came, from where but the direction of the Rulers would it come?

He breathed out fog—the visible warmth flowing from his body every time he exhaled. The landscape was eerily quiet. He could hear the other travelers snoring more than a bowshot away. But for those small noises, there was nothing, so much nothing that before long he could hear the blood rushing in his ears and the beating of his heart.

After a while, someone stirred and sat up, there by the smoldering fire. Was that Liv? Hamnet Thyssen's heart beat faster. Warmth flowed through him instead of flowing out. She got to her feet and walked toward him. A broad smile spread over his face. It still felt peculiar; his muscles just weren't used to shaping that expression.

She kissed him when she got out to where he was standing. But then she said, "Something's wrong," which spoiled his hope for anything more.

"What is it?" he asked. Instead of slipping under her tunic, his hand fell to the hilt of his sword.

"I don't know yet." Moonshadow made her look as troubled as she sounded. "But something."

"Should we wake the others?" Hamnet asked. "Should we wake Audun?" Something that roused foreboding in a shaman was bound to be sorcerous . . . wasn't it?

But Liv shook her head. "If he feels it, too, let him come," she said. "If not . . . not. I would say something different if we could talk together." She switched from her language to Raumsdalian. "Not know enough yet. And Audun Gilli not know Bizogot speech."

"You're doing very well," Hamnet said in Raumsdalian.

Liv returned to her own tongue to answer, "I should have started sooner. Then I would know more. And Audun Gilli should have started learning my language."

Not all Raumsdalians cared to learn the Bizogot tongue. Several of the guardsmen who'd come north with Gudrid also remained ignorant of it. Hamnet Thyssen had heard them muttering about braying barbarians— but never when Trasamund or Liv was in earshot. They might be arrogant, but they weren't foolhardy.

Hamnet put his arm around her—partly from affection and partly for warmth. "However you like. The company is good this way."

She nodded and smiled. "It is. If I was wrong . . . Well, we can see what happens then. But let's wait a while first."

"All right." Hamnet didn't want to wait. He waited anyhow. Pushing an unwilling woman wasn't a good idea any time. It made her think a man wanted her for only one thing—which was too often true. But pushing her when she said trouble was on the way had a special stupidity all its own.

If he were twenty years younger, he might not have cared. What man who was hardly more than a youth *didn't* think with his prong? Now, though, Hamnet could wait. Liv would still be here after the trouble, whatever it was, went away.

Motion in the sky made both of them swing their heads the same way at the same time. Silent and pale as a ghost, an owl soared past on broad wings. Or was it only an owl? To Hamnet's senses it was, but he would never make a wizard if he lived to be a thousand. "That?" he whispered.

"That," Liv said.

"What can we—what can you—do?"

"I don't know. I don't know if I can do anything," she answered, which wasn't what he wanted to hear. But then she went on, "I'd better try, though, yes?"

"I'd say so," Hamnet Thyssen said. "If you don't, the Rulers will think we're too weak to do anything about them."

"And they may be right to think that," Liv said bleakly, which was not at all what he wanted to hear. "But I don't care to be spied on night after night, and so . . ."

She reached into her pouch and drew from it something feathered, something clawed, and something that in the moonlight might have been a dark stone. "What have you got there?" Hamnet asked.

"The dried right wing of a screech owl, and his right foot, also dried, and his heart, likewise," the Bizogot shaman said.

"You didn't kill an owl on our travels," Hamnet said, and Liv shook her head to show she hadn't. He went on, "Then you've had them with you since we set out," and she nodded. He asked, "Why, by God?"

"Because these three things, taken together, will summon birds to them, which can be useful," Liv answered. "Also, the heart and the foot together, without the wing, will compel a man to truth if set above his heart while he sleeps."

"You did not use this magic against Samoth when he first spied on us," Hamnet said.

"No—he was in man's shape then," Liv said. "He took bird shape and flew away faster than I could have shaped the spell—faster than I thought anyone could do it. If he flies away now, the spell will fail. But if he gives me time to use it . . . If he does, I may give him a surprise."

"May it be so," Hamnet Thyssen said. "What can I do to help?"

"For now, just stand quiet," she answered. "The time may come, though, when you will want to put out an arm. If it does, I promise you will know it." He scratched his head, wondering what she meant. Meanwhile, she held up the wing and the foot in the right hand and the screech-owl heart in her left. "This spell must have come from the south," she remarked, "for the version we learn first says that these parts are to be hung in a tree." Even under the moon, her smile was impish. "Then we have to reshape it so that it works in our country. But the original still survives."

Hamnet Thyssen wondered why. Maybe the shamans needed the link with the original to ensure that their altered version still worked. He didn't know enough of magic to be sure of anything like that. He didn't have long to wonder, either, for Liv began to chant in a soft voice. He had everything he could do to stay quiet as she'd asked. He wanted to burst out laughing, for the tune she used was the same as a Raumsdalian lullaby. Sure enough, that charm had reached the Bizogots from the south.

Instead of laughing, Count Hamnet watched the owl. At first, he thought its soaring circles were unchanged, and feared the Rulers had some counterspell to deflect or nullify the charm Liv was using. But then he saw that the circles were getting narrower, and that they were centered on Liv and himself, not on the fire as they had been.

The owl called, a strange, questioning note in its voice. Liv answered—Hamnet could find no better way to put it. She gave back fluting hoots, still to the tune of that song that made babies in the Empire close their eyes in the cradle.

Down spiraled the owl. It flew right in front of Liv's face. She never flinched. Hamnet Thyssen didn't think he could have been so calm with that hooked beak and those tearing claws bare inches from his eyes. Then he remembered what she'd said. Before he quite knew he'd done it, he held out his right arm. The owl perched on it.

It stared from him to Liv and back again. Moonlight flashed from its great golden eyes. Despite that flash, though, it seemed confused. It looked back and forth again, as if wondering how it had got there. Hamnet didn't blame it—he was wondering the same thing.

"Do you understand me?" Liv asked in the Bizogot tongue.

The owl hesitated. Then it answered, "Yes, I understand." An owl's beak and throat were not made to speak any human language. The bird managed even so. Samoth, Hamnet recalled, was fluent in the Bizogot speech.

"You are from the Rulers." Liv didn't make it a question, or need to.

"I am from the Rulers," the owl agreed, and it nodded its round head, one of the eeriest things Count Hamnet had ever seen.

"Are you Samoth? Does his spirit dwell inside you?" The Bizogot shaman was thinking along the same lines as Hamnet himself.

"I am Samoth. It is not a matter of the spirit. I *am* Samoth," the owl said. To hear its words hoot and hiss their way forth made the hair at the back of Hamnet's neck want to stand up of its own accord, as if he were a frightened animal puffing up in the face of danger. *By God, what else am I?* he thought.

"And you flew here to spy on us?" Liv asked.

"To spy on you, yes, and to spy out the way south," said the bird that was also a wizard or a shaman or whatever the right word among the Rulers was.

"Hear me, Samoth." Liv's voice changed from questioning to commanding. If anything, the hair on Hamnet's nape stood higher and straighter. "Hear me," Liv repeated. "When you flew forth, you found no Bizogot or Raumsdalian travelers."

"When I flew forth, I found no Bizogot or Raumsdalian travelers," agreed the owl that was Samoth.

"You did not pass through the Gap at all—the snowstorm to the north was too strong."

"I didn't pass through the Gap at all—the snowstorm to the north was too strong," the owl echoed. Were its eyes duller than they had been when it landed on Count Hamnet's wrist? He thought so, but he couldn't be sure. He steadied his right arm with his left hand to make sure no quiver upset the owl or disrupted Liv's magic.

Her eyes, by contrast, shone as she thanked him with them. "You turned back and flew off to your camp because you could fly no farther," she said to Samoth.

"I turned back and flew off to my camp because I could fly no farther," the ensorceled owl agreed.

"And of course you remember nothing of this talk, for it never happened," Liv said. When the owl echoed her once more, she nodded to Hamnet Thyssen. He thrust his arm up and forward, as if launching a falcon against a quail. Like a hawk trained to the fist, the owl flew away. It arrowed off toward the north.

"That was—bravely done," Hamnet whispered, not wanting to disturb its flight in any way. "*Bravely* done!"

"My thanks," Liv whispered back. She let out a long, weary, fog-filled breath. "He is very strong. He almost slipped free of my magic four or five times, even as an owl. As a man . . . I don't know if I could stand against him as a man. This should have been easy, and it was anything but."

"You did it. What else matters?" Hamnet Thyssen was determined to look on the bright side. That felt strange for him, but it was true.

"Nothing else matters—now," Liv answered. "But if we see the Rulers again . . . When we see the Rulers again . . . How strong they are matters a lot."

He couldn't tell her she was wrong, for she plainly wasn't. "The way you sent Samoth off makes it less likely we'll see them anytime soon," he said. "It may mean we won't see them at all."

"I doubt that," the Bizogot shaman said. "What I wonder is whether he'll stay fooled, whether he'll believe the weather was bad or he'll realize he had a spell put on him. If he does realize I used magic against him, will he know how close his owl-self came to breaking free?" She sighed again, even more deeply than before. "Nothing is ever simple, however much we wish it would be."

Count Hamnet nodded; he couldn't argue there, either. But he said, "You did everything you could. It all worked, every bit of it. Be proud of that." He put his arm around her.

She leaned against him for a little while, drawing strength or at least consolation from his touch. Then she straightened and took her weight on her own feet again. "I am," she said. "But it should have worked better. It should have worked easier."

Hamnet Thyssen almost did argue with her then. At the very end, he held his tongue. He recognized that drive to have everything come out perfect, and the gnawing sense of dissatisfaction when any tiny little detail didn't. He had it himself. If anyone had told him not to worry so much, what would he have done? Ignored the advice and probably lost his temper. Why wouldn't Liv do the same? No reason at all, not that he could see. And so he kept quiet.

WHEN THE TRAVELERS rode south the next morning, Audun Gilli had the oddest expression on his face. He rode up alongside of Count Hamnet and asked, "Did anything strange happen in the nighttime?"

"Strange? What do you mean?" Hamnet couldn't have sounded more innocent if he'd worked at it for a year.

"I had the oddest dream," Audun said. "I was flying. I was a bird of some kind, not a flying man, the way you can be in dreams. I know I was a bird, because I looked down and saw myself. I don't know how I could, though, because it was night in the dream. But I did. And then—then I didn't. Then everything was all confused, as if I couldn't see at all. And I was flying away as fast as I could. But do you know what the oddest thing was?"

"No," Hamnet Thyssen said gravely. "You're about to tell me, though, aren't you?"

"The oddest thing was"—Audun Gilli ignored, or more likely didn't notice, his irony—"that in the middle of all this, your Grace, I somehow shook hands with you. Isn't that peculiar?"

"Yes, that *is* peculiar," Hamnet said. The wizard's occult senses, whatever they were, must have picked up some of what Liv was doing. But Audun never fully woke, and so had only a dreamer's confused notions of what had happened.

Audun sent him a quizzical look—or maybe a look a little more than quizzical. "You don't seem surprised by what I tell you."

"Nothing you tell me ever surprises me," Count Hamnet said—let Audun make of that what he would.

The wizard scratched his head. "When we get back to Nidaros, I will buy myself scented soap and a tub of hot water," he said. "And then . . ." He didn't go on, not with words, but his smile was blissful.

"Sounds good to me," Hamnet said, nodding. "Buy one more thing while you're at it."

"What's that?" Audun Gilli asked.

"A brush with at least medium-strong bristles," Hamnet answered. "We've been up here a long time, and the soap will need some help."

"You're right." Now Audun nodded, as if making sure he would remember. "I'll do that." Hardly noticing, he went on scratching.

Watching him made Hamnet scratch, too, the way someone else yawning might make him do the same. And once he started scratching, he also went right on. "You wizards don't have a sorcerous cure for bugs, eh?" he said.

"Not one that does much good," Audun Gilli said mournfully. "If we did, we'd be richer than we are, I'll tell you that."

Hamnet Thyssen scratched some more—thoughtfully at first, and then just because scratching felt good. "Speaking of rich . . . Meaning no offense, but Ulric Skakki found you in the gutter. How do you aim to buy your soap and your soak and your brush?"

Now Audun Gilli looked appalled. "Won't the Emperor pay us, reward us, for going beyond the Glacier in his name?"

"Well, I don't know." Hamnet made his hand stop scratching, lest he rub himself raw. It wasn't easy. He went on, "He may think we can live on fame." He could himself. Eyvind Torfinn could, easily. Jesper Fletti and the other guardsmen would go back to the duty they'd had before setting out. Ulric Skakki? Count Hamnet didn't know how much Ulric had stashed away, but Ulric was enough like a cat to be able to land on his feet no matter what happened.

Audun Gilli . . . wasn't. "I hope you're wrong," he said in what had to be one of the most desperately tense understatements of all time. "Times were . . . hard for me before I started this journey."

"I know," Hamnet said. "No matter what, you have a story people will want to hear, likely a story people will pay to hear. That will help you carry on your trade, too. You'll be a known man, even a famous man."

"Do you think that will stop me from ending up in the gutter again?" Audun asked. It was a serious question; he sounded as if he really wanted to know.

"Well, I can't answer that. Only you can," Hamnet Thyssen said. "If you can't keep yourself out of the gutter, who else will?"

"I suppose you're right." Audun Gilli sighed, almost as wearily as Liv had the night before. "I don't know whether it's good news or bad, though. Well, I expect I'll find out." As the Bizogot shaman's had, his breath filled the air with fog.

The travelers hadn't left winter behind. The wind didn't howl so hard on this side of the Glacier, but the cold still reached into Hamnet Thyssen's bones in spite of the furs that muffled him.

"Before long, we should run into bands of my folk and their herds," Trasamund said. "It will good to see my clansmen's faces again. It will be good to see the faces of the women, too," he added in a different tone of voice. Gudrid's back stiffened.

They started to run low on meat. Things might have got serious if they hadn't come upon a herd of musk oxen. Ulric Skakki slew one bull with an arrow through the eye, a perfect shot that dropped the big beast in its tracks.

"You couldn't do that again in a hundred years," Jesper Fletti said as they started the gory job of butchery.

Ulric studied him with a mild and speculative gaze. "Would you like me to try?" he asked in a voice so mild that no one could possibly take offense at it. Despite that mildness, Jesper was quick to shake his head. Maybe he didn't think Ulric was talking about shooting musk oxen. Hamnet Thyssen certainly didn't.

They gorged themselves on the meat once they cut it off the bones. People needed much more food in this climate just to fight the cold. Hamnet Thyssen was amazed at how much half-scorched, half-raw flesh he put away. It was as if he were doing hard physical labor even while only riding. When he actually did have to work hard . . . he needed even more.

The horses were in worse shape than their riders. They had trouble finding enough fodder under the snow. When one of them went down and would not rise, Trasamund knocked it over the head. The travelers butchered it as they'd butchered the musk ox. Hamnet had eaten horse before after similar misfortunes. It was chewy, almost gluey, but ever so much better than nothing.

Chewing—and chewing, and chewing—Eyvind Torfinn smiled wryly. "I don't believe my cook down in Nidaros has any recipes for this particular meat."

"I *hope* he doesn't," Gudrid said.

"It may not be wonderful food," Ulric Skakki said, "but any food is better than going hungry."

"All Bizogots know this, for we know how hard life can be when winter clamps down," Trasamund said. "I was not sure a man from the south, where you have bread and grain as a cushion against bad times, would understand it."

"I've been hungry a time or two, your Ferocity," Ulric answered. "Believe me, having food is better."

"To food!" Trasamund said. "A toast I will make in earnest when I can."

After they ate, they rode. Hamnet Thyssen had never spent so much time in the saddle before this journey. He wondered if he was growing bowlegged, the better to fit his shape to the horse's. He also wondered how long he would be able to go on riding. If the horses kept getting weaker, he and the other travelers might have to dismount and lead them. They might have to slaughter them one by one. The thought of more meals like the one he'd just eaten did not appeal. He patted the side of his mount's neck.

"Sizing up how tender the beast will be when the time comes to roast it?" Ulric Skakki asked.

"God, don't listen to this man!" Hamnet Thyssen exclaimed.

Ulric laughed. "Can't say as I blame you. Not the finest supper I've ever got down. But swallowing anything is better than not."

"Some people will certainly swallow anything," Count Hamnet said.

That drew another laugh from Ulric Skakki. "You're in a cheerful mood, aren't you, your Grace?" These days, he used Hamnet's title only for sardonic effect. They'd all traveled too far with one another for the formalities to matter any more.

"No." Hamnet wasn't laughing. "We've come an awfully long way. I'd hate to see us fall just short of getting back to . . . to Trasamund's clan." He almost said, *Back to civilization.* No matter how far he'd come, no matter what he'd seen, he wasn't about to confuse the way the Bizogots lived with civilization.

By Ulric Skakki's mischievous grin, he had a pretty good notion of what Count Hamnet didn't say. With his pointed nose and narrow, foxy eyes, he was good at sniffing his way past all kinds of deceptions and evasions. "Better to have the Bizogots with us than against us," he said, and

Count Hamnet could hardly quarrel with that. Then, looking even more sly than usual, Ulric added, "You've got one Bizogot on your side, all right."

Hamnet refused to rise to the bait. "You already teased me about that. If you do it over and over again, people will say you're boring."

"People? What do people know?" Ulric said. "Or did you mean the Rulers? They know everything—and if you don't believe me, you can bloody well ask them."

"I don't want to ask them anything. I hope I never see them again." Hamnet Thyssen feared that was a forlorn hope.

"Now that you mention it, so do I." But Ulric sounded no more hopeful than Hamnet. He looked to the east and to the west. The Glacier still loomed tall on both horizons, but a broad expanse of land lay between the two walls of ice—the Gap was widening out. Then Ulric Skakki stared south. "I never want to see the Rulers again, no, but I wouldn't mind meeting a Bizogot besides our ferocious jarl and the admittedly charming Liv."

"Neither would I," Hamnet allowed. "We're far enough south that we could any day now."

"There is some small difference between *could* and *will*," Ulric said. "You may perhaps have noticed."

"Why, no." Hamnet tried to play the game of irony himself. "Explain it to me, if you'd be so kind."

One of Ulric's gingery eyebrows rose. "I *could* say you're being difficult. I *will* say you're doing it on purpose."

"Very neat," Hamnet said with a mounted bow. "You should be a scholar."

"Thank you, but no," Ulric Skakki said. "No silver in it."

"Oh, I don't know. Look at Earl Eyvind." Hamnet Thyssen did look at him. Eyvind Torfinn was talking earnestly with Gudrid. For the moment, playing a subdued, demure wife seemed to suit her.

Ulric Skakki shook his head. "Earl Eyvind had silver before he decided he wanted to be a scholar. He's a scholar in spite of his money, not because of it."

"Well, not altogether," Hamnet said. "The silver he's got lets him do what he pleases. He wouldn't be able to buy his books and learn his lore without it."

"I suppose so," Ulric said. "But he isn't the kind of scholar I had in mind, anyway. I meant the hole-and-corner kind, the ones who have to stuff a rag into the toe of their felt boots in wintertime because they can't afford to patch them. That sort is good enough to teach boys how to read and write and count, but not for much more."

"Plenty of them around," Count Hamnet agreed. "They call themselves scholars, but I'm not sure how many other people do."

Ulric Skakki surely said something in reply. Whatever it was, Count Hamnet didn't hear it. His eyes went to an owl flying past the travelers from out of the north, white and swift and strong. Samoth? Hamnet's heart pounded. No wizard himself, he couldn't tell. His gaze went to Liv. She noticed him no more than he'd heard Ulric. All her attention pursued the bird till it streaked out of sight to the south.

Only then did she turn in the saddle and look for him. Even before she spoke, he saw the relief lighting her fine features. "Sometimes a white owl is only a white owl," she called.

"A good thing, too," Hamnet answered. They smiled at each other.

"Sometimes I think I don't know everything that's going on," Ulric Skakki said in tones full of mock self-pity.

Count Hamnet reached out and set a consoling hand on his arm. "Don't worry about it. Sometimes I don't think you know what's going on, either."

"Thank you. Thank you so much," Ulric said. Hamnet waved modestly.

On they went, farther and farther south. Another horse died, and another. They cut up the animals and ate them. The meat was strong-flavored and there wasn't a great deal of it; the horses had got very scrawny before finally failing.

"Do you think we'll make it?" Jesper Fletti asked Hamnet. The guards officer had never been up in the north before this journey. All things considered, he'd acquitted himself well enough. Hamnet Thyssen could . . . almost forget that he'd come along to protect Gudrid.

"I think so," Hamnet answered. "We can't be far from outriders from the Three Tusk clan. I would have guessed we'd run into them already, truth to tell." That they hadn't worried him, though he didn't say so. Had some disaster befallen Trasamund's clan while the jarl journeyed beyond the Glacier? That was the worst kind of bad news he could imagine.

The words were hardly out of his mouth, the thought hardly through his head, before Trasamund let out a bellow that might have come from the throat of a bull musk ox. That dot on the southern horizon was a mounted man, and he was riding toward them.

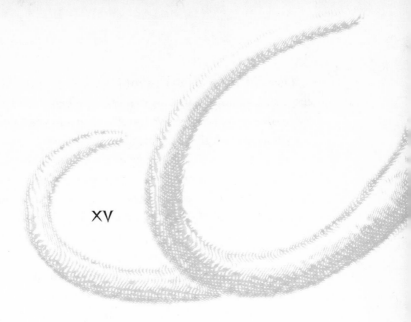

XV

Seeing a new face, hearing a new voice, felt strange to Count Hamnet. The Rulers hardly counted. Most of them hadn't spoken the Bizogot language, and the ones who did showed themselves to be outright enemies. Hilderic wasn't. He and Trasamund kissed each other on both cheeks in the usual greeting of Bizogots who hadn't seen each other for a long time.

"By God, your Ferocity!" Hilderic said. "By God! It's good to see you! You've been gone a long time. Some people were starting to wonder if you'd ever come back."

"Oh, they were, were they?" the jarl said. "I'm not so easy to get rid of as all that, and they'd best believe I'm not. Who are these fools who have no faith in Trasamund?"

Hilderic suffered a sudden coughing fit. "Uh, that is . . . Well . . . You see . . ."

Trasamund laughed. "All right. Never mind. You don't need to tell me. I can understand that you don't want a name as a snitch. But I'll find out sooner or later—have no fear of that. And when I do, I'll make those doubters pay." He thumped his chest with a mittened fist. "Yes, *I* will take care of them. You don't need to worry about it."

"May it be as you say, your Ferocity," Hilderic replied. Hamnet Thyssen and Ulric Skakki exchanged covert smiles. Trasamund always saw himself as larger than life. Because he did, he could make other people see him the same way most of the time. Hilderic, though plainly a seasoned man, certainly did.

Liv worried less about how important other people thought she was and more about things that really mattered. "Where is the camp you rode out of, Hilderic?" she asked. "We've traveled long and hard. We aren't at the end of our tether, but we aren't far from it, either."

"It's not far, lady," Hilderic said. Then he stopped and blinked. The face of every traveler who understood the Bizogot language must have lit up. Hamnet Thyssen knew how happy *he* was. Hilderic went on, "The guesting will be good, too. The herds have done well through the summer and into fall."

"Lead on!" Trasamund boomed.

Hamnet soon found that something he already knew remained true— what a Bizogot meant by *not far* was different from what a Raumsdalian would have meant. But they did reach the encampment just before darkness fell. Hamnet wondered whether he'd ever seen anything more beautiful than those black mammoth-hide tents.

Bizogots swarmed out of the tents to greet the travelers. "Welcome back!" they shouted. "Welcome home!" It was *home* only to Trasamund and Liv, but none of the Raumsdalians complained or contradicted. These tents might not be home, but they came much closer than the endless expanse of wilderness the travelers had crossed.

The Bizogots slaughtered and butchered a plump young musk ox. Spit flooded into Hamnet Thyssen's mouth. Trasamund scooped out a handful of the raw brains and ate it, blood running down into his beard. Hamnet did the same. He'd learned to tolerate the Bizogot delicacy on his first trip up beyond the tree line, years earlier. On this trip, he'd learned to enjoy it. And he was hungry enough now to find it delicious beyond compare.

Ulric Skakki took some of the brains, too. "Always glad when my stomach is smarter than my head," he said.

"Mine is most of the time, I think," Hamnet said, licking his lips.

None of the other Raumsdalians wanted anything to do with raw brains, though Liv came up to eat some. Trasamund clapped Hamnet and Ulric on the back in turn—gingerly, for his hands were still sore. "By God, the two of you make pretty fair Bizogots," he said.

"Thank you, your Ferocity." Hamnet knew the jarl meant it for praise, and some of the highest praise he could give.

"Thank you so much, your Ferocity," Ulric Skakki said. If Trasamund listened to the words, he would find nothing wrong with them. If he listened closely to the tone, he would find he'd given praise Ulric didn't want.

For a mammoth-herder, Trasamund was a sophisticate. Beside Ulric Skakki, he might have been a child; the irony went over his head. He was frank as a child, too, for he went on, "Maybe not as good as the real thing, but pretty fair even so."

This wasn't the Three Tusk clan's main camp—that lay farther south. These Bizogots had followed their herd of musk oxen into the Gap. Most animals went south for the winter. Musk oxen, shielded against cold and blizzards by their long, shaggy hair and soft, thick underwool, could head the other way if they chose.

Even though this was only a small band of Bizogots—a couple dozen men, fewer women, a handful of children—Hamnet Thyssen felt as if he'd suddenly come into Nidaros after a long sojourn in his castle. Unfamiliar faces talked about unfamiliar things in unfamiliar voices. So much chatter almost made him want to flee the tents for the quiet and solitude of the frozen plain beyond them.

Roasting musk-ox meat sent up a delicious aroma. Count Hamnet's stomach growled like a short-faced bear. Even if he did feel slightly over-whelmed, he decided to stay around.

He didn't mind half-raw meat at all. He did mind waiting for it to cook all the way through. So did the other travelers. He overheard one Bizogot say to another, "I thought these folk from the south couldn't put it away like real people do. I guess I was wrong."

"I thought the same thing," the second Bizogot answered. "Only goes to show you shouldn't believe everything you hear, doesn't it?"

Eyvind Torfinn stared in mild astonishment at the pile of rib bones in front of him. "I never could have eaten like this before I set out from the Empire," he said. "Never, I tell you. Amazing what practice will do, isn't it?"

"Amazing what hunger will do, isn't it?" Ulric Skakki said. Hamnet Thyssen thought that came closer to hitting the mark, though what Earl Eyvind said also held some truth. Without practice, Hamnet didn't think he could have gorged himself like this. Without being hungrier than he ever got down in the Raumsdalian Empire, he wouldn't have wanted to.

The Bizogots passed around skins of smetyn to celebrate the travelers' return. The fermented mammoth's milk tasted good to Hamnet, which only showed how long he'd been away from anything with a kick to it. It also mounted straight to his head, which showed the same thing.

Audun Gilli drank himself to sleep in short order. The Bizogots took such things in stride. They draped a mammoth hide over the sodden wizard and shoved him near the edge of the tent, where people were less likely to trip over him or step on him.

"Well, your Ferocity?" Hilderic said. "Tell us of the lands beyond the Glacier. Are there people there? Did you find the Golden Shrine?"

"There are people. There are indeed," Trasamund answered. He spoke of the Rulers, and of how they not only herded but rode mammoths. That made all the Bizogots buzz, as he must have known it would.

"Can we do that?" Three of them asked the same question at the same time.

"I don't see why not," the jarl said. "But we won't do it today, and we won't do it tomorrow, either. We'll have to figure out everything that goes into it, and we'll have to get the mammoths used to carrying men on their backs. The time will come, though, and I think it will come soon."

Gudrid and the Raumsdalian guardsmen who'd never learned the Bizogot tongue began to follow Audun Gilli's example. Hamnet Thyssen didn't suppose he could blame them—not in one sense, anyway. Listening to a language you couldn't follow had to be boring. But they'd traveled with Bizogots for months. They—and Audun—should have learned more than they did.

He glanced over to Liv. She'd waited longer than she might have to start learning Raumsdalian, too. But she was doing well with it now.

In the flames that came from butter-filled lamps, Hilderic's eyes glowed like a wild beast's. "If we learn this art, we'll ride roughshod over the rest of the Bizogots!" His fellow clansmen rumbled approval at the idea.

But Trasamund regretfully shook his head. "Once we learn this art, I fear we'll have to show it to the rest of the Bizogots."

"What? Why?" Hilderic demanded.

"Because the Rulers, God curse them, are full of greed," Trasamund said. "We see the opening of the Gap as a chance to go north, to see what lies beyond the Glacier. *They* see it as a chance to fare south, to lay hold of what lies below the Glacier."

"They can't do that!" Hilderic wasn't the only Bizogot to say that—far from it. Several of the big blond men shook their fists at the north.

"I hope they can't," Trasamund said. "But they have tricks we know nothing of yet. This mammoth-riding is bound to be but the beginning."

"The jarl speaks truly," Liv added. "One thing we saw while we were with them—their magic is strong, very strong, perhaps stronger than any we know ourselves. If the Raumsdalian shaman were awake, he would tell you the same."

"Still and all, they can be beaten," Hamnet Thyssen said. "His Ferocity proved as much."

A reminiscent smile spread across Trasamund's battered features. "Well, so I did," he said, and then waited till his people clamored for him to tell them more. He was indeed a sophisticate—for a Bizogot. He spoke of his battle with Parsh, finishing, "And after I beat him, the poor fool killed himself for shame."

"Killed himself? For what?" Hilderic said. "For shame, you say? What shame in losing a straight-up fight, as long as you gave your best? Did he?"

"He did." By the way Trasamund rubbed his chin, he had no doubt of that. He stopped smiling. "Oh, yes. He did."

"For shame of losing to a man not of the Rulers," Hamnet said.

"They are a serious folk, then, the Rulers." Hilderic sounded impressed in spite of himself. By the way several other Bizogots, both men and women, nodded, he'd put into words what they were thinking.

"They are a danger, a great danger," Liv said. "We would do well to put warriors at the narrowest part of the Gap, to make sure they cannot break through and come down into the richer country we mostly roam."

The Bizogots who hadn't traveled beyond the Glacier stared at her. So did Trasamund. "Meaning no offense, wise woman," he said, "but we of the Three Tusk clan have not the warriors to hold the Gap. Even if we sent all our men, I doubt we would have enough. And if we did that"—he chuckled as if humoring a madwoman—"who would tend the beasts?"

"Let everything be as you say, your Ferocity, but the Gap still needs to be held," Liv replied. "If we have not men enough to do it, let other clans send warriors to our aid. Let even the Raumsdalians send warriors to our aid, so long as we hold the Gap."

"Let other clans' warriors cross the land of the Three Tusk clan in arms?" That wasn't the jarl. It was Hilderic, horror in his voice. "Let the *Emperor's* warriors cross our land? By God, it cannot be!" Solemn nods from his clansmen said they agreed with him.

"I am one of the Emperor's warriors," Hamnet Thyssen said mildly. "You see others here beside you. What harm have we done?"

"He is right," Liv said. Trasamund's big head bobbed up and down.

But Hilderic said, "You are travelers. You aren't an army. While you're here, you obey the jarl. You don't follow the Emperor's orders. If an army came, it would come to hold us and conquer us and take our wealth away."

Count Hamnet almost burst into hysterical laughter. *What wealth?* he wondered. He had no idea how to say that without mortally offending not only Hilderic but also Trasamund and Liv. While he tried to find a way, Ulric Skakki beat him to the punch, saying, "No Raumsdalians would want to hold a land where trees won't grow." He put it more diplomatically than Hamnet could have.

"Ulric is likely right about the southerners," Trasamund said. "But I wouldn't care to let our own folk onto our grazing lands in arms. Who knows what they might do?"

"If we yield the Gap, if we don't fight there, we'll have to fight farther south—here, or in our very heartland." Liv sounded desperate. "We could put a stopper in the skin." A Raumsdalian would have spoken of a cork in the bottle, but it came to the same thing either way.

"What of the Golden Shrine?" another Bizogot said. "We asked about it before, but got no answer. Do the Rulers hold it?"

"They do not." Eyvind Torfinn spoke with assurance. "As far as I could tell, they know nothing of it. We did not find it, but it is safe. Believe me when I say this, for it is true."

"What does a foreigner know?" the Bizogot muttered.

"This foreigner knows more of the Golden Shrine than any Bizogot," Trasamund said before Earl Eyvind could even begin to speak for himself. "Don't argue with me, Wulfila, for I know what I'm talking about."

Wulfila bristled. Anyone who tried to tell a Bizogot what to do—even the jarl of that Bizogot's clan—was taking his chances, if not taking his life in his own hands. But then Liv said, "Trasamund is right," and Wulfila subsided. If a shaman said a Raumsdalian knew a good deal about occult matters, how could an ordinary Bizogot quarrel with her? Oh, a fool might, but Wulfila didn't seem a fool—not that kind of fool, anyhow.

"If I had to guess," Earl Eyvind said, "the Golden Shrine has ways to make sure that those who would trouble its tranquillity have no chance to do so. I cannot prove this, not with the little I know now, but I believe it to be the case." He sounded like a scholar even while speaking the Bizogot language. In an abstract way, Hamnet Thyssen admired that; he'd never imagined such a thing was possible.

Wulfila seemed impressed, but he asked, "If that's so, how do you know the Golden Shrine wasn't hiding from *you*?" That it might hide from a Raumsdalian seemed natural to him, where he never would have dreamt it might conceal itself from one of his own folk.

Eyvind Torfinn looked quite humanly surprised. "I do not know that, not for a fact. I do not believe it is true, but neither do I know it is not."

Count Hamnet was surprised in turn, for that seemed to satisfy Wulfila. Voice gruff, the Bizogot said, "Well, you seem honest, anyhow. Who would have thought it, from a man of the south?"

Trasamund upended a skin full of smetyn. He belched enormously, which showed good manners among the Bizogots. Then he yawned enormously. "Let us speak of all this another time. For now, I do believe I will die if I don't crawl under a skin pretty soon."

None of the travelers—those who'd stayed awake that long—argued with him. The Bizogots had hides and blankets to spare. The weather was cold, but not as cold as it might have been. Plenty of covers could make the difference between life and death when the Breath of God blew its hardest. Now the mammoth-herders shared them out to their guests. Hamnet Thyssen was as glad to slide beneath one as any of the others—and even gladder when Liv slid under the same one.

COUNT HAMNET WOKE in darkness. Liv was draped over him, smooth and bare, one arm flung across his chest, one thigh over his leg. One of his hands rested on the small of her back. He moved it, just a little. She murmured something wordless. It sounded happy. He hoped it was.

How long since he'd wakened with a woman in his arms before Liv? He knew that, down to the very day—since the last time he'd awakened so with Gudrid. After that, he'd bedded women, yes, but he hadn't slept with them, not in the literal sense of the words. He hadn't wanted so much intimacy.

Now . . . Now he had to remind himself not to wake Liv, not to rouse her as he was roused himself. He might want her, but she wanted sleep, and she'd earned the right to it. If she woke by herself . . . But that was a different story. So he told himself, over and over again, and made himself hold her quietly. It wasn't easy.

Then, just when he was on the point of drifting off again, she did wake—in surprise, more surprise than he'd shown. "What?" she said, and then, a long beat later, "Oh. Hamnet."

"Yes," he said, as if the two of them lying naked and entwined was the most natural thing in the world. *And why not?* he wondered. *Why not, by God?*

She smiled against his shoulder. "That's good," she murmured.

"Yes," he said again. He might have been announcing magic grander than any the most talented wizard could hope to work. He might have been—and, as far as he was concerned, he was.

Feeling her warmth against him made most of his warmth concentrate in one spot. Liv could scarcely help noticing. She laughed softly. "You're ready? So soon?"

He said, "Yes," one more time, and he might have been announcing another miracle. Again, he thought he was. He hadn't been so eager, so avid, for a very long time. At his age, he hadn't thought he could be. Getting *happily* surprised made a pleasant novelty.

Had he *ever* been so avid? He likely had, back in the first days with Gudrid. His arms tightened around Liv. She laughed again, and kissed him, and then twisted, limber as an eel, and suddenly they weren't just entwined but joined. "Shhh," she whispered as they began to move. By the nature of things, the Bizogots often made love in a tent with others present. That was all right. Waking others up while you did it, though—that was rude.

Hamnet Thyssen tried to remember his manners. Afterwards, he thought he did well enough, right up till the moment when joy overwhelmed him. He didn't think Liv remembered very well then, either. Neither one of them was inclined to be critical. He sighed with regret when he slipped out of her. A moment later, his eyes slid shut and he was asleep again.

IT WAS STILL dark when he next woke. If anything, he and Liv were even more tangled up than they had been before. He didn't pat her. *I am a virtuous man,* he told himself. *I can resist small temptations.* He hadn't tried—or wanted—to resist larger ones.

Other people were stirring now. Morning had to be close by, if so many were waking up. Liv came back to herself not long after Hamnet did. This time, she knew where she was, and with whom. She kissed him on the end of the nose. "We should dress," she said.

"Ah, too bad," Hamnet answered, which made her laugh.

They wriggled into their clothes under the hide. Anyone watching that from the outside might have guessed they were doing something else instead. No one seemed to be, though, and they weren't the only ones who'd celebrated returning to the Three Tusk clan. Trasamund hadn't always been perfectly quiet under his hide, either.

Roast meat left over from the night before broke their fast. The jarl left three or four of the weariest horses behind at the encampment, exchanging them for beasts his clansfolk had been using. "Sooner or later, we'll replace them all," he said, "but I don't want to leave a whole herd of screws up here. They might need sound horses."

"Sensible," Ulric Skakki whispered to Hamnet. "Who would have thought Trasamund had it in him?"

"Not fair. He's a good enough jarl—better than good enough," Hamnet said.

As if he hadn't spoken, Ulric went on, "Of course, by the noises last night, he had it in everything but the cat."

Ears heating (some of those noises might have been his), Count Hamnet said, "The Bizogots don't keep cats."

"That must be why he didn't, then," Ulric said blandly.

"Er—right."

Hamnet didn't have one of the fresh horses, but even the animal he was riding seemed glad of the longer than usual rest it had got the night before. The travelers hadn't been riding for more than a couple of hours before they came upon a herd of mammoths, with a couple of Bizogots steering it toward the best foraging. Trasamund shouted back and forth with the herders. He eyed the mammoths in a way he hadn't before. "How would you climb up on their backs without making them want to squash you flat?" he murmured.

"Personally, I wouldn't," Hamnet Thyssen said quietly. Laughing, Ulric Skakki nodded.

But Trasamund, with the thought in his mind, didn't want to turn loose of it. "How would you?" he repeated. "Do you suppose it takes magic, Liv? Do the Rulers spell their mammoths into quiet so they can mount them?"

"I don't know, your Ferocity," she answered. "I saw no sign of that, but I can't prove anything."

"I want to try it." Trasamund seemed ready to jump off his horse—he rode one of the fresh ones—and onto the back of the closest mammoth.

"This is perhaps not the ideal time for experimentation," Eyvind Torfinn said. "We have news to deliver, important news, and your untimely demise would assist only the raiders from beyond the Glacier."

"What untimely demise?" the jarl demanded indignantly. "Nothing would happen to me."

One of the mammoths swung up its trunk and let out a sound that reminded Hamnet Thyssen of a blaring bugle filled with spit. It also made him wonder if the enormous beast was giving Trasamund the horse laugh.

A glance at Ulric Skakki's raised eyebrow made him suspect the adventurer was thinking the same thing. "There's a time and a place for everything, your Ferocity," Hamnet said. "This probably isn't the time to try riding mammoths."

Trasamund glared at him. To the Bizogots, the time to do something was the time when you thought of doing it. But the jarl, unlike most of his countrymen, had gone down to the Empire and at least understood the idea of waiting, even if he didn't much care for it. "All right," he said grudgingly. "*All right.* It will keep, I suppose." He let out a martyred sigh that filled the air in front of him with fog. If he was going to pass up the opportunity, he wanted everyone around him to recognize what a fine fellow he was for doing it.

When the Bizogot herdsmen learned that the Rulers rode mammoths, they too were wild to try it for themselves. They weren't going anywhere important; they had nothing to do but guide the beasts in their charge. If they wanted to clamber aboard one of those beasts, they could . . . as long as the mammoth let them.

"I wonder if they're going to do something they'll regret," Ulric said.

"Well, if it goes wrong, they won't regret it long," Hamnet answered.

"A point. A distinct point," Ulric said. "But look at them. They think they'll be mammoth-lancers by the time the Rulers come through the Gap."

"The Rulers *shouldn't* come through the Gap—Liv's dead right about that," Hamnet said. "We ought to be able to stop them right there if they try."

"We ought to be able to do all kinds of things," Ulric Skakki said. "What we *will* do . . ."

Count Hamnet wished he hadn't put it like that. Plainly, the Bizogots and Raumsdalians wouldn't be able to do some things, no matter how obvious it seemed that they should. Trasamund's clansmen hated the idea of letting other Bizogots, let alone warriors from the Empire, cross their land even to fight the Rulers. Every other Bizogot clan would probably be just as unhappy to let its neighbors cross its grazing grounds. As for the Empire . . . Who could say whether the Empire would take the idea of a threat from beyond the Glacier seriously at all?

"We may have made the greatest journey in the history of the world for nothing, you know," Hamnet Thyssen said.

"Yes, that occurred to me." Ulric Skakki sounded surprised it had taken so long to occur to Hamnet. Then he glanced over toward Liv and smiled a little. "But you wouldn't say it was for nothing any which way, would you?"

"For myself? No," Hamnet answered. "I was talking about things bigger than any one person's affairs." He waited for Ulric to make some lewd pun on that.

The adventurer didn't. Instead, he asked, "How many people ever think past their day-to-day affairs?" And he answered his own question. "Not many, by God."

"Some do," Hamnet said. "Some have to, in the Empire. If they didn't, we'd be as barbarous as the Bizogots."

"Do you think we're not?" Before Count Hamnet could respond to that, Ulric Skakki held up a hand. "Never mind, never mind. I know what you're saying. But people like that are thinner on the ground than you think, your Grace. Not everyone comes with your sense of duty nailed inside his chest."

"You make it sound so wonderful," Hamnet Thyssen said.

"Oh, it is, it is." Ulric smiled a crooked smile that showed a great many sharp teeth. "If you don't believe me, ask Gudrid."

For a red moment, Count Hamnet wanted to kill him. Then, grudgingly, he nodded, saying, "You have a nasty way of making your points."

"Why, thank you," Ulric Skakki said with another carnivorous smile. Hamnet had no answer for that at all.

WHEN THE TRAVELERS found the Three Tusk clan's main encampment, everyone celebrated—everyone but Hamnet Thyssen. For him, it seemed more an end than a beginning, and an end he didn't want.

The smile on Liv's face flayed him. "This is my home," she said, and the words cut like flensing knives. "How I've missed these tents!" she went on, carving another chunk from his happiness. He wasn't used to being happy. Back before he was, he would have borne up under anything. Now . . .

"Would you like to see Raumsdalia?" he asked, and worked with his tongue to free a chunk of musk-ox meat caught between two back teeth.

She looked surprised. "I hadn't even thought of that. I hadn't thought of anything past coming back to the tents of my clan."

Ulric Skakki knew what he was talking about, sure enough, Hamnet thought. "I don't want to leave you," he said. "I . . . hoped you didn't want to leave me."

"I don't," Liv said, and peered at the dung fire over which the meat cooked. "No, I don't. But I don't think I can turn into a Raumsdalian, either."

"No more can I make myself into a Bizogot," Hamnet Thyssen said.

"Are you sure?" Liv asked. "You would be an ornament to my folk, an ornament to my clan. You are strong and brave and wise—and a *man,* as I should know." She looked at him out of the corner of her eye. "What holds you to the Empire?"

"Loyalty," he said at once. "I must go down to Nidaros and let the Emperor know what I have seen, what I have done, and what I think we need to do in times to come."

Liv gave him a nod that was almost a bow. "Your answer does you honor. But once you've shown your loyalty, why not come north again and lead the free life of the tents with me? What would you be losing?"

Hamnet had never thought of himself as a man who set much store by material things. But *things* were what sprang to mind when he asked himself why he didn't want to live the mammoth-herders' life for the rest of his days. Books. Beds. Linen. Bread. Ale. Beer. Wine. Mead. Even the language he'd known from his cradle was a *thing* of sorts. He could get along in the Bizogot tongue—he could, indeed, do better than get along—but it wasn't his, and never would be. He laughed a little when he thought of tobacco. It was Ulric's vice, not his; he'd smoked only enough to convince himself he didn't want more. But the herb came up to Raumsdalia from the south, and it hardly ever came any farther north. The only Bizogots who used it were men who'd learned the habit in the Empire. But never having the *chance* to smoke again . . . That seemed a bigger thing.

How much would he miss the society of his fellow Raumsdalians? Not much, not most of the time; he was honest enough to own up to that. But, most of the time, he stayed in his castle, and his countrymen had the courtesy to leave him the demon alone. Escaping the Bizogots if he came north to live would be much harder. It might well prove impossible. For all the vast plains they roamed, the barbarians lived in clumps and knots of people, especially in winter. If they were going to survive, they had to. Hamnet Thyssen imagined himself cooped up with a tentful of nomads for months on end. The picture didn't want to form. The more he thought about it, the less that surprised him.

He sighed. "You have your place; I have mine. Maybe you wouldn't fit in mine. I don't know if that's so, but I can see how it might be. But I'm sure I would never make a Bizogot. I need to be by myself too much."

He wondered if that would make any sense to her. To his relief, and a little to his surprise, she nodded at once. "Yes, I saw as much when we traveled," she said. "Few Bizogots have such a need. Is it common in your folk?"

"Not very," Hamnet admitted. Liv nodded again; all the other Raumsdalians up here, even hapless Audun Gilli and scholarly Eyvind Torfinn, were more outgoing than he. He continued, "But what others of my folk feel is not the problem. What *I* feel is."

"You seem to want *my* company." Liv didn't mean only that he wanted to sleep with her, though that was in her voice, too.

And now Hamnet Thyssen nodded. "I do," he said. "Aside from *that*"—he wasn't going to deny it was there; he hardly could, things being as they were—"I like talking with you. And one of the reasons I like talking with you is that you don't feel as if you have to talk all the time. You . . ." He groped for words. "You keep quiet in a pleasant tone of voice."

He waited. That would have said what he wanted to say in Raumsdalian. He wasn't so sure it did in the Bizogot language. When Liv smiled, so did he, in relief. "I thank you," she said. "I'm not sure I ever got higher praise."

Now Hamnet wasn't sure whether she was sincere or sarcastic. "I meant it for such."

She smiled again. "I know you did. Bizogots *do* live in each other's pockets, don't we? We can't help it, you know. If we didn't help each other all the time, if we didn't stay close so we could help each other, we couldn't live up here at all."

"No, I suppose not," Hamnet said. "Now I've seen how you live. Don't you want to come down to the Empire and find out what life is like there? You wouldn't have to stay. I don't think I'll stay forever myself." He drummed his fingers on the outside of his thigh. "I don't think the Rulers will let me peacefully stay there."

Liv bit her lip. "Part of me would like to, but . . . I don't know. It's a far country, far away and very strange."

"You went through the Gap. You went beyond the Glacier." Hamnet gestured toward the towering ice mountains that shaped the northern horizon. "After that, what is the journey to the Empire? A stroll, a nothing. The way south gets easier, not harder."

She shook her head. "The travel might not be hard. The travel probably isn't hard. But when I went beyond the Glacier, I was still myself. What would I be when I came to the Empire? Nothing but a barbarian." She spoke the last word in the Raumsdalian she was slowly learning.

"If anyone calls you a barbarian, turn him into a lemming," Hamnet Thyssen said. "That will teach the next fool to mind his manners. Or if it doesn't, he's a big enough fool to deserve being a lemming."

"You don't understand." Liv sounded almost desperate. "Chances are no one will call me a barbarian to my face. You people don't come out and say the things you think the way we do. But you think them whether you say them or not—and what can I do about that?"

Count Hamnet grunted. She wasn't wrong. Raumsdalians did think Bizogots were barbarians. He thought so himself. He had good reasons for thinking so. He also had good reasons for making exceptions now and again—as with this shaman with tears standing in her eyes. Would his countrymen make those kinds of exceptions? He feared not.

And what he feared must have shown on his face, for Liv said, "You see? It would be the way I told you." She started to turn away, then looked back at him in angry defiance. "Give me one good reason why I should go down to the Empire. A *good* reason, I tell you."

She was afraid. He could see that, but for a moment he could find no reasons anyhow, not reasons of the kind she meant. Then he did—and in finding one he discovered Liv was not the only one who could be afraid on this cold autumn morning. If he told her what the reason was . . . But he would lose her if he didn't. He could see that.

Even so, his heard pounded like a kettledrum in his chest as he answered, "Because I love you."

Her eyes widened. Maybe she had some small idea of how hard that was for him to say. She couldn't possibly know all of it, not unless she knew everything about him and Gudrid. Even not knowing everything, she said, "You look as if that was harder than going into battle."

"Maybe it was," Hamnet said.

"How could it be?"

"In a battle, all they can do is kill you. If you love someone and it goes wrong, you spend years wishing you were dead." Hamnet knew how true *that* was.

"You mean it," Liv said, wonder in her voice.

"I usually mean what I say," he answered. "I meant what I said when I told you I loved you, too. And I meant what I said when I told you I wanted you to come down to the Empire with me. Will you?"

"I don't know," she said, which made him want to shout in frustration. He made himself keep quiet; if he pushed too hard, he would push her away. He could feel that. Instead of pushing, he waited. Slowly, she went on, "But I don't see how I can say no, not with things the way they are, not when I love you, too."

"Ah," he said—a small sound, one that didn't come close to showing how his heart exploded in rainbow delight.

Liv's nod was altogether serious. "Yes," she said. "I do. And because I do, it seems only right I should go south. You've seen how Bizogots live. I should at least see your way, too." She made it sound only reasonable. Hamnet was much too glad to care how it sounded.

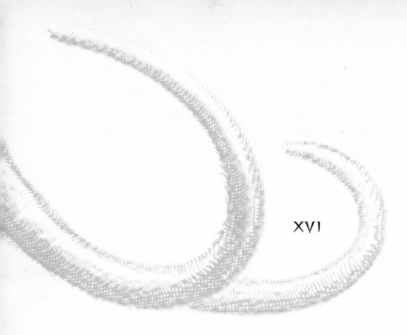

XVI

Setting out across the broad plains of the Bizogot country with winter's frozen fingers gripping tighter every day should have chilled Hamnet's heart. It should have, but it didn't.

Snow and sleet and likely hunger and Bizogots who couldn't stand Raumsdalians or the Three Tusk clan or both at once? Hamnet Thyssen didn't worry. Not worrying felt strange, unnatural, almost perverse. All the same, he didn't. He was with someone who mattered to him more than all the possible worries put together.

"I hardly know you with that smile on your face," Ulric Skakki said.

"Ah, well," said Hamnet, who hardly knew himself. "With this smile on my face, I hardly know you, either."

"What's that supposed to mean?" Ulric asked.

"Just what it said, and not a bit more," Count Hamnet answered. Ulric Skakki rode off shaking his head, which suited Hamnet fine.

Gudrid left him alone at the start of the journey south from the Three Tusk clan's encampment, which suited him fine. He waited for her to try to find some way to make him less happy, as she'd done whenever she caught him smiling after she left him.

He'd always stolidly pretended not to care about her, never with much success. Now, though, he truly didn't, an armor he'd never enjoyed before. He was tempted to flaunt his happiness with Liv to get Gudrid's goat.

He wouldn't have minded revenge; Gudrid had put him through too much to leave him immune to its charms. But what he wanted even more was freedom from the hooks she'd set in his soul. She'd been harder to break away from than poppy juice, mostly because he'd always wanted her back more than he'd wanted her to go away and leave him alone.

She couldn't go away now, not till they got back to Nidaros. She could keep on leaving him alone, though. He wanted no more from her—and no less.

But not long after he found what he wanted, Gudrid suddenly decided she couldn't stay away from him. It would have been funny . . . if he didn't have so much trouble keeping his hand off the hilt of his sword.

She guided her horse alongside his as they rode south. When he made as if to steer his mount away from her, she stayed with him. "So slumming makes you happy, does it?" she asked.

He looked at her—looked through her, really. "No, I didn't end up happy with you," he replied.

Gudrid laughed. "If you were half as funny as you think you are, you'd be twice as funny as you really are."

"If you don't care for my conversation, you're welcome to find someone else to annoy," Hamnet Thyssen said.

"Here I try to give you good advice, and this is the thanks I get." Gudrid sounded convincingly wounded—but not convincingly enough.

"The only good advice you'd give me is which poison to take and how to jump off a cliff," Count Hamnet said.

"Oh, I expect you can figure out that sort of thing for yourself." Gudrid pulled off a mitten for a moment so she could flutter her fingers at him. "You're clever about matters like that. It's people you have trouble with."

"No doubt," Hamnet Thyssen said. "Look how long I put up with you."

"Just so," Gudrid said placidly as she returned the mitten to her hand. "What makes you think you'll do any better this time around?"

"Well, I could scarcely do worse, could I?" Hamnet said.

"You never know, not till it happens."

"I'll take my chances," Hamnet said. "Why don't you go back to telling Eyvind Torfinn what to do? He's your sport these days, isn't he?"

"You're more amusing, though. It's harder to make him angry."

"I'm sure you could manage if you set your mind—or something—to it."

"Meow," she said. "Jealousy doesn't become you."

"I'm not jealous of Eyvind Torfinn." Hamnet listened to himself. It was true. He *wasn't* jealous. It so surprised him, he said it again: "I'm *not* jealous of Eyvind Torfinn, by God. If he wants you so much, he's welcome to you."

Gudrid stared. She must have heard the conviction in his voice, and it must have surprised her as much as it surprised him. She yanked hard at her horse's reins. The luckless beast snorted as she jerked its head away and rode off.

Hamnet Thyssen went on alone for some little while after that. For the time being, he was free from the longing for what once had been. He wasn't sure she entirely believed that, even now, but she would surely begin to suspect it might be so. And when she decided it was . . . What would she do then?

WHENEVER THE TRAVELERS met other Bizogot clans, Trasamund would go on—and on, and on—about their wanderings beyond the Glacier. He'd come with them precisely so he could speak with each clan's jarl as an equal. He talked about the Rulers, and about the way they rode mammoths. That always made the Bizogots, chieftains and clansmen, sit up and take notice. Everyone who heard about it seemed wild to try it. "Why didn't we think of that?" was a refrain Count Hamnet heard over and over again.

Then Trasamund would talk about how the Bizogot clans needed to band together against the invasion that was bound to come before long. Every other jarl who heard that would smile and nod politely, and then would go on with whatever he'd been doing before Trasamund raised the point. Riding mammoths interested the Bizogots. Taking steps against what hadn't happened yet . . . didn't.

"What's wrong with them?" Trasamund growled when yet another jarl refused to get excited about the threat.

"I can tell you, your Ferocity," Ulric Skakki said. "And I can tell you something else—you won't like it."

"Try me." Trasamund turned it into a challenge.

"Suppose a jarl from near the border with Raumsdalia came up to the Three Tusks country and told you the Empire was going to invade his grazing lands when spring came. What would you do about it?"

The jarl frowned. "Me? Probably not much, not by my lonesome. It's a long way off, and . . ." His voice trailed away. He sent Ulric Skakki a perfectly poisonous glare. "You have a nasty way of making your point."

"Ah, God bless you, your Ferocity. You say the sweetest things," Ulric crooned. Trasamund muttered into his beard. Not for the first time, Ulric's gratitude for things that weren't meant as compliments succeeded in confusing the person who'd aimed the unpleasantry his way.

"He's right, I'm afraid," Hamnet Thyssen said gloomily. "When the

Rulers bump up against these clans, they'll worry about them. Till then, folk from the far side of the Glacier don't seem real to them."

"But they ought to," Trasamund said. "You Raumsdalians can see the problem even though it isn't right on top of you."

"Well, we've gone beyond the Glacier, too," Hamnet said. "We *hope* the Emperor will see it. But you need to remember—" He broke off, not wanting to offend the jarl.

"Remember what?" Trasamund asked. "What, by God?"

Hamnet Thyssen knew he needed to pick his words with care. What he meant was that the Bizogots were nothing but barbarians, and so of course they didn't worry much about what would happen in a few months. No matter what he meant, he didn't want to say that. For one thing, it *would* anger Trasamund. For another, he had no guarantee that the future meant anything more to Sigvat II than it did to a fleabitten mammoth-herder.

He scratched. Plenty of fleas had bitten him, too. How he looked forward to a long soak and, best of all, to clean clothes!

He still had to answer Trasamund, who waited impatiently. "You need to remember, the Rulers will seem less real to the Emperor than even to your own folk. Nidaros is much farther away from the Gap than your camps are."

"And so the Raumsdalians will try to use the Bizogots as a shield, the way they bribe the southern clans now to help hold out the fiercer men from the north." Trasamund thumped his own chest with a big, hard fist, reminding Count Hamnet he was one of those fiercer men himself.

"How can you imagine we would do such a thing?" Hamnet said, as innocently as he could.

The Bizogot jarl laughed in his face. "By God, your Grace, I would if I lived in Sigvat's palace. We are mammoth-herders—you think you can get away with being Bizogot-herders. But there is a difference. The mammoths don't know what we're doing to them. Bizogots aren't blind men, or deaf men, either. Sooner or later, you Raumsdalians will be sorry."

He was likely to be right. No, he was bound to be right. Once upon a time, back in the days when history and legend blurred together, the Raumsdalians had roamed the frozen steppe (in those days, it ran much farther south than it did now). Hamnet Thyssen's distant ancestors had torn the meat from the bones of the empire that preceded Raumsdalia. One of these days, maybe the Bizogots would storm Nidaros and set up their own kingdom on its ruins.

Or maybe the Rulers would swarm down through the Gap and beat the

Bizogots to the punch. Hamnet Thyssen didn't know that the barbarians from the far side of the Glacier could do any such thing. He didn't know they could, no. But he didn't know they couldn't, either, and that worried him.

"*I* can see that the Rulers are a danger," Trasamund said. "If Sigvat II can't, maybe he doesn't deserve to be Emperor anymore. Maybe something will happen so he isn't. One thing God does—he makes sure fools pay for their folly."

"Well, you're right about that." Hamnet wasn't thinking about Sigvat and the Rulers.

"Liv . . . likes you." Now Trasamund spoke hesitantly. Even a jarl took care talking about a shaman.

"Yes," Hamnet said. "I like her, too."

"Be careful with her. I don't want her hurt. She isn't just a good shaman. She's a good Bizogot, and a good woman, too."

"If she weren't a good woman, I wouldn't like her the way I do." Hamnet Thyssen hoped that was true.

"If you were a Bizogot . . ." Trasamund's voice trailed off. A moment later, he tried again, saying, "If you were a *Three Tusk* Bizogot . . ."

"I'm not," Hamnet said. "I'm never going to be. You know that as well as I do, your Ferocity. I don't expect Liv to turn into a Raumsdalian. That won't happen either. I know it."

"I should say not. But she would lose something if she turned into one of your folk. You would gain something if you turned into a Bizogot."

"My folk would say it the other way around, you know," Count Hamnet said. Trasamund laughed uproariously. He thought that was the funniest thing in the world. Hamnet Thyssen had known he would. If barbarians recognized that they were barbarians, they wouldn't be so barbarous any more.

He, of course, was right and full of reason when he declined to think about becoming a Bizogot. That was as plain as the nose on his face. At the moment, the nose on his face had a muffler over it, to keep the blizzards from freezing it off him. He rode on toward the south, but winter rode ahead of him.

IN SPRING, SUDERTORP Lake had been a marvelous place, full of ducks and geese and swans and waders and shore scuttlers—every manner of bird that lived in or near the water seemed to want to breed in the bushes and marshes and reeds that lined the immense meltwater lake. In winter, though . . . Hamnet Thyssen had never seen Sudertorp Lake in the wintertime before. He was sorry to see it now.

Under a gray sky, the water and ice of Sudertorp Lake in winter were the color of phlegm. The north wind—the Breath of God—whipped the water to waves and whitecaps that tossed sullenly . . . where they could. Toward the shore, the surface of the lake was frozen. Count Hamnet supposed the ice would advance across the water till the turning of the sun made it retreat once more.

Right now, that turning looked a long way off, a long, long way indeed.

The bushes and reeds and rushes were yellow and brown and dead. The turning of the sun would also bring them back to life, but that seemed likelier to be legend than truth. Hamnet would have been sure of it if he hadn't come through here in the springtime.

In spring, the Leaping Lynx clan camped by the eastern shore of Sudertorp Lake. The Bizogots of that clan lived off the fat of the land then. So many birds bred and foraged here, a clan's worth of hunting mattered no more to them than a mosquito bite to a man.

In winter, though, the Leaping Lynxes' lakeside houses stood empty. The Bizogots had to go forth and follow their herds and flocks like any other clan. Trasamund surveyed the empty stone buildings with a certain somber satisfaction. "Serves them right—you know what I mean?" he said. "In the springtime, Riccimir gets above himself. He might as well be a Raumsdalian."

"A Raumsdalian?" Ulric Skakki said.

"That's right." Trasamund nodded. "He doesn't have to move around so much, so he thinks he's better than the people who do."

"If I thought not moving around made me better, would I have gone beyond the Glacier?" Ulric asked. "Twice?" he asked to himself.

"But you are a man of sense," the Bizogot jarl said. "Riccimir is an overstuffed mammoth turd."

"What does he call you?" Hamnet Thyssen asked.

"Who cares?" Trasamund answered, which might have meant he truly didn't care or might have meant he couldn't see the boot might fit on the other foot as well. Hamnet would have bet on the latter; Trasamund was better at seeing other people's weaknesses than at noting his own.

The travelers came upon the Leaping Lynxes' winter encampment, their wandering encampment, a day after the pause by Sudertorp Lake. It seemed like any other Bizogot camp—but, then again, it didn't. The mammoth-herders were doing the same sort of things as all their fellows did, and doing them about as well as the other Bizogots did. But every other clan

Hamnet Thyssen had seen took those labors altogether for granted. The Leaping Lynxes seemed faintly embarrassed at living in tents and following the herds. They knew another way of life. They not only knew it, they preferred it.

When Riccimir gave his guests roasted musk-ox meat, he said, "It's not fat goose, my friends, but it's what we have."

"Nothing wrong with musk ox," Trasamund said, his lips shiny with grease.

"Nothing wrong with it, no," the jarl of the Leaping Lynxes agreed. "But it's not as fine a flesh as waterfowl. I'm not just speaking of geese, mind you, though they're common and they're easy to take. But when you eat snipe and woodcock through the fat season of the year, you aren't so happy with the leaner days." He shrugged broad shoulders. "It can't be helped. I know it can't be helped—it's the way God made things work for us. But I wish it were different, and I don't know a Leaping Lynx who doesn't."

"You like living soft," Trasamund said, without rancor. Hamnet Thyssen wouldn't have put it that way. He would have said the Leaping Lynxes took advantage of their springtime abundance. Maybe those amounted to the same thing. He wasn't sure, and he would have bet Trasamund wasn't, either.

As for Riccimir, he replied, "What if we do? You'd live the way we do, too, if only you could. Will you call me a liar?"

"No," Trasamund said. If he'd said yes, it would have meant a fight to the death. But he went on, "Be careful how soft you get, or some other clan will drive you away from Sudertorp Lake. Then you'll go back to wandering all through the year, if you're lucky enough to hold together as a clan."

"We've been attacked before," Riccimir said. "We still hold our lands. Anyone who ever tried to take them came to grief. What does that tell you?"

"That you've done what you needed to do—so far," Trasamund said. "But you have to win every single time. If you lose even once, you're ruined."

"And for which Bizogot clan isn't that so?" Riccimir said. Trasamund had no answer for him.

Neither did Hamnet Thyssen. What Riccimir said spoke of the differences between the Bizogots and the Raumsdalian Empire. The riches of Sudertorp Lake in springtime let the Leaping Lynx clan approach civilization, but it *was* still as vulnerable as any other clan. One defeat meant disaster. The Empire could draw upon more resources. Losing one fight wouldn't—or wouldn't have to—mean collapse for it.

What about the Rulers? Hamnet wondered. *How much in the way of failure can they stand?* Before too long, he worried that he would find out.

DOWN TOWARD THE tree line, where the frozen plains ended and forests began, the Bizogots yielded to the Raumsdalian Empire. Hamnet Thyssen knew how tenuous Raumsdalian rule over the northern part of the Empire was. In the north, everything was tenuous; there wasn't enough food and weren't enough people to make life as relatively safe and secure and rich as it was down by Nidaros.

Trasamund kept looking back over his shoulder and shaking his head. Even when the weather was clear, the Glacier had fallen below the horizon. "Doesn't seem natural," he said. "The north looks naked."

The cold wind that blew down from the Glacier left Hamnet Thyssen in no doubt that it hadn't gone away. He said as much, adding, "It won't, either, not for many, many generations."

"Even to think that it might one day is as strange as thinking God might get old and die," Trasamund said.

Eyvind Torfinn rode close enough to hear him. "Some men in the Empire have been known to wonder about that, your Ferocity," he said. "They argue that everything else grows old and dies, that even the Glacier is falling back and may leave us one day, so why should the same not hold true for God?"

"Really?" Trasamund said. "What do you do with men who ask things like that?"

"Yes, what?" Hamnet Thyssen echoed. "I don't remember hearing about men with those ideas, and I'd think it would kick up a scandal."

"It did," Earl Eyvind answered. "This was about a hundred and twenty years ago, you understand, in the reign of Palnir I. If I remember rightly, one of the philosophers got fifty lashes, the other two got twenty-five apiece, and they were all exiled to a town in the far southwest, where they could watch ground sloths and glyptodonts and hope the Manches didn't nip in and cut their throats."

"I'm surprised they got away with their lives," Hamnet said.

"Palnir had a name for being merciful," Eyvind Torfinn said. "He told them he wouldn't kill them himself—he would leave that to God."

"You Raumsdalians are softer than the Leaping Lynxes," Trasamund said. "But what's a glyptodont?"

"Do you know what an armadillo is?" Hamnet Thyssen said. The Bizogot shook his head. Hamnet wasn't surprised; armadillos and their bigger cousins liked warm weather and didn't come up anywhere near Nidaros. He went on, "Imagine a pot with a long handle. Turn it upside down. Make the handle its tail—sort of a bony club. Give it a head and four short legs, also armored in bone. Make it ten feet long from nose to tailtip, and three or four feet high. It's not very bright, and it only eats plants, but a sabertooth will break his fangs before he can puncture it."

"You're having me on," Trasamund said. "That's the craziest beast I ever heard of."

"No, he's telling the truth," Eyvind Torfinn said.

"I don't believe it," Trasamund said stubbornly. "You figure you've got a fool of a Bizogot here, and you think you can tell him funny stories and have a laugh afterward."

"Go ask Ulric if you don't believe me," Hamnet said.

The Bizogot jarl shook his head again. "Not me. You probably all cooked it up amongst yourselves beforehand." He rode away, his head still going back and forth. Not much later, though, Hamnet watched him riding along next to Jesper Fletti. Trasamund might have thought Hamnet wouldn't conspire with Gudrid's chief bodyguard—and if he did, he was right. By Jesper's gestures, he knew what a glyptodont was. Trasamund threw his hands in the air.

Hamnet Thyssen began looking for border stations. They were thinly scattered, and wouldn't have been easy to spot if not for the smoke that rose from them all through the winter. A lot of Bizogots skirted the stations when they came down into the Empire. Some succeeded in smuggling their goods or themselves into Raumsdalia. Others ran into customs inspectors in the small northern towns and paid duty there.

A smoke plume led the travelers to a border post. The guards wore furs that made them look like Bizogots. One of them stared at the newcomers and said, "If you're not the raggediest-looking bunch of buggers I've ever seen, bugger me with a pine cone if I can think of who is."

"If you're not a disgrace to the uniform you aren't wearing, God's more merciful than I thought," Hamnet Thyssen retorted.

Hearing unaccented, educated, angry Raumsdalian burst from the mouth of the shaggy ragamuffin in front of him gave the border guard pause. "Uh, who are you, anyway?" he asked, his own voice suddenly much less scornful.

"You might have wondered sooner. I am Count Hamnet Thyssen. With my companions here, I've traveled beyond the Glacier, and I have come back to tell the tale—but to the Emperor, not to the likes of you."

The guard's jaw dropped. "You're the people who went beyond the Glacier? You really did?" He turned to his comrades. "God let them come back, Vigfus!"

"Somebody did, anyhow," Vigfus allowed. "Or so they say. Do you suppose we ought to believe 'em?"

"If you do not believe Trasamund, jarl of the Three Tusk clan of Bizogots, God may not punish you," Trasamund said. "God may not, but I will." He made as if to draw his great two-handed sword. "Do you call me a liar? Who will mourn for you when you die? Anyone? Or will your flesh feed foxes and teratorns?"

"Keep your hair on, pal," said Vigfus, who'd surely heard Bizogot bluster before. "If you really made it through the Gap, more power to you."

"We were supposed to keep an eye out for you people, but I never figured you'd come through here," the other guard said. "What are the odds?"

"Whatever the odds may be, here we are," Eyvind Torfinn said. "We have done much, we have traveled far, and we have seen strange things. His Majesty Sigvat II needs to hear of them as soon as we get to Nidaros."

Vigfus and his friend looked at each other. At the same time, they asked, "Did you find the Golden Shrine?"

"Well, no," Eyvind Torfinn answered. "But that doesn't mean it isn't there. We'll go back one day, and maybe we'll find it then."

"We did find white bears, and deer that men ride like horses, and beasts like lions, only without manes and with stripes," Hamnet said.

"And we found men who ride mammoths," Trasamund said. "By God, I will ride a mammoth before too much time goes by. I *will*." He folded his right hand into a fist and brought it down hard on his thigh.

"Men who *ride* mammoths?" said the guard whose name they didn't know. "Are they very brave or very stupid?"

"Yes," answered Ulric Skakki, who'd kept quiet till then.

"What's that supposed to mean?" the guard asked.

"What it says," Ulric told him. "I'm like Count Hamnet here—I usually say what I mean. People have a better chance of understanding me when I do. The Rulers are very brave. And, by God, they're very stupid, too."

"The Rulers? What kind of name is that?" Vigfus said.

Hamnet Thyssen, Ulric Skakki, Eyvind Torfinn, and Trasamund all shrugged together. "It's what they call themselves, or how they say it when they use the Bizogot language," Hamnet said. "I don't know what you want us to do about it."

Gudrid rode up to the guards. "Why are you wasting our time here?" she demanded. "Why don't you let us go back to civilization?"

Vigfus looked at her. It wasn't the way a man looked at a pretty woman. With half a year's grime on them, none of the travelers was pretty any more. "Who the demon does she think she is?" the border guard asked no one in particular.

"She thinks she's my wife," Eyvind Torfinn said. "She's right, too." Did Gudrid think that? Hamnet had his doubts. When she felt like it, maybe she did.

"Huh!" Vigfus said. "She's a mouthy one, she is. You should belt her more often, teach her to behave."

Gudrid's squeal was pure rage. "You are speaking to, and of, an earl's wife!" she said shrilly. "Show the proper respect!"

"Oh, shut up," Vigfus said. Gudrid's jaw dropped; that wasn't what she'd had in mind. She was used to getting her way with men with a wave of the hand and a wink of the eye. Not here, not now. Vigfus went on, "I'm a guard at the most godforsaken post in the Empire. What can you do to me that's worse? Send me to prison somewhere farther south? I'll get down on my knees and kiss your hand, or whatever else you want kissed, if you do. But the way things are, I'll talk however I cursed well please."

She stared at him. Some men in the Empire were strong enough to take no notice when she said something. She'd never imagined a man who could be weak enough to do the same thing, and neither had Hamnet Thyssen.

"May we pass on?" he asked.

Simple respect was the only thing the guards were looking for. "Yes, your Grace," replied the one who wasn't named Vigfus. "Pass on to the south. Tell the folk there what you've told us. See if they believe you any more than we do."

With that less than ringing endorsement, Hamnet did ride south with the rest of the travelers. Once they got out of earshot of the border post, Ulric Skakki said, "By now, I hardly care whether I tell the Emperor what we've seen or not. All I care about is finding a town with a bathhouse. Did you see those guards? Some time not too long ago, they had baths. Both of them! Isn't that something?" He scratched.

As usual, that made Hamnet scratch, too. How many different kinds of bugs was he carrying around on his person and in his clothes? Too many—he was sure of that.

Liv stared at the firs and spruces through which they rode. "So big," she murmured in an awestruck voice. "Are they really alive?"

"They really are," Hamnet assured her, his voice grave. "We make things from the wood, and we use it for fires instead of dung."

"Yes, I can see how you might. So much of it in each tree, there for the taking," the Bizogot shaman said. "Truly this is a rich land."

Hamnet Thyssen's jaw dropped. These northern provinces were heartbreakingly poor—backbreakingly poor, too, if you had to try to claw a living from them. Woodsmen and trappers were almost the only people who could. He eyed Liv with something that went deeper than astonishment, because what she said spoke volumes about how different they were. In her eyes, this miserable country seemed rich beyond compare.

And why wouldn't it? Summer here probably lasted six weeks longer than it did up where she lived, hard by the Glacier. The ground wasn't permanently frozen. Liv had never seen a tree before in all her life. A land warm enough to let them grow . . . was a land richer than any the Bizogots inhabited.

Realizing that almost left Hamnet embarrassed to be a Raumsdalian. How much his own folk took for granted! They sneered at the Bizogots for all the things the mammoth-herders lacked. But that wasn't the Bizogots' fault; it was the fault of the country in which they lived.

The Rulers lived even farther north than the Bizogots. Hamnet had seen that they used iron. Did they forge it themselves, or did they get it in trade from some unknown land far to the west and south, as the Bizogots got it from the Empire? Hamnet didn't know—by the nature of things, how could he? But he was sure of one thing. If the Rulers reached Raumsdalian territory, even these hardscrabble provinces along the northern border, they would think the land was as rich as Liv did.

That wasn't good news, not as far as Raumsdalia was concerned.

Up in a tree, a blue jay screeched at the travelers. "What makes that noise?" Liv asked.

"A jay." Hamnet Thyssen pointed up to it. The bird didn't like that—maybe it thought his outstretched arm and hand were an arrow aimed its way. Screeching still, it flapped off to another fir farther away.

Liv laughed and clapped her mittened hands. "It's a piece of the sky with wings!" she exclaimed. "I've never seen anything so pretty. How many other birds do you have that we never see up by the Glacier?"

"How many? I don't know. Earl Eyvind might be able to tell you, or one of the savants down in Nidaros," Hamnet answered. "But there are lots of them. Jays, warblers, orioles, woodpeckers . . ."

They were only names to Liv. "Woodpeckers?" she echoed uncertainly. Count Hamnet translated the word into the Bizogot tongue. Then he told how they pounded their bills into trees, going after insects and grubs. Liv laughed when he finished. "You're making that up," she said, as Trasamund had when he heard about glyptodonts. "You're telling me a story because I don't know any better, the way we might talk about a musk ox with a trunk if we were making sport of a Raumsdalian who thought he knew it all."

"It's not a story—it's the truth," Hamnet said. "By God, it is. Ask any other Raumsdalian you please. Ask your jarl—chances are he's seen them, or maybe heard them drumming."

"Drumming." Liv repeated that, too. "Why don't their heads fall off from all that banging, if they do what you say they do?"

"I don't know." Count Hamnet had never worried about it. "And we have bats, too, though not this far north. Think of a vole or a lemming. Give it big ears and sharp teeth and wings that are all bare skin—no feathers or anything. That's what bats are. They hunt at night, and they eat bugs."

"Next you'll probably tell me you have things that live in the rivers but aren't fish," Liv said with a scornful sniff.

"We do." Hamnet talked about frogs. He talked about turtles. He talked about alligators and crocodiles, finishing, "Those live only in the far south. There are probably a few alligators in the southern part of the Empire, but not many."

Liv eyed him. "You aren't making these things up."

"No, I'm not. By God, I'm not," Hamnet Thyssen said. "We have lots of creatures you don't, because your winters would kill them." He talked about toads and salamanders. He talked about lizards. He talked about snakes. This time, he finished, "Some of them have poisonous fangs. If they bite you, it can kill. If it doesn't, it will make you very sick."

He wondered if she would think he was lying about those. Her face thoughtful, she said, "A trader from the Empire came up to the Three Tusk country a few years ago and talked about creatures like those. We all thought he was the biggest liar in the world, even if we didn't say so."

"Why didn't you?" Hamnet asked. "You Bizogots are quick enough to call Raumsdalians liars most of the time."

Liv wrinkled her nose at him. "Well, a lot of the time you *are* liars. But no, we didn't call him on his stories. They were new to us, and they helped make the time go by. We didn't believe them? So what? We still enjoyed them."

"Fair enough, I suppose," Hamnet said with a smile of his own.

"Your Ferocity!" Liv called—Trasamund was half a bowshot ahead of her on the trail through the forest. He looked back over his shoulder and waved to show he'd heard. She booted her horse up into a trot to catch up to him. Hamnet Thyssen sped up, too. When Liv got close enough to the jarl to talk without shouting, she said, "Remember that Raumsdalian trader who told us tales about the legless things with the poison teeth?"

Trasamund threw back his head and laughed. "I'm not likely to forget him. He could spin them, couldn't he?"

"He was telling the truth," Liv said. "He must have been. Hamnet here just told me about the same creatures."

"Oh, he did, did he?" The Bizogot jarl eyed Count Hamnet. "Who's to say he's not lying through his beard, too?"

"I could tell you the chances of two men making up the same strange animal are slim," Hamnet said. "Or I could just tell you I'm not lying, and if you want to make something out of it and say I am, go ahead."

Trasamund eyed him. "You wouldn't fight over a no-account thing like a story. A Bizogot might, but a Raumsdalian wouldn't. So I suppose you *are* telling the truth. Who would have believed it? These beasts are real?"

"They are," Count Hamnet said. "Have you ever heard the phrase 'a snake in the grass'?" He shifted to his own tongue for the last few words.

"Yes. It means something sneaky and dangerous."

"That's right. Snakes crawl around in the grass, and it's easy to miss them. With the poison in their fangs, though, they can make you sorry if you do."

"Well, well." Trasamund plucked at his beard. "How many 'snakes in the grass' do you suppose we have with us?" Hamnet Thyssen found no good answer for that, in Raumsdalian or the Bizogot tongue.

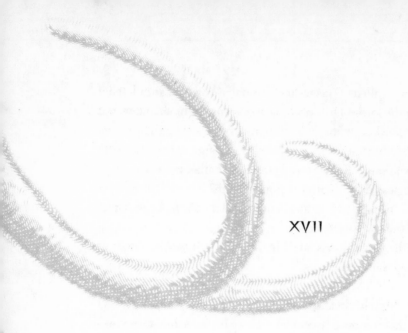

XVII

B y the standards of Nidaros, the hostel in the northern town of Naestved would have been third-rate at best. But even a third-rate hostel boasted a bathhouse. A big, hot fire blazed in a hearth near the two copper tubs that sat side by side. The travelers rolled dice for the order in which they would bathe. Hamnet Thyssen and Ulric Skakki had to wait far into the night. Hamnet didn't care.

Neither did Ulric. "Did you hear the landlord squawk about how much water he'd have to heat?" he said, and then ducked himself and scrubbed at his hair. He came up blowing like one of the whales seacoast people talked about. "The poor dear."

"You'd think we weren't paying for the wood," Hamnet Thyssen said, doing some scrubbing of his own. The steaming bathwater had been clean when he stepped into his tub. It wasn't clean any more. It was grayish brown and scummed with soapsuds. His own skin, by contrast, was getting toward the color he remembered its being once upon a time.

"Oh, but we're making his servants work for their living. They don't like it any better than anybody else would." As usual, Ulric Skakki had enough cynicism for two or three ordinary people.

"I want to wallow here for the next week," Hamnet said. "This is almost as wonderful as I thought it would be." Only two things separated him from perfect bliss. For one thing, the soap the landlord gave them was harsh and strong-smelling. For another . . .

Ulric leered at him. "You wish Liv were in this tub instead of me. Or more likely you wish she were in that tub along with you."

Hamnet's ears heated. That was exactly what he wished. He wondered if Liv had ever had a real bath before. He doubted it. Among the Bizogots, hot water, except for cooking, was hard to come by. They washed their hands and faces. Sometimes they steamed themselves, pouring water onto fire-heated stones. But he was sure they'd never heard of bathtubs.

She would have to bathe with Gudrid. That filled Hamnet with misgivings. Gudrid might try to lead Liv astray for the fun of it. But if Liv watched what Gudrid did herself, she wouldn't go far wrong.

"These tubs are narrow to fit two," Ulric went on. "Of course, if you fit one on top of the other . . ."

"Oh, shut up," Hamnet told him.

This time, Ulric didn't leer. He just grinned—he'd wanted to get under Hamnet's skin, and he'd done it. "Down in Nidaros," he said, "they make tubs a little wider, because they know people will want to sport in them."

"Do they?" Hamnet said. "And is this something you've heard, or have you tried it for yourself?"

"Oh, I've tried it," Ulric Skakki said cheerfully. "Doing things is a lot more fun than talking about them. Some people will tell you the opposite, but they're liars—or if they're not, I'm sorry for them."

"Doing *some* things is more fun than talking about them," Hamnet said. "I'd sooner talk about lice and fleas and bedbugs than deal with them in person." He looked at the specks floating in his bathwater. How many of them were drowned bugs? Too many—he was sure of that. Had he killed them all? He was just as sorrowfully sure he hadn't.

"Have to take the bad with the good." Ulric's shrug made water slosh out of his tub. "Not everyone sees that." He paused. "Sometimes I think hardly anyone sees that."

"Everyone sees why the other fellow needs to take the bad with the good," Hamnet Thyssen said. "Why he needs to do it himself . . . That's a different story."

Somebody banged on the bathhouse door. "Haven't you two turned into prunes yet?" Jesper Fletti called through the spruce planks. Almost all the wood up here was fir and spruce, drawn from the enormous northern forests. "Some of the rest of us want to see what color we really are, too," Jesper added.

"All right. All right. We'll get out," Ulric said regretfully. Under his breath, he went on, "Talk about taking the bad with the good."

"Or after the good, anyhow." Hamnet sighed as he got out of the tub. The water was starting to get cold, but it hadn't got there yet. In spite of the fire roaring in the hearth, the air in the bathhouse was chilly. He went and stood in front of the flames to dry off and warm up. Ulric Skakki stood beside him. Hamnet was the bigger man, but saying which of them was harder wouldn't have been easy. Hamnet eyed Ulric's scars. "You've been in a scrape or three, haven't you?"

"Oh, you might say so." Ulric Skakki surveyed Hamnet's hairy arms and torso. "Now that you mention it, so have you."

"The other fellows will fight back now and again," Hamnet said. "Treacherous dogs, but what can you do?"

"Kill 'em fast, before they have the chance to do anything to you," Ulric answered.

"Good advice. Anyone would know you were a fighting man." Hamnet ran a comb through his hair and beard. Then he stared at the bone tool. "I hope it's not covered with nits. If it is . . ."

"If it is, you'll know about it before long." Ulric, who was also combing himself, paused to mime scratching. "At least we can bathe now. That will help. And if we soak our hair in oil, that will help more."

"I suppose so." Count Hamnet put on a robe the landlord swore was pest-free. Ulric Skakki donned another one. The Bizogot-style clothes they'd worn on their travels were being fumigated with burning sulfur. The stinking smoke would kill most of the pests the garments carried. As for the ones that survived . . . Well, now that the travelers were back in civilization, they could always fumigate the furs again. They could even get new clothes.

The Bizogots would have thought nothing of skinning and tanning hides up on the frozen steppe. Hamnet might have tried it himself in a pinch, but he was glad he hadn't had to. The mammoth-herders were bound to be better at it than he was.

When he and Ulric opened the door, Jesper Fletti and Eyvind Torfinn glowered at them. "Took you long enough," Jesper said.

"Wait till the next pair start yelling at you," Hamnet said. "And they will. They will."

"I suspect he may be right," Eyvind Torfinn said.

"I don't care if he is," Jesper Fletti said. He turned and shouted in the direction of the kitchens. "Where's that clean hot water, by God? Do you expect me to soak in somebody else's swill?"

"So charming," Ulric Skakki murmured. Hamnet Thyssen carefully didn't smile. Jesper Fletti gave Ulric a sharp look. But the bathhouse attendants came up just then, and Jesper went back to yelling at them instead. Count Hamnet thought that wise. Jesper Fletti was a large, strong, tough man. If he got into a fight with someone ordinary, he would win, and win easily. If he got into a fight with Ulric, his size and strength and toughness might keep him alive an extra half minute or so. Or, on the other hand, they might not.

Eyvind Torfinn didn't quarrel with the attendants. He eyed them as if they were the most wonderful people he'd ever met. "To be clean," he said. "I shall be clean." Hamnet Thyssen walked down the hall before Eyvind could finish the conjugation. Not that he didn't sympathize, but he already knew how the verb worked.

Next morning, he found fresh bites. In a way, that infuriated him. In another way, it showed he'd made progress. For weeks, for months, he'd been bitten so often that he hardly noticed new marks—one itch blended into another. Now he had few enough that they stood out. Maybe one day before too long, if he kept bathing and went on fumigating his clothes, he wouldn't have any. Wouldn't that be something?

FAT SNOWFLAKES FRISKED on the breeze as the travelers rode out of Naestved. Liv looked back over her shoulder, watching the palisade disappear behind them. When she sighed, the wind blew her breath, too. "Everyone talks about how rich the Empire is," she said, and sighed again. "Trasamund has come down here before, and I've listened to him go on about it. But I never imagined it could be as rich as . . . this." Her wave encompassed both the town they were leaving and the dour forest around it.

"Naestved isn't anything much," Hamnet Thyssen said truthfully.

Liv stared at him, sure he was joking. When she saw he wasn't, she sighed one more time. "I think you have so many . . . things . . . that you take them all for granted." Plainly, she chose her words with care.

"Maybe we do," Hamnet said. "Plenty of priests would be happy to tell you how right you are—you can bet on that."

What she said about priests would have horrified any of them who heard her. It made Eyvind Torfinn and Ulric Skakki whip their heads around in astonishment. "I did not mean anything that has to do with my comrades here," she went on in more moderate tones. "But you Raumsdalians do have so many things that I wonder how you can stand to do without them when you come up to the Bizogot country."

That thought had also crossed Hamnet Thyssen's mind. "A lot of us wouldn't want to," he admitted uncomfortably. "A lot of us wouldn't be able to. But things are only things. Either you own them—or they own you. If you can't do without them, they own you. I don't want to be owned, thank you very much."

"You even talk like a Bizogot," she said. "How? You say Naestved is nothing much. That means you must have seen better, though I don't know what could be finer than that. Hot water to bathe in . . . Things to put the hot water in . . ."

"Tubs," Count Hamnet said helpfully.

"Tubs," Liv repeated. "Soft things to sleep on . . ."

"Beds."

"Beds," she said. "And the food made from ground grain . . . Bread." She found the word before he gave it to her. "And the tents with wooden walls . . . Houses. So much wood everywhere. Even wood around the town to keep out enemies." She shook her head in wonder.

To keep out the Bizogots, Hamnet Thyssen thought. Here in the north, there were no other enemies. He shook his head. There hadn't been any other enemies, not till the Gap melted through. Now the Rulers would come through, come down onto the Bizogots' frozen plains—which would seem familiar enough to them—and then, if they got this far, into the Empire.

"So many things," Liv went on. "This is because you don't have to wander, to follow the herds, isn't it?"

"Partly. Maybe even mostly," Hamnet answered. "It would be hard to carry bathtubs around in a mammoth-hide tent. But also partly because the country is different. It would be hard to herd mammoths and musk oxen through the forest."

"I think so!" Liv exclaimed. "I look at these . . . trees . . . and I think they all lean toward me. I think they all want to fall on me. We go through them, and I feel they are all squeezing in on me." She gestured with her hands.

"Some Raumsdalians, when they come up into the Bizogot country, they feel the land is too big. They feel like flies walking across a plate." Hamnet Thyssen gestured, too. "They feel the land is so wide and they are so small that God has forgot them."

She laughed. "Really?" After Hamnet nodded, she asked, "Did you ever feel this way?"

He thought she expected him to say no, but he nodded again. Sure enough, she looked surprised. "On the Bizogot plains, I feel small," Count Hamnet said. "If a mammoth could think, it would feel small out on the Bizogot plains. But some of my countrymen have it worse than I do. Some of them feel as if they're about to disappear."

"How funny. How strange," Liv said. "But the forest doesn't bother them?"

"I've heard Raumsdalians say they feel crowded here," Hamnet replied. "Farther south, we have forests and fields, all mixed together. We have towns that make Naestved look like nothing beside them. We have rivers that stay unfrozen all year long—well, except in hard winters, anyhow— and we have boats that travel on them."

"We have boats," Liv said proudly. "We make them from hides, and use mammoth bones to give them their shape. We use them for fishing, and to cross streams too deep for fording."

So there, Hamnet Thyssen thought. *I'm no savage—my people can do these things, too,* Liv was saying. "Ours are bigger," he said gently. "They're mostly made of wood, because it floats on water." He felt odd saying that—how could anyone not know it? On the other hand, how *could* she know it, living so far north of the tree line? Up where the Three Tusk clan roamed, willows and birches were little shrubs, hardly taller than the middle of a man's calf. The forever frozen ground wouldn't let anything larger grow.

Her eyes went wide, so wide that he saw white all around the blue of her irises. "It floats, you say? Then you can make boats as big as you please, and they stay on top of the water?"

He'd already seen she was clever. She understood right away what things meant, even when they weren't things she'd had any reason to think about before. "We do make big boats," he said. "They carry people and goods up and down the rivers. Most of the grain trade in the Empire goes by boat, be- cause it's so much cheaper to ship by water than by land."

"Up and *down* the rivers? How do you go against the current?"

"Our boats have *sails,*" Hamnet Thyssen answered. They were mostly us- ing the Bizogot tongue, but the new word had to come out in Raumsdalian. As best he could, he explained what sails were and how they worked.

Liv's eyes widened again. "How marvelous!" she breathed. "This is one of the most wonderful sorceries I ever heard of—more marvelous than any- thing I ever imagined myself, believe me."

"If you think this is magic, then I didn't make myself plain," Count Hamnet said. "It's a craft, a skill, like tanning leather or carving bone."

"Is it? Are you sure?" Liv asked. "Suppose the wind doesn't blow the way you wish it would, the way you need it to. Won't a shaman call up a wind to take the boat where it needs to go?"

"More likely the crew will use oars, or will have horses to tow the boat upstream." Hamnet plucked at his beard. He was no wizard. He didn't know everything a spell might do. If any of the travelers did, Audun Gilli was the man. "Hi! Audun!" Hamnet called, and waved to draw the sorcerer's notice.

"What is it, your Grace?" Audun didn't seem as enthusiastic about going back to Nidaros as the rest of the Raumsdalians. Up in the Bizogot country, he'd been able to set aside the cruel memories that haunted him. Now he was returning to them again. He couldn't be looking forward to that.

"If the breeze is against him, can a wizard raise enough of his own wind to send a boat upstream?" Hamnet asked.

"Well, it depends on the boat and the wizard," Audun Gilli answered. "If it's a little sailboat and it doesn't have to go too far upstream, a lot of wizards can manage. I could do that myself, I think. If you're talking about a great wallowing barge with a couple of hundred head of cattle aboard, that's another story. Maybe a team of strong sorcerers could bring it off, but chances are there's some easier way to do it. Try that and fail, and the wizards might not be worth much afterwards."

"How much did you understand?" Hamnet asked Liv.

"Most, I think," she said in her own language, then switched to Raumsdalian to ask Audun, "Why not make better spells for such a useful thing?"

"Because most of the time, like I said, you can go upstream without using much magic," he replied. "Don't you know spells you could use, only most of the time you don't because they're more trouble than they're worth?"

That got too complicated for her to follow easily. Count Hamnet translated it into her language. She thought it over, then nodded. "Yes, there are some," she said, again in Raumsdalian. "But for something this wonderful—"

"Ah, there we have it," Hamnet Thyssen broke in. "You think boats and sails are marvelous and wonderful because they're new to you. Down in the Empire and the lands farther south yet, we've been using boats for as long as anyone can remember, and probably for longer than that. We take them as much for granted as you take mammoth-hide tents."

"How sad," Liv said in Raumsdalian.

"Sad?" Hamnet and Audun both asked at the same time.

She nodded. "Sad. Very sad. Wonders *should* be wonders. To take them for granted is to waste them. Do you take making love for granted?"

Audun Gilli shook his head. "By God, I hope not!" Hamnet said.

Liv didn't claim he did, which was a relief. She just said, "Well, then," as if she'd proved her point.

"To people who are used to them, boats aren't as important—or as wonderful—as making love," Hamnet said stubbornly. Audun Gilli coughed. Hamnet sent him an annoyed look, not least because he had a point of sorts. Men who skippered boats and men who made their living from them probably did think what happened aboard them was as important as what went on in bed. "You know what I mean," Hamnet said. Audun didn't deny it. If he had, Hamnet would have looked around for something to clout him with.

"Well, it's not worth the argument," Liv said.

Hamnet Thyssen stared at her, as surprised as if a short-faced bear had spoken to him. He'd never heard those words from Gudrid. *And what about you?* he asked himself. He'd never been known to back away from any argument. He'd kept this one going. He wondered why. Who was right and who wrong counted for nothing, not when you thought for a little while. But he hadn't. He wanted to be right, whether he was right or not.

When you got down to it, that was . . . pretty stupid. And he'd only taken forty-odd years to realize it. The really scary thing was, he was doing better than most. A lot of people went to their graves without ever figuring that out.

"No, it's not," he said, and neither Liv nor Audun Gilli had the slightest idea how much effort getting those three words past his lips took.

By Raumsdalian standards, the northern forests changed very slowly. But Liv noticed differences at once. "What are those trees with the white . . . ?" she asked, and gestured because she couldn't remember the Raumsdalian word she needed.

"Trunks," Count Hamnet supplied, and she nodded. "Those are birches," he said.

"They look like skeletons." Liv took off her mittens and raised her hands with fingers widespread. "How do they live? Where are their leaves?" The last word came out in the Bizogot language.

"They'll grow them in spring and keep them into fall," Hamnet answered. "They do that every year. The leaves fall off. They turn brown and die. Most of them are buried under the snow now."

"Why do they do that?" she asked. "It seems like a waste. The . . . the firs and the spruces keep their leaves in this time. Why not the birches, too?"

"I don't know. Maybe you'd have to ask the trees," Hamnet Thyssen said. She made a face at him. He called out to Eyvind Torfinn. "Why do birches and oaks and willows lose their leaves in the fall?"

Eyvind stared on him. "What on earth makes you think I'd know something like that?"

"Well, *I* don't, your Splendor," Count Hamnet said. "Of all the people here, I thought you had the best chance to tell me. You know all sorts of strange things."

"Not that one, I fear."

"Too bad." Hamnet Thyssen turned back to Liv. "If Earl Eyvind doesn't know, you really do need to talk to the trees."

"I wonder if I could magic out the answer." The Bizogot shaman sounded completely serious. "Use the law of similarity to compare leaf to leaf, branch to branch . . ."

Eyvind Torfinn was no wizard, but he knew a good deal about sorcery—he knew a good deal about anything that happened to catch his interest. "I don't see why you couldn't," he said, surprise and what sounded like wonder in his voice. "I don't believe anyone has ever used wizardry like that. I don't believe anyone ever thought to use wizardry like that."

"What are you going on about in that horrible language?" Gudrid asked. Most of the time, she paid as little attention to her husband as she could. Seeing him talking with Liv, though, drew her notice—and her ire.

"Deciduous and evergreen trees," Eyvind replied in Raumsdalian.

"What about them?" Gudrid still sounded suspicious.

"Why there are such things, why they're different, and how one might go about finding out through sorcery."

His wife stared at him. "You're joking."

"No. Why would I be?" Eyvind Torfinn sounded confused.

"Because if a man talks to a woman, only a sap talks about trees." Gudrid rode down the path ahead of Eyvind and Liv and Hamnet Thyssen.

"What was that all about?" Liv asked. "She talked too fast for me to follow much."

"You're lucky," Hamnet said.

"My wife has a short temper sometimes," Eyvind Torfinn said. "Once in a while, she lets it get away from her."

Hamnet Thyssen coughed a couple of times, in lieu of snorting or breaking into wild—into mad—laughter. What Earl Eyvind said was true. And the Glacier was chilly, and the sun warm, and this forest rather wide. Sometimes understatement was the most effective way to lie—even to yourself.

Did Eyvind know—did he even suspect—she was no more faithful to him than she had been to Hamnet? *I can't very well ask,* Hamnet thought. This wasn't the first time he'd wondered, though—far from it.

Usually, the man was the one who wandered, and also the one who bristled if the woman so much as looked at anybody else. Count Hamnet did laugh then, even if not in the gales he'd almost loosed a moment before. Trust Gudrid to do things backwards.

And then she screamed, and he forgot about his musings.

He didn't need to hear the short-faced bear's growling roar to guess what was wrong. The great bears haunted these northern woods, and often didn't sleep through the winter. A horse—and a woman—would be just what a hungry bear was looking for.

Gudrid screamed again. No, this time it was more of a shriek. She'd bragged about what an archer she was, but that seemed forgot now—or maybe she never had a chance to string and draw her bow.

Hamnet Thyssen yelled, too, as he rode toward her. He drew his sword—no time for him to string his bow, either. Maybe he could distract the bear, keep it from attacking. . . . He shouted once more, and laughed while he did. The world turned upside down again. More often than not, he would have been happy to see Gudrid dead. And here he was, riding to her rescue. If that wasn't insane, what was?

The short-faced bear had Gudrid's horse down. If the horse had tried to run, it didn't have much luck. Short-faced bears had longer legs than grizzlies and ordinary black bruins. A horse with a running start might escape them. But if the bear was already charging and the horse just ambling along, the bear could—and this bear had—outrun its intended prey before the horse got up to speed.

When the horse went over, Gudrid had jumped or been thrown clear. But she wasn't running. Was she paralyzed with fear, or had she hurt herself? Hamnet couldn't begin to guess. It hardly mattered. She was easier to kill than a kicking, thrashing horse. Before long, the bear would figure that out.

Hamnet Thyssen shouted at the top of his lungs. The short-faced bear ignored him. It started eating the horse before the other animal was even dead. If dinner kicked and squirmed and screamed, so what? The bear's muzzle was crimson almost to the eyes. How close to starving was it?

And if it did pay attention to Hamnet and his onrushing horse, what would it do? Run off? He hoped so. Suppose it didn't. Suppose it went for his horse—and him—instead. What would he do then? *Think of something fast,* he told himself. He'd be on the bear in another few heartbeats.

An arrow hissed past his head—someone had managed to string his bow, or perhaps was traveling with it strung. The shaft thudded into the short-faced bear's hindquarters. *That* got the beast's attention, where Hamnet's shout hadn't. The bear jumped and reared and roared again, this time in pain and surprise rather than in fury.

As it reared, he swung his sword. The stroke wasn't perfect. He'd intended to strike its muzzle and badly wound it, and all he managed to do was shear off the tip of one ear. Then his horse thundered past. He tugged hard on the reins and guided the horse around with pressure from his knees and thighs. If he had to make another pass at the bear, he would.

He didn't. Two wounds at opposite ends were more than enough for the animal. With a final snarl, it limped off into the forest again. It left a trail of blood behind. Had Hamnet wanted to hunt it down, he would have had an easy time tracking it. He was content to let it go.

"Bravely done!" Ulric Skakki called. He had an arrow nocked and ready to shoot, so Hamnet supposed he'd let fly with the first one. He didn't shoot again as the bear withdrew; like Hamnet, he thought driving it off counted for more than killing it. With a wry grin, he added, "Foolhardy, maybe, but bravely done."

Looking back on things, Hamnet thought he was foolhardy, too. But he'd got away with it. "Are you all right?" he called to Gudrid.

"That horrible monster didn't eat me, so I'm a lot better than I might be. I hurt my ankle when I went off the horse, though." She looked up at him from the snow. "You're the last person I expected to come riding up and save me."

The same thing had gone through his mind while he was booting his horse forward. Shrugging, he said, "I would have done it for anyone. I would have done it for the horse, come to that."

"Nice to know where I stand—er, sprawl," Gudrid said. "What's worse is, I believe you."

"Do you think the ankle's broken or sprained or just twisted?" Hamnet asked.

"I don't know. I think it would hurt more if it were broken, but I never broke one before, so how can I be sure?" Gudrid eyed him again. "Do you want to feel it and find out? God knows you've wanted to get your hands on me again for long enough now."

"Around your neck, maybe," Hamnet Thyssen said grimly. "Around your ankle? No, thanks. Somebody else can check." The poor horse still writhed feebly. He dismounted, bent beside it, and cut its throat—the last favor he could give it. The horse let out a sigh that sounded amazingly human and died.

Trasamund rode up. He glanced at the horse. "Well, the bear didn't get a whole lot," he said. "It can feed us now." Bizogots didn't waste much—didn't waste anything if they could help it. The jarl pointed to Gudrid. "How bad is she hurt?"

"I don't know," Hamnet answered. "Enough so she couldn't run, anyhow. Do you want to see if that ankle's broken?"

"Well, why not?" Trasamund leered. The way he prodded and tugged at Gudrid's ankle was all business, though. She gasped a couple of times, but she didn't scream or burst into tears or even swear. Trasamund looked up from his work. "I think it's sound, but she should lie on her back for a while when she—*Mmpf!*" Gudrid threw a snowball in his face.

"Serves you right, you nasty man," she said. Trasamund scrabbled at himself. Even after he got rid of some of the snow, he still looked like a frozen ghost.

Hamnet Thyssen turned away so neither Gudrid nor Trasamund would see him laugh. He still had little use for his former wife. He didn't think he ever would. But she had a point—that snowball *did* serve Trasamund right.

WHEN THEY CAME out of the northern forests, the sun was shining brightly. The weather wasn't warm, not by Hamnet's standards, but it was above freezing. Some of the snow on the ground had turned to slush. Some had even melted, exposing patches of bare black earth. They weren't on the Great North Road, but somewhere to the west of it.

Liv laughed out loud. She threw back her hood to let the sun shine on her head. "A thaw in wintertime!" she said. "Who would believe that up in Three Tusk country? Why, the Breath of God hardly blows at all here."

"When it blows, it can blow hard," Hamnet said. Liv laughed again, right in his face. He held up a hand. "Oh, it can. Believe me—it can. Not the way it will in your country at the worst, but bad enough. The difference is, it doesn't blow all the time here. This is about as far north as south winds can reach during the winter."

"South winds in the winter?" A smile bright as the sun, and much warmer, still lit Liv's face. It might have been the funniest thing she'd ever heard. "In the winter, in Three Tusk country, there is no wind. Or, more often, there is the Breath of God." She gave a melodramatic shiver. "Now you have met the Breath of God in truth."

"A lazy wind," Hamnet Thyssen agreed gravely.

"Lazy?" Liv started to scorch him, but then very visibly checked herself. "Wait. You mean something by that. Tell me what."

"What we call a lazy wind is one that blows straight through you because going around is too much bother."

"Ah." She thought it over. After a few heartbeats, her smile came back— she must have decided she liked it. "Truth. That is a truth. Has Trasamund heard it?"

"I don't know," Hamnet answered. "If he has, he hasn't heard it from me."

Liv called to the jarl. "What is it?" Trasamund rumbled.

"Do you know what a lazy wind is?" Liv asked.

"Is that what happens when Jesper Fletti talks?" Trasamund said with a sly grin. Jesper wasn't close enough to hear himself slandered. If he had been, if he'd chosen to take offense . . . Count Hamnet would have bet on Trasamund in a fight.

Liv made a face at her clan chief. "No," she said when they got done scowling at each other. She told him what a lazy wind was.

He weighed it. Then he nodded. "Not bad. No, not bad at all. The Raumsdalians don't lack for wit—no one would ever say they did. Some other things, maybe, but never wit. I wouldn't have come down to Nidaros for help with the Golden Shrine if I thought different." Even on that relatively warm day, steam surged from his lungs when he sighed. "Turned out we didn't need help with the Golden Shrine after all."

"Not this trip," Hamnet Thyssen said. "But chances are we'll go beyond the Glacier again. It may be there. If it is, Eyvind Torfinn knows more about it than any other man alive."

"Eyvind Torfinn knows all sorts of things," Trasamund allowed. Then he spoiled it by asking, "So why doesn't he know his wife disgraces him whenever she pleases?"

"Maybe he doesn't choose to look," Hamnet said. "That can happen, especially when a man who isn't so young has a wife who isn't so old. Or maybe he doesn't care."

"Doesn't care? Do you say he has no ballocks at all, then?" Trasamund demanded.

Count Hamnet shook his head. "No. I wondered about that myself before I got to know him on this journey, but no. He isn't a warrior—he doesn't pretend to be a warrior—but he's no craven, either."

"Well, then, what *do* you say?" Trasamund's frown was half anger, half incomprehension.

"That men and women and how they get along—or don't get along—are more complicated than you'd guess," Hamnet answered. "I won't judge Eyvind Torfinn, and I hope he won't judge me. Sometimes *not* judging someone is the biggest kindness you can do him—or her."

"It sounds very pretty," the Bizogot said. "Tell me this, then—do you *not* judge Gudrid?"

He was a boor, a brute, a barbarian. He was a shrewd boor, a clever brute, a sly barbarian. Hamnet Thyssen's lips tightened. His hands also tightened on the reins, as if the leather straps were Trasamund's neck . . . or possibly Gudrid's. He didn't want to answer the question, and didn't see how he could help it. "I judge her," he said after a pause he hoped wasn't too long. "Yes, I do. But just because I do, that doesn't mean someone else has to. If Eyvind Torfinn wants to, he may. If he chooses not to, who am I to tell him he should? Who are you?"

Trasamund opened his mouth. *Someone who spread his wife's legs.* That was what he was about to say, that or something like it. But at the last moment, instead of saying anything, he jerked his horse's head to one side and rode off.

"He shouldn't have put you through that," Liv said quietly.

"The only way I could make him stop was to kill him," Hamnet said with a shrug. "It isn't worth that. I've killed one man over Gudrid, but I was married to her then. Now? Now it's Earl Eyvind's worry, if he feels like worrying about it."

"How did it happen that you killed him?"

"About the way you'd expect. I found out he was bedding her. No room for doubt. No room to look away—I'd already done too much of that. We fought a duel. Swords. He would have killed me, too. You've seen that scar on my left arm, up near the shoulder, and the one that streaks my beard with white?"

She nodded. "Oh, yes."

"Ingjald gave me those. Ingjald Oddleif, his name was. But I killed him anyway. I was proud of myself. What a man I was! Gudrid acted like I had a cock the size of a bull mammoth's. For about a week, she acted that way. Then she went out and found somebody else to sleep with. She must have decided I wouldn't kill her."

"You loved her," Liv said.

"So I did." Hamnet Thyssen shook his head like a musk ox the Bizogots were slaughtering. They'd herded it and tended it and warded it all its life—why were they doing this to it now? The beast couldn't understand. Even after all this time, part of Hamnet couldn't, either. "So I did," he repeated heavily. "And much good it did me, eh?"

"Maybe for a while," she said.

He shook his head again. "I used to think so, but I don't any more. What good is love when the person you love is laughing behind your back? You're only fooling yourself. I was a fool. I'm not the first. I won't be the last, God knows." He rode on.

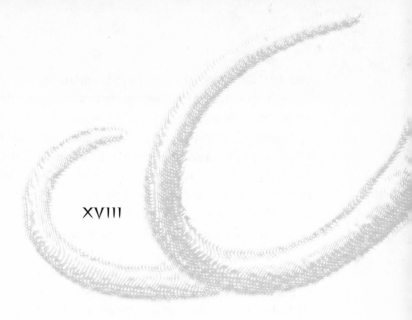

XVIII

As Liv went deeper into the Raumsdalian Empire, as the travelers made their way over to the Great North Road and went down it, she saw plenty of towns larger and finer than Naestved. Each seemed grander than the one just farther north had been. Each time, she would ask, "And is Nidaros like this?"

And each time, Hamnet Thyssen would smile and say, "No, not really. Wait till you see the capital. Then you'll understand."

But when at last they came to the city on the long-vanished shore of long-outflooded Hevring Lake, Liv could see very little, and neither could any of the rest of the weary travelers. The blizzard roaring down from the north would not have been despised in the Bizogot country—would not have been despised in the land of the Three Tusk clan. The Breath of God *could* reach all the way down to Nidaros and beyond. It didn't always, but it could.

Hamnet got a glimpse of Nidaros' great gray frowning walls through swirling snow, but only a glimpse. Of the towers and spires that showed above the walls in good weather, he could see nothing at all. As they neared the city, Liv said, "The wall is very tall, isn't it?" A little later, she added, "The gate seems very strong."

"It is," Hamnet said. She might as well have been examining a mammoth by closing her eyes and feeling first its trunk, then a tusk, then a leg, and finally its tail. She would know something about mammoths after she did that, but probably not as much as she thought.

The guards had as much trouble spying the travelers as Count Hamnet and Liv did seeing the city—maybe more, for the guards had to peer straight into the storm. The travelers were almost on them before they cried, "Halt! Who comes?"

"I am Earl Eyvind Torfinn," Eyvind said. "With me ride Count Hamnet Thyssen, Jarl Trasamund of the Three Tusk clan, and the rest of our comrades. We have come to report success to his Majesty. We have gone beyond the Glacier, and we are here to tell the tale."

"Well, they're here to tell *a* tale, anyhow," one of the guards said to another, not bothering to keep his voice down. "You really think there's anything beyond the Glacier?"

"How could there be?" the other guard returned. "You keep on going north, it's just Glacier forever. Only stands to reason."

Audun Gilli muttered to himself. His hands twisted in a few quick passes. One of the soldiers' spearheads grew a face that was a nasty caricature of the man holding it. "D'you suppose there are really such things as guards?" it asked in a shrill, squeaky voice.

"How could there be?" the other guard's spearhead answered. It too now looked like its owner . . . its owner as seen by somebody with a wicked sense of humor. "We fly through the air all by ourselves. Birds do, so we must. Only stands to reason." It crossed its eyes and stuck out an iron tongue.

Both guards goggled. So did their sergeant. Hamnet Thyssen and Ulric Skakki looked at each other. *Told you so,* Ulric mouthed. Hamnet nodded, remembering when Audun Gilli worked that same spell on their winecups.

"I think you had better pass on in," the sergeant said. "They can deal with you at the palace, by God." *His* spearhead blew him a wet, slobbery kiss. He looked as if he wanted to wring its wooden neck. The other guards' spearheads made more sarcastic gibes.

"Maybe you'd better let them quiet down," Hamnet Thyssen murmured as the travelers rode into the city.

"They will as soon as I get far enough away," Audun Gilli answered. "That spell takes work to keep up, and I'm not going to bother."

"It is a good magic, a funny magic," Liv said in her new and halting Raumsdalian. "You teach me? Make people laugh when I go north again."

Not *if I go north again,* Hamnet noted. *When.* She sounded very sure of what she wanted to do. And he couldn't suppress a stab of jealousy when Audun walked her through the spell step by step. Her face was bright and shiny, full of excitement. She and Audun shared something she never could with him.

He scowled and muttered and clasped the reins tightly. He hadn't left himself open to a woman's wounding since Gudrid left him. Liv wasn't hurting him on purpose, which didn't mean she wasn't hurting him.

"I thank you," she told Audun Gilli when he finished. "It is clever. I can do it. I am sure I can do it."

"Not hard," Audun said. "Not good for much, but fun."

"Fun is good." Liv looked around, seemed to come back to herself, and nodded to Count Hamnet. "I begin to see what you mean. This city is . . . very large. Look at all the big buildings, and at all the people in the streets. And not just people. All the beasts, too."

A string of loaded mules was coming up toward the north gate. The plump merchant leading it had some pungent things to say about the travelers who blocked his path. Then the lead mule screwed up his face and said, "Oh, sure, you think they're as bad as you are, don't you? Fat chance!"

It spoke clearly, distinctly, loudly. The merchant's jaw hit his chest with what should have been an audible clank. The travelers squeezed past the column of loaded mules. The animal in the lead went right on telling the merchant what it thought of him. He didn't stand there gaping long. When anyone—anything—insulted him, he shot back hard. Telling off a mule? He didn't mind. He'd likely done it countless times when the beast couldn't say anything.

"You've got more demon in you than I thought," Hamnet told Audun Gilli.

"Who, me?" the wizard said modestly. "What makes you think that had anything to do with me?"

"I'll tell you what—if Liv tried it, the mule would have had a Bizogot accent."

"I was going to do it," Liv said. "Audun did it first."

"Well, you've got more demon in you than I thought, too," Hamnet said. Liv stuck out her tongue at him. They both laughed, his jealousy dissolving.

Behind them, the merchant called the mule something really unlikely. The mule called the merchant something even worse. Chances were they were both right. Before long, the mule would lose the power of speech as Audun Gilli moved too far away to sustain the spell. The merchant was guaranteed the last word, and all the words after that. But Count Hamnet would have bet the man would never trust the mule not to tell him off again one day.

They moved deeper into Nidaros, streets zigzagging to blunt the Breath of God. The farther they went, the wider Liv's eyes got. "There really is . . . quite a lot of it, isn't there?" she said. "How do you feed so many people?"

"Me? I don't," Hamnet answered. "You've seen the way I cook. These folk would sooner starve than eat that."

She sent him a severe look. "And you said I had a demon in me."

"All right, then. A lot of food comes up from the south. We have markets. We have storehouses. Meat mostly keeps fresh through the winter, though that's shorter than it is up in the Bizogot country. Grain will last a long time if you store it where mice and rats can't get at it and it can't go moldy."

"How long is a long time?"

"I don't know exactly. Years, anyhow."

"Years," she echoed. "You *are* luckier than we are. These are the riches that let you build the things we can't, aren't they?"

"I suppose so," Hamnet said. "We have more left over at the end of a year than you do—unless the year is very bad, I mean."

"There's something else about having extra food," Ulric Skakki put in. "We don't all have to hunt or gather all the time. Some of us can make the things Bizogots don't have, yes. And some of us can try to think up new things, things even we don't have, things it would be nice if we did have."

"New things." Liv frowned. "Like what? When you have all this, what more could you want?"

"If I knew, I'd think up new things myself," Ulric said.

"Old men say that when their grandfathers were boys no one made lamps with mirrors behind them to shed more light. I've heard that more than once," Hamnet Thyssen said. "It's a small thing, but it's the kind of thing I mean. Every craft probably has secrets someone thought of not so long ago. Wizards make new spells all the time. Audun Gilli would know more about that than I do." There—he'd said it.

"Thank you, your Grace. That's what I was talking about, sure enough," Ulric Skakki said.

"We do come up with new spells now and then," Liv said. "The rest of the way we live . . . That hasn't changed much, not so far as anyone can remember."

"Ah, but the Three Tusk clan lives hard by the Glacier," Ulric said. "The Bizogot clans farther south trade with the Empire." He turned to Hamnet Thyssen. "Remember those ugly wool caps the Musk Ox Bizogots wore?"

"I'm not likely to forget them," Hamnet said with a shudder. To Liv, he went on, "You're lucky we came back farther west, so you didn't have to see those. But some of the Bizogots take things we make and use them in ways we'd never think of. And the Leaping Lynxes, up by Sudertorp Lake—the shorebirds they take there let them live in a town half the time. They're having to figure out how to do that when most of them have never seen a real town."

"I see." Liv nodded. "Every folk has clever people and fools in it. But in the Empire your clever people have more room to be clever than they do up on the plains."

"Yes, I think that's likely so," Count Hamnet said.

"Maybe. Or rather, sometimes," Ulric Skakki said. "Just remember, most people in the Empire live on farms, not in towns. They're born on a farm, they grow up on a farm, they get old—*if* they get old—on a farm, and they die on a farm. The clever ones might make better farmers than their stupid neighbors, but that's about it. Farmers don't change the way they do things any faster than Bizogots do. Sometimes they don't change any faster than their beasts."

"You sound like you know what you're talking about," Hamnet remarked. Ulric was always chary of talking about his own past. Was he doing it now without naming names?

His foxy features were perfectly opaque as he smiled at Hamnet. "Well, I try to do that. Harder to be taken for a fool when you do, eh?"

"Er—yes." Hamnet had to drop it. Ulric left nothing on which to get a conversational grip.

The street zigzagged again. Jesper Fletti, who was riding ahead of Hamnet and Liv and Ulric, let out a war whoop no Bizogot in the world would have been ashamed to claim. "The palace!" he shouted. "The palace!" He might have spotted water in the southwestern desert. In an instant, all the guardsmen who'd gone north with Gudrid were shouting the same thing. *"The palace! The palace!"* They'd come home at last, and probably all of them had wondered if they ever would.

Come to that, Hamnet Thyssen had wondered if he would come back to Nidaros, too, even if he was still a long way from his castle in the southeast at the forest's edge. A moment later, very much to his surprise, he found himself shouting, too.

SIGVAT II DIDN'T stint. He let the travelers use the imperial bathhouse. That was luxury by anyone's standards. Soft robes waited when the newcomers emerged. The gown the Emperor's maidservants presented to Liv told Count Hamnet what a fine figure she really had. Seeing her clean and dressed so was a far cry from the grubby woman in Bizogot-style furs and leathers. Those clothes, the same for women as for men, hardly showed which sex she belonged to. The wine-colored gown left no room for doubt.

It also flustered her. "How do your women stand outfits like this?" she asked Hamnet. "It's *drafty*!"

The gown did reveal more of her than he'd seen except when they were making love. "It shows the world how beautiful you are," he said.

Liv blushed. Now that she was clean, he could watch the flush rise from her throat all the way to her crown. "It's none of the world's business," she said, which alone would have proved her no Raumsdalian.

"Well, I like the way you look," Hamnet said.

"That's different. You already know more than this. But—" Liv waved her bare arms. "I feel like I'm naked in front of everyone. And it *is* drafty, even though more fires burn in this palace than in all the tents of the Three Tusk clan put together."

"Which bothers you more? The cold, or everyone looking at you?" he asked.

"Everyone looking at me," Liv said at once. "What will people think?"

"The women will think, *I wish I looked that good*," Hamnet Thyssen answered. "And the men? The men will think, *I wish she were on my arm, not that gray-bearded count's*."

Liv flushed again. "Your beard isn't gray," she said. "Only streaked."

"A matter of time." Hamnet didn't worry about his own looks. They were what they were, and he couldn't do much about them. "If things really bother you," he went on, "ask the servingwomen for a fur stole. That will warm you up and cover you up. I think it would be a shame, but do what you like."

"You're a man," Liv said, more or less tolerantly. "Of course you like to look at women."

"Pretty ones, yes."

"There is a what-do-you-call-it at sunset tonight," Liv said. "Could I really come to it dressed like this?"

"A reception. Gudrid will, or in something that shows even more of her," Hamnet answered. "So will plenty of other noblewomen, and noblemen's mistresses. And they'll all say, *Who is that fair stranger?*"

"You're making that up." But Liv's back stiffened. Hamnet smiled to himself. She liked the idea of outdoing Gudrid, and she thought she could, too. He judged she was right—she was a fine-looking woman with about a twelve years' head start. If they were born on the same day? Count Hamnet wasn't so sure. But, while the calendar might not be fair, it was part of life.

Liv did wear the gown to the reception. She wore it with a stern, jut-jawed determination that warned people not to dare to look at her twice. Because of that, some didn't look at her even once. Others, of course, couldn't get enough.

Hamnet Thyssen proved right about that, and about Gudrid. Her gown revealed and emphasized instead of concealing. She had a lot to show, and showed it to best advantage. When she strode into the reception hall with Eyvind Torfinn, the men already there gave her a couple of heartbeats of . . . respectful . . . admiration. Then most of them had to turn to the women they were with and pretend they'd done no such thing.

There, at least, Count Hamnet had no problem with Liv. She knew he was content—more than content—with her, and not ogling the woman to whom he'd once been married. All she said was, "Well, you knew what you were talking about." A bit later, she added, "If she tried to wear that up in the Bizogot country, she'd freeze."

"No doubt." Hamnet hid a smile. "But you're not in the Bizogot country anymore."

"Yes, I'd noticed that," Liv said.

"It has its advantages," he told her. "Come drink some wine."

She'd put up with beer and ale on the way south from the frontier. They were different from the smetyn she was used to, but not necessarily better. Wine, even in Nidaros, was an expensive imported luxury. One thing being Emperor meant, though, was not worrying about expense.

The tapman dipped her up a cup of wine red as blood, and another for Hamnet Thyssen. Liv's eyes widened as her nose caught the bouquet. "It even smells sweet," she said, and Hamnet nodded. She raised the silver cup to her lips. "Oh," she whispered.

Hamnet took a pull at his own cup. He nodded again. Nothing else was like wine, not even mead. Some of the southern Bizogots, who lived in country where bees could survive the year around, knew of mead. Liv's clan, though, wouldn't be able to brew it. Hamnet wondered if they ever got any in trade. He hadn't seen or heard of any while he was with the Three Tusk Bizogots.

Liv emptied the cup as fast as she could and held it out to the tapman. Face impassive, he filled it again. She made a good start on the refill, then said, "With this wonderful stuff to drink, why don't Raumsdalians stay drunk all the time?"

"Some of us do." Hamnet thought of Audun Gilli. He looked around for the wizard. As often happened, his eye slid past Audun and had to come back. Audun was drinking, or holding a silver cup, anyhow. He didn't seem drunk—but then, the night was still young. He was talking with a woman who wasn't wearing a great deal more than Gudrid. Maybe she would give him an incentive to stay somewhere within shouting distance of sober.

Ulric Skakki materialized at Hamnet's elbow. So it seemed, anyhow—one heartbeat, he was nowhere near; the next, there he stood, a winecup in hand, a slightly mocking smile on his face. "Not a bad bash," he said.

"No, not bad at all," Hamnet agreed. "I'm getting used to beef and mutton and pork again, after so long eating musk ox and—"

"And worse," Ulric finished for him. Maybe he was thinking of the direwolf liver he'd downed on the frozen plains. Hamnet Thyssen had no trouble calling it back to mind. Ulric went on, "How much do you suppose the Rulers would enjoy a spread like this?"

"Oh, maybe a little," Count Hamnet answered. "Yes, maybe."

"I think they might, too." As Hamnet had before, Ulric Skakki looked around. But he wasn't seeking Audun Gilli—he wanted Sigvat II. "I wish his Majesty would come in," he said when he didn't see him. "He hasn't wanted to hear about the Rulers, has he?"

"Not as much as I hoped he would," Hamnet Thyssen said. "As soon as he found out we didn't find the Golden Shrine and we weren't bringing home any treasure, he stopped being interested. I think this reception is a consolation prize."

"I was thinking the same thing," Ulric said. "Pretty soon, he'll throw us out of the palace—either that or he'll start charging us rent."

Hamnet shrugged. "If he does, I'll go back to my castle, that's all. I can give you a room and a bed, if you like."

Liv set a hand on his arm. "But what about the Rulers? You said it yourself. If they come through the Gap, they aren't just the Bizogots' fight. They're the Empire's fight, too."

"I know," Hamnet said. "But if they turn into the Empire's fight, it won't matter if I stay here or go back to the castle. I'll have to fight them either way. We may not be so ready if his Majesty doesn't care to listen to Ulric and Earl Eyvind and Audun and me, but we'll have to meet them ready or not."

"You're more likely to lose," Liv said.

"I can't *make* the Emperor see that. I can't make the Empire do anything about it, either." Hamnet shrugged again. "What I can do, I've done and I'm doing." Liv bit her lip but nodded; she knew that was true.

Musicians struck up a sprightly air. They distracted the Bizogot shaman. She knew about drums and flutes. She even knew about horns, though the Bizogots made theirs from the natural horns of musk oxen, not out of brass. But she'd never seen viols and basses and lutes before coming down to Nidaros. The look of them and the sounds they made fascinated her.

A courtier in a gaudy satin jacket spoke to the musicians' leader. He in turn gestured to his comrades. The strings suddenly fell silent. Horns and drums blared out a fanfare. "His Majesty, Sigvat II, by God's grace Emperor of Raumsdalia!" the courtier bawled into the silence that followed.

Sigvat wore ermine. Liv and Trasamund seemed much less impressed with his robe than his own subjects were. Up on the frozen plains, weasels wore their white coats far longer than they did inside the empire. Those splendid furs were commonplace to the Bizogots, even if they weren't to Raumsdalians.

Hamnet Thyssen and Ulric Skakki bowed low when Sigvat strode into the reception hall. So did the the rest of the men there. The women dropped curtsies. Liv's was smoother than Hamnet expected. "Who taught you?" he whispered as she straightened.

"The maidservants," she answered, also in a whisper. "This is another strange notion you people have, to use people to serve other people. Among my folk, we can all do everything for ourselves." She drew herself up very straight indeed. In her own way, she had as much Bizogot arrogance as Trasamund did.

"As you were, everyone," Sigvat II called with a wave. "For the rest of the evening, let the thought be taken for the deed." He made for the tapman, who handed him a cup of golden wine from the far southwest.

"Shall we beard him?" Ulric Skakki asked.

"Do you think it'll do any good?" Count Hamnet asked in return.

"How can it hurt?" Ulric said.

Since Hamnet couldn't answer that, he approached the Emperor with Ulric. Sigvat was talking and laughing with a tall, black-haired woman whose gown displayed at least as much of her as Gudrid's. He was married, but who was going to tell the Emperor he couldn't amuse himself where and as he pleased? Not the Empress, certainly; she wasn't even at the reception. Sigvat II saw Hamnet and Ulric coming up to them. He seemed more interested in the black-haired woman. In one sense, Hamnet didn't blame him. In another . . .

"Your Majesty?" the nobleman said, politely but firmly. No one who knew him ever thought he wouldn't take the bull by the horns.

Sigvat's mouth tightened. With ill-concealed annoyance, he told the woman, "Please excuse me."

"Of course, your Majesty," she murmured in tones that said she would excuse him anything. Her curtsy almost made her fall out of that gown. Abstractly, Hamnet wondered why she didn't. Some sort of paste holding it to her? He wouldn't have been surprised.

"Thyssen. Skakki." Sigvat acknowledged the two of them with their family names—the least politeness he could give. No, he didn't like being interrupted. He muttered to himself, then went on, "Well, what can I do for you gentlemen?" That was better—a little, anyhow.

"Your Majesty, we wish to thank you for this reception in our honor," Ulric Skakki said. He was smoother than Hamnet, and sly enough to remind the Emperor that the reception *was* in the travelers' honor.

"My pleasure." Sigvat unbent—again, a little. When he spoke of pleasure, though, his eyes slid back to the woman waiting beside him. He sipped from his winecup, then went on, "You did something marvelous when you went beyond the Glacier."

"Thank you again, your Majesty," Ulric said.

Before he could go on, Hamnet interrupted him, saying, "One of the things we did, your Majesty, was find danger in the far north. The Rulers are not foes to be despised."

By the way Sigvat II said, "Maybe so," he didn't believe it for a minute. He went on, "Whatever else the so-called Rulers are, they're very far away. I don't think we need to worry about them for a long time—if we ever have to."

"With respect, your Majesty, that may be so, but it may not," Count Hamnet said. "Both our Raumsdalian wizard and the Bizogot shaman who went north with us from the Three Tusk clan believe they have new magic, magic the likes of which no one on this side of the Glacier has ever seen, magic we may not be able to match."

The Emperor's eye found Liv. Even in this hall full of lovely women, she stood out. "While I admire the shaman's, uh, opinions," Sigvat said, "she is not necessarily expert on what Raumsdalian sorcerers know. And neither she nor, uh, Audun Gilli is expert on what the barbarians beyond the Glacier can really do."

Don't bother me about this now. That was what he meant, all right. Hamnet Thyssen didn't care. Stubbornly, he plowed ahead. "We would do better, your Majesty, to meet this new threat as far from our own borders as we can."

"*I* decide what we would do better to, uh, do." Sigvat II made a face. That didn't come out the way he wanted it to. But even if it didn't, what he meant was only too clear. "If you'd found the Golden Shrine, now . . ."

He cared more about what wasn't there, or wasn't found to be there, than about the real danger. "Your Majesty—" Ulric Skakki began.

"I have spoken." Sigvat II sounded most imperial indeed. "If this people—if these Rulers—show themselves or itself or whatever the right word may be, then Raumsdalia will deal with it or them. Till that time, the Empire has enough real troubles without borrowing imaginary ones. Good evening, Skakki."

That was dismissal, harsh as a slap in the face. Expressionless, Ulric Skakki bowed. "Your Majesty," he said, and stepped away.

When Hamnet Thyssen didn't join him in withdrawing, Sigvat raised an eyebrow. "Your Majesty, you are making a mistake," Count Hamnet said. Then he bowed and turned away without giving the Emperor a chance to reply.

If Sigvat were a different kind of ruler, that could easily have cost him his head. He was too angry to care. But Sigvat, if he didn't want to look north, also wasn't vindictive for the sake of being vindictive. He just went back to the statuesque brunette in the revealing gown. "Sorry to keep you waiting there," he said.

"It's all right, your Majesty," she replied, her voice like a crystal bell.

It wasn't all right, or even close to all right, but Hamnet Thyssen couldn't do anything about it. Savagely, he stalked over toward the tapman. Ulric Skakki was right behind him. "I aim to get as drunk as Audun Gilli ever did," Hamnet warned.

"Good," Ulric said. "We can end up in the same gutter, because I aim to get that drunk too. Maybe we'll keep each other warm."

Hamnet Thyssen wasn't usually a man who drank to oblivion. He'd done it a couple of times after Gudrid left him, but he hadn't seen that it helped him much. He was in the same mess when he sobered up, but with a headache and a sour stomach besides. Once in a while, though, the world seemed too idiotic to stand. This was one of those times.

Eyvind Torfinn and Gudrid had been talking, for all the world like any married couple. Eyvind left her and came over to Hamnet and Ulric, both of whom were getting their cups refilled by the impassive server who took care of the wine. "No luck?" Eyvind asked.

"Not a bit of it, your Splendor. Not one bloody bit," Hamnet growled. "Haven't you tried explaining things for him?"

"Of course I have," Earl Eyvind answered. "Whatever happened beyond the Glacier doesn't seem real to him. God may know why—God must know why—but I don't." He sighed. "Maybe we should have lied. Maybe we should have said we did find the Golden Shrine. That would have kept his interest, anyhow."

Ulric Skakki shook his head. "Jesper Fletti and the rest of Sigvat's hounds would have given us the lie." He wasn't drunk yet, but he didn't care what he said. He had to be disgusted with the world; he didn't usually let himself go like that.

"I suppose you're right," Eyvind Torfinn said with another sigh. "It's most unfortunate."

"It'll be worse than unfortunate if we have to deal with the Rulers here toward the end of next summer," Count Hamnet said.

"Maybe the Bizogots will hold them in check." Eyvind didn't sound as if he believed they could, either.

Hamnet gulped his wine. As he drank, he watched Gudrid out of the corner of his eye. He wished he could stop doing that, but getting what he wished for, even after falling in love with the woman from the north, wasn't easy.

His former wife said something to Liv. Across the room, Count Hamnet couldn't tell what it was. The Bizogot shaman answered. Again, Hamnet couldn't tell how. Gudrid said something else. This time, Liv just shook her head.

Gudrid stuck her nose in the air. Hamnet Thyssen had seen that gesture more times than he could count. Whatever Gudrid heard, she didn't like it. Maybe Liv was rash enough to have said something nice about him. Or maybe she said something rude about Nidaros. Whatever it was, it roused Gudrid's ire, or at least her contempt.

If she'd walked away with her nose held high, everything would have been fine. But she decided she had to do more than that. So as she turned to go, she stepped on Liv's foot. It might have been an accident. It might have been—but it wasn't.

His own anger inflamed by the strong wine he'd poured down, Hamnet Thyssen started over toward them. He hadn't gone more than a couple of strides before he found, not for the first time, that his present beloved could take care of herself.

Liv's lips moved. Hamnet could see that. Gudrid didn't turn back, so the Bizogot woman's words weren't intended for her ear—which didn't mean they weren't intended for her. Gudrid made a fundamental mistake. She forgot the lesson she'd had to learn far to the north—getting on the bad side of a wizard or shaman was a long way from smart.

One heartbeat, Gudrid's minimal gown held together as well as over-strained fabric could reasonably be expected to do. The next, things fell apart, literally and spectacularly. They had no obvious reason for falling apart. It might have been an accident. It might have been—but it wasn't.

Gudrid looked down at herself, first in surprise and then in horror. The involuntary squawk she let out swung every eye in the reception hall toward her. That was just what she didn't want. There was more of her to cover up than she had hands to cover it.

She started to pick up what was left of the gown, then seemed to realize she couldn't put it back together again. She took a step toward a table full of trays of appetizers, but must have decided the trays weighed down the tablecloth too much for her to grab it. With another squawk, she kicked out of the remnants of what she'd worn and fled the reception hall.

"Oh, dear." Eyvind Torfinn hurried after her.

"Well, well. There's a dressmaker who won't live to grow old," Ulric Skakki predicted. "But I'll bet half the men here want to know who he is so they can get him to make gowns for their lady friends."

"I wouldn't be surprised," Count Hamnet answered, but didn't think it was the dressmaker's fault. When he walked over to Liv, he carefully detoured around the bits of fabric still on the floor. He wagged a finger at her. "That was naughty of you."

"Too bad," she said. "Did you see what happened?"

"I saw, yes. I couldn't hear what the two of you said, but I know she stepped on you on purpose."

"If she did that in the Three Tusk country, I would have killed her," Liv said. "But I know you Raumsdalians are soft when it comes to such things, so I thought I'd embarrass her instead."

"You did," Hamnet said. Gudrid might have arranged for her own wardrobe to fail, but she would have gloried in her nakedness if she did. To get surprised . . . *That* was embarrassing.

"She's spent a lot of time tormenting you, so she thinks she can torment me, too, because I make you happy," Liv said. "She won't get away with that, no matter what she thinks. I can make her more unhappy than she makes me." Her eyes flamed.

"Chances are she's got the message now," Hamnet said.

"She'd better." Liv glanced over toward Sigvat II, who was happily chatting with the well-made brunette. "Did the Emperor get the message about the Rulers?"

"No, curse it." Hamnet shook his head. "He says he'll worry about them when they bother the Empire, if they ever do. Till then, he doesn't care."

"Well, why should he? He has more important things to worry about." The Bizogot woman's voice was tart. Sigvat's companion laughed at something he said. If the Emperor made a joke, of course it was funny.

"I don't know what to do about it. I don't think I can do anything about it—except bang my head against a stone wall, I mean," Hamnet Thyssen said. "I've done that before. By God, I've made a career out of it. But this time I can see it won't get me anywhere."

"So what will you do, then?" Liv asked.

"Well, I told you I was thinking about going back to my castle and waiting for the sky to fall," Hamnet answered. "Sooner or later, it will. We both know that. And . . . I was hoping you'd come with me." He had to work to say that, but he got it out. Now to see what happened next.

"I like being with you. You know that. I like it better than I ever thought I could like being with anyone," Liv said. "And the Empire has more . . . more *things* in it than I thought there were, there could be, in the whole world. But—"

"But?" Hamnet broke in harshly. As soon as Liv started saying nice things, he knew trouble lay ahead.

"But," Liv said again. "The sky will fall here sooner or later, yes. For the Three Tusk clan, the sky will fall sooner. We roam nearest the Gap. The Rulers will strike us first. By the nature of things, they have to. The Three Tusk clan . . . They are my folk. I will do what I can to help them. I have to do that, Hamnet—don't you see?"

He started to ask if anything he could do or say would make her change her mind. He started to, but he didn't; he could see it was hopeless. Not without admiration, he said, "You're as stubborn as I am. Do you know that?"

She nodded again. "That was one of the things that drew me to you. I wondered if we would bang heads, the way musk-ox bulls do in rutting season. But we never did, did we? Not till now."

"You *will* go north?" Hamnet asked.

"I will. I have to," Liv said.

He thought about his castle, about the estate surrounding it, about the game-filled woods to the east. He thought about how many Raumsdalians, starting with his bailiff, could care for the castle and estate as well as he could. He thought about the Gap, and the building storm beyond it.

"Would you put up with a half-baked Bizogot if I came north with you?" he asked.

Liv stared at him as if she didn't believe her ears. Then she threw herself into his arms. Naked Gudrid might have made a bigger spectacle at the reception, but not by much. *Well*, Hamnet thought dizzily as the embrace went on and on, *at least I know why I'm doing this.*

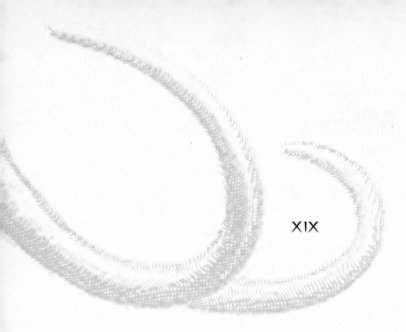

XIX

HAMNET THYSSEN DID have a hangover from the drinking he'd done at the reception the night before. Maybe his own headache and touchy stomach made him think Ulric Skakki seemed especially jaundiced-looking the morning after. Or maybe Ulric *was* as astonished and dismayed as he seemed to be.

"You're really going back to the barbarians?" he yelped in what certainly sounded like pained disbelief.

"That's right." Count Hamnet took a cautious sip from a mug of wine. The hair of the dire wolf that bit him might ease his pangs. He sent the adventurer a defiant stare. "What about it?"

"You mean, besides your being out of your bloody mind?" Ulric was also nursing a mug. He was eating a sticky roll with candied fruit, too. Hamnet wasn't ready for food yet. Ulric Skakki went on, "You're the last man on earth I would have looked for to think with his cock."

"By God, I'm not!" Hamnet said, loud enough to make his own head throb. More quietly, he continued, "Sigvat's not going to do anything about the Rulers. You know that as well as I do. He rubbed our noses in it last night. So what does that leave me? Either I go home and wait for the world to go to the demons or I try to do something about it. I thought about sitting on my hands, but I just can't."

"An idealist?" Ulric Skakki asked sardonically. Hamnet Thyssen's nod was as defiant as his stare. Ulric laughed in his face and said, "Sitting on your hands, eh? How idealistic would you be if the Bizogot girl weren't sitting on your—"

"Watch your mouth, Skakki." Hamnet Thyssen folded his right hand into a fist. "It's early for a brawl, but you can have one if you want." He wondered if he was bad-tempered because of his headache or because Ulric's gibe held more truth than he wanted to admit, even to himself.

The adventurer shook his head. "No, not me. I'm a peaceable chap," he said. Count Hamnet snorted. Ulric Skakki went on, "Seriously, though, would you think of doing something like this if you weren't in love with Liv?"

"I hope so," Hamnet answered. "It's the right thing to do—or will you tell me that's not so?" If Ulric tried, Hamnet intended to walk away.

But Ulric didn't, not straight out. He was practical instead, practical and devious. "It's only the right thing to do if you think the Bizogots can beat the Rulers. Otherwise, seems to me you'd do better waiting for trouble here. Besides, *do* you want Trasamund for your overlord? I mean . . ." He rolled his eyes.

But Count Hamnet refused to back down. "Better Trasamund than Sigvat," he said. "Trasamund doesn't pull his head into his shell and sleep through the winter at the bottom of a pond the way the Emperor does."

Ulric Skakki looked alarmed, not because he hadn't told the truth but because he'd told it too loud. "Keep your voice down, or you won't have the chance to go north!"

"Why not?" Count Hamnet said. "His Majesty should be as glad to get rid of me as I am to go, and that's saying a lot."

He got only a shrug from Ulric, as if to say, *On your head be it.* The foxy-faced man asked, "And how do you think Trasamund will like having you for a subject?"

"I haven't talked with him yet," Hamnet answered with a shrug. "He put up with me all the way through the Gap and past it. He ought to be able to stand me from here on out. It's not as if I'm likely to try to take the jarl's job away from him."

"If you could get the Bizogots to listen to you, you'd do it better." Ulric Skakki held up a hand. "I know. I know. Nobody can get the Bizogots to listen to him. That's one more reason what you're doing is madness."

Count Hamnet looked at him—looked through him, really. "I have two questions for you. Are the Rulers the biggest trouble we have, or is something else?" He folded his arms across his chest and waited.

Ulric let out a snort of his own, but he answered, "Well, the Rulers are. I don't think there's any way around that."

"All right. Very good, in fact." Hamnet Thyssen clapped his hands in mocking applause. Ulric looked more exasperated than ever. Ignoring his sour expression, Hamnet went on, "If the Rulers *are* the worst trouble we have, would you rather do something about them or do nothing about them?"

Ulric Skakki opened his mouth, closed it, then opened it again, but still didn't speak for some little while. At last, he managed, "That's not fair."

"Fine. Have it your way. But why shouldn't I have it my way, too?" Hamnet said.

"Because you won't do what you think you will?" Ulric suggested.

"Fine," Count Hamnet repeated. "But I'll do something. I want to do something. I need to do something. If you want to do nothing, that's your business."

"And you'll be laying your pretty little Bizogot—except she's not so little, is she?—in the meantime," Ulric jeered. Hamnet Thyssen swung on him. The next thing Hamnet knew, he was flying through the air upside down. He hit the stone floor on his back, hard. Ulric Skakki wasn't even breathing hard. "You all right?" he asked. "You rushed me a little there."

Count Hamnet needed several heartbeats to take stock of himself. His right wrist was sore. So was the back of his head, which had also thumped the floor. "I . . . think so," he said slowly as he climbed to his feet. "What did you do there? Can you teach it to me?"

"And spoil my air of mystery?" Ulric said archly.

Before either of them could say anything more, a servant stuck his head into the room. "What happened?" the man asked. "It sounded like the castle was falling down."

"Oh, I dropped my winecup." Ulric's voice was bland as butter without salt. "It was empty, so I didn't even make a mess."

"Your *winecup*?" The servant thought he was lying or crazy or both. The man was right, too, but Ulric wouldn't let him prove it. The adventurer just nodded and smiled. The servant looked at Hamnet Thyssen, then quickly looked away. Hamnet's expression was probably terrifying. Thwarted, the man withdrew. Ulric Skakki winked. "Where were we, O winecup of mine?"

"Oh, shut up," Hamnet muttered. He gathered himself. Standing on his dignity wasn't easy, not when he'd just been flipped and thrown. "*Will* you teach me that trick?"

"Come at me again and you'll learn more about it than you ever wanted to know," Ulric Skakki answered.

"Keep my woman out of your mouth, then." Hamnet set a hand on his swordhilt. "And don't even start to make the joke that's in your filthy mind."

"You can't prove it," Ulric said. He didn't make the joke, so Hamnet didn't have to try.

EYVIND TORFINN WAS even more surprised and even more dismayed to learn Count Hamnet intended to go north with Trasamund and Liv than Ulric Skakki had been. What Gudrid thought, Hamnet didn't inquire.

No matter what she thought, Eyvind Torfinn arranged a gathering of his own to see Hamnet and Liv and Trasamund off to the Bizogot country. That he was able to arrange it left Hamnet impressed. Earl Eyvind was more his own man than Gudrid's former husband had imagined before setting off for the north with him.

"Are you sure we should come here?" Liv asked as she and Count Hamnet rode up to Eyvind's large, rambling home. "Will that woman poison the food? Or will hired murderers greet us when we go in?"

"I doubt it," Hamnet answered. "She hasn't tried to murder me—that I know of—since she left me. And I expect she'll put up with you. She knows you're dangerous, and she knows me well enough to fear my revenge."

"Ah." Liv nodded. That, she understood.

Like all entrances in Nidaros, Earl Eyvind's faced south. The bulk of the large home shielded Hamnet Thyssen and Liv from the Breath of God. Even so, the knocker had frozen to the door. Hamnet had to tug on it to free it.

Eyvind Torfinn opened the door himself—no hired bravos. "Your Grace," he said to Hamnet, and then, to Liv, "My lady." He remained polite to her. Maybe Gudrid hadn't told him everything that happened at the reception. *Just as well if she hasn't,* Hamnet thought.

"Your Splendor," he and Liv said together. They smiled at each other, the way people will when they do that.

"Come in, come in," Eyvind Torfinn said. "You are both welcome here . . . in spite of your foolishness, your Grace."

"I thank you," Hamnet Thyssen answered. "I don't look at it as foolishness, you know."

"Yes, I do," the older man told him. "It makes you the only one in Nidaros who doesn't."

Liv squeezed Count Hamnet's hand. "No, your Splendor, it doesn't," she said firmly in her new, slow, precise Raumsdalian.

"I stand corrected, my lady." Earl Eyvind bowed to her. He bowed more readily than he would have before setting out for the Gap and the lands beyond the Glacier; he'd lost most of the comfortable paunch he'd carried then. Hamnet guessed he would get it back soon enough, but he hadn't yet. As he straightened, he went on, "I should have said, the only Raumsdalian in Nidaros who doesn't."

"Oh, there must be some sot in a gutter somewhere who hasn't heard the news," Hamnet said with a wry smile.

"You make light of it, but you shouldn't." Eyvind's smile was just as sour. "Well, come along, come along. We will celebrate what you have done and hope you may yet do more in days to come if you return to your senses."

"I'm not dead yet. I don't plan on dying any time soon, either," Hamnet Thyssen said in some annoyance. "By God, I'm doing what I think is right."

Trasamund was already in Eyvind Torfinn's reception hall, drinking wine and gnawing on a leg cut from a roast goose. *His* belly was thicker than it had been before he got down to the Empire. He enjoyed the good things of life when he could get them. He sent Hamnet Thyssen something more than a wave and less than a salute. "You *are* a brave man," he boomed to Count Hamnet. "To put yourself in my hands, you must be."

"I'm going north anyway," the Raumsdalian nobleman answered. Liv smiled. Trasamund laughed. Audun Gilli watched in wide-eyed fascination. Ulric Skakki's face was unreadable; he was better at keeping it that way than anyone else Hamnet had ever seen. Jesper Fletti plainly thought Hamnet had lost his mind—but, with a cup of wine in one hand and a mutton rib in the other, he didn't seem to care much. If he hadn't gone north, he never would have been able to get an invitation to Eyvind Torfinn's home.

As for Gudrid . . . She had on almost as little as she did at Sigvat II's ill-fated fête. Was she reminding Hamnet of what he would be missing?—not just her, but also a city such as Nidaros, where there were dressmakers who turned out gowns like the one she was almost wearing.

Liv made a small noise, deep down in her throat. A lioness spotting prey might come out with a sound like that. If Gudrid had heard it, she would have been wise to take herself elsewhere as fast as she could go.

But she didn't. She swayed toward Hamnet Thyssen, a smile on her reddened lips. She leaned forward and stood on tiptoe to kiss him on the cheek. Liv made that noise again, louder this time. Gudrid ignored it, saying, "So you're going away, are you? Well, I hope you enjoy the bugs and the smells."

Had some of her paint come off so he was branded to the eye as well as to the touch? He would wipe his face . . . soon. For now, he said, "I can put up with them. And I'll be where I need to be. And"—he put his arm around Liv—"the company is better."

Gudrid didn't lose her smile. Her face went ugly for a moment all the same. "Who would have thought someone like you would run away for love?" she said. *Someone boring like you* but hung in the air.

Hamnet shrugged. "I'm not running away. I'm running toward. You met the Rulers. You know what they're like."

"Ah, the brave hero, sure he can charge off and save the day where nobody else has a chance. You sound like someone out of the romances *dear* Eyvind can quote for hours at a stretch." Gudrid jeered at her present husband, too.

"I'm not sure of anything of the kind," Hamnet answered steadily. "I'd rather not pretend there's no trouble, that's all."

"Really?" Gudrid tilted her head to one side. "Since when?"

"You ought to know—you taught me the lesson." He kept his voice even. "Will you excuse me, please? I'd like to get something to eat and something to drink."

"So would I, please," Liv said.

Gudrid had to notice her then. "How could I say no to you? Who knows what would happen if I did?"

Liv shrugged. "How do I know there is no . . . no poison in the food and drink?" She had to search for the word she wanted, but she found it.

Hamnet Thyssen watched Gudrid closely. If Liv's sarcastic comment turned out to be not a sarcastic comment but the truth, he thought his former wife's face would betray her, if only for a heartbeat. But Gudrid just shook her head. "I wouldn't poison you. You're going back to your tents, and you're taking Hamnet with you. That's a better revenge than poison ever could be."

Instead of answering, Liv walked away and got a cup of wine. Count Hamnet lingered long enough to say, "We're going off to fight the Rulers, and this is the thanks we get?"

"As if you care a fart about the Rulers," Gudrid said. "You're going off to screw yourself silly—sillier—and to collect lice and drink sour smetyn. And you're welcome to every bit of it, too."

He growled, down deep in his throat. But then he turned away. Gudrid looked . . . disappointed? If he'd hit her, there in front of everybody, he would have stirred up a terrific scandal. Was that worth getting slapped? Gudrid would probably think so.

He gulped the wine a polite servant gave him. And then, out of the blue, Liv said, "She's jealous of you." She used her own language, so most of the people who might overhear her wouldn't understand.

"Who? Gudrid?" Hamnet Thyssen didn't laugh in her face, which was a small proof of how much he cared for her. But he did say, "You must be joking."

"No. No, indeed," Liv said seriously. "You're doing something important. And you've found—I hope you've found—someone who matters to you. Whatever else she is, she is no fool. She has to know all this"—her wave took in Eyvind Torfinn's mansion—"is empty. We don't have so much up in the Bizogot country." Scorn edged her voice. "We don't have so much, no, but we know what we need to do."

Count Hamnet glanced over toward Gudrid again. She was laughing and flirting with Jesper Fletti. Hamnet wondered if Liv was right. He didn't want to argue with her, but he couldn't believe it. Because the Bizogot shaman had such a strong sense of purpose, she thought everyone else did, too. She couldn't grasp that Gudrid really was as shallow as she seemed.

Well, why should she? Hamnet thought. *I had to get my nose rubbed in it before I understood.*

"Having fun?" Ulric Skakki had that gift for appearing at someone's elbow—and for disappearing just as readily.

"Me? No. But I knew I wouldn't," Count Hamnet answered.

"Why did you come, then?" Ulric asked.

"Well, I didn't want to disappoint Eyvind Torfinn. He's doing something nice to see me off, and he's a pretty good fellow, even if—" Two words too late, Hamnet broke off.

Ulric Skakki knew what he was about to say, and said it for him: "Even if he's married to Gudrid."

"That's right. Even then." Hamnet Thyssen's shoulders went up and down. "And if *I* can say that about him, then chances are he's really better than a pretty good fellow, if you know what I mean."

"He's not as smart as he thinks he is." Ulric could always find something unkind to say about someone—and something that was true at the same time, too.

"Well, who is?" Count Hamnet said. This time, Ulric was the one who shrugged. Hamnet pointed at him. "Are *you?*"

"I like to think I am." Ulric Skakki laughed. He *could* laugh at himself, which made him much easier to get along with than he would have been otherwise. "Of course, maybe I'm not so smart myself." He bowed to Hamnet. "Yes, I do see your point, your Grace."

"I'm so glad," Hamnet said dryly, and Ulric laughed again. Hamnet asked, "Are you smart enough to come north with me?"

"I'm smart enough not to," Ulric answered. Hamnet Thyssen raised an eyebrow. Unabashed, the adventurer went on, "I'm not a hero. I never wanted to be a hero. I've done my share of . . . interesting things. But I don't have to do this one, and I don't intend to. If you think you can save Raumsdalia up by the Glacier, be my guest. I wish you good fortune, and that's the truth. I aim to enjoy what you're saving, though. I like wine better than smetyn and spiced mutton better than roast musk ox. I confess to a weakness for real buildings and real beds and women who take baths. If that makes me a lazy, good-for-nothing weakling, well, I'll live with it."

He was about as far from being a weakling as any man Hamnet Thyssen knew. That was part of the reason Hamnet so badly wanted him to go back to the Bizogot country. "I don't suppose I can do or say anything to make you change your mind?"

"Not likely, my dear," Ulric Skakki said. "When have you ever known anybody to change somebody else's mind? The only person who can change my mind is me, by God." He jabbed a thumb at his own chest.

Someone Hamnet Thyssen barely knew came up to him then. The man wore expensive clothes and had a big belly. He carried himself with the confidence of somebody who'd done well for a long time, though Hamnet couldn't remember what he did well in. No doubt he was a friend of Eyvind Torfinn's, which said something unflattering about Earl Eyvind's taste in friends.

"So you're going off to the Glacier again, are you?" By his accent, the near-stranger was born and raised in Nidaros. By the amused contempt in his voice, he thought too much of himself.

"That's right," Hamnet answered. People like this made him wish he'd declined Eyvind's invitation after all.

"By God, you must be daft," the fellow said cheerfully. "You'll freeze your stones off, and for what? For nothing, that's what." He sounded altogether sure he was right—altogether sure he had to be right.

"Oh, I think going up to the Bizogot country may be worthwhile after all," Count Hamnet said.

"Ha! How could it possibly be? Eh? Tell me that." Eyvind Torfinn's rich acquaintance was convinced Hamnet Thyssen couldn't.

But Hamnet could. "Well, for starters, it takes me away from jackasses like you."

The other man's face flushed ominously. "Here, now! What the demon is that supposed to mean?"

"I usually mean what I say," Hamnet answered. "You should try it one of these days. It works wonders."

"You can't talk to me that way! Do you know who I am?" the big-bellied man said.

"I've been trying to remember your name, but I'm afraid I can't." Hamnet Thyssen shrugged. "If you push me a little more, though, I suppose I can always find out from your next of kin."

"From my—?" The prosperous fellow must have drunk a good deal, because even that message took longer to penetrate than it should have. "You wouldn't—" He broke off again, because Hamnet plainly would. The big-bellied man gaped, discovering some things gold couldn't dissolve. "You *are* a barbarian!" he burst out.

Count Hamnet bowed. "At your service. And if you keep wasting my time and fraying my temper, I will be more at your service than you ever wanted. I promise you that." He shifted his feet as if getting ready to draw his sword.

Although the prosperous man also wore a blade, he seemed to have forgot about it. That was wise, or at least lucky; whatever else he was, he was no trained warrior, and wouldn't have lasted long against someone who was. "Madman!" he blurted, and took himself elsewhere.

"You still know how to win friends, don't you?" There was Ulric Skakki again.

"Winning him as a friend is a dead loss, by God," Hamnet answered. "And you *want* to spend your time with people like him? Why?"

"Oh, he's no prize. There are plenty here in Nidaros who aren't. Don't get me wrong, Hamnet—I don't say anything different." Ulric paused to snag a cup of wine from a pretty maidservant passing by with a tray. After sipping, he went on, "But you can't tell me the Bizogots are any better, not at that level. People are people no matter where you find 'em, and a lot of them anywhere will be boastful, blustering saps."

Did his eyes travel to Trasamund? Or, instead of following Ulric's, did Hamnet Thyssen's go to the jarl on their own? "Trasamund's no sap," Hamnet said. Whether the Bizogot was boastful and blustering was a different question, one he didn't try to answer.

"Mm, not all the time, I suppose," Ulric Skakki said generously. "But often enough to make him a pain in the posterior."

"He knows the Rulers are dangerous. You know the Rulers are dangerous. Does his Majesty know the Rulers are dangerous?" Hamnet said.

"He will by the time he has to do something about them. I hope he will, anyhow," Ulric said.

Hamnet turned away from him. "Enjoy yourself, then."

"That's what I'm here for." Nothing fazed Ulric Skakki—or if anything did, he didn't let on.

AFTER THE UNFORTUNATE feast, Hamnet took leaving for the frozen plains much more seriously. He bought everything he could think of that might be useful—a second sword, knives, iron arrow points, wooden arrow shafts (lighter and straighter than the bone arrows the Bizogots commonly used), a spare helmet, poppy juice, horse trappings, a pillow, soap, insect powder (which probably wouldn't work, but you never could tell), and several sets of flint and steel for making sparks and starting fires. A man could find flint up in the Bizogot country, but not much steel went up there.

"You get no clothes. You get no feathers for fletching or bowstrings," Liv said, accompanying him as he spent his silver.

"I don't seen any need for those. You Bizogots make better cold-weather gear than anything I could buy here," Count Hamnet answered. "Sinew will do for bowstrings, and I can get feathers and fletching tools up on the plain. What I want here are things I can't get there."

"Ah." Liv nodded. "This is wise."

"Well, I hope so." Hamnet sometimes fancied his own cleverness. Usually it turned and bit him when he did.

"On some of these things, you could also turn a fine profit," the Bizogot woman said.

"I'm not going up there to be a trader," Hamnet told her. "If the Rulers don't come, maybe I'll trade what I don't need, but that's not why I'm bringing it." *If the Rulers don't come, I'll look like an idiot. If they don't come, I'll feel like an idiot, too.*

"You should have things to trade. It will help you live among us," Liv said seriously. "You ride well and you fight well, but you have no practice herding musk oxen or mammoths. Sooner or later, you need to learn."

"Yes, I suppose so," Hamnet said with no great enthusiasm. She was right; he couldn't lie around waiting for a war that might not come and eating what the rest of the clan gave him. He wouldn't be a guest now—he would be one of them. And the Bizogots didn't have enough to spare for idle hands. Children worked at whatever they were big enough to try. Men and women who got too old to work—not that many lived so long up there—went out on the plains to die a cold but mostly merciful death. It wasn't cruelty; it was a harshness the land imposed.

"Not many Raumsdalians would be able to do it," Liv said. "You, though—once you learn, I think you'll do as well as if your hair weren't dark."

"Thank you so much," he said. Many Raumsdalians sneered at the Bizogots because they were so fair—though not many Raumsdalian men, from all Hamnet Thyssen had seen, sneered at Bizogot women. Amusing to find the mammoth-herders looking down their noses at their southern neighbors.

Most of the time, Liv recognized his irony for what it was. She took him seriously here. "I mean it," she assured him. "You can do the work. Ulric Skakki, I think, could do the work—but he would rather find ways to get out of it instead. The rest of the Raumsdalians who traveled with us? The ones I've seen here?" She shook her head.

"Each cat his own rat," Hamnet said. "Up in the north, everyone has to be able to do everything, near enough. You said that yourself. Here, we pick one thing and get good at it. That leaves a lot of us not so good at other things. It's the price we pay."

"If the Rulers come this far . . ." Liv said.

"If the Rulers come this far, they'll see that some of us make good soldiers, too," Count Hamnet said.

"I hope so." Liv didn't sound convinced. "From what I saw of Jesper Fletti and the other Raumsdalian soldiers who came north, though . . ." Her voice trailed away again.

"No, no, no, no." Hamnet Thyssen shook his head. "Don't judge our soldiers by them. They're imperial guards. Part of their job is to look pretty while they take care of Sigvat. They can fight some, or they'd be useless. But they have to be impressive while they're doing it. Most soldiers don't bother with that nonsense."

"I hope so," Liv repeated, still seeming dubious.

"Look at it like this," Hamnet said. "Never mind the Rulers. If all our soldiers were like the ones you saw, who'd stop the Bizogots from overrunning the Empire?"

Liv grunted thoughtfully, the way a man would. She squeezed his hand. "Fair enough. You have a point. I always thought it was because the southern Bizogots were too weak and puny to be worth much themselves, but your soldiers have to be able to fight, too. Do you think they'll be able to fight warriors who ride mammoths?"

It was Hamnet's turn to grunt. "I don't know," he admitted. "The Bizogots will have to worry about that, too."

"At least we *know* mammoths," Liv said.

Hamnet Thyssen started going on, in Raumsdalian, about two Bizogots and two mammoths gossiping about the clan that lived next door to theirs. For a little while, Liv didn't understand what he was doing. When she did get it, she was affronted at first. Then, in spite of herself, she started to giggle. "I didn't mean we know them like *that*," she said.

In the voice of one of the mammoths—a snooty one—Hamnet said, "Well, *we* don't say we know Bizogots like that, either." He made an indignant gesture with his arm, as if it were a trunk. Giggling still, Liv hit him. It was a most successful shopping trip.

It was snowing when Count Hamnet and Liv and Trasamund set out from the imperial palace. That seemed fitting to Hamnet. It also seemed fitting to Trasamund, who said, "Now we go back to a land with proper weather, by God."

"If you say so, your Ferocity." Hamnet didn't feel like arguing with him.

One of the stablemen said, "Good fortune go with you, your Grace."

"Why, thank you, Tyrkir." Hamnet Thyssen was surprised and touched. "I thought everybody here was glad to get rid of me."

"Oh, no." Tyrkir shook his head. "You know how to take care of a horse, and you always treat us like people when you come to the stables. We aren't just—things that can talk, not to you. Not like some I could name."

Another attendant hissed at him. He left it there. Hamnet found himself wondering as he rode off. Was Tyrkir talking about the Emperor like that? He couldn't very well ask, but it made for an interesting question all the same.

"Nidaros is a fine place to visit. Nidaros is a wonderful place to visit, in fact," Trasamund said as they rode out, with a smile like a cat's that has fallen into a pitcher of cream. "I wouldn't want to have to stay here, though."

"Neither would I," Hamnet Thyssen said.

"Plainly not, or you wouldn't come with me," the jarl said.

Count Hamnet shook his head. "I've always thought so. Too many people crowded together. Too many ambitious people crowded together. Whenever I could stay away from the place, I would. Sometimes you can't help it, though."

"It's not just the people crowded together. It's all the *things* crowded together, too," Liv said. "The houses and the shops and everything in the shops . . ." Her shiver had nothing to do with the weather. "It's marvelous, I suppose, but I'd go mad if I stayed here much longer."

As if to prove her point, they got stuck behind a wagon that had overturned on the icy road, spilling sacks of beans or barley or something of the sort. The driver tried to keep people from darting in and stealing the sacks, but some would distract him while others did the taking.

"We Bizogots don't steal inside the clan," Trasamund said loftily.

"Why do these people do it?" Liv asked.

"Maybe to sell what they grab. More likely because they're hungry and they need something to eat," Hamnet answered.

"Here, some have too much and many have not enough. That is not good," Liv said. "Among the Bizogots, if someone goes hungry, it's because everyone in the clan goes hungry. That way is better, I think."

"Maybe so," Hamnet said. "Things are more equal among you—you're right. But you've seen we can do things you can't."

"Oh, yes." The shaman nodded. "We talked about the price you pay for being able to do them. This is another part of that price, wouldn't you say?"

Although Hamnet Thyssen hadn't thought of it like that, he found himself nodding, too. "Yes, I'd have to say it is."

"Let's turn around and take another road," Trasamund said. "Otherwise, we'll be here till they steal the wheels off that poor fool's wagon and the tail off his horse."

"I can get us to the north gate on side streets, I think," Hamnet said. "We'll have to do some zigzagging, but we would anyway." A boulevard that ran straight north would have given the Breath of God a running start. Raumsdalian winters were milder—or at least less regularly frigid—than the ones the Three Tusk clan knew, but people still had to do all they could to fight the cold.

Hamnet would have embarrassed himself if he'd got lost in the maze of lanes and alleys that sprouted from the main road. He knew more than a little relief when he got back onto it. With luck, neither of the Bizogots with him noticed.

If it was snowing here, what was it like up by the Glacier? *Do I really want to know?* he wondered. He shrugged. Ulric Skakki had gone that way, and gone by himself, without the Bizogots' knowing. *What he can do, I can do, by God.* Hamnet Thyssen muttered under his breath. He still wished Ulric were coming along. The adventurer was a good man to have beside you when you ran into trouble—or when it ran into you.

He pointed. "There's the gate."

"So it is." Trasamund nodded in satisfaction. "On the way home at last. Even getting out of Nidaros, getting into the countryside here, will feel like an escape. It's not the plains, but I won't feel closed in all the time, either, the way I do now."

"Closed in. Yes, by God!" Liv said. "When you leave the tents, there's a whole big world around you, and you can see it. When you leave a house, what do you see? More walls!" She shuddered. "It's like being tied up, like being caged."

"All what you're used to," Hamnet Thyssen said. "I told you before—out on your plains, sometimes I feel as if there's too much nothing around me." He mimed curling up into a little ball.

The gate guards asked their names. When the sergeant heard them, he said, "Oh, you're *that* lot. Yes, you can go through. By all we've heard, it's good riddance to the lot of you."

"We love you, too," Hamnet said mildly. He *had* offended Sigvat, then. Well, too bad. And as a matter of fact, it *was* too bad. Trasamund said something even more unflattering in the Bizogot language. Luckily, none of the guards understood him.

Liv really did sigh with relief when they put the gray stone walls of Nidaros behind them. "Free!" she said, and threw her arms wide. Her horse twitched its ears, doubtless wondering why its rider was acting so strange.

Hamnet Thyssen wondered why two horsemen—tough-looking rogues, he thought, peering at them through the swirling snow—sat waiting by the side of the Great North Road. Was Sigvat angry enough to set bravos on him to make sure he didn't get to the Bizogot country? He wouldn't have thought so, but . . . When he got a little closer, his jaw dropped. "Ulric!" he said. "Audun! What the demon are you doing here?"

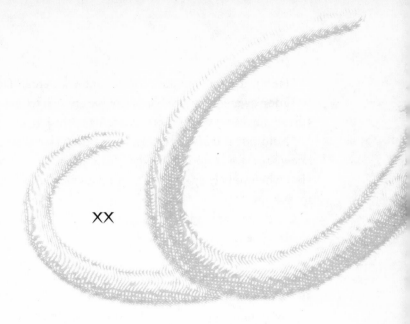

XX

ULRIC SKAKKI TILTED back his head so he could look down his long, straight nose at Hamnet. "You're more persuasive than you have any business being, Thyssen," he said severely. "If you set your mind to it, you could probably sell snow to the Bizogots."

"I don't need to sell it." Hamnet held out a mittened hand till a few flakes fell on it. "It's right here. And I'm glad to see you, even if I didn't think I'd put any horse traders out of business." He sketched a salute to the wizard. "I'm glad to see you, too, Audun—you'd best believe I am. What made you decide to come?"

Audun Gilli's nondescript features lit up when anyone paid attention to him. "I thank you, your Grace. What made me decide to come? Ulric here kidnapped me."

For a moment, Count Hamnet believed him. Then Ulric Skakki laughed. "Well, it's nice to know I'm innocent of *something,* anyway. We got to talking after Eyvind Torfinn's gruesome bash, and we decided we'd do better going north than staying here after all. Yes, curse you, you were right. There—I've said it. Now how much more snow are you going to sell me?"

"You *will* remember that I am the jarl of the Three Tusk clan?" Trasamund thumped his chest with his right fist and glowered in turn at Ulric and Audun.

"Yes, your Ferocity," Audun said. He wasn't likely to raise that kind of trouble any which way.

Ulric pointed toward Hamnet Thyssen. "Why aren't you thundering at him?"

"He already understands," Trasamund answered. "Do you?"

"I don't want to be jarl. I have trouble enough telling myself what to do," Ulric Skakki answered. "You're welcome to the job, as far as I'm concerned."

"I did not think you wanted to lead my clan. You are no witling. You know they would not follow you." Trasamund gave Ulric his fiercest stare. "But when you are among my clansfolk, will you follow me? That is what I must know."

Ulric thought hard before saying, "Unless I think you're wrong enough about something to make a real mess of it."

"That's not good enough," the Bizogot said.

"You'd better take it," Ulric Skakki advised. "It's as much as you'll get, and a lot more than I'd give most people."

Trasamund went right on looking fierce. Hamnet Thyssen could have told him that was the wrong way to go about intimidating Ulric. Luckily, Hamnet didn't need to tell him; he figured it out for himself. "I would kill any Bizogot who was so insolent to me," he snarled.

"Well, you're welcome to try," Ulric Skakki said politely.

Trasamund muttered into his thick, curly beard. Then he booted his horse up the Great North Road. So did Liv. So did Count Hamnet and Audun Gilli. And so did Ulric Skakki. And if he had a smile on his face, he often had a smile on his face. He wasn't openly mocking Trasamund—not so the jarl could prove it, anyhow.

For the first hour or so, Trasamund rode as if trying to shake off pursuers. Then he seemed to decided Ulric really was on his side, or would be if he let him. He slowed down. That had to relieve his horse; the Bizogot was a big, beefy man, and couldn't have been easy to carry.

Liv pointed to little sparrowlike birds hopping around on the snow-covered ground off to the side of the road. "Larkspurs!" she said. "So this is where they go during the winter."

"I suppose so." Hamnet thought for a few heartbeats. "We did see them up in the Bizogot country in summertime, didn't we?" He hadn't paid much attention to the birds. They were too wary to be easily caught, and too small to be worth eating unless a large batch of them were baked in a pie or something of the sort.

"We saw them beyond the Glacier, too," Liv said. "Do those birds fly through the Gap to come here? Do they fly over the Glacier? Or do they winter in the lands we don't know, the lands to the far southwest?"

There was an interesting question. "I don't know," Hamnet admitted. "How would you go about finding out?"

"You might be able to enchant a bird in the summer and then use the spell to see where it went in wintertime," Liv answered. "Of course, something might eat it between the time you cast the spell and the time you tried to check it. And you might not be able to tell anything if the larkspurs beyond the Glacier do go to that other land. God only knows how far away it is."

That was liable to be literally true. No man on this side of the Glacier knew; that was certain. Maybe the Rulers did. And, come to that, maybe the larkspurs did. "*You* might be able to enchant a bird in the summer," Hamnet said. "*I* never could." He paused, then added, "You enchanted me."

Liv blushed and shook her head. "That was no magic, not the way you mean. It was . . . the two of us."

"Well, good." Hamnet had always believed that was so. But he'd believed things about Gudrid that didn't turn out to be true. Could he stand it if he and Liv went sour?

Slowly, he nodded. He could stand their going sour. That was the chance you took, the risk you had to accept. Life wasn't perfect; neither were people. If Liv lied to him, though . . . He would be a long time getting over that, if he ever did.

He didn't think she would. He hoped she wouldn't. And, right now, what else could he do? On he rode, after Trasamund, toward the Bizogot country, toward war with the Rulers, away from Nidaros, away from the Empire, away from everything he held dear. Sometimes you had to break the patterns that had run your life—and run it into the ground. Was he doing that here? Again, he thought so. He hoped so. Whether he was right or not . . . sooner or later, he'd find out.

STOPPING AT THE first serai north of Nidaros made him nervous. He breathed a silent—or maybe a not so silent—sigh of relief when there was no sign of Gudrid in the common room. The only women in the place were barmaids and slatterns.

The men in there fell into two groups: merchants on their way down to Nidaros, and merchants on their way up from Nidaros. They ate and drank together, gossiping and doing their best to find out what lay ahead. They all eyed the party with two Bizogots in it with curiosity they hardly bothered to hide. Hamnet Thyssen supposed he accounted for some of that curiosity, too. He might have been a great many things, but few men would ever have accused him of buying and selling things for a living. Everything about him, from his face to the very way he walked, said he had no compromise in him.

He and his comrades squeezed their way onto the benches at a long table near the hearth. Merchants sat closer together to make room for them. Half a dozen men asked one of two questions—"Where are you from?" and "Where are you bound?"—at more or less the same time.

Before answering, Trasamund shouted an order for a fat roast goose. A passing barmaid waved to show she heard. "And mead!" Trasamund added. "Plenty of mead, by God!" The woman waved again.

"We're out of Nidaros, heading for the lands of the Three Tusk clan and the Gap," Ulric Skakki said.

That couldn't have been better calculated to make everyone else blink and gape. "At this season of the year?" asked a grizzled merchant who found his tongue sooner than the rest. "What will you do there? Besides freeze, I mean?"

Ulric looked not at Trasamund but at Hamnet Thyssen. *Why not?* Hamnet thought. *The more who know, the better. If Sigvat doesn't like it, too bad for him.* "Some of you will have heard the Gap has melted through," he said. "It's true. There's land beyond the Glacier. There are folk beyond the Glacier, too—the Rulers, they call themselves. They're warlike and dangerous. Chances are they'll try to come down into the country we know. We aim to try to stop them."

"You by yourselves?" The gray-bearded trader laughed raucously.

Audun Gilli murmured to himself. Count Hamnet thought his chant sounded familiar. He was right, too. A moment later, the merchant's plate grew a face that looked like a twisted version of his own. "*You* wouldn't have the ballocks to come along, that's certain sure," it jeered.

He stared at it. So did several of the men around him. Their laughs were even coarser than his had been. He picked up his pewter mug and slammed it down on the plate, which shattered like the cheap earthenware it was—or had been.

"You'll pay for that, by God!" a barmaid said. "You can't go breaking crockery for the fun of it."

"It called me a coward!" the trader exclaimed.

The barmaid rolled her eyes. "I didn't figure you for one who saw snakes and demons when he put down too much ale," she said. "Only shows I'm not as smart as I thought I was, doesn't it?" She strutted away, swiveling her hips in magnificent scorn.

Another merchant turned to Hamnet and said, "Next thing you'll tell me is that you went and found the Golden Shrine off beyond the Glacier."

"No." He shook his head. "We looked, but we didn't see any sign of it. It may be there, or it may not. I can't tell you one way or the other."

"I'd like to go back and look again," Ulric Skakki added. "I didn't believe there was any such thing till I went beyond the Glacier. I didn't believe you *could* go beyond the Glacier till I went and did it."

"Neither did I," Hamnet Thyssen said.

"Nor I," Trasamund rumbled. "I didn't know what would happen when I rode up into the narrowest part of the Gap the first time. But I kept going, and I found there was another side after all."

"What about the—what did you call them?—the Rulers, that was it?" yet another trader asked.

"Yes, the Rulers," Count Hamnet said. "What about them? They're dangerous, that's what. For one thing, they ride mammoths to war. They carry lancers and archers aboard the beasts. For another, they're stronger wizards than any we have on this side of the Glacier."

"That's so," Audun Gilli said quietly.

"It is," Liv agreed in her deliberate, newly acquired Raumsdalian.

"The other reason the Rulers are dangerous is that they're sure God or whatever they worship wants them to go out and rule all the other folk around them," Ulric Skakki said. "They don't want to talk to other folk. They just want to tell them what to do. And they may be tough enough to get away with it, too."

"Huh!" the trader said. "They haven't bumped into Raumsdalians before."

"Or Bizogots." Trasamund's tone and the warning gleam in his eye challenged the merchant to argue with him.

The man didn't rise to the challenge. "Or Bizogots," he said quickly. Trasamund subsided.

"Why isn't the Emperor doing anything about these Rulers?" somebody said.

"You would have to ask his Majesty about that." But Hamnet couldn't leave it there. "I wish he would have seemed more interested," he added.

"You . . . talked to him?" the merchant said slowly.

"I talked to him." Hamnet's voice was hard as stone, cold as the snow-drifts outside. He waited to see if the merchant called him a liar, and how. Whether the man went on breathing after that depended on such things.

Before the trader could speak, Ulric Skakki said, "This is the famous Count Hamnet Thyssen. If he says a thing is so, you may rely on it. You'd better rely on it."

Some of the men at the long table had plainly never heard of Hamnet Thyssen, famous or not. To others, he was famous for the wrong thing. "He's the one whose wife . . ." one of them whispered to his neighbor, not quite quietly enough. The trader who'd asked if Hamnet had spoken to the Emperor didn't challenge him. Part of him was relieved, part disappointed. Sometimes fighting was simpler than talking.

"What can we do about the, uh, Rulers?" a merchant asked.

That meant more talking. Count Hamnet sighed. Maybe it would help, maybe it wouldn't. "Spread the word," he said. "The more people who know trouble's coming, the more who know what kind of trouble it is, the better off we'll be." He could hope that was true, anyhow.

He paid the seraikeeper extra for a private room with Liv. "Do you think they believed you?" she asked as they got ready for bed. "Or was it all another traveler's tale to them?"

"Some of them believe some of it, anyhow." Hamnet smiled at his convoluted answer. "Maybe spreading the news will do some good. Maybe some more people will ask Sigvat questions he doesn't want to hear. That may help, too. Who knows? Who knows if anything we do means anything at all?"

Liv lay down on the bed. The frame creaked under her weight. "I've got used to sleeping soft," she said. "It won't be so easy to lie on a mat or wrapped in a hide on the ground when we get back to the Bizogot country."

Hamnet lay down beside her. "Well, then," he said, "you can always lie on me instead."

Her eyes glinted. "I can do that now." She blew out the lamp. And she did.

TWICE UP THE Great North Road in the same year. Twice up into the Bizogot country. Count Hamnet had stayed in his castle most of the time after Gudrid left him. He traveled because he had to, not because he enjoyed it for its own sake. He would get where he was going, and he would try to do what needed doing.

Ulric Skakki, now, savored each new day, each new sight. He couldn't

stand doing the same thing all the time. Everything interested him—the
fading of the fields, the approach of the forest that stretched north to the
tree line. Trasamund and Liv were the same way. They were nomads from a
nomad folk. Where Ulric came by his wanderlust was harder to fathom.

Audun Gilli? The wizard was always hard to fathom, at least for Hamnet.
He rode along, never saying much. Sometimes he got drunk when the travelers stopped at a serai. If he did it all the time, Hamnet would have tried to
make him stop or sent him back to Nidaros. But he didn't. Some nights he
stayed sober. If he drank for amusement and not because he had to, Count
Hamnet didn't see that he had any business complaining.

Serais grew fewer, too. They'd done the same thing the last time Hamnet
came north, but he didn't notice it so much then. In spring, mosquitoes
were the only things wrong with camping outdoors. They could come inside, too, as he had reason to know. If you didn't have a good notion of what
you were doing during the winter, though, you could easily freeze to
death—and the more easily the farther north you went.

Hamnet Thyssen wasn't bad at tending to himself in winter weather. He
freely admitted the Bizogots and Ulric Skakki were better. When they ran
up tents, no cold air got inside. They built snow barriers north of the tents
to blunt the force of the Breath of God. They made the most of fur blankets
and small braziers.

Audun Gilli seemed much more lackadaisical. Count Hamnet wondered
if he should scold the wizard or worry about him. Liv shook her head when
he raised the question. "He uses spells to keep himself snug," she said. "I
wouldn't do that. It would make me tired, and I have enough things making
me tired already. Easier just to do things right the first time. But if you have
the spells, you can use them if you choose."

"All right," Hamnet said. "I won't bother him about it, then. I didn't
want to wake up one morning and find we had an icicle instead of a wizard,
that's all."

"He won't freeze," Liv assured him. "Not unless someone overpowers all
his wards, and who would want to do anything like that?"

"The Rulers?" Hamnet said.

Liv's breath caught. She hadn't looked for an answer to her question.
"How could they reach him here, inside the Empire?" she asked. "How
could they even know he's coming north again?"

"I'm no wizard—I can't tell you that," Hamnet Thyssen said. "But we
saw they know more of magic than we do. Just because we can't imagine

how they would do something doesn't mean they can't do it. Or am I wrong?"

Plainly, Liv wanted to tell him he was. As plainly, she couldn't. Her voice troubled, she said, "Maybe you should speak of this with him tomorrow. I don't know if you're right or wrong. Either way, though, Audun should think about it."

"I'll do that." Hamnet blew out the candle that lit their tent. As darkness descended, he added, "Tomorrow."

He almost forgot about it the next day. Audun Gilli didn't draw attention to himself. He seemed to do everything he could not to draw attention to himself. Eventually, Hamnet did remember. The wizard heard him out; Audun was seldom rude. "Well, there's a cheery notion," he said when Hamnet finished.

"What can you do about it? Can you do anything?" the Raumsdalian noble asked.

"I don't know. I don't know how much I have to worry about it, either," Audun said. "Maybe I'll tighten up my wards, just in case. Maybe your lady friend ought to do the same thing, too."

Hamnet grunted. He hadn't thought about that. But if the Rulers could know Audun was on the move, they could know the same thing about Liv. "I'll tell her," Hamnet promised.

"Me?" Liv said when he did.

"Why not? Who here besides Audun knows as much about their magic as you do?" Count Hamnet said. "If they *can* reach this far, doesn't that give them a reason to go after you? Do you want to take the chance that they can't?"

He admired the way she thought it over and then shook her head. She really did think things through; she didn't start with her mind closed, the way so many people did. "No, I don't want to take that chance," she said. "If they marked Audun, they might have noticed me, too."

"If they didn't notice you, they were blind," Hamnet Thyssen said.

That flustered Liv much more than the idea of sorcerous attack from the Rulers did. "You!" She wagged her hand at him; it would have been an angry finger if she weren't wearing mittens. "Why do you say such things?"

"Because they're true?"

She ignored him. He smiled, which only seemed to annoy her more. He wasn't a great one for fancy speeches and praise of women's beauty. But any praise at all seemed more than Liv was used to.

They came to a serai not long before the sun went down. There would be a few more in the towns in the north woods. After that, the travelers would have to arrange their own shelter or pay the price for failure. A roaring fire and greasy roast mutton suited Hamnet fine after a long day on the road.

He ate more mutton for breakfast, and washed it down with beer mulled with a hot poker. "Not fancy, but it sticks to the ribs," Ulric Skakki said, and Hamnet nodded.

The travelers were about to go out to the horses when a newcomer walked into the serai. Hamnet and Ulric looked at each other. Had the stranger traveled through the frigid night to get here? By the way he yawned and rubbed at his red-tracked eyes, he probably had. "Do I see Count Hamnet Thyssen here?" he asked.

Hamnet got to his feet. His hand rested on the hilt of his sword. "You see me," he said. "Why do you care?"

"I am an imperial courier." The newcomer handed him a rolled parchment held closed by a ribbon and by the imperial seal stamped into golden wax. "This is an order recalling you to Nidaros at once."

"Give it to me." Hamnet broke the seal and read the order. It was exactly what the courier said it was. He recognized Sigvat's signature; the document was genuine. Nodding to the man, he said, "All right—I have it. Thank you."

"You will accompany me back down to the capital, then?"

"No."

The courier's jaw dropped. "But . . . But . . ." He tried again. "You are *ordered* to return. *Ordered*. By the Emperor. Sigvat II." He added the name as if Count Hamnet might have forgot who ruled Raumsdalia.

"No," Hamnet said again. "He's welcome to exile me. Why not? I'm leaving the Empire anyhow. And I *am* leaving. I'm not going back to Nidaros. If he wants to confiscate my castle down in the southeast, he can do that, too. I'm in no position to stop him, God knows. I hope he'll treat my retainers well. I haven't seen them since last spring, and they have nothing to do with this."

"But . . . you're disobeying a direct imperial command." The courier didn't seem to think such a thing was possible, or even imaginable.

"I am, all right." Count Hamnet nodded, as if to encourage him. "You catch on fast."

"You can't do that." The young Raumsdalian sounded absolutely certain.

"Watch me," Hamnet Thyssen said calmly. Being clear in his own mind about what he aimed to do brought a wonderful sense of freedom. He was his own man, not Sigvat's man or even the Empire's man. He would do what *he* chose, and hard luck to anyone who didn't like it.

"What am I supposed to do?" the courier bleated.

"Tell the Emperor you delivered his order. Tell him I told you no. Here, wait." He borrowed a quill and ink from the seraikeeper, who watched the drama with wide eyes. *I have read this order. I decline to obey it. Do not blame the messenger—it is not his fault,* Hamnet wrote, and signed his name in a fine round hand. He gave the parchment back to the courier. "There you go. It shouldn't have anything to do with you. This is between his Majesty and me."

"This won't help," the courier predicted, voice full of gloom.

"Would you like the wizard here and me to witness whatever Count Hamnet wrote?" Ulric Skakki asked.

Even more gloomily, the courier shook his head. "I could have God witness it, and it wouldn't do me any good."

If Sigvat was in one of *those* moods, the man might be right. "Tell me something," Hamnet said. "Did Earl Eyvind Torfinn's wife have anything to do with getting this order sent?" The courier looked blank. Hamnet added, "Her name is Gudrid."

"Oh. Her. I know who you mean. The one who's like *that* with the Emperor." The courier twisted two fingers together. But then he shrugged. "I don't know anything about it. A clerk gave me the order and told me what was in it in case it got wet or something, that's all."

The one who's like that *with the Emperor.* Hamnet Thyssen wasn't much surprised; he'd already had a good idea that that was so.

"All right, then. You'd better head south, then, and let Sigvat know." Hamnet had a second thought. "Unless you'd sooner come north with me?"

"No, thanks. I'm not a crazy man. I'm not a rebel." Shaking his head, the courier walked out of the common room.

Ulric Skakki patted Count Hamnet on the back. "You crazy man, you," he said affectionately. "You rebel."

"Do not mock this man," Trasamund growled. "He has done what a free man should. He has done what a Bizogot would. He's shown he is worthy to come north, worthy to take his place in the Three Tusk clan."

"However you please, your Ferocity." Now Ulric seemed as indifferent as a dead man. He could assume any tone, or none, in the blink of an eye. "See how much you like it when Hamnet tells you where to head in instead of the Emperor."

"He would not do that." But Trasamund sounded doubtful.

"Don't be an idiot. Of course he would." Ulric turned back to Hamnet Thyssen. "Wouldn't you, your Grace?"

"Probably." Hamnet knew he would be lying if he said anything else. "I would if the jarl made the same sort of mistake Sigvat's made, anyhow."

Trasamund beamed. "Then we have nothing to worry about." He thumped his chest. "Me, I do not make mistakes like this. I am too clever."

"And too modest, too," Ulric Skakki remarked.

"Yes. And that," Trasamund agreed. Liv raised an eyebrow. Audun Gilli looked up at the ceiling. Count Hamnet looked down at his hands. Ulric whistled a snatch of something or other. Trasamund wouldn't have recognized irony if he were a lodestone.

"I think we'd better leave," Hamnet Thyssen said.

As he went out the door, he wished he were wearing chainmail instead of furs and leather. If that courier decided to exact punishment for disobeying an imperial order, he could be waiting out there with a bow, looking for a good shot. He could be, but he wasn't.

The travelers hadn't gone far from the serai before the Great North Road plunged into the forest belt. Liv sighed. "All these trees," she said. "We could do so much with them—and they even smell good." Her nostrils twitched. Then they twitched again. The wistful smile left her face. "That's not just trees I smell."

Hamnet Thyssen sniffed, too. "I know what that is—it's the musk of a short-faced bear."

"It is," Ulric Skakki agreed. "No doubt about it. "Maybe a sow that had a litter, and now she's out of food." He strung his bow. "Much as I hate to mention it, we qualify. If a short-faced bear would try to eat Gudrid, it only goes to show they'll eat anything."

That jerked a laugh out of Count Hamnet. Trasamund visibly started to say something. Then, just as visibly, he changed his mind. Hamnet strung his bow, too. Short-faced bears were hard to kill with arrows. Sometimes, though, they would run away if they got hurt. And sometimes getting hurt would only infuriate them and make them attack all the more ferociously. You never could tell.

"Audun, Liv—if you know any charms for fighting off animals, this would be a good time to dust them off," Hamnet said.

"These don't always work," Liv said. "Animals are more deeply connected to nature than shamanry can ever hope to be."

"Well, see if you can make this beast unbearable all the same," Ulric said. Audun Gilli and Hamnet Thyssen winced. Liv was too new to Raumsdalian to get the pun or realize how bad it was.

The horses snorted and sidestepped. They smelled the bear, too, and didn't like it. "The wind is blowing from it to us," Hamnet said. "Maybe it won't realize we're here."

"I hate to tell you this, your Grace, but bears have eyes as well as noses. They have ears, too," Ulric said.

"Really? Tell me more about these things, and I'll taste what you have to say." Unlike Trasamund, Hamnet Thyssen didn't miss sarcasm aimed his way. He didn't put up with it, either.

"There!" The Bizogot jarl pointed. "I saw something move behind that tree."

Hamnet peered in that direction. He wasn't sure which tree Trasamund meant, but he didn't see anything moving. Was a short-faced bear clever enough to hide behind a tree trunk and peek out at its intended prey? He wouldn't have thought so, but maybe he was wrong.

Then the bear came out. It wasn't very big, not as far as short-faced bears went, but they went a long way in that direction. When it rose on its hind legs to growl at the travelers, Hamnet saw it wasn't a sow, as Ulric Skakki had guessed—and as Hamnet had thought himself—but a boar.

Ulric let fly. His bowstring thrummed. The bear dropped down in that same instant, so the arrow hissed over its head and thumped into a tree trunk, where it stood thrilling. Ulric swore. He reached over his shoulder to grab another shaft from his quiver.

At the same time as the short-faced bear ducked under the arrow, Liv gasped and Audun Gilli let out a wordless exclamation. Then he said, "Magic!" and her hands twisted in a sign Bizogots used against evil.

All that Hamnet noted only out of the corner of his ear, so to speak. His attention centered on the bear. If he gave it an arrow in the face, that might hurt it enough to make it run away. He drew his bow—and the bowstring snapped. His curses made Ulric Skakki's seem a beginner's beside them.

The bear let out a deep growl and sprang forward, straight toward him. Ulric shot again in that same moment, but only grazed the bear's right hind leg. Count Hamnet just had time to draw his sword before the bear was on him. It reared again, perhaps to smash him off his horse.

He swung first. His blade bit into its right paw, severing three claws.

Blood spurted and splashed the snow with red. The bear roared, opening its fang-filled mouth enormously wide. As it did, Ulric shot an arrow straight into that inviting target. This time, the short-faced bear's roar was more like a scream. It came down on all fours, raking Hamnet's horse with the claws on its left paw as its forelegs lowered.

The horse screamed, too, more shrilly than the bear had. It sprang away. Hamnet Thyssen tried with all his strength to keep it under some kind of control, and also tried to stay on its back. The bear lumbered after him. The wound on its front paw must have slowed it; short-faced bears could usually outsprint horses.

Ulric Skakki had a perfect shot this time—right at the bear's heart. But his bowstring also broke. This time, he outcursed Count Hamnet.

Trasamund rode up and slammed his sword down just behind the bear's ears. The animal had hardly seemed to notice his approach—all its attention was on Hamnet Thyssen. It let out a startled grunt and slumped to the snow, dead. No wonder—Hamnet heard its skull break.

And then all the travelers swore at once. The dead bear writhed in the snow. Its shape changed. After a couple of minutes, it was a dead bear no more, but rather a dead man. "That fellow comes from the Rulers," Audun Gilli said. No one tried to contradict him; that strong-featured, heavily bearded face plainly belonged to one of the men from beyond the Glacier.

"What in blazes is he doing here?" Ulric said, fitting a new string to the bow that had let him down.

Hamnet Thyssen was doing the same thing. "The way it looks," he said, "I think he was trying to kill me."

"You don't think well of yourself, do you?" Ulric Skakki mocked as automatically as he breathed.

"I think Thyssen is right," Trasamund said. "When it was a bear, it let you shoot it. It let me strike it. It wanted only the count. No one else, nothing else, mattered to it."

"Why would that be?" Ulric asked.

"I see only one answer—they think he is dangerous to them." That wasn't Trasamund, who'd raised the point. It wasn't Liv, who might have been expected to take Hamnet's side. It was Audun Gilli. His objectivity helped make him convincing.

"Aren't we all dangerous to them? By God, we'd better be," Ulric Skakki said. "Should I write them an angry letter complaining that they don't think enough of me to try murdering me? I'm tempted, if only I could find some-body to deliver it." He sounded affronted that the Rulers might not find him worth killing.

"Believe me, I could do without the honor," Hamnet Thyssen said as he dismounted to look at the wounds the bear had scored in his horse's flank. They were long but not deep—plenty to pain and frighten the animal, but not crippling. He thought they would heal well. The horse trembled when he put his hands anywhere near the gashes. He bent down, scooped up some snow, and pressed it against the animal's wounds. The horse snorted and started to shy. Then it seemed to decide the cold felt good, and let out what sounded like a sigh of relief.

"Bear grease might help," Ulric said.

"How about shaman grease?" Trasamund said. "You can slit that bas-tard's belly and use what he's got." He wasn't joking, not in the least. Bizo-gots wasted nothing. They couldn't afford to.

"This would be the same sort of spell that wizard used when he turned into an owl, wouldn't it?" Hamnet asked Liv.

"I would say so, yes," she answered, her voice troubled. "It is a more thorough spell than we use. It is a more thorough spell than we know, though some of ours do the same thing."

"How did he get down here?" Trasamund said. "A long way from the far side of the Gap to this forest."

"Maybe he was an owl till not long ago. Maybe he flew," Audun Gilli said.

"I doubt it," Liv said. "With us, at least, a shaman has a spirit animal. If the animal is a dire wolf, say, the shaman may howl when the moon is full. But he will not hop like a snowshoe hare, and he will not take wing like a ptarmigan."

"Is it the same for the Rulers? Would it have to be?" Audun asked.

"If it is not the same, they are even stranger and darker than I thought." Liv sounded more troubled than ever.

"This one was a bear, and now he's dead," Trasamund said. "We still live, no matter how strange and dark he was, the son of a scut. And we'd better get up to the north and put a stop to the trouble the Rulers are causing."

Hamnet Thyssen wondered what Sigvat II would have done if he knew the Rulers were already inside the Empire. He laughed bitterly as he re-mounted. Seeing that the wizard or shaman or whatever he was had tried to kill him, Sigvat might have congratulated the fellow, or even ennobled him.

"Will the horse be all right?" Ulric asked. "We still might be able to buy you another one."

"I think he will," Hamnet said. "I think Trasamund's right, too. We need to get up to the Gap as fast as we can."

"Why?" Ulric Skakki said. "The Rulers are already here." On that cheery note, the travelers rode north again.

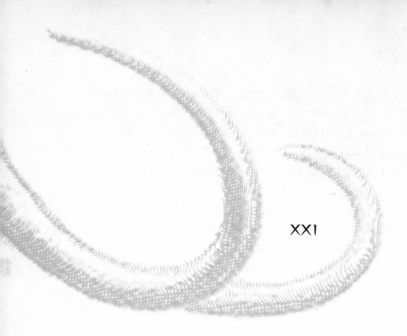

XXI

IN THE MIDDLE of winter, Hamnet Thyssen saw only a little difference between the Bizogot country and the Glacier farther north. Snow blanketed everything. On days when the sun shone, the reflections from all that white could dazzle and overwhelm the eye. Trasamund and Liv had no goggles, but rubbed streaks of ash from a campfire under their eyes to cut the glare. Before long, the Raumsdalians with them started doing the same thing. It was ugly, but it helped.

"I'm wearing musk-ox dung." Ulric Skakki sounded more cheerful than he had any business being.

"Well, we've been eating it whenever we cook up here," Hamnet said. "Why not wear it, too?"

"I wish you hadn't reminded me," Audun Gilli said.

"I wish for all kinds of things that won't come true—good sense from the Emperor, for instance," Ulric said. "What's one more wasted wish?"

Hamnet Thyssen looked around, as if to see who might have overheard Ulric. Down in Raumsdalia, someone could have betrayed him to the Emperor's servants, in which case he would not have a happy time of it. Up here, he was among friends, and had the sense to realize it before Hamnet did.

Trasamund saw the Raumsdalian's glance, and knew what it meant. "No spies up here, your Grace," he said. "No informers. You're in Bizogot country again. You're in the free lands. Breathe deep. Breathe free."

"What if someone back in the Three Tusk clan has been talking about you behind your back, your Ferocity?" Ulric Skakki asked in his most innocent tones.

Beneath the dirt and ashes on his face, Trasamund turned red. "If I hear about it, I'll knock the son of a mammoth turd's teeth out!" he growled.

"Welcome to the free lands. Welcome to Bizogot country," Ulric said.

"And what's that supposed to mean?" the jarl demanded.

"What do you think it means?" Ulric asked.

"I think it means you're making fun of me on the sly, you Raumsdalian hound," Trasamund said, and he wasn't wrong. "Didn't I ask you when you chose to come north if you would obey me?"

"How am I disobeying you? Did you ever tell me not to make fun of you? Did you ever tell me not to make fun of silly ideas?" Ulric sounded mild, which didn't mean he wasn't serious.

"If you obey, you have to respect. You are not respecting," Trasamund said.

Ulric Skakki went to his knees before the jarl. Then he went to his belly, knocking his forehead in the snow. "Your Ferocity! Your Wonderfulness!" he cried. "Your Highness! Your Majesty! Your exalted Magnificence! May I please be allowed to kiss some of the musk-ox dung from the sole of your boot?"

Liv giggled helplessly. That meant Trasamund's venomous glaze divided itself between Ulric and her, and lost some of its effect. He stirred Ulric with the toe of his—with luck—clean boot. "Get up, you fool. Give me the respect I deserve, not this stupid show of more."

"I was trying to do that." The adventurer brushed snow off his front. "You didn't seem to like it very well, either."

"No one likes to be made fun of," Trasamund said accurately.

"Well, your Ferocity, if you say something silly, can't I let you know I think it's silly?" Ulric Skakki asked. "If I can't, what's your famous Bizogot freedom worth? I might as well have stayed in the Empire after all."

Trasamund started to answer, then stopped. This time, Ulric got the full force of his glare. He seemed to have no trouble enduring it. "You twist things up," Trasamund complained. "I am the jarl. I know what I can do, and I know what I am not supposed to do. And I know what my clansfolk can do, too. You go past that."

"He is a foreigner, your Ferocity," Liv said. "He did not suck in our ways with his mother's milk."

"Do you follow all our Raumsdalian customs when you come down into the Empire?" Hamnet Thyssen added. "I don't think so."

"Maybe not," Trasamund said. "But I don't dance on them for the sport of it, either. Ulric was trying to pull my prong for the sport of it. I won't put up with that." A Raumsdalian would have talked about getting his leg pulled. As usual, the Bizogot idiom was gamier.

And the jarl was probably right. Ulric Skakki *did* make trouble for no better reason than that he liked making trouble. He'd certainly annoyed Count Hamnet more than once. Now he said, "I'll be mild as milk. You can rely on it."

"You'll be as mild as smetyn, and like smetyn you'll make everyone around you wild," Trasamund predicted. "The only reason I tell you to come along is the hope you will madden the Rulers more than the Three Tusk clan."

"That's good enough," Ulric Skakki said cheerfully, and on they went.

THE BREATH OF God reached down to Raumsdalia in the winter. Hamnet Thyssen thought he knew what blizzards could do. After the first couple he went through on the plains, he owned himself an amateur.

He was as warmly dressed as any man could be, in furs with mittens on his hands and baggy felt boots with more loose felt in them on his feet. Only his eyes showed. His hood came down low on his forehead. A thick musk-ox wool scarf covered his nose and mouth. When snow came roaring down from the north riding a wind almost strong enough to knock a man off his feet, it hardly seemed to matter.

Trasamund and Liv took being out and about in such weather for granted. "We're still a long way from the Glacier," Liv screamed in Hamnet's ear, that being the only way to make herself heard through the wind's howls. "This is nothing."

"It seems like something to me," he shouted back. Her eyes showed amusement, or he thought they did. When they were the only part of her he could see, he had trouble being sure.

It was blowing too hard for them to hope to set up their tents when they stopped for the evening. Trasamund and Liv started making snow huts, lumping snow into blocks and building inward to form a dome. They left a tiny opening in the roof to let smoke out. The entrance faced south and had a dogleg to break the force of the wind.

"What about the horses?" Audun Gilli asked.

But the Bizogots were already piling up more snow blocks into a windbreak. Liv used a little magic to melt some snow on the ground and let it refreeze as ice around the poles she used to tether the horses. "They won't be able to go anywhere," she said confidently.

"Suppose bears come? Or wolves? What do we do then?" Audun asked.

"We walk," Trasamund answered with withering scorn. The idea didn't seem to worry him. It worried Hamnet Thyssen, but he didn't say anything about it. What *could* he say? The wizard also kept quiet.

No one said anything about how the travelers would occupy the snow huts, either. But Hamnet and Liv ended up in one, with the other two Raumsdalians and Trasamund in the other. Just getting out of the ravening wind made Hamnet feel warmer. He fumbled for flint and steel in the darkness inside. He had a little leather pouch with tinder in it on his belt. The sooner he got a fire going, the happier he would be.

Liv did it before him. A few murmured words were enough to set a lamp alight. He gave her a seated bow. "Handy traveling with a shaman," he said.

"Up here, any Bizogot will know that spell," she said. "We need it too often, and not knowing it can kill."

"Can Bizogots who aren't shamans work it?" Hamnet asked. "Is the power in the spell or in the spellcaster?"

"This spell works most of the time for most people," Liv answered. "Whether that means most people have some power or the spell itself is strong . . . I don't know. I never thought about it."

Most of the time, Hamnet wouldn't have thought about it, either. It was the kind of question more likely to interest Eyvind Torfinn. But here, in the snow hut, fire was naturally on his mind. He and Liv didn't need much of a blaze. The heat from their bodies warmed the cramped space surprisingly well. The lamp gave more light than heat.

Liv even had a chunk of musk-ox meat with her. As she sliced off frozen strips, she sent Hamnet a sly look. "Can you eat raw meat?"

"If I'm hungry enough, I can—" He broke off. He almost said he could eat anything if he got hungry enough. But, since the Bizogots ate stomachs and guts with their contents still in them when they got hungry enough, that might prove more bragging than he cared to back up.

To his relief, Liv took what he did say for a complete sentence. She started passing him strips of meat. He had no trouble eating them. They might even have been a delicacy down in Nidaros. And the company here was better than any he would have known in the imperial capital.

"What's it like making love when the wind is screaming outside?" he asked.

Liv smiled. "You want to find out, I suppose. Well, why not? It's warm enough, and the work will make us warmer."

As long as they lay on their clothes and blankets, it was fine. When Hamnet stuck his foot in the snow for a couple of heartbeats, it put him off his stroke, but he quickly recovered. Afterwards, he dressed in a hurry, and so did Liv. They wrapped themselves in their blankets and fell asleep.

It was dark inside the hut when Count Hamnet woke—the lamp had gone out. The wind still howled and screeched outside. Within the hut, though, it was snug and more than warm enough. The Bizogots knew what they were doing, all right. He yawned, twisted, and went back to sleep.

The next time he woke up, a little light was coming in through the smoke hole. He needed a moment to realize the storm had died. It was almost eerily quiet. Beside him, Liv said, "It's blown itself out. I hoped it would."

"I wondered if it would bury the hut before it did," Hamnet said.

"No—too windy for that. The snow wouldn't stick enough," she said. "We may have to dig out of the entrance, though."

They did. As they shoveled snow with mittened hands, Hamnet Thyssen said, "I hope the horses came through all right."

"So do I. They're your southern beasts, not the ones we breed ourselves." Liv went on digging as she spoke. She broke out into fresh air. "We'll know soon."

Standing up came as a relief to Hamnet. He'd felt as crowded in the snow as he felt small and insignificant traveling across the frozen plains. Everything was frozen now, the ground as far as the eye could see robed in white. Even his furs and Liv's had snow all over them.

He trudged through snow that crunched under his boots to the windbreak Trasamund and Liv had built. The horses were still there, still alive, and eager for food. He had a little sugar made from maple sap down in the Empire. The animals snuffled up the treat and snorted for more.

Liv started digging out the snow in front of the other hut's entrance. Somebody inside said something. Hamnet couldn't make out what it was, but Liv's tart answer told him. "No, I'm not a bear," she said. "It would serve you right if I were."

Audun Gilli, Ulric Skakki, and Trasamund emerged a moment later. "Good thing the sun's in the sky," Ulric said. "Otherwise we wouldn't have any idea which way north was."

"I could use the spell with the needle," Audun said. "It wouldn't be perfect, not up here"—he was ready to admit that now—"but it would give us the right idea."

"If the water didn't freeze before you could finish chanting." Trasamund sounded altogether serious. Hamnet decided he had a right to be. With the air this cold, water would turn to ice in a hurry.

"We've got the sun," the Raumsdalian noble said. "Let's use it." They mounted and rode north. The southern horses did know enough to paw forage up from under the snow. Hamnet hadn't been sure they would. One less thing to worry about, anyhow.

ONLY LAST SUMMER'S frozen marsh plants sticking up from the snow here and there told the travelers they'd come to the edge of Sudertorp Lake. No screeching waterfowl now—nothing but the silent grip of winter. Count Hamnet looked west, then east. The frozen lake stretched as far as he could see in either direction.

"Which is the shorter way around?" he asked.

"They both look pretty long," Ulric said.

"That both will cost us time," Hamnet said fretfully. The sense that it was slipping away gnawed at him.

"See the southerners," Trasamund said to Liv in the Bizogot language. She grinned and nodded. Whatever amused the jarl, she found it funny, too.

"What's the answer, then?" Hamnet Thyssen asked with as little sarcasm as he could.

"We don't go around," Trasamund answered. "We go straight across, by God. This season of the year, musk oxen and mammoths cross lakes and rivers. If the ice holds them, it will hold us, too."

Hamnet and Ulric and Audun exchanged glances. Hamnet had skated on frozen ponds in winter—what Raumsdalian hadn't? But sending horses across? That was a different story.

"What happens if we fall in?" Audun Gilli asked the question on Hamnet's mind, and surely on Ulric's, too.

"If we're close to shore, we drag you out, get on dry land, build a big fire fast as we can, and maybe you live," the Bizogot jarl answered. "If not so close, you freeze before we can do it." Like a lot of mammoth-herders, he was callous when it came to things nobody could do anything about. He went on, "It won't happen, though. The ice now is as thick as Jesper Fletti's head, and even harder."

That made both Ulric and Hamnet Thyssen smile. Audun Gilli just nodded seriously and said, "I hope you're right."

"I'm betting my neck, too," Trasamund said. The wizard nodded again.

The horses went out onto the ice without much fuss. They placed their feet carefully. Even with horseshoes—one more thing the Bizogots, who didn't smelt iron, went without—the going was slippery. But Trasamund proved right about one thing—the frozen surface of the lake was more than solid enough to bear the heavy animals' weight. Except for the smoothness, Hamnet couldn't tell he wasn't riding across solid ground; there was no shaking under him to suggest water yet unfrozen lay beneath the ice.

Sudertorp Lake was a long way across. Going around would have been three or four times as long—Hamnet understood as much. But he still felt peculiar with nothing but ice all around. He felt as if he were riding across the top of *the* Glacier.

When he spoke that conceit aloud, Ulric Skakki clapped his mittened hands. "Now there's a sport no one's likely to try soon," he said. "Men might get to the top, I suppose, but not horses. Your Ferocity!"

"What do you want?" Trasamund often suspected Ulric of laughing up his sleeve at him—and often was right.

But the adventurer sounded serious as he asked, "Have any Bizogots ever tried climbing to the top of the Glacier?"

"Not in my clan," the jarl answered. "Not so anyone remembers. I've heard that men have tried farther west. I don't think anyone ever made it, though. There are mountains that stick up through the Glacier. Some of them are topped with green in the summertime—but what grows on them no one knows. How would you get to them to find out?"

Count Hamnet whistled softly. That wasn't a small thought. Those mountain peaks above the Glacier—*what* might grow up there? Anything at all. How long had they been there, each by itself? Eons. Could there be people up there, people who did roam the top of the Glacier and had no more hope of coming down than the Bizogots and Raumsdalians did of going up? What would they eat? The top of the Glacier made the Bizogot plains seem paradise by comparison.

"Probably rabbits and lemmings and voles up there," Ulric said when Hamnet put that into words. "Bound to be birds, too, at least in summer. But I wouldn't want to try to live up there, and that's the truth." He shivered.

So did Hamnet Thyssen. And then, unmistakably, so did the ice beneath them. Hamnet thought he heard a crackling noise far below. He pointed at Trasamund, not that pointing with a forefinger in a mitten did much good. "You said this couldn't happen!" he shouted at the Bizogot.

"It can't!" Trasamund shouted back, even though it was.

The crackling grew louder. "I don't know about you people, but I'm making for shore as fast as I can," Ulric Skakki said, and booted his horse up to a trot and then to a gallop.

That seemed like such a good idea, Count Hamnet did the same thing. So did Trasamund and Liv and Audun Gilli. But the crackling followed them and got louder still, even through the drumming thunder of their horses' hooves. "This is sorcery!" Audun shouted. "Someone is *making* the ice break up!"

"Well, for God's sake make it stop!" Hamnet shouted back. He thought about what the jarl said about going into the icy water. Having thought about it, he wished he hadn't. To die like that . . . It would end fast, but not fast enough.

And *someone* could only mean *someone from the Rulers*. How did the folk who lived beyond the Glacier track the travelers here? Hamnet had no idea. He wished Audun Gilli or Liv did.

Liv began to chant in the Bizogot tongue. She took her left hand from the reins so she could use it for passes. "I know that spell," Trasamund said.

"Do you?" Hamnet Thyssen looked back over his shoulder. What he saw made him wish he hadn't. Cracks in the frozen surface of the lake stretched toward him like skeletal arms wanting to hold him in an embrace that would last forever.

"I do, by God," the jarl answered. "When snow is very dry, it won't hold together for things like huts. That spell clumps it, you might say."

"Will it do the same for ice?" Hamnet asked.

"I don't know," Trasamund said. "We're going to find out, don't you think?"

Audun Gilli rode up alongside Liv. He reached out and set a hand on her leg. Most of the time, Hamnet would have killed him for that. Now, though, he understood the wizard wasn't feeling her up. Audun was lending her strength. He didn't know the spell; it wasn't one Raumsdalians were likely to use. But he was doing what he could to help.

Would what he was doing, what Liv was doing, be enough? Count Hamnet looked over his shoulder again. Those grasping cracks were still coming forward as fast as a horse could run—but no faster, or so he thought. So he hoped. He looked ahead. That rise had to be the beginning of solid ground, real ground. It also had to be most of a mile away. Could Liv hold back the sorcery from the north long enough, slow it down enough, to let them all win to safety?

If the horse stumbles under me, I'm a dead man, Hamnet thought. Even so, he booted it on as fiercely as he could. If the cracks in the ice caught up with him, he was also dead. When he looked back one more time, he gasped in dismay. He could see black water there where the cracks had widened. No, he didn't want to go into that. "Come on, horse!" he called. "Run, curse you!"

And the horse did run. And its hooves thudded up the slope of Suder-torp Lake's northern bank just as the cracks and black water reached the edge of the lake. Ulric and Trasamund were ahead of him, Liv and Audun just behind.

For a bad moment, he wondered if the spell could tear land asunder as it tore ice. But it *did* stop at the lake's edge. He reined in, breathing almost as hard as his horse was. Then he pulled back his hood in lieu of doffing a cap to salute the shaman and wizard. "I think you saved us," he said.

Liv was panting, as if she'd run a long way. "I think I did, too," she said. "And I know—I know—I had help from Audun."

"You knew the spell," Audun Gilli told her. "It worked . . . just well enough." He looked back toward the cracks in the frozen surface of the lake.

So did Liv. Her shiver had nothing to do with winter on the Bizogot plains. "Just well enough is right," she said. "I couldn't stop the spell. I didn't have a chance in the world of stopping it. All I could do was slow it down a little."

"How did the Rulers reach so far?" Hamnet Thyssen asked.

"I don't know!" she blazed, sounding angry at him and herself and the Rulers all at once. "I don't know, I tell you. If I knew, I'd be able to do something like that myself, and I can't. Nobody can."

"Nobody except them." Audun Gilli pointed north.

"What does that say?" Count Hamnet had a pretty good notion what it said, but hoped he was wrong. "Does it say we'd better not quarrel with them, or else we'll lose? Does it say we should bend the knee to them, because that's the best we can hope to do? If it does, why are we fighting?"

"We're fighting because we're free, and we're going to stay free," Trasamund answered before Liv could speak. "If that's not why you're fighting, go back to the Empire, because I want nothing to do with you."

"I'm not going anywhere," Hamnet said. "Except north, that is."

"Next frozen lake we come across, we ought to go around it and not over it," Ulric Skakki said.

"I wonder if it matters," Hamnet said. "If the Rulers know where we are, if they can strike as they please, they'll find some other way, some other place, to try to kill us."

"Foolish to give them the same chance twice," Ulric insisted.

"Why? They've seen it didn't work, so wouldn't they think it's not worth trying again?" Count Hamnet said. "We haven't seen any more wizards pretending to be short-faced bears after we killed the first one."

"That man was not pretending." Liv and Audun Gilli said the same thing at the same time in two different languages.

"Whether he was or not, they only tried it once," Count Hamnet said stubbornly.

"Are we as safe as we can be now?" Trasamund asked. The only answers the others could give were shrugs. How could they hope to know? But even shrugs satisfied the jarl. "Either we let them scare us, or we don't," he said. "And if we don't, we keep moving."

"Spoken like a nomad," Ulric said.

"I *am* a nomad," Trasamund answered proudly. "I am on the way back to my clan's grazing grounds. And you had better be, too." He urged his horse north. The others came with him. Having ridden so far, what else could they do?

HAMNET THYSSEN DIDN'T like his dreams. They'd mostly been happy after he and Liv became lovers. The dreams he'd had since returning to the frozen steppe, though, were muddled and grim, and they got worse the farther north he traveled.

When he finally complained about it, Liv looked surprised. "Yours, too?" she said. "Mine have been the same way. I don't care for the omen."

They soon found they weren't the only ones with ugly dreams. Ulric Skakki made light of his, saying, "What do you expect after you eat musk-ox chitterlings two days running?"

"What's wrong with musk-ox chitterlings? They're good," Trasamund declared. "And besides, they're a lot better than going empty."

"I won't argue with the second part of that," Ulric said. "The first . . . is a matter of opinion, and it isn't mine."

Even though Trasamund liked what he was eating, he also had bad dreams. He put it down to worry. "I keep wondering how things are with the clan," he said. "I imagine everything that could go wrong. Do that long enough and you'll start doing it whether you're awake or asleep."

Audun Gilli said, "If my dreams are bad, it's because someone is trying to make them bad. And someone is doing it, too."

"The Rulers?" Hamnet said.

"I can't think of anyone else it's likely to be," Audun said. "Can you?"

"*I* can't." Liv's voice was worried, too. "None of the other Bizogots hate the Three Tusk clan enough to bring a sending down on us."

"What about his Imperial Majesty?" Ulric Skakki, as usual, was full of pleasant ideas.

However much Count Hamnet wished he could, he couldn't dismiss that one out of hand. The most he would say was, "I don't like to think that of Sigvat."

"Well, neither do I. But I don't like nightmares, either. I don't like waking tireder than I went to sleep," Ulric said. "How do we know for sure our own wizards weren't cracking the ice on Sudertorp Lake?"

"How do we know? Because they cursed well weren't, that's how," Audun Gilli said. "I know what our sorcery feels like. I ought to, by God. This had nothing to do with that. It felt strange, strange and strong. Whoever worked that magic has been making spells in a tradition, in a style, separate from ours for . . . for forever, as best I can tell."

"He's right," Liv said. "I know Bizogot shamanry. I know some of what Raumsdalian shamanry feels like. This was different, as different as blackberries and musk oxen."

Ulric spread his hands. "All right, I was wrong about that. But are you sure I'm wrong about the sending?"

Liv and Audun looked at each other. "I thought it was coming from the north," she said slowly. Audun Gilli nodded. But Liv went on, "I'm not *sure* of that, not the way I was with the spell on the lake. I still think it's likely, but I'm not sure."

"My dreams have been cold. All of them have been cold," Audun said. Thinking back on it, Hamnet realized his had, too. Audun continued, "That doesn't prove it's the Rulers and not the Emperor, but I'd bet on them."

"When we get back among the good folk of the Three Tusk clan, we will be troubled no more," Trasamund said. "By being what they are, they will shield us from this nuisance."

"What? We're not good folk ourselves?" Ulric asked. "If that's all it takes . . . We don't have some of the people who came along with us last time here now, you know." He named no names, which was just as well. Hamnet Thyssen's mind immediately turned to Gudrid.

But he hadn't had nightmares about her up here, not even once. That struck him as odd. He'd had plenty of them before.

Trasamund's thoughts ran in a different direction. "Nothing wrong with

Eyvind Torfinn," he said. "Jesper Fletti and the other soldiers—I don't miss them so much."

He thought Earl Eyvind was a good fellow because the aging noble either didn't see his sport with Gudrid or pretended not to notice it. Hamnet didn't think Eyvind Torfinn a bad fellow, either, but he esteemed the other Raumsdalian despite his ties to Gudrid, not because of them.

Trasamund sent Ulric Skakki a sly glance. He didn't say anything about Ulric. He didn't say the adventurer wasn't a good man. Whatever he thought, he thought. And if Ulric growled and muttered, he didn't—he couldn't—do any more than that. Trasamund . . . smiled.

Who would have thought a Bizogot could show such subtlety?

THE RED DIRE Wolves—not to be confused with the Black Dire Wolves, who dwelt far to the west—fed the travelers to the bursting point. They'd just killed a bull mammoth, and for the time being had more meat than they knew what to do with. Baked mammoth, stewed mammoth, mammoth fritters, roasted mammoth marrow—a delicacy, that, even without toasted bread on which to spread it—mammoth blood sausage, mammoth head cheese . . . Anything you could do to and with a mammoth's carcass, the Red Dire Wolves did.

"I'm surprised we didn't see mammoth eyeballs and mammoth ballocks," Audun Gilli said during a pause in the orgy of eating.

"Oh, the jarl gets the eyeballs," Trasamund said seriously. "They help make him farseeing, or so the hope is. As for the ballocks, the clansmen slice them up and roast them first thing. Same with the pizzle. You can figure out why."

"Er—yes." Audun raised a leather jack of smetyn to his lips. He was on his way to getting drunk, but so were the rest of them. He didn't get drunk when he needed to stay sober, which was all that really mattered.

Hamnet Thyssen gnawed more meat off a chunk of mammoth rib. Some enterprising Raumsdalian trader had sold the Red Dire Wolf clan several bone saws, of the sort surgeons used down in the Empire. For the Bizogots, they made first-rate butcher's tools. Hamnet wondered who his clever countryman was. The fellow had found an odd way, but a good one, to meet his customers' desires.

A big, burly graybeard named Totila ruled the Red Dire Wolves. He eyed Hamnet and Ulric and said, "Some of you foreigners can fill yourselves almost like real people." He didn't include Audun in that. The wizard was small to begin with, and didn't seem to have an infinitely extensible paunch.

"Practice, your Ferocity," Ulric Skakki answered. "The mammoth brain is very tasty, but now I keep wanting to wave my trunk and wiggle my ears." He *did* wiggle them, something Hamnet hadn't known he could do.

Totila stared, then laughed and laughed. "As long as thinking like a mammoth doesn't make you want to shit in the middle of my tent, eat all the brains you please."

Ulric did eat some more, then mimed pulling down his trousers. Totila laughed harder than ever. In Raumsdalian, Hamnet Thyssen said, "I see you've found your true level."

"I'll cut your heart out and eat it for that," Ulric answered. "And what kind of fool will I act like then?"

"A jealous fool, I'd say," Hamnet answered. "And I ought to know about those." He remembered the feel of his point grating off the ribs of Gudrid's first lover—the first one he found out about, anyhow—and then sliding deep to pierce the man's heart. He remembered the anguished surprise on Ingjald Oddleif's face. *This can't be happening to me,* he must have thought, there at the end. But it was.

Totila found girls for Trasamund and Ulric Skakki. He would have found one for Audun Gilli, too, but the wizard was using the bits of the Bizogot tongue he'd painfully acquired to try to talk shop with the deaf old man who was the Red Dire Wolves' shaman. Audun would have liked to find someone to translate for him, but the rest of the travelers were otherwise occupied—Hamnet and Liv had crawled under a mammoth hide together, too. Audun had to do the best he could on his own.

WHEN THE TRAVELERS rode out of the Red Dire Wolves' encampment the next morning, the wizard said, "I *think* Odovacar told me there were changes in the north."

"Their shaman? Has he had bad dreams, too?" Ulric Skakki asked. By his self-satisfied smirk, whatever dreams he'd had after enjoying the Bizogot woman weren't bad at all.

But he sobered when Audun Gilli nodded. "He has. I'm almost sure of it," Audun said. "That makes it more likely the Rulers are sending the dreams, not the Emperor. Why would imperial wizards trouble a shaman's dreams?"

"Why would the Rulers?" Hamnet Thyssen asked in turn. "If they're plotting something, wouldn't they want to keep shamans in the dark as long as they could?"

In the dark was the right phrase. The sun rose late and set early, scuttling across the sky from southeast to southwest and never rising high above the southern horizon. Beyond the Glacier, it wouldn't come up even this far. Hamnet remembered Ulric's account of winter up there.

"Sometimes spells wash out farther than you wish they would," Liv said in Raumsdalian, and Audun Gilli nodded. She went on, "Odovacar may have felt bits and pieces of what was aimed somewhere else."

"Aimed at us?" Hamnet asked.

"It could be," Liv said. "Or maybe—" She broke off.

"Maybe what?" Audun Gilli asked.

She didn't answer. She stopped speaking Raumsdalian. In her own language, she called out to Trasamund, saying, "I fear the Rulers may have struck at our clan. God grant it not be so, but I fear it."

"Would they dare?" the jarl said.

"Never doubt what the Rulers would dare," Ulric Skakki said in the Bizogot tongue. "They may not always get everything they want, but they want a lot."

"God be praised we come in time to stop them here, then," Trasamund said.

"If we do," Hamnet Thyssen said. Trasamund sent him a horrible stare. He looked back steadily. The Bizogot was assuming that what he wanted was true. But was it really? *We'll find out soon,* the Raumsdalian thought.

On they rode. The weather was clear but very cold. Totila had given them some mammoth meat to take with them on their journey. They also killed hares. Even so far north, though, those had next to no fat on them, relying on their thick white fur for warmth. They would feed a man, but wouldn't keep him going indefinitely by themselves. In such weather, people needed fat for fuel to keep from freezing.

"Now we ride into the lands of the Three Tusk clan," Trasamund said a couple of days after they left the Red Dire Wolves' encampment. "Now we join the grandest clan among the Bizogots." He looked around. "I see no herds, not yet. They will be wandering elsewhere, no doubt. Our grazing range is vast."

And needs to be, Hamnet Thyssen thought. If the land up here by the Glacier were better, the musk oxen and mammoths could have lived on less of it. By the ironic glint in Ulric Skakki's eye, he saw the same thing. Neither of them pointed it out to Trasamund. That would have enraged him without being able to change anything.

Late in the afternoon, Liv pointed north across the snow-covered plain. "Those are people, I think, heading our way."

They were no more than wiggling dots at the edge of visibility to Count Hamnet. "If you say so," he told her.

"My own folk, coming to greet me." Smug pride rang in Trasamund's voice.

Before long, he got a closer look at his clansfolk, and pride changed to horror. They weren't welcoming him—they were fleeing disaster. Some were wounded, others terribly burned. "Invaders!" Gelimer gasped when he saw his chieftain. "Invaders from the north!"

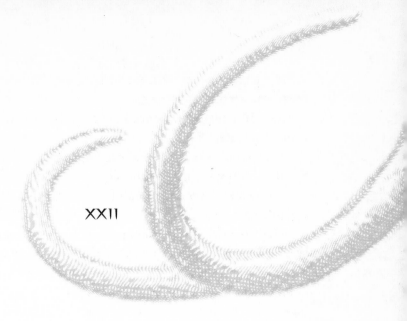

XXII

Not all the survivors from the Three Tusk clan even wanted to linger long enough to talk with Trasamund and his comrades. The Bizogots wanted to flee, lest worse befall them. They had been struck, and they had been broken. They'd never imagined such a blow could fall on them, not from that direction. Even though Trasamund spoke of the Rulers on the far side of the Glacier, the danger must have seemed no more real to his folk than to Sigvat.

"Why didn't you patrol the Gap?" the anguished jarl asked Gelimer.

"We did—for a while. But the hunting is bad up there, so the men came back," Gelimer answered. He had a new cut across his forehead and a bandage on his left arm. "We didn't look for invaders, not at this season of the year." He grimaced. "I wish we would have."

"The Rulers . . . can do all kinds of unpleasant things," Hamnet said. Gelimer nodded, and then bit his lip. Moving his head had to hurt.

"How far behind you are they?" Ulric Skakki asked—a good, relevant question.

"Not far enough, by God!" the Bizogot exclaimed. "But they aren't chasing as hard as they might be. Why should they bother? What's left of us can't do them any harm, and they have to know it."

"My clan!" Trasamund howled. "You threw away my clan because you wouldn't listen to me. What I ought to do to you . . ."

"What's the point, your Ferocity?" Hamnet Thyssen said wearily. "Whatever you want to do, the Rulers have already done worse."

"If I'd stayed—"

"It might not have mattered," Ulric said. "They still would have surprised you, eh?"

"I would have beaten them anyhow." Even in disaster, Trasamund clung to his arrogance.

"They had—riding mammoths. Riding mammoths with lancers on them!" Gelimer said, for all the world as if the travelers hadn't told him about that when they came south from the Gap, as if he hadn't wanted to ride mammoths himself. "How could we hope to stand against them? And the ones who weren't on mammoths rode deer. They might as well have been horses! And their shamans—their shamans blasted our camp with lightning."

Liv put her face in her hands. "I might have stopped that if I were there," she said in a broken voice. "I've met the Rulers. I have some notion of what they can do. Anyone who didn't . . . would have been easy meat for them." She swiped at her eyes. "I can't even cry, not now. My eyelids will freeze shut."

"What . . . do we do?" Audun Gilli asked in a very small voice.

"We can't keep riding north—that seems plain enough. If we do, we run into the Rulers, and then . . ." Ulric Skakki didn't go on, but he didn't have to. The rest of the travelers could draw their own pictures.

"How many other clansfolk got away?" Trasamund asked Gelimer. "Are there parties in back of you, or did they flee in different directions?"

"I don't know, your Ferocity," Gelimer said miserably. "I think the only ones behind us are those horrible, God-cursed demons from beyond the Glacier."

"I wish I could know for sure," the jarl said. "I don't like to leave anyone behind who might somehow get away. If I go forward—"

"You throw yourself away," Hamnet Thyssen broke in. "Will you charge a squadron of war mammoths singlehanded? Some people would call that brave. But isn't it stupid? What would you do afterwards? Nothing, because you'd be dead."

"With my clan murdered, I deserve to be," Trasamund said.

"No." Count Hamnet shook his head. "This war is all the Bizogots, all the folk below the Glacier, against these invaders. The Three Tusk clan has lost a fight. But the Bizogots are still your folk. They need you. They need what you can do. They need what you know. Ulric's right. If we charge now, we lose. We have to regroup and figure out what to do next, how to fight the Rulers."

"Talk, talk, talk. This is what Raumsdalians do," Trasamund said. "Not Bizogots. Bizogots go out and fight."

"And then wish later that they'd done some talking instead," Ulric Skakki said. Trasamund scowled at him—and at the world.

"The Raumsdalians are right, your Ferocity," Liv said.

"Not you, too!" the jarl howled.

She nodded. "I'm sorry, but yes. Going forward, charging ahead, is useless now. We need to save ourselves for a fight we can hope to win."

"Our grazing grounds! The mammoths! The musk oxen!" Trasamund beat his fists against his legs in misery.

"They're lost now, your Ferocity," Ulric said. "If we win, you can reclaim them. If you lose now, will you ever see them again? How likely is it? Tell me the truth, not what your heart wants to hear."

Trasamund growled like a wild beast, down deep in his throat. "Better to die than to live the exile's life!" he cried.

"If you really want to die, it won't be hard," Ulric said. "If you're just making noise because things hurt so much right now, that's a different story. But be careful what you say, because you may decide to do something your mouth means but your heart doesn't."

"He is right," Liv said again. "What we really need is vengeance. Don't throw yourself away before we can take it."

Trasamund turned his ravaged gaze on Hamnet Thyssen. "Well, Raumsdalian? Are you going to preach me a sermon, too?" He spoke in the Empire's language; his own had no word for *sermon*.

"No," Count Hamnet answered. "The only thing I'll tell you is, I know what watching your world crash down on you feels like. It's happened to me, too. You have a hole where your heart used to be, and you go on anyway. What else can you do?"

"*Kill!*" Trasamund roared.

"If you kill a little now, your Ferocity, you will die right afterwards." Audun Gilli was almost maddeningly precise. "If you wait for your moment, you can work a great killing on the foe, and still live to hear him mourn. Which would you rather?"

"I want to kill now, and I want to kill later," the jarl answered. "I want to kill and kill and kill. If I drowned the world in blood, it wouldn't glut me. Do you understand, you and your talk of killing? What do you know of death?"

Audun Gilli bit his lip. "I came home one night to watch my family burn.

Is that enough, your Ferocity, or do you want something more? Did you ever smell your wife's charred flesh when you lay down to try to sleep?" He almost quivered with fury. Little weedy man that he was, he was on the point of hurling himself at the burly Bizogot, magic forgot, simply man against man. And Hamnet Thyssen might not have been astonished if he prevailed.

Trasamund stared. In his own moment of agony, he seemed to have forgot that others could know, had known, torment, too. Where Ulric's sarcasm and Hamnet's stolidity failed to remind him of it, the wizard's rage did. Trasamund seemed to slump in on himself like a pingo melting in an uncommonly hot summer. "I will live," he mumbled. "I will avenge. And I will hate myself every heartbeat till I do."

Hamnet Thyssen and Audun Gilli both nodded. "Oh, yes, your Ferocity," Hamnet said. "*Oh*, yes. That comes with the territory. For now, though, we see about living."

Dully, Trasamund nodded as well.

AUDUN GILLI KNEW a weatherworking spell that seemed stronger than any Liv had. He used it to call snow down on the travelers' tracks. Maybe that would let them and the survivors from the Three Tusk clan give the Rulers the slip. Or, then again, maybe it wouldn't.

"If you like, I'll ride off by myself," Hamnet said. "The wizards from the Rulers seem to want to kill me in particular, fools that they are. I don't want to bring my troubles down on anyone else."

"You'll do no such thing!" Liv's voice went high and shrill. *She* does *care for me,* Hamnet thought. That seemed a stranger, stronger magic than the one Audun used to fill their trail with snowflakes.

"Stay with us, Thyssen," Trasamund said. "Stay with us. If the Rulers want you so much, it follows that you can hurt them if you live. And so we'd better keep you alive if we can." He cared for Hamnet, too, cared for him the same way he cared for his own weapons. Anything he could aim at the Rulers, he would.

Count Hamnet didn't want to leave Liv. And he didn't want to leave Trasamund, either. The Bizogot jarl wanted to hit back at the invaders. That was more than Sigvat II did. Hamnet Thyssen was in the right place, and in the right company. "If you don't think my coming along will endanger you, I'll gladly stay."

"Good. That's good. We need all the enemies of those lion turds to ride together." Trasamund could see that, even if Sigvat couldn't. "And we need to hit back at them as soon as we can without throwing ourselves away."

"How?" Once more, Ulric Skakki asked a bluntly practical question.

He asked it, and the Bizogot waved it aside. "I don't know yet. But we need to do it when we see the chance. We need to show the rest of my folk that we *can* hit back. If we don't, what's to stop them from rolling on their backs like a dire wolf that's lost a fight and giving the cursed Rulers whatever they want?"

"A point." Ulric didn't sound happy about admitting it, but he did. He was no more honest than he had to be, but was in his own way scrupulous.

"Gelimer!" Trasamund boomed. The other Bizogot nodded miserably. Trasamund went on, "You will know where the herds are, not so?"

"I know where they were, your Ferocity. Where they were before the thunderbolt from the north hit us, I should say," Gelimer answered.

"We warned you. By God, you should have listened." But Trasamund let that go—for a Bizogot, a rare show of magnanimity. "The Rulers will be feeding off the beasts closest to your camp. Guide us to a herd farther away. It will feed us for a while. And, sooner or later, the invaders will come to steal. When they do"—he smacked his hands together—"we strike!" He made it sound simple. Whether it would be . . .

Gelimer seemed to gain a little life at the thought of hitting back. "Off to the west is where most of the musk oxen were. The mammoths roamed closer to our camp. I don't know if those . . . Rulers are breaking them to ride. Even after you said they could do that, who would have thought it was true?"

"You should have," Hamnet Thyssen answered before Trasamund could speak. "Did you think we were making up stories to pass the time?"

"With Raumsdalians, who knows?" Gelimer said. "All you people lie all the time, so how can we tell what to believe?"

Hamnet looked at Liv. She was looking back at him. They both remembered Eyvind Torfinn's paradox. Hamnet wished the Bizogots here hadn't taken it so literally; it might have cost them dear. Or, then again, it might not have mattered. Who could say whether the Rulers would have beaten them anyhow?

"Am I a Raumsdalian? Is the jarl a Raumsdalian?" Liv asked Gelimer. "When *we* say something is true, you can rely on it. You can, but you didn't. And now you see what happened."

"You don't need to make me feel any worse, Lady," Gelimer said. "I'm already lower than a maggot's belly."

"Killing the enemy will make a man of you again," Trasamund declared. "West, you said the musk-ox herds were? Then west we shall ride, west and north, back into our own lands again."

ENOUGH FATTY ROAST meat made the cold all around much easier to bear. The furnace inside Hamnet Thyssen, stoked with such fuel, burned harder and hotter. He seemed warmer, and supposed he really was.

The Bizogots had no trouble cutting an old bull musk ox, half lame and slow, out of the herd and leading it downwind so the smell of blood wouldn't panic the other animals. Killing it took a lot of arrows, but they had them. When it went down at last, bawling in pain and incomprehension, Trasamund finished it with a headsman's stroke from his great two-handed blade.

Gore crimsoned the snow. Some of the hungry Bizogots snatched up that bloody snow and stuffed it into their mouths. They couldn't wait for butchery, let alone a fire. Bodies needed food of any sort in this weather. The nomads grinned with blood on their lips and running down their chins.

Hamnet Thyssen, having eaten better lately, left the blood alone. After the dung fire began to burn, he roasted his meat and gulped it down— burnt on the outside, raw in the middle. He didn't care. You couldn't be very fussy in the Bizogot country, not if you wanted to go on living. He supposed he would eat bloody snow if he got hungry enough. He didn't think he would grin afterwards, though.

Trasamund seemed to gain strength with food, too. "Where are the Rulers?" he roared. "Let them come now. Yes, let them come, by God! We will kill them by the hundreds, by the thousands!" The remnant of his clan had no more than twenty warriors, counting the newcomers up from the south.

"Let them come, yes—but not too many of them." Wherever you put him, Ulric Skakki had good sense.

"Let them leave their wizards behind, too." That wasn't Trasamund scorning Liv and Audun Gilli. That was Audun himself. "They are stronger than we are, however much I hate to admit it."

"Maybe we can take them by surprise," Liv said. "They'll think we're weak." *And they'll be right, too,* Hamnet Thyssen thought. The shaman went on, "And they'll think we're afraid. And we will show them they're wrong."

"We're not afraid of them. We were never afraid of them." Gelimer's voice was blurry, because he talked with his mouth full. He was too busy eating to pause very much. "But they beat us. They were too many and too strong."

"They won't come against us with everything they have. That's bound to be true. They won't think they'll need to. And they'll be gathering strength for a raid farther south. That's what I would do if I were one of them, anyhow. They'll push through the Bizogot country so they can attack the Empire."

"What makes you so special?" demanded one of the Bizogots who'd lived through the Rulers' onslaught. "What are you doing here, if you think you're better than we are?"

"I didn't say anything about better. I don't say anything about that," Ulric answered. "But we're richer than you are. Our lands are richer than yours. Our weather is warmer than yours. The Rulers *will* strike south." He defied the Bizogot to disagree with him.

The man wanted to. Hamnet Thyssen could see as much. But the fellow only muttered into his gingery beard and went back to stuffing himself with meat.

Down in Raumsdalia, the musk ox's stones would have been called prairie oysters. Trasamund toasted them over the fire and ate them. "As the bull battered down his rivals and won his mates, so will I beat down the Rulers," he vowed.

"So may it be," Liv said softly.

ULRIC SKAKKI HAD to remind Trasamund to put scouts out to the east. The jarl still wasn't at his best, or anything close to it. "If we had another leader here to follow, I would," Ulric told Hamnet Thyssen.

The way the adventurer looked at Count Hamnet alarmed him. "I don't want to lead anybody," Hamnet said. "I didn't want to do it down in Raumsdalia with my own folk. I really don't want to do it here. The Bizogots wouldn't follow me anyhow."

"You might be surprised," Ulric said. "You're large and you're tough and you don't spend all your time going on about how wonderful you are."

"I'm a foreigner," Hamnet said with a patience not far from desperation. " 'All Raumsdalians are liars,' remember?"

"And Bizogots aren't?" Ulric Skakki threw back his head and laughed. "That's the funniest thing I've heard since I don't know when."

"It's their country. They can do whatever they want in it," Count Hamnet said. "And one of the things they'd want to do is knock any Raumsdalian who tries to tell them what to do over the head with a lump of frozen mammoth dung."

Liv came up to the two of them, the snow crunching under her felt boots. "What are you arguing about?" she asked. They spelled it out for her. She didn't need long to make up her mind. "Count Hamnet is right," she said. "We Bizogots must have our own to lead us. Do you plot against the jarl?"

"No, but I want someone who isn't sunk in grief in charge," Ulric answered. "If Trasamund can't do it, who can?"

"Who says Trasamund can't?" Liv returned. "When the Rulers come, his spirit will rouse. You wait and see."

"What if the Rulers came and we didn't even know they were on the way?" Ulric asked. But Liv didn't want to listen to him, and neither did Hamnet Thyssen. Ulric sighed out a small cloud of fog, threw his hands in the air, and gave up.

Whoever persuaded Trasamund to set scouts out, it was as well that he did, because two days later one of them rode back to the musk-ox herd so hard that his horse steamed in the frigid air. "They're coming!" he shouted. "Those murderous thieves are coming!"

Liv proved to know her jarl. He might have been sunk in gloom before he got the news, but he revived with a roar. "Oh, they are, are they?" he boomed. "By God, we'll teach them this isn't their country!"

When he gave orders, he seemed to know which ones to give. He sent a few Bizogots out as herd watchers, to give the Rulers something to focus on. The rest, along with the Raumsdalians, he stationed at the edge of the herd, ready to ride out and strike as the chance offered. He put Liv and Audun Gilli with that group.

"If you find a spell to confound the Rulers, use it," he said. "If you find they're using spells against us, block them. Is that plain?"

"If we fail . . . ?" Audun asked.

"You won't. You can't," Trasamund said. "Too much riding on it. No place to run away any more. No place to hide. We beat them here or we die here. Is *that* plain?" Biting his lip, the Raumsdalian wizard nodded.

"They're coming!" The shout came from several throats at once.

Count Hamnet looked east. Those moving dots . . . At first, he took them for horses, or for the large deer the Rulers rode instead. Then he realized they were bigger and farther away than that. *Mammoths,* he thought. The chill that ran through him had nothing to do with the icy weather. He was honest enough to call it by its right name—fear.

"Can we really fight them?" The same noxious beast filled Gelimer's voice.

"By God, we can. We will." Trasamund sounded confident, or at least un-afraid. "If we die, what do we lose? Nothing, for the clan is shattered and we are nothing without it. But if we win, we have the start of our vengeance. And so we shall win. We have nothing else left to do."

"I don't think Eyvind Torfinn would like the logic," Ulric Skakki mur-mured to Hamnet.

"Bugger Eyvind Torfinn. He's down where it's warmer," Hamnet an-swered. "We're doing his work for him up here, so let's do it."

Behind him, Audun Gilli began a soft chant. "A masking spell—just a small one," he said into a pause. "So they don't look at the musk oxen too closely and don't notice whatever they happen to see along with them."

"Good. Good," Trasamund rumbled. "Let us surprise them if we can."

The Rulers had stronger magic than folk on this side of the Glacier. But Audun's spell didn't have to be strong. It didn't aim to draw attention to it-self. The opposite, in fact. Hamnet Thyssen hoped that meant the invaders wouldn't notice it—and wouldn't notice him and the rest of the warriors.

He strung his bow and nocked an arrow. Here came the mammoths. Now he could see the deer-riders flanking them. "So you want some more, do you?" a lancer atop one tusker shouted in the Bizogot tongue. "We'll give you more, all right—see if we don't!"

The Bizogots who seemed to be ordinary herders did what Hamnet Thyssen would have done in their place—they wheeled their horses and fled. Laughing and jeering, the Rulers came after them. Hamnet discovered something he didn't know—mammoths could move at least as fast as horses with snow on the ground.

Some of the Bizogots turned and shot over their shoulders at their pur-suers. Most of those arrows went wild. The Manches and other tribes in the far southwest practiced that shot and made it deadly. They would have laughed themselves sick at how little use the Bizogots got from it.

When a mammoth caught up with a horse, by contrast, the Rulers knew just what to do. They speared one Bizogot out of the saddle, then another. And they went on laughing while they did it.

"Now!" Trasamund bellowed. The Bizogots and Raumsdalians concealed by the musk-ox herd and by Audun Gilli's magic thundered forward.

Bowstrings thrummed. These archers weren't making an unaccustomed shot, but one they used all the time. They aimed for the mammoths' eyes and ears and trunks—the sensitive spots where wounds would pain even those gigantic beasts. And they aimed for the warriors atop them.

One thing mammoths couldn't do was turn as quickly as horses. The Rulers cried out in surprise and dismay at the unexpected flank assault. Their enormous mounts went wild when wounded, just as horses would have. One plucked a rider off its back with its trunk, dashed him to the ground, and stepped on him. His scream cut off abruptly. Red stained the snow.

With shouts of rage, men of the Rulers on deer tried to close with the horsemen. The deer lowered their heads and charged, ready to use their antlers as secondary weapons. But ferocious archery kept most of them at a distance, and the horses overbore those that did manage to close. Hamnet and Ulric and the Bizogots chopped down at the enemy riders with their swords.

"Revenge!" Trasamund shouted over and over again. "The Three Tusk clan! Revenge!"

Ulric Skakki made a lucky shot: he hit a mammoth not just near the eye but in it. No, Hamnet decided—it was a great shot, not lucky; Ulric had done that before. The arrow must have pierced the thin, fragile bone behind the eyeball and reached the brain, for the mammoth crashed to the ground, stone dead. One of the men atop it survived the tumble, but not for long. A Bizogot ran up and dashed out his brains with a hatchet.

"Revenge!" Trasamund yelled once more, and all the Bizogots took up the cry. "*Revenge!*"

Seeing the mammoth topple seemed to suck the spirit from the Rulers. They still outnumbered their foes, but they lost stomach for a fight that wasn't a walkover. The ones who could rode back toward the east as fast as they could go.

"They don't look like such heroes when you see their arses, do they?" Ulric Skakki remarked.

"Not a bit of it," Hamnet Thyssen answered, thrusting his blade into the snow to get blood off it. "We ought to round up the ones who are still breathing but couldn't get away."

"Yes, the Bizogots will have fun with them, won't they?" Ulric said.

Count Hamnet's mouth twisted. The adventurer was bound to be right about that, and what happened then wouldn't be pretty. *Revenge, yes,* Hamnet thought. "They shouldn't just be sport," he said. "We ought to squeeze answers out of them, too. Some of them speak the Bizogot tongue."

"Who knows what kind of noises they'll make by the time the Bizogots get through with them?" Ulric said. "Do you want to be the one to tell Trasamund he can't have all the revenge he craves?"

"I'll do it." After a moment, Count Hamnet amended that: "I'll see if he wants to listen, anyhow."

Trasamund wasn't paying much attention to captives when Hamnet came up to him. He was directing the butchery of the mammoth Ulric had slain, and of the deer and horses that had fallen in the fight. "When we go off to join up with another clan, by God, we won't come empty-handed," he shouted. "We'll have meat for their larders, so much meat that they'll want us worse than we want them."

That was bravado. He had to know as much, too. But it was a bravado the surviving Three Tusk clansfolk needed. Along with the fallen men of the Rulers, Bizogots lay in the snow, cold and dead and rapidly getting stiff. The ones who yet lived had to be convinced the others didn't die for nothing.

The Bizogots were already starting to abuse the prisoners they'd taken. "We should question them, not torment them," Hamnet said.

Trasamund looked as if he hated him. "Easy for you to talk like that," the jarl growled. "They didn't wreck your clan."

"Not yet," Hamnet Thyssen answered, which brought the Bizogot up short. He went on, "If we learn all we can, we'll save other Bizogot clans, too. Or we can hope we will. Would you rather waste them? Think of them as food—for the sword."

That got home to Trasamund. Considering how the Bizogots ate every bit of every animal they killed, from snout to tail, Count Hamnet had hoped it would. The jarl went on scowling at him, but then turned aside and started bellowing orders.

And he needed to bellow. Having started in on some of their captives, the Bizogots had the rest trussed and waiting and watching. They didn't want to be deprived of the pleasures of vengeance.

Trasamund said, "If they tell us the truth, maybe we let them live, or at least give them a quick end. That will give them a reason to talk to us. If we catch them lying, then we do as we please."

"Some of them don't know any of our tongue," Gelimer said. "We might as well slay them—we can't talk to them."

"Keep them breathing for now," Trasamund said. "Maybe we can ransom them or make the Rulers do something to keep us from hurting them."

"You've spent too much time in the south," Gelimer said. "You're getting soft."

Trasamund hit him in the face. The jarl's mitten cushioned the blow, but it knocked Gelimer down even so. He got up smiling—Trasamund had proved himself still ferocious. Hamnet Thyssen would have thought that a perfect Bizogot attitude if he hadn't known Raumsdalians who worked the same way.

He went over and squatted down by one of the captives. "Tell me your name," he said in the Bizogot tongue.

"I am a dead man," the warrior of the Rulers answered in the same language.

Count Hamnet drew back a fist. "Tell me your name, I said." He wouldn't take nonsense from the prisoner no matter what.

Wearily, the shaggy, hatchet-faced warrior replied, "You can call me Karassops."

That wasn't quite the same as telling Hamnet Thyssen his name. But Hamnet accepted it; Karassops likely feared his real name, if he gave it, would be used in magic against him. "Why did you invade this land, Karassops?" Hamnet asked.

Wounded, battered, and captive though he was, Karassops eyed the Raumsdalian as he would have eyed any other fool. "Because we could, of course."

"It doesn't belong to you."

"Some of it does now. All of it will." The warrior spoke with frightening confidence.

"Much good coming here did you. You will die here," Hamnet said.

"I told you—I am already dead. All of us you captured are dead. You surprised us. You caught us. You disgraced us. We are dead. We cannot show our faces around the fires of our folk ever again. Give me a weapon, and I will end myself now." Karassops sounded eager for the chance.

"If you are dead, you won't mind answering my questions," Count Hamnet said. "What harm can answering do the dead?"

Karassops made an argumentative corpse. Eyeing Hamnet, he said,

"Who are you? You are no Bizogot. You must be one from that other herd."

"Never mind who I am. You don't ask questions. You answer them," Hamnet said.

"One from that other herd . . ." Karassops followed his own line of thought. "Which one? We knew some of you were stupid enough to come back and stir up more trouble." He laughed. "I know! You must be the one who kept mooning over the woman he couldn't have any more."

Hamnet Thyssen hit him two or three times before even realizing what he was doing. Blood ran from Karassops's nose and started freezing in his mustache and beard. Hamnet looked at his hands in some surprise. They seemed to have minds of their own.

"My women are none of your business," he growled.

"I got the idea." Karassops turned his head and spat red into the snow. "And you were the one who didn't want to torture us."

"I didn't want you mouthing off, either," Hamnet said. "You'd better remember who won this fight and who lost."

"I am not likely to forget. I am disgraced forever." Karassops couldn't have looked any more forlorn. "I am outcast. I am outlawed. I can never take my place among the Rulers again. I am dead."

Now Hamnet wished he hadn't lost his temper and hit the man. If Karassops was dead to the Rulers, he might decide he could be alive and have a place among the Bizogots. But as things were, Hamnet didn't try to turn him. Even if Karassops said he would join the folk who'd defeated and captured him, how far could he be trusted? *Not far enough, not now,* the Raumsdalian thought regretfully. Maybe he or the Bizogots would have better luck with some of the other men from the Rulers.

Meanwhile, though, Hamnet could still learn from Karassops, even if he didn't try to get him to turn his coat. "How many of your folk came through the Gap?" he asked.

Despite the blood on his face, Karassops bared his teeth in a saucy grin. "Enough."

When Count Hamnet made as if to hit him again, he didn't flinch. He had courage. The Rulers seemed to. They were enemies, but far from cowards. "How many of your folk still dwell off to the north?"

Karassops's grin got wider. "More than enough. We are tigers. You are prey."

"It could be," Hamnet Thyssen said. That startled the warrior from beyond the Glacier. Hamnet went on, "We can build tiger traps, though.

Would you be here if we couldn't? You would be trying to squeeze answers out of me instead."

"You got lucky this time," Karassops said. Hamnet Thyssen feared he was right, but didn't say so. Karassops added, "How long do you think you can go on being lucky?"

"How long do you think it will be before the Bizogots join together and hurl you out through the Gap?" Hamnet returned. The warrior from the Rulers laughed in his face.

Shrugging, Count Hamnet got to his feet. Startled again, Karassops asked, "Aren't you going to kill me?"

Hamnet thought of Parsh after he lost the stand-down with Trasamund. He had killed himself to efface the shame of losing to a foreigner, to someone who didn't belong to the Rulers. The Raumsdalian noble grinned, too, as unpleasantly as he could. "Live," he said. "Live with knowing how you failed. What worse thing could we do to you? Live long, and brood on what you should have done."

That struck home where nothing else had. The Rulers might disdain physical torment, but Hamnet knew he'd found a vulnerable spot even so. Karassops yammered at him in his own harsh, guttural language. Hamnet didn't understand him, but knew rage and fear when he heard them.

"You don't deserve to use that tongue any more, do you?" Hamnet said sweetly.

He thought he was only mocking the warrior, but Karassops took him literally. The captive bit down hard. He groaned in agony, then spat something pink and red into the snow. Blood poured out of his mouth. He gulped frantically, swallowing more so he wouldn't drown.

"You idiot!" Hamnet Thyssen cried.

You could bandage and close off a gash on an arm or a leg, maybe in the neck, maybe even, if you were very lucky, in the chest or belly. But on the tongue? How? Count Hamnet stared helplessly as Karassops's face went gray. The warrior slumped over. His eyes sagged shut. In a few minutes, he'd bled to death.

Ulric Skakki eyed the corpse, and the chunk of meat next to it. "I don't think I could make myself do that," he said, shaking his head. "Why did he?" After Hamnet explained, Ulric shook his head. "If you'd just told him to watch his tongue, he'd still be here?"

"Who knows?" Hamnet pointed to the severed organ. "He died watching it."

"Heh," Ulric Skakki said. "Either I laugh or I heave. And you were the one who said to go easy on the Rulers we'd caught."

"I thought I was," Hamnet Thyssen answered. "I didn't mean for him to do . . . that." His stomach wanted to turn over, too. He'd never been seasick, but this helpless nausea had to come close to that feeling.

"Well, we're rid of him now," Ulric said. Was that callousness, practicality, or, most likely, both at once? The adventurer went on, "If he was the kind who would do something like that, he was the kind who would have caused us all sorts of trouble. Meanwhile, we can take the prisoners we do have and head on down to the Red Dire Wolves. They'll prove the invasion is real, and they'll make Totila get off his backside and fight the Rulers."

That was pure practicality. Count Hamnet found himself nodding. "Good enough. And we'd better use Audun's magic to cover our tracks again, or we'll have lancers on mammoths right behind us. They won't be so easy to surprise twice."

"I wasn't sure we could surprise them once," Ulric Skakki said. "But it turns out they can be overconfident fools just like anybody else. That's good news, of a sort."

"Huzzah," Hamnet said, and Ulric laughed. But it *was* worth remembering. The Rulers were powerful and dangerous, but they were also human. They made mistakes. They could be made to make mistakes.

So could Trasamund. He was wild to storm to the attack after his small victory. He didn't want to wait and gather strength before hitting back. He didn't want to listen to Count Hamnet, either. Then Liv said, "Your Ferocity, this is bigger than the Three Tusk clan."

"Nothing is bigger than the clan! Nothing!" the jarl shouted.

"The Bizogot folk is. The Empire is. All the lands on this side of the Glacier are," Liv said. "Hamnet does not tell you not to fight back. He tells you to pick your time."

Trasamund snorted. "He worries more about Gudrid and Eyvind Torfinn and Sigvat more than he does about us."

"For better or worse—for better *and* worse—they are my folk. So are the rest of the Raumsdalians," Hamnet Thyssen said steadily. "No matter what Sigvat thinks, they'll join this fight before too long. They'll have to."

"So you say," the Bizogot rumbled. After a moment, though, he gave a grudging nod. "To the Red Dire Wolves, then. We will . . . pick our moment." He made it sound like picking his nose. But when he said, "The fight goes on," Liv and Hamnet Thyssen both nodded with him.